CONTENTS

PART 1 MOONCAT!

Prologue

~*~

Karl Vandyl put down his copy of Faulkes's translation and chuckled to himself at the thought that even after almost a thousand years, he was still listed there in the Skaldskaparmal, on page 157. Of course, that too was part of Karl's problem. Too many people were beginning to delve into the old legends, and the old faith was coming back. That was dangerous to Karl and his kind, few as they might be. Karl was one of the ancient races of beings known as the Jotuns, or giants. Of course, giant was really a misnomer; Karl and his kind were not truly giants in the sense of huge beings thundering through the land grinding Englishmen's bones to make their bread, although they could be that if they chose to. But, they were elemental forces, which had existed since the dawn of time-- who'd come to be born in the same primal ice and fire that spawned the hated Gods.

A thousand years ago, the Christian church had managed to wipe out the followers of those Gods-- or at least convert them to religion where they were easier to manipulate. But now, in this land of tolerant America, and across Old Europe, the men of Midgarth were rediscovering their heritage, and that was something Karl and his brethren were sworn to prevent. It was something they'd been actively working against since the Puritan witch hunts of the seventeenth century. The men of Midgarth would not again be allowed to make contact with the likes of Ymir's Slayer.

Vandyl sat down at his desk, swivelled in his chair and

looked out over the city below him. Cincinnati was not a large city, nor was it a small one, but one of the many average-sized cities cropping up all over this extraordinary country of average people. Vandyl was at the heart of the city. In one of any number of guises, he had a Brandt in almost every fire in the city and therefore spread his influences across most of the Midwest and Appalachia.

He picked up the folder lying on his desk and perused it. The report- one that few people would be able to read for it was written in the language of the Jotuns, and then in the Runic form- about a recent mission his thralls had carried out for him. The man and woman in the file had been eliminated. The boy, their son, however, had escaped after killing one of his thralls. In the old days, during the era of the Sagas, this would have been seen as a fatal mistake- the kind that would have led to the singing of a new saga. However, these days, revenge was not a dish often served, and the death of the boy would have simply spurred on the rest of the investigation. By leaving him alive, Vandyl had cast doubt on what had really happened on that camping trip and left the authorities wondering if the boy had had something to do with his parents' death. After all, nobody would believe his wild tales about werewolves.

He smiled to himself. Two more followers of the Old Gods had been eliminated, and a third discredited. It was a good day's work. He'd have to be sure to send Matthias a little something extra in his paycheck. All in all, it promised to be a good week.

CHAPTER 1

Van put down his suitcase next to a large cast-iron bed and looked around. The room itself wasn't quite as big as his old one back in Lexington, but it was homey. It was made smaller by the score or so boxes stacked in various piles around the room, boxes that held what of his belongings he had kept out of storage after the executor had sold his parents' home.

Rough-hewn blond pine panelling covered the walls, and a dormer looked out over the backyard from the other side of his bed. A heavy bookcase was centered on the wall opposite the bed, with a desk next to it- a perfect place for his computer. A large overstuffed chair sat next to the dormer with a free-standing floor lamp. A large woven rug covered half the hardwood floor giving the whole room a cozy mountain cabin atmosphere-- which in a way it was.

Aunt Linda had had the log home built with the insurance settlement she received after her parents- Van's grand-parents-- had died. Her husband had been killed a few years before in Afghanistan, leaving just her and her sixteen-year-old daughter, Shelby alone in the huge rambling farm in northeastern Kentucky. Outside of a distant great uncle in Mississippi they were the only family Van had left, so he'd come to stay with them after his parents' death in that terrible camping trip.

"This will be your room, Van," his Aunt Linda said. "You can decorate it any way you like, just keep it clean. You share a bath with Em, so if the door's locked that means she's probably going to be in there for a few hours." There was a tone of bemusement in her voice with the last comment.

"Thank you, I appreciate it," Van told her, trying hard to feel something. Since that night two months ago, he'd felt nothing- just a cold ice deep in his chest keeping the pain that threatened to stab at his heart at bay. In reality, this was the first time he'd really been comfortable in a home since then. He'd spent the last two months-- all of his summer vacation-- either in the hospital, or being held in Juvenile Detention until the authorities had checked his story. He knew that the police didn't believe him about the huge wolf-like beasts that had attacked them in the Colorado Mountains. He knew that they considered him a suspect and that if it hadn't been for the body they'd found with the knife buried in its neck, a knife he'd put there himself, he'd be in jail right now, awaiting trial. As it was, they chalked his tale of werewolves up to the shock of having seen his parents murdered and having killed one of the attackers himself, and were still looking for the gang that had attacked them. Still, they couldn't deny the tracks and the wounds on his parents' bodies.

As if sensing his discomfort, his aunt quietly withdrew from the room. Before backing completely out of the door, she said quietly, "We'll discuss the house rules a little later, when you've gotten settled."

Van simply nodded and said, "Yes ma'am." Closing his eyes, he let himself relax. He could almost feel the warmth and comfort of his aunt's home reach out to him. It was a feeling he hadn't felt in a long time, and he was surprised to realize just how much he missed it.

Finally, opening his eyes, he went about unpacking his things with meticulous fastidiousness. Everything had to have its own place, and he could almost feel where each item should go. Lastly, he came to the box he'd been dreading. In it were his most personal keepsakes: his karate trophies, his yearbooks, and his photos-- photos of his parents. These were the things that were part of his old life, things that could melt the ice around his heart, and that melting threatened pain. He wasn't sure if he was ready for that pain just yet.

Steeling his mind and pushing the pain back into the ice, he sat down on the bed, ignoring its softness, and forced himself to open the box. Pulling out each item he gently placed it on one of the shelves, making himself relive the memories it represented in his past. It was a brutal way of facing his new life, but it was a way around the pain, a way to do what was needed to move on.

Two hours later found him sitting quietly in the chair looking out over the backyard as the sun dipped behind the mountains. In a blaze of reds, oranges and yellows glowing against the cerulean of the late summer sky, Van allowed himself to drift off into a relaxed sleep for the first time in months.

~*~

"So, your cousin get moved in yet?" Brett asked.

"Yeah, he got here today." Nodding, Shelby looked up from where she was sitting quietly eating at one of the many outdoor tables at Jeroldan's and indicated the bench across from her. Of course, all the tables there were outdoors because it really wasn't a sit down inside kind of place, but instead a little quick-stop and barbeque joint across the street from Wade Elementary, where most of the teens in Wellman hung out.

"How's he holding up?" Brett asked. He'd met Van a couple of times in the past, when the other teen's parents had visited Shelby and her mom, for the occasional Blot with the kindred.

Shelby smiled again, a smile that didn't quite reach the green orbs of her eyes. "I don't know. Mom said to go kind of easy on him for the first few weeks. He's still adjusting to his folks being gone."

Brett nodded, "Yeah, I understand. I don't know how I would handle it if something happened to Uncle Alex." It was his turn to shrug as he absently toyed with the small gold acorn on a chain around his neck, "My parents I'm not too worried about, but Uncle Alex has been there for me when nobody else was."

"Still worried about being sent back to Georgia?"

With a sad smile he shook his head. "No, not really, I guess I 'm just still bitter about everything that went down."

"Well, you're definitely in a better place now."

"Believe me, I'm not arguing the point with you," he told her. "It's just that sometimes I get angry about it all." Shelby was one of the few people who really knew about his parents and everything that had happened that Christmas his grandfather had died, how in just a span of a few days, his whole life had turned around when his Uncle Alex had for all intents and purposes bought him from his parents.

"You're brooding about it again," Shelby interrupted

his mental self-flagellation session. She did that quite a bit. It was one of the reasons they were such good friends, and the fact that while he showed a talent for galdr, she had an obvious gift for seidr. The innate intuition that came with that particular form magic gave her a better insight into what her friends were feeling. That helped her keep him centered.

"Sorry," he told her, chagrined. "I guess it still irks me that I was so much an embarrassment to my dad that he was willing to just send me off to live with someone else for a few thousand dollars. You know, it's sort of strange knowing that there's a dollar amount that you're worth to your parents."
Shelby reached out and touched his hand. "Look at it this way. At least there was someone more than willing to pay that amount in order to give you a shot at a better life."

He nodded and said, "I know, but still it..." He found himself choking up at the thought and let the words hang there for long moments. Finally, the frustration became too for him and he slammed his fist down on the table, "Damn it! Why did they have to be that way!" He spun from his seat and turned his back on his friend so she wouldn't see the tears standing in his eyes.

Finally, he felt Shel's warm hand gently on his arm. He could literally feel the calm and warmth spread up from his wrist to infuse him, to sooth his hurt. She said softly, "I don't know, Brett. But, here you've got people who care about you. Your Uncle Alex cares about you, and I care about you."

Without turning around, Brett could see her teasing smile in his mind's eye as she added. "You drive me up the wall sometimes, but I do care about you. So does Alex."

He gave her a nod, "I know. If he didn't he wouldn't have been willing to do what he did. In a lot of ways that puts even more pressure on me. I mean, how can I let myself disappoint him, after all he's done to turn my life around." He thought of all the changes in his life since he'd come to live with his uncle at the beginning of last year.

Back home in Georgia, he'd been an outcast in his own

family. All his life he'd been alone, even with two sisters and a brother, he felt like he didn't belong with the rest of his family. They wanted so little out of life-- for themselves and for him- and he wanted so much. His loneliness had been compounded by his smaller size, his intelligence, and innate strangeness. He hid his differences as much as he could. He hid from the poverty in which he lived; from the scorn and apathy of his father for his lack of sports prowess; from the overbearing mother that insisted that he be the caretaker of his siblings while she lost herself in her soap operas.

He hid himself in a hundred fantasy worlds born of his deep love of science fiction, fantasy, and comic books. In his own mind he wasn't Brett Bond, poor kid from north central Georgia; he was really an alien commander sent to Earth to protect it from an evil empire; he was a hidden sorcerer trying to fight off the forces of darkness from overwhelming the world as people understood it; he was a superhero who couldn't reveal his identity to the world for fear of being persecuted. He was all of these and many more. He was anything but what reality and his family kept telling him he was- a nothing; never going to amount to anything; a dreamer; unworthy of being part of the family much less of friends; a drain on the family.

Here, things were different.

Now, he was living with his mother's brother, Alexander Falkstal, in of all places Wellman, Kentucky. He was more than five hundred miles from where those that had tried to hurt him lived. Here, he was safe. Sure, he was living in an unusual community, a kindred of fellow heathens in a hollow outside of town, but it was a community where he was accepted--a community where he was considered a valuable member. His soul was finally free to explore everything he wanted. Not only was he free to ask the questions his inquisitive mind kept generating, he was encouraged to do so. His uncle seemed to revel in Brett's new found sense of wonder as much as Brett himself did.

Since coming to Wellman his life had turned around. Now he didn't have to worry about being embarrassed that his clothes were hand-me-downs from older cousins-- they weren't. He actually HAD money for lunch and didn't have to worry about others finding out he was on the free lunch plan-- he wasn't. Mostly, he had his library. That had been small back home out of the necessity of keeping his mother and father from finding it and burning it. Now he could read to his heart's desire.

"I can imagine, but I don't think he expects you to be anything other than who you are." Shelby said as she touched his shoulder bringing him back to reality. She gently turned him around, "And I mean completely who you are." Locking eyes with him, she said, "You know you didn't have to convert. Alex would have been perfectly happy if you'd stayed with your parent's faith."

"Shel, my parents didn't have a faith. I mean they mouthed the words and I guess they considered themselves to be Christian, but I never saw them practicing it. The first time I went to a Blot here with the Kindred I suddenly felt like I'd come home. I could feel the Gods call me; I could almost see the Allfather's presence around me. I didn't convert because I wanted to please Uncle Alex. I simply came home."

"And you *are* home. You don't have to go back there if you don't want to. You know, I wonder if your Uncle heard the Elderkin calling you before you did. I wonder if he could sense that inside you, and was willing to go to bat for their sake as much as yours." She gave his shoulder a squeeze and smiled. Suddenly remembering the reason he'd sought out his best friend, Brett asked, "So is he going to be starting school on time?"

"Who?" Shelby asked sitting back at the table and looking down innocently at her barbeque sandwich. It was a not so well kept secret that Jeroldan's had the best pork barbeque in the Tri-State area.

"You know who I meant," he told her, his voice in a mock warning tone.

"I suppose so," she asked. "Why are you worried about it?"

He replied with a grin, "Because, it'll be nice to have someone else from the Kindred at the school." Leaning back he added meaningfully, "He'll make nine of us."

"There you go again with that nine thing. Don't try to read more into it than is there." She gave him a smile. "I think maybe your interest may have more to do with other things than just having an extra set of eyes around to watch your back at the high school." The Kindred to which Brett and his uncle as well as Shelby's family belonged was one of the largest in the Appalachians. It was certainly one of the most concentrated east of the Mississippi. Two-dozen or so families had purchased land from the Kindred's Gothi in an isolated mountain valley just east of the small city of Wellman.

"Maybe," he said noncommittally. "I wouldn't tell if it was."

Shelby shook her head with a wry smile, "You've really got to work on your social skills, Brett. Remember what my mom keeps trying to tell us: We are not apart *from* the culture, we are a part *of* it."

He smiled, "I know, I know. Still, whatever I might be interested in would just serve to put me further apart from the rest of the school anyway."

"Yeah, but this one you can't help. It's part of who you are. How you deal with school *is* something you can help. You don't have to keep picking fights with the Crispies. After a while, that just makes the rest of us look bad."

Changing the subject, he asked, "So, how is he really doing?"

Shelby smiled and gave in. "He's adjusting, I guess. He's been in what amounts to custody in Colorado for the last two months."

"Custody, why?"

Shelby carefully controlled her own emotions. She'd heard the tales, and she wasn't sure what she believed. She did know one thing though: There was *no way* Van had murdered his parents. She knew it down in her bones. The other stuff, the werewolves, she wasn't so sure about, but she knew he was innocent of murder. She locked eyes with Brett and kept her voice very neutral. "Because for a while they thought he was the murderer."

"What?" Brett asked lowly sitting back down next to her. He couldn't say that he knew Van *that* well. Heck, the two had only spent time with each other whenever Van's family visited the Kindred-- mainly major holidays and such. But, he couldn't see the other boy as a killer.

Shelby leaned in close, "Look Brett, just drop it for now. I'm sure Van wouldn't want it to get around school. Just keep it to yourself, and if Van wants you to know about it, he'll tell you."

"Van's no kin killer," Brett said patting her on the hand.

She smiled up at him. "No, he's not. But I think something so horrible happened out there that he's blocked it out of his mind.

~*~

Terror so intense that it paralyzed him into immobility locked Van's limbs in place as a snarling bloody maw loomed over his face. He could feel the creature's hot fetid breath as it sniffed him up and down. With a primal scream he broke the grip that fear had on his heart and hurled himself to the side to avoid the beast. The soft straw that littered the forest floor suddenly turned to a hardwood as he rolled painfully into the pine paneling of the dormer. His aunt started at his reaction and leaped backward, her auburn hair piling behind her head as she backed against the door.

"You were dreaming," she managed to stammer. "I'm sorry, you called out." Van could almost hear her heart beat in fear at his reaction to her. He could almost smell it on her.

Shaking his head, Van forced his mind back to the present. "I'm sorry." He fought back the wave of memories that threatened to crash over him, drowning him in their deluge. "I was dreaming about…, about…," he couldn't bring himself to even mention the night that those creatures had murdered his parents. "I had a nightmare," he finally said.

His aunt nodded and straightened her blouse. She gave him a sad smile and said, "I understand. I'm sorry I startled you."

"I'm not," Van said. "I'm glad you woke me up. If I never sleep again, I don't think I would care," he added as he got up and sat on the edge of the bed.

She came over and sat down next to him. "It's okay," she told him. "If you need someone to talk to, I'm willing to listen."

He shook his head, "You wouldn't believe me," he told her. "Nobody else believes me." He gave her a painful look. "Everyone thinks I'm crazy."

"Van, I don't think you're crazy, I know something happened out there in those woods. I know it was so horrifying that it's given you nightmares." When Van went to protest, she gently touched his lips with her fingertips, "I also know what the FBI told me you told them. Do I believe in werewolves?" She shrugged and said, "I don't know. The Eddas and the sagas talk about them a lot, but I can't really say I've seen one. Alex tells me that there are legends of men and women who've mastered both seidr and galdr who can project themselves into a fylgia form to travel about the world. Do I believe these things? Maybe on some level, but mainly I believe in kin." She squeezed his hand. "You are my sister's son. You and Shelby are the only family I have left, and I'm going to stand by you. You tell me you were attacked by werewolves, I'll believe that on some level that's the truth."

Van smiled up at his aunt and said, "Thanks, Aunt Linda. That means a lot." And it did mean a lot to him. Just knowing that he was loved, that there was someone left in the world who cared about him was for some reason very important just now. He turned to look out the window to see the first stars of the evening twinkling against the velvet blackness of the mountain night. Something deep inside him began to stir as he saw the tiny sliver of a waning moon peek over the mountains to the east of the hollow.

~*~

As the rising sun painted rich reds, oranges, and gold across the eastern sky, a low hazy late summer mist settled across the land. The day was just awakening and Shelby could feel in her blood the flow of life across the farm as she led Van toward the barnyard at the base of the mountain where the farm sat.

She gave her cousin a careful look. He hadn't really changed that much physically since the last Yule celebration but there was something definitely different about him. He was still a looker, albeit a little thinner than she remembered. His jet-black hair was longer than the last time she'd seen him but that just gave him a slightly roguish boy-band look. She realized that it was his eyes that were different. There was a dark pain behind those electric blue orbs that hadn't been there before, and that pain seemed to reach out and touch some fierce fraternal chord in her. It was something that had hurt her childhood playmate deeply, and that gave his normally fair features a tragic air.

"Morning chores aren't really that difficult," she told him. "We don't have any cows or nanny goats, so we don't have to worry about milking them."
Van chuckled.

"That's good. I don't think I'd be very good at milking one anyway. Especially a goat; how do you milk a goat?"

Shelby could still feel the deep hurt in him, but there was something else too. Something that was starting to heal and she could feel the life of the farm reaching out to him. "It's not too different from milking a cow. Just smaller udders." The mixture of smile and grimace that brought to his face told her he was at least trying.

"You've milked one before, then?" he asked.

She grinned at him, "Oh, yeah. Mom used to have several to help keep the grass on the north lawn eaten, but they got to making too much a mess around the place so she sold them."

"Too much a mess?" Van asked.

"Yeah, all that grass goes in one end, but she forgot to consider what had to come out the other. Goats aren't exactly easy to housebreak if you know what I mean. Every time they'd get out, they'd make a beeline for the carport and leave us a mess. After a while mom just got tired of the crap."

Van chuckled, "In more ways than one I take it."

"Exactly," she replied, nodded back at him and smiled as she walked up to a paddock where they kept her favorite animal on the entire farm, Faxi, her mother's quarter-horse. She couldn't help but smile at the teasing her mom had caught over owning a quarter-horse in thoroughbred country. Her mom had just simply smiled at it and commented on the notorious bad tempers and high spirits that Arabians had. She smiled and turned as the animal came up to nuzzle her. "This is Faxi. He's mom's horse, but my responsibility."

"Looks like he's your mom's in name only," Van commented at the horse's antics.

Shelby chuckled at the insight and smiled at him as she stroked the horse's withers. "You're probably right. I ride him more than mom does, and since I'm the one who feeds and grooms him, we have a closer relationship than what he has with mom."

As Van cautiously approached the large animal Shelby could almost feel the concern rise in Faxi. She could feel his muscles tightening under her hand, his nostrils flared, and he took a nervous half step backwards from her cousin. Van seemed to sense that the horse wasn't comfortable with him and came to a gentle and graceful stop. "I don't think he likes me," he said.

Shelby looked into the horse's eye and saw the pupil dilated. "That's strange, he's not usually this high-strung."

Van shrugged and suggested, "Maybe I don't smell right to him." He smiled and backed off, "After all, I am sort of new around here."

She nodded and said, "You're probably right." She

didn't really believe the explanation, but this wasn't the time to explore it. Something about the whole situation didn't sit well with her, and that little voice inside her said that this was important. There was something wrong here, and she wasn't sure what it was.

"So where do you keep his feed?" Van asked. "Maybe he won't be so nervous if he's eating." It was a good suggestion, and it showed an insight that surprised Shelby coming from someone raised in the city.

She nodded, "Good idea." Gesturing toward the barn with her head, she said, "Over there, in the feed room. We're going to need to get in there anyway to feed the other animals." She patted Faxi on the shoulder and then led the way toward the building.

As they turned the corner, she halted and held an arm out to stop Van. She wondered when that dumb dog was going to learn. "Shh," she told her cousin. "Watch," she gestured toward the edge of the barn where the family dog, a huge Great Dane named Viking, was slowly stalking Shadow, their gray mouser who lived in the barn. The cat had its back arched up against the red barn wall as it hissed at the dog.

"He'll eat your cat alive," Van whispered.

Shelby turned and looked at her cousin and whispered, "Just watch."

Suddenly Viking lunged forward, his jaws snapping at the cat. Shadow leapt high into the air, letting the larger animal's head pass harmless under him and slam into the barn. Coming down in a gray flurry of hissing and spitting claws, Shadow landed on the dazed Viking's head, delivering several painful blows.

Shelby winced as one lucky shot managed to open the dog's face from lip to nostril before the bigger animal could even get turned around and head toward the gate yelping in pain. She chuckled as the cat rode Viking to the edge of the yard and as the dog passed through it, leapt to the ground and immediately began an emergency bath as if nothing had happened.

"Now that was a surprise," Van said somewhat in awe.

"Viking never seems to learn that the cat has sharper claws and is a whole lot faster than he is." she told him. Shelby shook her head as she once again made her way toward the barn. Opening the door, she basked in the sweet smell of hay, and feed that permeated the building.

Walking over to the feed storeroom Van laughed. "I was sure you were about to have to get a new cat."

"Not this time," she told him. "The day most full grown cats can't fight off a single dog is a day that cat is either very sick or injured or is ready to die." Shelby could sense that for some reason the exchange they just witnessed had affected Van on a profound level. Smiling over at him she added, "C'mon, the sooner we get finished, the sooner we can tear into mom's pancakes. She doesn't make them often, so let's get to 'em before they get cold."

Van nodded and set to work as Shelby showed him where each of the feeds were stored and the chart on the wall where Shelby and her mom kept up with what they'd fed each animal. "Be sure to mark when you feed something. That way nobody comes behind you and over feeds them. This stuff can get expensive."

Van nodded and grabbed a pail of oats and barley as they headed out to where they were to feed the other livestock. Reaching the edge of the paddock, she looked over at her cousin and asked, "How'd you sleep last night?"

Van smiled at her, "Better than I have in a long time." Looking around to where the sun was finally peeking over the mountains on the eastern horizon, he said. "There's something about this place that's just restful."

"I know what you mean. This really is a very special place. I mean with the Kindred here, it's a place where we can really build a heathen community."

"How does that work for you in school?" he asked. "I mean do you catch a lot of grief from the non-heathens?"

She shook her head, "Not really. That is not most of us. Brett seems to go out of his way to pick a fight with the Crispies, and that can sometimes cause problems for the rest of us."

"That doesn't sound like him. I mean, Brett's the last person I would think would pick a fight," Van replied.

Shelby snorted, "It's not so much that he picks fights as he tends to wear his faith on his sleeve, and reads more into things than are really there sometimes."

There must have been more venom in her voice than she intended because he asked, "I thought you two were best friends?"

She smiled and nodded, "We are. It's just sometimes our best friends can drive us up the wall."

Van smiled over to her as he poured the pail into the trough. Shelby noticed that the smell of food seemed to overcome Faxi's reticence toward Van and he approached cautiously, keeping one eye on the stranger. After a moment, Van said, "I'm sorry to hear that Brett's having a hard time fitting in. I really like him."

Shelby raised an eyebrow at that, "You do?"

Van just smiled at her, "Yeah, I do. He's a good friend and from what he's told me about his past, he deserves a break. I just wish he wasn't having so many problems with being different."

"We all have problems being different, Van. It's whether or not we go looking for those problems by using our differences to dare people to say something about them."

Van smiled as the horse began to eat while it was keeping a weather eye on him. He sighed and stepped away to allow the animal to have its meal in peace. "I know. Some things are harder to hide than others." Shelby had a feeling where he was going with this. They'd talked about his differences on occasion in the past. It had been hard for him to tell her his secret, and she was glad he trusted her enough with it.

"You don't have to hide, Van. Nobody in the kindred

will say anything to you," she told him.

He smiled at her, "I know. That's what mom told me."

"You finally told the 'rental units?" she asked.

Van nodded and replied, "Yeah. The night they were...," he seemed to struggle to find a word. Finally, he changed tack and said, "The night we were attacked."

"What did they say?" she asked carefully. She knew they'd gone into the mountains for a mini-vacation just before Midsummer as a family celebration. Van's mother had been a very gifted vitki and seidrworker and had helped lead several Blots for the Kindred in the past. Shelby halfway suspected that she'd been working some kind of magic that night. Van's revelation was the kind of thing that could seriously throw off her center and skew any spell. She also realized that he probably never told the police what he'd told his parents. If he had, they probably would have never let him go. They'd think he might have murdered his folks over their not accepting him.

Van shrugged and set the pail down. "They told me that I was their son and they loved me anyway." Something in his tone said there was more.

"But?" she suggested.

"But that they still expected me to continue the blood. That they expected to have someone to remember them along the line besides just me," he told her.

They knew! It suddenly hit her like a load of bricks. In an instant flash of memory her aunt's favorite perfume permeated the air around her and she knew in her bones she was right. *They knew they were going to die and they were trying to tell him not to forget.* Of course this was not the kind of thing that she could say to him right now. She could feel that the wounds were still a little too raw to deal with that kind of knowledge. Instead she said, "They were right you know. Nobody in *this* Kindred would have a problem with it. Not as long as you manage to remember that we're supposed to make sure that we're the ancestors of somebody. Otherwise, there'll be nobody to Blot to us in a hundred years."

Van nodded to her. "I know." He smiled, "But let's face it, I'm sixteen now. That's something I'll worry about in ten years or so."

She smiled back, "That's good to hear. I think mom would kill either one of us if we got too much of a jump on that particular duty to the Kindred." She stopped a moment and thought about what they were discussing. "Do you plan on telling her?"

Van shook his head, "I hadn't planned on it. You're mom has enough to worry about without this to add to it."

"It's not a burden, Van. You're family, and we take care of family." She grinned at him and punched him in the arm like she used to do when they were ten and their biggest worry was whether or not there was going to be a new Ranger on the team this upcoming season. "Besides, mom can handle it. She's a strong woman," she told him. Then, with a mischievous grin she added "Like her daughter."

Van grinned and picked up the pail and headed back to the barn. "You know I think you might be right about that."

"I know I'm right, Van Griffin. Didn't you know that we seidr-workers are always right?" she teased him.
"When did that become a law?" he asked over his shoulder.

She smiled and followed, "Last night while you were asleep."

He chuckled and reentered the barn, setting the pail in the feed storeroom. "Still, I wonder if I could help Brett with his social skills," he suggested.

"I don't know, I think he might be willing to listen to you. I know he needs friends," she told him.

"I think I can do that for him," Van suggested with a strange unreadable expression.

CHAPTER 2

Under hooded lids Shelby watched her cousin as the two walked quietly down the halls of Wellman High School. She wasn't sure what she was watching for, but something told her that it was important. A tingling at the back of her skull seemed to warn her something significant was in the making. Wellman was not a large school. Between the high school and junior high, which were housed in the same building, it had only about 400 or so students, but it was a very good school, which was one of the reasons the kindred's gothi had chosen this area for the community in the first place. Most of the students all knew each other, and by the end of the year, even the faculty tended to learn most of the students' names by sight. All in all it was a very good place to grow up, even if it was dull and boring, which of course was something for which it wasn't to be forgiven. Nothing interesting ever happened here.

As the two exited the main office, Shelby looked down the hall and groaned at what she saw. Two senior football players, Dallas and Craig, each had Brett by an arm and were making their way toward one of the larger garbage cans at the intersection of two halls. It was obvious that they thought the whole situation to be quite amusing. Brett on the other hand was anything but amused and was kicking futilely at the air.

Van followed her gaze as he too saw the smaller blond being manhandled. "Wait right here," he said, handing her his schedule. Striding with easy steps he put himself between the garbage can and the trio like some tall brooding piece of dark granite.

Dallas raised an eyebrow at the sudden obstacle. Shelby

watched as his eyes seemed to measure up Van and then glanced over at Craig. With a nod, he turned back to Van. "What's up man?" he asked casually as if he didn't have one half a kicking sophomore in his grip.

Van smiled at him and then turned to address Brett, "Hey man. How's it hanging?"

Brett looked at his friend incredulously and then answered in a sarcastic tone as he looked down at his feet. "About six inches off the floor right now." Shelby did notice that he stopped kicking.

Van turned back to Brett's captors, "I'm sort of new at the school, and need my friend here to help show me around." He indicated Brett with his head. "Do you mind?"

Dallas gave him a long look and the two locked eyes. From her vantage point, Shelby couldn't see her cousin's eyes, but she could see something else dawning in Dallas's. She could almost feel the primal fight or flight reaction build in the boy. Something on an animal level seemed to pass between him and Van: A challenge was thrown down, and Dallas had let it pass uncontested. He let go of Brett as a result and said, "No problem."

"Thanks, man," Van said. Then he turned to Craig, "Do you mind?"

Craig seemed confused by Dallas's reaction. His face revealing that confusion and a building anger, he turned on Van and growled, "Why don't you just stay out of it, pretty-boy?"

Still not losing his calm, Van reiterated, "Brett here's a friend of mine. I sort of would like to have him around not smelling like stale milk and pencil shavings."

"So?" Craig challenged. "We don't always get what we want."

In an even voice that dripped controlled violence, Van answered, "I usually do. Especially when it comes to my friends and their safety." He stepped forward and gently pulled Craig's hands from around Brett's upper arm.

Shelby watched as the color drained from both Brett's

and Craig's face at the sight of whatever they saw in Van's eyes. Brett quickly scampered meekly around behind Van and stood there, obviously trembling. "Okay, man," Craig backed away, never taking his eyes off Van. "Take the little weirdo," he growled at Van. Once he was sufficient distance to feel safer, he called back loudly, "This isn't over!"

Van shrugged and said, "It is as far as I'm concerned." Turning to Dallas, he asked, "You?"

Dallas smiled warmly if a little uneasily, "Sure man. We were just playing."

Van smiled back. "It's cool." He then added less warmly, "As long as it doesn't happen again."

Dallas just nodded, looked sheepishly over at Brett and said softly, "Sorry, man." Brett gave him an incredulous look and muttered something Shelby didn't quite catch. With that acknowledgment, the senior turned and left the trio standing there.

"What was that all about?" Van turned and asked Brett.

Brett shrugged and said somewhat bitterly, "Just Craig and Dallas's favorite game of smear the heathen." He looked over at Van and said, "Thanks, man."

Van smiled at him, and for the first time since he arrived in Wellman, Shelby saw it reach his eyes. "Not a problem." He shook his head, "But you gotta stop picking fights with football players."

"I can't help it if they're intellectually challenged," Brett protested.

"No, but you can help by not pointing it out to them," Van suggested. "C'mon, buddy. I know you. You probably said something that brought attention to yourself."

Brett looked down at the floor and Shelby could see the blood rise in his neck and face as he blushed deeply. Finally, to Shelby's amazement, he said softly, "You may be right."

Van smiled hugely, put an arm around the smaller blond boy and said, "See? All you gotta do is think about what you're about to say before saying it."

Brett nodded, "I'll try."

"Good," Van said.

Shelby looked over at Brett and asked, "How come I can tell you that and you fight me. Tall dark and gorgeous here tells you and you say okay? What's up with that?"

Brett looked over at her and smiled weakly before glancing over at Van. What she saw in that glance made her wonder just how much trouble Brett was going to get himself into before it was all over. Turning back to her, he shrugged and said, "Don't know. Maybe something about all those karate trophies you were telling me about?"

~*~

Dace Yarnvid hung up the phone and looked over toward his brother Logan and their cousin Vic with a feral grin. "Found him," he told the others. "He's living in Northeastern Kentucky in some place called Wellman."

"Who?" Vic asked from where he was sitting across the legs of an armchair, a soda in hand.

"The boy. The one who killed Greg," Dace replied. He'd been searching for the little punk for the past few weeks but hadn't had much luck. Finally, a few well-placed questions to a buddy who ran with a pack in Denver had turned something up.

"Vandyl said to leave him alone," Vic said as he sat up.

"Well, it wasn't Vandyl's brother the boy killed either," Logan interjected, the anger evident in his voice.

Dace nodded in affirmation and turned to Vic and said, "We answer to Granny before we do Vandyl, and you know she'd skin us alive and rub silver in the wound if we let Greg's killer get away."

Vic shook his head, "I don't know, Dace. Getting Vandyl upset doesn't sound like too good an idea to me."

"Well, letting that little punk get away with killing' one of ours don't sound too good to me either," Logan said with a growl. Even in the dim light, Dace could see his brother's features grow more feral. The wolf was always close to the surface in Logan.

Vic shrugged, "Okay, okay. You want to' eat the kid; we'll go eat the kid. I was just pointing' out that Vandyl'll get mad."

"We'll let Granny deal with Vandyl," Dace told him. "Nobody gets away with killing one of my brothers, no matter what."

"You going to' tell 'Thias where we're going?" Vic asked.

"Tell him where we're going' not what we're doing'." Logan said. "This is family business and 'Thias ain't family."

"Maybe he isn't family, but he's the pack leader," Dace told him.

"He's Vandyl's pack leader, not Granny's and not ours. When Vandyl sends us to do something then he's the pack leader. When we're on our own, I'm the pack leader," Dace said daring his cousin to contradict him.

Vic gave him a look like he didn't believe him but said nothing about it. "Fine by me. When do we leave?"

He grinned at Vic and said, "Tonight. Get rid of that girl sniffing around you and be ready to go by sundown." Turning to leave the room, he stopped at the door and told his brother, "Get online and find out where the nearest airport to Wellman is and then book us three tickets. We're going hunting." He watched as both men nodded and then left to talk to Mathias.

~*~

Caleb zipped up his lettermans jacket against the un-usually cold late September morning chill as he walked through the festival. He reached back and undid the tie hold-ing his long brown hair to let it fall to the sides of his head in hopes that it might keep his ears a little warmer. The festival impressed him with its focus on a subject near and dear to the hearts of many Eastern Kentuckians: crafts. There were lines of tents set up along either side of slate stepping-stones that ran in paths down the middle of the large well-mown field. Each tent held a small display with all sorts of hand-made items including brooms, pottery, weaving, and various kinds of metal work. There was even a sword shop that seemed to be doing a brisk business.

In the center of the field was a small stage where a band named *Something Rose* was playing what sounded like an old Irish song. The field was set between rows of houses and small farms that dotted the road through the valley that the locals had renamed Mountain Hearth Hollow.

Lots of people were moving in and about the tents, buying wares, discussing various points of interest and for the most part just visiting. He smiled at himself at the costumes some of them wore. Traditional Pre-Industrial Revolution costumes seemed to be the norm of the day. There were so many men in kilts that on occasion he had to remind himself that he wasn't in Scotland. In some ways he was reminded of a Renaissance Festival he'd once attended in North Carolina. He also wondered how they weren't freezing their junk off.

He'd never really been out to what the local residences called the Kindred, even though it was just down the road from the parsonage. Of course he wouldn't admit it to him-self but his interest in the festival had less to do with seeing what these people with the strange religion was about than it did with spreading his wings, and rebelling a little from his father's profession. There was also another reason, one that he would at least admit to himself if no one else, a reason that had long auburn hair and deep green eyes.

Stopping at a small snack shop, he paid entirely too much for a sausage and biscuit and a glass of apple cider- which unfortunately wasn't hard but was at least warm- before wandering further along. Snacking on the biscuit, he drifted over toward the stage and listened to an amusing song about the virtues of dating pagan girls. The band was good, there was no doubt of that, and he thought he might pick up their CD.

"Didn't expect to see you out here," the sound of Dallas Howard's voice caught his attention from the crowd.

He looked over to see Craig Blankenship turn to his fellow senior and reply, "I'm not really. Mom wanted to come out and look at the crafts and I got drafted into coming along. What about you? You turning into one of these pagan wannabes?"

"Nah, just didn't have anything better to do and Van suggested I stop by. He scored me a free ticket to the pig roast this afternoon, and you know me, I don't turn down good barbeque." Both seniors laughed as Dallas patted his trim stomach.

Craig shook his head and asked warily, "What are you doing hanging around that freak Van for?"

"Hey, Van's cool," Dallas said.

"He's one of these weird pagans..."

"Heathens," Dallas corrected him. "From what he and Shelby tells me, they don't really like to be called pagans."

"Pagans, heathens, what's the difference?" Craig said dismissively.

Caleb watched as Dallas gave his friend a long look before asking, "You really want to know, or do you just want to be difficult?"

Craig shrugged, "Don't really care. They're all going to hell anyway."

Dallas just shook his head and said, "That's what you believe, not necessarily them."

"When did you get in so good with them?" Craig asked.

"I mean a month ago you didn't give a damn about these weirdos and now you suddenly seem to be their best friend."

It was Dallas' turn to shrug. "Don't know. Since I took the time to get to know 'em I guess. Van seems to be pretty cool."

"Most of the girls think so at least," Craig said with a hint of bitterness in his voice. Caleb too had noticed that half the girls in the school suddenly had the hots for the tall newcomer to Wellman High. Fortunately for him, stereotypes notwithstanding, Van wasn't Caleb's competition for his cousin Shelby, just a possible obstacle. "I wouldn't mind re-arranging that pretty-boy face of his," Craig added.

"I wouldn't try it," Dallas told him. "You might lose that chance at playing for Kentucky if you got a broken leg."

Craig smiled wickedly and in a tone of voice that suggested there might be more than just speculation involved, replied, "You never know. Some of us may just decide to take him out in the woods and give him a good ol' country-boy butt-kickin'."

Dallas grunted with mild disgust, "I wouldn't try it." Then looking around he seemed to notice that Caleb had been listening and nodded to him. "Look there's Caleb. I need to talk to him about last night's game. Catch you later."

"Sure," Craig said as Dallas left him for Caleb's direction.

"What's up man?" Caleb asked as the senior approached.

Without speaking, Dallas took him by the arm and guided him some distance from Craig. Finally stopping just outside the sword shop, he looked back over his shoulder and sighed. "Nothin' really. Just needed an excuse to get away from Craig. He's gotten really weird about this place since school started back in August."

Caleb nodded, "Know what you mean. It's like he's got a hate on for anything to do with them. Any idea why?"

Dallas nodded, "I think so."

"Care to let me in on it?"

Dallas blushed and looked around, "It's nothing really. Just that Van stopped him, uh... us, from having a little fun with Brett, and ever since he's acted weird."

"I heard about that," Caleb said. Cautiously he added, "Gotta' say, I was a little surprised to hear you'd given up your favorite pastime of smear the heathen." One didn't bring up the football captain being bested without some caution.

Dallas chuckled, "Well, we were being jerks."

"Don't take this wrong, Dallas, but what's happened to *you* lately? You've taken a hundred and eighty degree turn in attitude about the Kindred since then," Craig asked.

Again Dallas blushed. He shrugged his shoulders and said, "Don't really know. After that, the fun just seemed to go out of it."

Caleb nodded, still not understanding but not about to let Dallas know that. "So why are you here today?"

He smiled, "Van scored me some tickets to the barbeque, so I thought I'd stop and see what was going on. What about you?"

"Nothin' better to do on a Saturday morning, and I thought it might be interesting." He tilted his head toward the stage and said, "Besides I heard that the band was good."

Dallas turned and listened for a few bars and then nodded in agreement. "Now that you mention it, they are- in an Enya sort of way."

Both boys chuckled as they wandered on down toward the head of the field. They slowly browsed through the shops commenting on various crafts and goods available as they went. After a while, the regular hum of the crowd, and then the steady ring of steel striking steel slowly drowned out the sounds of the band. There was a peculiar rhythm to the ringing, one beat followed by two half-beats.

The ringing was coming from a large tent set farthest from the bandstand. It was a big pavilion number enclosed on three sides. From the backside where he and Dallas stood,

Caleb couldn't tell what sort of shop it enclosed, but there was an acrid coal-burning scent coming from it. The boys exchanged a quick glance and walked around to the front.

With a smile, Caleb realized that it was a blacksmith and farrier shop. What surprised him was to find a tall auburn-haired woman slowly pounding on a piece of red-hot steel. As they entered, she looked up, smiled, blew a strand of hair off her eyes and said, "Hey guys. What's up?"

Dallas smiled and said, "Hi, Mrs. Stein. Is Van around?" He looked around the shop, held his hands out toward the forge and said, " You know, I think this is the warmest place in the whole festival."

"He's up at the house changing, she told him as she put the piece back into the forge. Turning back she smiled at Dallas warming his hands, "You should try being around the forge in the summer, you'll get plenty warm."

"I'll bet," Caleb said. "Why is he changing clothes?" Looking around at the forge he asked, "He didn't get burned or anything did he?"

Mrs. Stein laughed and answered, "No, he didn't get burned, a little surprised but mainly muddy and bloody, but not burned."

"Bloody?" Dallas asked, suddenly alarmed. "How?"

Mrs. Stein just smiled at them. "This morning, he went out bow hunting with some of the other men in the kindred."

"Nobody got hurt did they?" Caleb worried.

She shook her head, and Caleb realized that it was obvious she was trying to hide her amusement at whatever had happened. "No, not really. It's just that they went deer hunting, but Van came back with a wild hog, a sow I'm told." By now she was openly grinning. "According to what I've heard, the sow came charging out of the bushes, and Van shot it at pretty close range. Supposedly it was a clean shot right through the heart, but was so close that the thing's momentum carried it right into him. According to Brett, Van was knocked down and it died on his chest."

"Weird," Dallas said.

Mrs. Stein said, "No kidding. He was covered from head to toe in blood and dirt. When he first came in I didn't recognize him." For a second her eyes drifted upwards as if she was remembering the scene, an enigmatic smile on her face. "He left about half an hour ago, so he should be back any minute now."

"I thought he was hunting deer. I mean, don't you get in trouble if you kill something not on your license?" Caleb asked.

"Not in this case. Wild hog is an invasive species so it's legal year round," Mrs. Stein explained.

"Cool," Dallas replied. "So, is that what's being roasted today?"

Mrs. Stein shook her head, "No, there's not enough time to dress it and then cook it. It'll be butchered and then preserved for later in the year."

"Sweet" Dallas said, and Caleb wondered if he'd been invited to dinner.

"What are you making Mrs. S?" Caleb asked, indicating the metal that was heating up in the fire.

"I'm working on a new draw bar for the tractor. It broke last week when I loaned it to Mr. Falkstal."

"You fix tractors?" Caleb asked surprised.

"I fix as much as I can around the farm, Caleb. Being self-reliant is one of our Nine Noble Virtues."

Caleb laughed and told her, "It just surprises me to see such a nice lady working with hot iron."

"What?" she asked. "You think it's supposed to be man's work or something?"

"No! Not really," Caleb quickly interjected as he realized he might be in dangerous territory. "It's just, you don't look like a tractor mechanic or a blacksmith."

She just grinned at him, "I'll take that as a compliment."

"So what you boys got planned today?"

"Thought we'd hang around the fair, see what's to see,"

Caleb said. "See if Brett and Shelby wanted to join us."

Mrs. Stein gave him a look that made him wonder if she knew he was more interested in spending time with her daughter than with Brett or Van. Finally, she said with a twinkle of mischief in her eyes, "I think you'll enjoy it. Don't forget to stop by and get some of that barbeque, Dallas mentioned. Brett's uncle has been in charge of the barbeque since they put it in the pit last night."

"Mr. Falkstal is cooking?" Dallas asked. "I didn't know he could cook." The high school counselor didn't exactly have a reputation as being that domestic. He'd once heard that the confirmed bachelor knew a widow that he exchanged work around her house for hot meals and such.

Mrs. Stein shrugged and said enigmatically, "He can cook, it's just he usually doesn't have time to. He fixes some of the best barbeque you'll ever put in your mouth."

Dallas grinned beside him, "Then I can't wait."

"Can't wait for what?" Van's voice asked from behind them as he, Brett and Shelby entered the tent.

At the sight of the leggy redhead, Caleb felt something knot up in his stomach. He could literally feel his pulse start to throb in his chest. Caleb swallowed and forced his attention on her tall good-looking cousin and replied, "The barbeque, Mrs. Stein here was telling us how good Mr. Falkstal's barbeque is."

Van gave him a long look, his eyes seeming to follow Caleb's gaze dancing back and forth between himself and his cousin. Finally with a light chuckle and a knowing smile, he said, "You'll just have to come and find out for yourself then."

~*~

It felt good to be on the hunt, and Dace knew that it was only going to get better, before the night was over. The target they'd been sent after was going to be sweet; he could almost taste the fear and the death in anticipation.

'Thias had already spread the pack out long before they got too close to the campfire. Greg and Matthias were to come in from the south, Dace was to cover the north side of the campground, while Vic and Logan took the east and west. It pretty much left the kill for the pack leaders and the rest of 'em got what was left.

Dace could smell the food cooking on the campfire. He could hear their conversation, even a good half mile away. His senses were alive with the spoor of the hunt as he loped through the forest in his half wolf- his battleform. He heard the son's confession to his parents. He heard their support of him, and it turned his stomach. There were some things that he'd never accept, even if they were understood by the old ways.

He approached the edge of the campsite silently as he watched the family carefully. He could see the altar to the hated Shining Ones off the side, the hammer- it looked like the standard three pound sledge used by so many these days- and a blot bowl were sitting there along with a large knife lying next to it. The targets were sitting near the altar talking softly, the parents trying to comfort the son. Dace could smell the weakling boy's tears on the soft breeze.

At a signal from 'Thias, Dace howled into the campsite, raised himself up to his full height and stood there in the light of the full moon. With a deliberate slowness designed to create fear in the prey, he leaned down into the face of the boy and growled. Both of the parents turned to face him, which gave 'Thias and Greg the time they needed to close for the kill. The humans never knew what hit them.

Seeing him, the boy however did something that no human had ever done. He dove out of the way and came up next to the altar. Moving faster than Dace ever expected to see a human, he whipped the knife and hammer from the altar and tore into Thias and Greg.

Out of the corner of his eye, Dace could see Logan and Vic closing the circle so the boy couldn't escape.

Dace heard the crunch of bone as the hammer slammed into Greg's skull. He knew that the blow would have killed an ordinary human or wolf, but that it was only going to make his older brother angry. With two quick lopes across the campsite, Dace lunged at the boy. Again moving with a speed and grace Dace had never seen in a human, the kid danced out of the way as he raked the knife down Logan's back. From his younger brother's howls of pain, Dace knew that the knife had to be made of silver.

Dace's own blow already committed slammed directly into the open wound on Logan's back. Logan reacted the way he does to anything that hits him; he attacked Dace.

By the time Dace was able to clear himself from Logan's attack and chase his brother from the melee, the boy had managed to get outside the circle. But instead of running he stopped and turned. There was no fear in his eyes; there was no spoor of the hunted on him, there was only hurt and rage. If Dace hadn't known better, he would've sworn the boy was about to go through a first change as his lips drew back in a feral snarl.

With a roar of defiance the boy charged forward toward Dace. Dace was fast, but somehow the boy was faster. Dace swung hard at the kid's head. The boy ducked and wasn't there. Then he was there again delivering a painful kick to Dace's groin, followed by another to his knee that was accompanied by the sound of snapping bone. As Dace bent over in pain he felt the icy fire of the silver blade spread across his body as it bit deep into his lower back.

Turning as he fell, Dace saw the boy zigzag so that only one member of the pack could get at him at a time. He ducked a blow from 'Thias and drove the blade into the pack leader's armpit. 'Matthias' howls of pain could be heard for miles.

The boy closed with Greg, who was feeding on the kill. Dace could see the disbelief in Greg's eyes as the boy actually charged. With a low growl, Greg swung a backhanded blow toward the kid. Again the kid ducked as he stopped cold and stared into Greg's face. "I'm going to kill you," came the boy's voice. "It doesn't matter if I *die or not, I'm going to kill you for what you did."*

Greg growled again and leapt low at the boy to bring him down. The kid sidestepped the attack and with a great overhand blow drove the hated dagger down into the base of Greg's neck. Dace could hear his brother's spinal column snap from the force of the blow.

Suddenly Vic was telling him to switch to wolf form as 'Matthias howled the retreat. Retreat?! Dace couldn't believe that "Thias was going to let the boy get away with killing a packmate. He started to argue with him, but seeing the pack leader's face decided against it. He obeyed and switched forms as the pack, or at least what was left of it, loped away, their mission only partly completed.

Dace's last memory of that mission was seeing the boy kneeling by the bodies of his parents. "No good can come of leaving an enemy behind," he'd told himself.

A sudden lurch from the jet landing pulled Dace out of his memories. The pretty young attendant was giving instruction on deplaning. Dace growled lowly to himself. "I will not let him get away with killing Greg."

CHAPTER 3

Van felt better than he could remember feeling since that horrible day this past summer. Time had indeed begun to heal the wounds of his loss. Still there was a dull ache in his soul, but no longer did even the most minor event remind him of his parents. He still thought of them daily, and missed them terribly, but he was moving on with his life.

His talks with the Kindred's gothi and with the school's counselor, who happened to be Brett's uncle and guardian, Alex, had helped him greatly to put things in perspective. He was slowly coming to realize that he was still a part of the greater family that was the Kindred.

Today had been a case in point. While traipsing through the early fall woods at dawn, bow in hand, he'd felt a connection to the land like never before. He felt as if his mind had reached out to become one with his surroundings.

He'd known the sow was going to charge- known that it was there- before he'd ever seen it. There was a feeling as if something had guided his hand, and his arrow. He hadn't even realized he'd loosed the arrow until the creature's death throes had been stilled atop him. He remembered struggling out from under the huge beast and looking around for the woman whose laughter was like tinkling glass that seemed to surround him. Whatever the sound was, it was gone, leaving him to stand silently over his kill.

"Earth to Van," Shelby asked from his side.

"Huh?" he turned and asked.

"You sure you didn't hit your head when that hog

charged?" she asked. "You were wool-gathering."

He laughed and smiled over at his cousin, "No, I was just thinking."

"About?" she asked.

He shot her a look that he knew she'd understand: *later, not here.*

"So tell me about what's going on here, this weekend, Van," Dallas asked, seeming to sense the uncomfortable moment.

Van smiled. Since he and the football captain had become friends, Dallas had shown more of an interest in learning about the community as a whole. "It's the Allthing. People from various kindreds from all over the area come here to meet, to discuss business, to settle disputes, and to gather."

Dallas gave him a questioning look and asked, "I thought it was Frey-something-or-another?"

"Freyfaxi," Shelby interjected. "The Allthing is for business and just fellowship. Freyfaxi is the religious ceremony."

"Who's Freyfaxi?" Caleb asked. "I've heard of Frey, and Freyja, but never Freyfaxi."

"Freyfaxi was a horse," Brett told him.

"You're having a religious ceremony for a horse?" Dallas asked incredulously.

"No," Van shook his head. "We're having the ceremony in remembrance of what happened with the horse, and the lesson it teaches us about the importance of oaths."

"Okay Van, so what's the story?" Caleb asked.

Van smiled as he looked over at Brett. The smaller boy was quiet as they walked along toward the creek bank that wound along the valley at the foot of the northern mountains. Van couldn't help but notice how his hair was shining bright gold in the fall sunlight. "Brett, why don't you tell him? You're a better storyteller than me."

Brett gave him a startled look and gazed back at him, as if searching for some kind of trap. Immediately, Van understood. In the past too many other people had set him up for teasing this way. Van gave him a gentle smile, did his best to project the sincerity he felt toward the smaller youth. Brett *was* an excellent storyteller, and Van loved to hear him weave a good tale. Sensing his honesty, Brett smiled his thanks and nodded. What Van saw in his eyes made him swallow as his heart skipped a beat. "Okay," Brett said and launched into his tale.

"It's an old Icelandic tale about a very devout farmer who had dedicated himself to Frey, whether or not he was trui I don't know, but we do know that he was so dedicated to the God, Frey that he gave half his horse to the him, swearing that nobody but himself or Frey would ever ride him. He named the horse Freyfaxi."

"What's trui?" Caleb asked.

"Trui, is when a follower of our faith takes an oath swearing himself to the service of a single As or Van."

"As or Van?" Dallas asked.

Brett looked over at him and sighed, "Sorry, sometimes I forget that not everyone knows the technical terms of the Lore. There are two clans of our Gods. The Vanir, such as Frey, his sister Freyja, Njorth, and Nerthus, are deeply tied to the land and the cycles of life. The Aesir are the other clan. Odin, Frigg, and Thor represent them and they're a bit more war-like."

"Anyway, there was this farmer named Hrafnkell, who had a horse that he gave half of to Frey. Like I said, he swore that nobody but himself or his God would ever ride Freyfaxi. Now, Hrafnkell was a farmer and somewhat wealthy. He had lots of sheep that needed to be looked after, and a herd of mares ruled over by Freyfaxi, so he hired a local boy about our age to named Einar to watch after them."

"Hrafnkell explained to Einar that he could have the service of any of the horses except Freyfaxi to use to keep up with the sheep he was supposed to watch. He went on to explain to Einar the reasons that he couldn't ride Freyfaxi so there would be no misunderstanding."

"One day there was a great storm brewing and Einar found himself high up in the mountains watching the sheep, but there were thirty missing. Of course at that time and in that culture, thirty sheep represented a lot of money, so Einar knew he was in trouble."

"After spending a lot of time looking for the sheep, he realized that the weather was getting worse, and that he could cover a lot more ground on horseback. So, he went down to where the herd of horses were, and tried to catch one. But with the wind being up and the weather being bad, the horses were spooked and he couldn't catch any of the mares to ride. Freyfaxi however, simply stood there watching him as he approached."

"Einar considered his position. He could try to ride Freyfaxi and save his employer's sheep, or he could tramp around all day in the wind and rain, and mud, and maybe never find them. After a while, he decided that what Hrafnkell didn't know, wouldn't hurt him, so he approached Freyfaxi with a bridle and caught him. The horse didn't seem to mind, so Einar swung up on his back and headed off in search of the sheep."

"After a long search, Einar was able to find all of them, and return them safely to his employer's lands. However when he got down from Freyfaxi's back, the horse bolted before Einar could get the bridle off him. Shrugging to himself and satisfied that his employer's sheep were safe, Einar went into the little cabin Hrafnkell provided for him to use while he was up in the mountains and waited out the storm."

"Meanwhile, down at his home, Hrafnkell was having dinner when his housekeeper told him that Freyfaxi was at the door whinnying for him. Getting up from his table, Hrafnkell went out to see about his horse. When he got there, he was upset to see Freyfaxi had obviously been ridden hard, and still had the bridle on him. He told the horse, "I'm sorry that you've been misused this way. I will get to the bottom of it." He then instructed his house servants to take the horse to the barn and feed him."

"The next day, Hrafnkell took his axe with him up into the mountains as if to cut some wood. He came upon, Einar working around the cabin and asked him straight out, "Did you ride Freyfaxi?"

Einar was an honest boy and nodded, "Yes I did," he told Hrafnkell. He then explained about the sheep.

"Hrafnkell nodded, and said, "It's good that you were honest about this." Then before Einar could say or do anything, Hrafnkell ran at him and killed him with a single blow from the axe."

"That's a little harsh isn't it?" Dallas said. "I mean, he did save Hrafnkell's sheep, and it was only a horse."

Brett nodded, "It was but it wasn't. You have to understand that Asatru take oaths very seriously."

"So this is a story that celebrates murder in order to fulfill an oath?" Dallas asked.

Brett shook his head, "No. It's a story about the dangers of making them in the first place. The moral isn't: keep your oaths at all costs. It's: be careful what oaths you make, because the cost of keeping them may be more than you want to pay."

"What happened to Hrafnkell?" Caleb asked.

"He eventually became a very powerful Jarl in Iceland. He set up a very nice barrow and monument to Einar. Not all turned out great though. Freyfaxi was killed in retribution for Einar's death, and a whole clan war was sparked. However in the end, Hrafnkell was a very wealthy and happy man."

Van broke in, knowing that Brett was likely to go into a long description of Icelandic history if he didn't. "So what we do at this time is to remind us that we should be careful what kinds of oaths we make. Oaths aren't to be taken lightly. We don't make them easily, but when we do, we'll make sure they're kept."

"So it's sort of a negative example?" Caleb asked.

Brett chuckled, "You could call it that. Hrafnkell was a good and honest man who kept his oath, but came to realize that making them lightly isn't a good idea."

"I guess that means if you guys promise something, it's going to be kept," Caleb commented.

Shelby nodded at him and replied, "Oaths and promises are two different things. I can't speak for Brett or Van, who I've never known to break a promise, but I know that if I promise you something, I'm going to keep it."

"She just doesn't make very many promises," Brett teased her.

"Exactly," she smiled back. "Our word is our bond. Oathbreaker is one of the worst insults you can throw at us."

"I'll keep that in mind," Caleb said as they walked along. Van noticed the other boy watching his cousin closely. He knew that Caleb's father was the minister of the little church just outside the Kindred. He wondered how much of Caleb's interest in Shelby was part of the whole bad-boy preacher's kid thing.

"So what do you guys want to do today?" Dallas asked.

"Well, I don't know about you guys, but I'm hungry. How about we grab some funnel cakes and some cider and go listen to the band for a while?"

"Sounds good to me," Shelby replied.

Both Caleb and Brett both jumped at the suggestion.

~*~

Dallas got the feeling that there was a lot more going on with his friends than any of them were really willing to let on about. *Friends.* That word hit him hard. When had these people become his friends? Three months ago, his favorite pastime had been giving them hell, especially Brett. Now, after the scene on the first day of school, he'd found himself being drawn to them.

He wasn't sure why they suddenly held such fascination for him. Maybe it was when Van had stood up to him. He hadn't told a soul, but he couldn't identify whatever it was he'd seen in the tall raven haired youth's eyes that day, but whatever it was, it had shaken him badly. There was a controlled violence there that was both awesome and terrifying at the same time.

Maybe it was when Brett had come to him alone, full of hard won courage and humility all rolled into one. He'd actually apologized to Dallas for picking fights, and told him that it was not going to happen again. For some reason the sheer courage that it took to do that had impressed Dallas as much as what Van had done.

Now he found himself spending the day hanging out with them at one of their festivals and enjoying the heck out of it. He caught himself smiling at Caleb's attempts to get Shelby's attention. He didn't blame him either. She was pretty, smart, and had a fire and will about her that was extremely attractive. Dallas though, had learned a long time ago to avoid red heads, and from what he'd heard, she had the temper to go with the hair.

He looked over to where Van seemed to be watching Brett out of the corner of his eye. Again, he wondered about his friends and how he ended up here. "So you want to go?" Caleb asked.

"Huh?" Dallas replied.

"To Brett's house, they asked us over next Friday night,

for movies and pizza."

Dallas shook his head and realized that Van wasn't the only one who'd been wool gathering. "Uh, sure. It shouldn't be a problem. What about you? How late can the preacher's kid stay out?"

Caleb shrugged to him, "As long as I'm home in time for church on Sunday and he knows where I am, Dad doesn't mind."

"So are *you* going?" Van asked. Then he looked over at Shelby and added, "Forget I asked that."

Caleb chuckled. "I guess I'll be there."

"Uh Caleb?" Dallas asked.

"Yeah?"

"What did I just agree to go to?"

"It's just a get together at my place. We're going to sit and talk, eat pizza and watch some horror movies," Brett told them.

"Sounds good," he told him.

"Good, glad to see you there," Brett told him.

"Uh, just curious about something though?" Dallas asked.

"What?" Van asked.

"Why us? I mean, since when do you invite outsiders in?" Dallas asked.

"What outsiders? This isn't about the Kindred or Frey-faxi, or the Allthing. It's just a bunch of friends spending some time together," Brett answered. Then giving him a strange look, he added, "You *are* a friend aren't you?"

The question caught Dallas off guard. He had to admit that he hadn't realized that these guys had become his friends, but somehow they had. He smiled over at the smaller boy and said quietly, "Yeah."

"Good," there was genuine pleasure in the smaller boy's eyes. Then turning back to the others, he asked, "So, what dya guys want to do with the rest of day?"

"I don't know," Shelby replied as she slipped up beside

Caleb and smiled at her fellow sophomore. "Why don't we just hang around the festival, do some shopping, and just chill?" The others nodded in agreement and Dallas found himself following along.

~*~

At sumbel later that night, Linda watched her daughter and nephew from the corner of her eye as they sat quietly listening as the horn passed from person to person. Secretly, she was very proud and pleased with the way he'd managed to find a niche inside the kindred. His success with finding friends outside the kindred was also a good sign. Maybe his influence would help Brett learn to not wear his faith on his sleeve so much. She knew that Alex worried about his ward and how much trouble it had caused him professionally. It was difficult being the high school counselor when your own nephew and ward was constantly pointing out that you followed an alternative religion. It was a good thing he had tenure. However, today, all three teenagers had comported themselves with the honor and dignity appropriate for the situation.

First round of the sumbel each of them had raised the horn in honor of a specific God who they felt was touching their lives. She'd been a little surprised, and maybe just a little worried by Shelby and Van's toast to Freyja, but it had been Brett's that had been the most revealing. Somehow, the small teen just didn't strike her as a Thor's man, but it was to Red Beard that he'd raised the horn.

As the horn was passed to her for the second time she stood and cleared her throat to fight back the emotions that even now, five months later, threatened to choke her voice from her. This was the round of toasts to heroes, friends, and ancestors, and she already knew to whom she would lift the horn. With the strong clear voice that surged from her soul she said, "As many of you know, my sister and her husband took the long walk this summer. Both, had been to these halls many times before and had lifted a horn to the Gods, to honored ancestors, and to the disir alongside us. Now it is our turn to raise this horn to them as they have gone to be with our ancestors. Hail Ellen and Dane Griffin, may your souls find peace in the Halls of our Elderkin!"

Beside her, she heard her daughter say, "To Aunt Ellen

and Uncle Dane."

From the Shelby's other side, Van's voice added, "To Mom, and Dad."

Many in the hall added their sentiments and stood in honor of her family. She'd always known that they were welcome here, and the show of support from her kindred made that tangible. She raised the horn to her lips and drank deeply, savoring the taste of the wassail before passing it to her daughter.

Shelby looked at her mother, and then to Van. Something seemed to pass between them and she lifted the horn with both hands and said, "To my Dad who died on the battlefield and to all the Einherjar!"

Again there was much assent as Van reached out and put a hand on her shoulder saying, "To Uncle Max and drank from his own cup." At this rate, Linda expected the kids to be more than just a little inebriated by the end of sumbel.

Next, it was Van's turn to take the horn. With a respectful bow of his dark head, he lifted the horn high and simply said, "Mom and Dad." Maybe it was something in the way he said it, maybe it was the solemnity of the moment, or maybe it was something higher, but for just an instant, Linda smelled her sister's favorite perfume, and images from their childhood together came rushing. Then it was gone, and the moment passed.

Linda shook her head as Brett took the horn and surprised her again when he said, "To Uncle Alex, who gave me a home, who introduced me to the Shining Ones, and who taught me what it means to be part of a family." Again there were several toasts of assent and the horn passed on down the table.

Linda considered the surprises she'd witnessed today and wondered why they surprised her. After all, it was their first sumbel and she was sure they, like all teenagers, wanted to be taken seriously. Why should that surprise her? But something at the back of her mind kept telling her there was something else. This was no ordinary group of teenagers. There was glory to be won here, and that thought scared her more than she wanted to admit.

It was the third round, the one coming up, which worried her the most however. Third round of sumbel was called Oaths, Boasts, and Toasts, and it was here that boasts were made, oaths taken, and life, people, and friends were celebrated. It was the oaths part that had her worried. What was said over the horn was considered to be part of the Well of Wyrd, and for good or ill was considered binding to all present.

She hoped and prayed to the Gods that listened that the children had paid attention to the lesson of Freyfaxi. She knew that Van was still hurting over his parents' death, which was as it should be. She was somehow terrified that Van might do something, make some foolish oath about revenge that he would regret. It had not escaped her attention that many of the great tragedies and sagas from the lore came from people making foolish oaths.

However, she had her own oath to make on this round as well. It was important to her. It was important to the kindred, and she knew it was in some ways important to Van. It would be his official welcoming into the kindred and into her family- and it was just as binding. For long moments, as the horn passed its way down the rest of the length of the table, and then back up the other side, she fretted.

It was traditional for the persons highest up in the hierarchy of the kindred to sit closest to the head of the table. As was also traditional, her own place as a community elder was not far from that head. Most people would be surprised to learn that women played a much more important role in ancient Nordic society than in other cultures, and that they had pretty much the same rights and responsibilities as the men. It was only with the coming of Christianity to Northern Europe did they lose many of their rights. The church went out of its way to destroy the worship of such Goddesses as Freyja and

Frigg because the idea of a strong female upset the sensibilities of the patriarchy of the church.

This nearness to the head of the table gave her some time to think about how she was going to word her oath as the horn went on down away from her, across the table and then back up the other side. Mountain Hearth Kindred was no small kindred, and therefore sumbel could take quite a while. There were also a great many fresh new faces here today. At her decision to allow Van and Shelby to participate as adults, she'd noticed that many other parents had also taken that same step. She secretly wondered just how many hangovers they were going to be dealing with tomorrow. After all, the wassail- a combination of apple cider mulled with honey and spices, and then mixed with vodka or rum- was pretty powerful stuff.

Finally, Gareth, the kindred's gothi stood and cleared his throat, a bit of childlike mischief glinting out of his good eye. Tale was, he'd lost the other in a hunting accident back when he was a teenager, because he now wore a patch over it. Linda always thought that the missing eye and the gray hair and beard gave him the look of the Allfather. His gnarled hands took the cup as it was refilled and he said, "Third round of sumbel is traditionally called Oaths, Boasts, and Toasts. It is a time when we boast of what we've accomplished or will accomplish; when we take oaths to bind ourselves more strongly to the Gods, and to each other, and a time when we toast any all we feel are worthy. It's also a time for gift giving, as gifts strengthen our connections to each other as well. The Sayings of Har tell us, *If friend thou hast whom faithful thou deemest, and wishest to win him for thee: ope thy heart to him, nor withhold thy gifts, and fare to him often.* Well, you are all my friends, and my family, and today I want to do a little of all four."

"We started this community together nigh on thirty years ago. Like a family we've had our prosperous years and those that were not so prosperous. We've made it this far sometimes quietly, often argumentatively, with more better than worse by being a family of families, and by being friends. We are what is discussed in many of our circles as the best example of a modern tribe that I can imagine. As a boast, I like to think that I've had not some small part in that." He smiled again and raised the horn.

"I look out today and see a room of family that is growing and prospering. We have several new faces here- our next generation of Asatru, and I have to say that I'm impressed with what I've seen. So as a toast, I'd like to tell all you parents out there, good job; you've raised a fine crop of kids. A great deal of the acceptance we've received from the local community has come through your children. By the values you've taught them, they and you have shown us to be good neighbors who work with our surrounding community for everyone's benefit; as opposed to being some weird devil-worshiping cult. It is you, the parents, and you the young people here today that I want to toast. " He chuckled and paused.

Linda remembered the times when she first arrived in the kindred when several of the local churches had preached against them, and made life difficult on those who bought land and settled here. Of course her own theory about the turning point of the attitude toward them had as much to do with the festival that invited others in to see how they lived. And of course there was the flood of '93 when the whole Kindred turned out to help man the sandbags when the Ohio threatened to put most of the community of Wade, including the upper elementary school, under water.

Gareth continued, "I believe that this community will continue to grow into the next generation. I believe that our faith as a whole will continue to grow and prosper, and as such I want to take an oath to do everything reasonable in my power to help this growth along."

"Finally, I want to make this gift to the young people here. To each of the nine of you, I am gifting two acres of land at the mouth of the valley for you to use to build a home when the time comes." He grinned outrageously, and lifted his cup first to the Gods and then drank deeply from it as the whole table stood and joined in the toast. Linda knew that there were several people inside the kindred who'd already approached him about purchasing some of that land for their kids. Many were afraid that the lure of the larger cities like Lexington, Columbus, and even Huntington would take their children away. This was the kind of gift that would indeed strengthen the community ties. She knew that Gareth was a shrewd old man and it was this kind of thing that confirmed her knowledge.

After the toast and the room settled down the horn passed back down the table toward her. Finally, as it reached her she smiled and stood. Holding the horn under her mouth to make sure that the words would go into the Well. She smiled over at Shelby and then at Van beside her before saying, "Van, you are blood of my kin and that makes you kin. You have come into my home and become part of my family. I know that I can never replace your parents, and I would never try. However, you are part of my family and I will do my best by you as if you were my own son." She raised the horn and drank deeply.

Linda understood that this really didn't have to be said. But to say it here, to say it now, over the Well of Wyrd made it binding and made it real. From this point on, the kindred would recognize Van as part of her family and as part of the kindred. She passed the horn to Shelby whose eyes were just a little droopy.

The girl stood and looked down over the horn and said, "Here's to Gareth. And thank you." As other cups were raised, she took a sip and then passed it to Van.

This was it. This was the moment she'd feared. She had no idea what her nephew was going to say, and that worried her. He looked at the horn, and then over to her. He smiled softly and spoke over it. "Thank you for everything. Thank you for giving me a home. Thank you for giving me a place to live and a chance to heal. But most of all, thank you for just being here when I needed you. Here's to you, the Mountain Hearth Kindred." Then as the weight lifted from Linda's shoulders, he passed the cup to Brett.

"I too want to offer my gratitude and thanks to everyone here. I especially want to thank Van for helping me see some of the mistakes I've been making, and I promise to try to do better." He drank and the horn moved on. Linda's fears abated and drained away.

CHAPTER 4

Craig smiled at the pretty young sophomore who'd agreed to do some digging for him. Felicia Ballenger was in the perfect position to pull it off too. Her dad was an FBI agent assigned to the Huntington office. And of course meeting here at Jeroldan's was the perfect cover. Nobody would think twice about a smart, pretty girl, helping one of the football players out with some homework.

She shook her head as she pulled the file from her back pack. Craig took a moment to study the girl. Her black hair had been highlighted with bits of brown and was braided into long strands that stuck stylishly out from the wool hat she was wearing. Her skin was the color of his mom's favorite milk chocolate and her mouth was wide with a smile that always seemed to be reflected in her brown eyes. He decided that if she was a senior, he'd definitely date her. Other things went without saying. The girl was smoking!

She made to hand it to him, but then pulled it back. "You can't tell anyone where you got this. If my dad found out he'd ground me until I'm an old maid."

Craig gave her his best "captain of the football team" smile and said, "I'm not going to tell where I got it, Felicia. I promised you and I always keep my promises."

She nodded and handed the folder to him. "It's some pretty messed up stuff in there. To be honest I wouldn't push him. He's already killed one person."

Craig raised an eyebrow in surprise, "Who?" That was something he wasn't expecting.

"One of the gang bangers who attacked and killed his folks. Stuck a thirteen inch blade through the back of his skull, after nearly beating him to death with a sledge hammer," she said.

"Damn," Craig said. "That's messed up." Shaking his head as he considered the news he added, "So our pretty-boy isn't all that nice after all."

"Don't know if I'd go that far," Felicia replied as she zipped up her backpack again and settled into one of the tables sipping at her shake. "I can't say I wouldn't kill someone who hurt my folks. Now the other stuff though. That's fair game."

"What other stuff?" Craig asked.

"The doctors think that it may be some kind of post traumatic stress- you know, hysteria. But he claims that they were attacked by werewolves."

Craig gave her an incredulous look, "You're kidding?"

Felicia shook her head and replied, "No. The scary thing about it is that the bodies showed signs of an animal attack and there were at least four sets of large wolf prints in the area."

Craig gave her another incredulous look and asked, "Don't tell me you actually believe this stuff? Didn't you say it was a motorcycle gang that attacked them?"

"That was the one who was dead- he was a member of a West Coast gang. They found him naked with the blade stuck in his neck. There's no other evidence that the rest of the gang was there."

Craig suppressed an involuntary shudder. "This is starting to sound like something out of X-Files. Why didn't they charge him for the murder?"

"Not enough evidence mainly," Felicia told him. "It was his word against a dead man with a record of violent attacks."

"Any idea how our pretty-boy managed to kill someone like that?" Craig asked.

"Karate?" she asked. "He's got the background- a black

belt in combat style Shoto-khan karate from one of the most exclusive dojos in the Lexington area. And the rumors that are floating around about that group he lives with is that they teach their kids to use guns, bows, knives, swords, and even axes."

"And evidently sledge hammers," Craig said as he glanced over the file. He was starting to have second thoughts about the plan he'd let slip to Dallas that he and some of the other seniors had for tall, dark and brooding. He wasn't sure he wanted to take on a guy that had already killed one hardened criminal. He was going to have to seriously reconsider his options.

~*~

Brett swallowed hard as he entered his Uncle Alex's office. He couldn't think of anything that he had done to get himself in trouble. On the contrary, he'd been going out of his way to behave himself ever since Van stopped Craig and Dallas from dumping him in the garbage can. His grades were as they always were: blowing the curve. "You wanted to see me sir?" he said to the school's counselor.

Alex smiled up from under the shock of blond hair that always seemed to curl at his forehead, "Sit down Brett. I want to talk to you about something important. Just let me get this filled out."

Brett raised an eyebrow but said nothing as he settled into the uncomfortable waiting-room style chair in his uncle's office. He took a moment to look around the room. He smiled at the poster of the kitten clinging to a rope with the words: HANG IN THERE on the wall. It was the exact same poster as was in one of his favorite movies. Behind the desk hung his uncle's degrees from various colleges and universities in Kentucky. He briefly wondered how his uncle- born and raised in Georgia had managed such deep ties in the Bluegrass State. He also noticed several photos on the filing cabinet. One was of him, Shelby, Van, Dallas, and Caleb at the pig roast. Another was of him and his uncle at Six Flags Over Georgia this past summer. They were standing with several park employees dressed as the Justice League. Brett noticed his uncle was trying not to ogle Power Girl's impressive endowment.

Drawing him out of his reverie, Alex closed the file in front of him and smiled. Finally speaking he said, "Mrs. Devlin came and talked to me the other day. She wants to test you for Talented and Gifted classes. I want to know what you think of the idea."

"Tag classes, the ones that do all the cool field trips and stuff?" he asked surprised.

Alex chuckled and nodded. "Yeah. She does a lot of outside projects." He leaned back in his chair, steepled his fingers and added, "It'll also be a lot more work, but I think you can handle that." His voice became serious as he said, "Let's face it, Brett, you're IQ is off the charts. You're breezing through high school like it's not even here. I think Mrs. Devlin's classes will challenge you."

Brett shrugged but remained silent. His intelligence had been the cause of this problems with his family back in Georgia. It was what set him apart there, and what he'd only recently been struggling with not letting it set him apart here- thanks to Van. Sighing, he asked, "Can I think about it?"

Alex smiled and said, "Of course. I understand your need to consider all your options."

~*~

Shelby settled into her regular table at lunch and opened the insulated lunch pack she'd brought. Since the new nutrition regulations came down from the government, nobody ate the school lunch anymore- not even the people on the free lunch program. People found a way to bring their own lunches, even if it was only an apple and a peanut butter sandwich. Of course, now there was talk of banning peanut butter sandwiches because of nut allergies.

As she pulled the lid off the thermos full of her mom's venison stew she opened her can of soda and looked around for her friends. The first person to settle across from her was Brandt Snow- he was a handsome blond with a brain that gave Brett a run for his money. She knew there were quite a few girls at school that were quietly crushing on him, but so far most of them were a bit afraid of the hammer he wore around his neck. Some of the local ministers could be real asses.

As if to punctuate that thought, Brandt was joined by of all people Caleb Johnson. "Mind if I join you guys?" he asked, settling in across from Shelby?

"Not at all," Brandt said. "Did you get that homework for Mr. Mercer finished?"

"Yeah," Caleb replied. "Took me a while to figure out exactly what he was talking about. I mean, come on. It was such a little comment in the story that you thought it was a throw away line."

"That's the way Straczynski writes," Brandt said. "A character will make an off-handed comment that will become important or at least a watershed moment later. Vir's comment to Morden is a perfect example of that."

Caleb shook his head and said, "I'm sorry. I don't get the reference."

Shelby elbowed Brandt gently and said, "Don't pay him any attention. He's just geeking out."

"Speaking of geeking out," Brandt said. "Did you hear the good news about Brett?"

Shelby raised an eyebrow that suggested she wouldn't appreciate any comments at her best friend's expense. "What?"

Brandt smiled and said, "I'll wait and let him tell you then."

"You are just evil, Brandt," she told him.

"Well, it's his news, and it's good news and I agree with Brandt, he deserves a chance to tell it," Caleb interjected. She couldn't help but notice the look he gave her. She recognized that Caleb's interest in her was more than just someone to hang out with- she wasn't stupid. She also realized that their two situations could create problems for both of them. His dad wasn't known as a fan of the kindred. Hel's Bells, he'd resigned from the city's Interfaith Council over Gareth being accepted onto it. And her own faith was important to her. It was part of who she was and what had shaped her. She wasn't going to turn her back on that just because some boy smiled at her, no matter how cute he was. Still the comment about Brett said a lot about his character.

Before she could reply, Brandt's sister, Allison as well as Brett settled into seats at the table. As they began digging into their lunches, Shelby felt something primal touch her mind. She looked toward the door to the cafeteria to see where Dallas Howard was putting his life in danger by standing between Van and Craig Blankenship. Both boys were squaring off over something.

"Oh crap!" Brett said and got up from his table as Caleb joined him.

"What?" Shelby asked, getting up.

"I'd say that Craig's mouth has finally written a check his body can't cash," Caleb said heading in that direction.

Van stepped toward the other boy, and suddenly something primal rushed through Shelby's mind, literally staggering her. It was like looking directly into the eyes of an animal that was about to eat you. She heard a mental growl and looked over to where both Dallas and Craig were standing with their eyes wide in fear. A yellow puddle was forming around Craig's shoes. He looked down and realized what had happened. Then out of nowhere he screamed and leaped at Van. He had the look of a man who was going to die, but was going to die fighting.

Her cousin stepped sideways and for an instant, Shelby was convinced that Dallas was going to simply miss his target. At the last moment, Van's hand lashed out with lightning speed and grabbed the other boy by the back of the belt. He pivoted on his heel and with one hand slung the much bigger senior back down the hall toward where Mr. Mercer was coming down to break up what was going to be a fight.

Dallas hit the floor hands and face first, bounced once, twisted sideways and rolled into the Sophomore English teacher, taking the older man's feet out from under him. Someone in the crowd looked to where Dallas was standing and said, "Craig peed himself!"

Shelby pushed her way through the gathering crowd and put her hand on Van's shoulder. He spun on her, faster than any human had a right to move and for a brief moment she saw the pupils of his blue eyes morph from a near slit to their normal round form. She looked down at the hand at his side and could have sworn that she saw something sharp and dark glitter at his fingertips. Realizing who she was, her cousin suddenly relaxed and looked back over his shoulder where Mr. Mercer and Craig were picking themselves up off the floor. "Maybe you should call Aunt Linda. I get the feeling that I'm going to be in trouble."

Shelby just nodded and pulled out her cell phone to make the call.

~*~

The forest was alive with sights, sounds, and smells. The light of the nearly full moon gave everything an eerie glow. Van was surprised at exactly how well he could actually see. All the colors of the world were muted, but at the same time, he could make out surprising detail in the low light.

At the same time all his other senses were alive, more alive than he could possibly imagine. The forest around him was brimming with unknown scents and sounds. Gone was the sense of dread he had when he'd gone to bed. A feeling of freedom and power poured through his limbs, as he ran across the forest floor, sometimes dropping to an almost four-limbed gait. In the distance he could smell the spoor of a frightened deer, and something else. Something primal, like himself. Something vaguely canine, and there were lots of them crisscrossing the forest floor. He heard a howl in the night and recognized it as a call to the hunt- but not a call for him.

He leapt high onto a ridge and then with a preternatural agility scrambled up the trunk of a tall ash tree, the claws in his fingertips and toes biting deep into the old tree's bark. Stretching out on a limb, he waited. Why should he chase his prey when the wolves would send it toward him.

It wasn't long before he heard the panicked sounds of animals scattering in all directions. A large buck came bounding over the ridge and under the tree. Muscles like steel springs launched him into the air and onto the buck's back. With a single stroke of the claws at his fingers he opened up the deer's throat. As it stumbled to the ground under his weight he felt the life go out of the magnificent creature.

With a quick prayer of thanksgiving to the Keeper of Cats, he began to dig into the creature's chest, burrowing for the heart. Finally ripping the organ free he began to feast on its thick muscle. For long moments, the only sounds in the forest were the sounds of the tearing of flesh as he gorged himself on not just the flesh but on the spirit of the animal itself.

Suddenly a low growl came from below the ridge. Looking down he saw several wolves standing on all fours in a semi-circle

*around him. He threw his head back, roared and then bounded off
into the night. He had what he wanted from the beast, its heart and
spirit that tied it to the land itself. Behind him, he could hear the
wolves begin to fight and growl over the carcass.*

~*~

Gareth Bjargeir ran the cotton cloth over the hard wood as he looked up from his counter at The Eye in the Well Antiques as the bell on the door went off. He looked up with his good eye and immediately knew this was not going to be a pleasant visit. The ulfhedinn did not come to visit him often, and when they did, it usually meant some kind of problem with the kindred.

The fact that one was much older than the other suggested that they had come expecting trouble. The older man looked around the store as if he was shopping for something specific. When he was sure that the three of them were alone, he approached the counter and tossed something on the glass surface.

"You've got a problem Gareth," he said. "We and the Council of the Tree agreed to let you found a kindred here, you agreed to keep your people out of our business."

Gareth looked down at the small silver hammer on a chain. He immediately recognized it. Only one member of the kindred wore that particular design on the face of their hammer. "Where did you get this?"

"Something took the vaedvaettir last night. It wore a coat like none I've seen before. It was not one of us. After eating the heart of the stag, it took off faster than the pack could follow. It left that," the younger man said, his gray eyes blazing with an inner fire only those chosen of the Allfather could know.

Gareth picked up the hammer and asked worriedly, "It took the hunt-spirit, what does that mean?"
"It means that one of yours has bound himself to the land in the same way we are. But he's not ulfhedinn."

"How do you know?" Gareth asked.

"Because he was more human than animal, and the spoor was wrong," the younger man said. "The Allfather gave us this land to guard. We can't do that without that connection to the landvaettir. You are close to breaking our pact,

Gareth." He leaned over the counter and growled low. Gareth noted the three interlocking triangles of the volknut he wore swung from under his shirt.

"I did not send anyone from the kindred to interfere with your Wild Hunt,"Gareth said, staring back at the man with his one good eye. He knew exactly what effect his eye could have- especially on those who had told the Allfather where to put the spear. "But, I will get to the bottom of it." He turned back from the counter and picked up the hammer and chain, he added, "We have a new member. He may interest you."

"We know about the Griffin kid. He kicked the crap out of old man Blankenship's brat yesterday. I heard he made him lose control of his bladder," the older man said pulling the younger one away from Gareth.

"Did you know he killed a managarm?" Gareth asked.

The younger man gave Gareth a double-take, before asking, "How do you know?"

"Four managarm and a werewolf attacked him and his family in Colorado. They killed his parents, but he killed one of the managarm with the family seax," Gareth told him, dropping the hammer into his vest pocket.

"How do you know they were managarm?" the old man asked.

"They were in a half man form, and they had tails," Gareth told him. He and Van had relived that night many times when they'd talked. The boy had a remarkable memory for details. "You know what that means."

"And the other didn't have a tail?" the old man asked.

Gareth nodded and added, "And he was in the man-wolf form, so he wasn't ulfhedinn either."

"This changes everything, Gareth," the old man told him. "Why didn't you tell us about this?"

"I had no idea that the boy had been infected- or for that matter if he's been infected. More importantly, I'm probably the only person that he's told the tale to that believes him. The police wanted to pin his parent's murders on him."

"Do you think the boy has become a moon-wolf?" the old man asked seriously.

Gareth shook his head and replied, "I don't know. He's showing some signs of irritability, but that could just be from being a teenager." He gave the younger man a knowing look. "His aunt has grounded him for fighting, so that means he's going to be inside for the full moon cycle."

"That could be dangerous for her," the old man said.

Gareth nodded. "I've asked her to let him stay with me for the next few days so that I can get to the bottom of his anger issues."

"Has she agreed?"

Gareth shook his head and said, "Not yet."

"Well, something was out last night and it has either purposefully, or by accident tied itself to the spirit of the land. Like it or not, it's now the guardian for the next year."

"Can't you call another hunt?" Gareth asked.

"We could, but all it would do is tie us to it," the older man said. "I prefer to keep my wolf-skins under my control for now."

Gareth nodded again. "I will see what I can find out."

"Do that old man," the younger man said, reaching for the door.

Gareth just grinned at him and touched the scar running down his face. "I will. But you keep in mind how I got this scar cub. We can work together on solving this problem or we can make both our problems more dire. It's up to you."

CHAPTER 5

Van smiled as Faxi kept a watchful eye on him as he fed the animals on the farm. He'd offered to take Shelby's chores as a form of penance for losing his temper and getting into a fight. The school had suspended him for three days- which he guessed was fair. Craig had gotten the same. Mr. Mercer told him that he'd not have been suspended at all if he'd just let Craig leap past him, but because he caught him and slammed him down the hall, he had to face the same punishment. The bad part for Craig was that he was going to miss Friday's game against Greenup County.

"Wanna talk about it?" his Aunt's voice came from the hay loft of the barn.

Van nearly jumped out of his skin when he heard it. Instinctively he stepped back into a defensive stance. Realizing who it was and that she'd been watching his reaction he forced his heart rate to slow and shrugged, "What's there to talk about? I screwed up."

"Gotta give you credit where it's due, Van Griffin, you don't avoid taking responsibility for what you've done, and you don't make excuses. But there's more going on here and I'd like to know what it's about."

Van shrugged and told her, "He called me a name."

"Must have been some name," she said.

Van looked at the ground as his aunt climbed down from the loft. As she stepped off the last rung of the ladder she said, "What I want to know is what you said to him that made him lose control of his bodily functions." She put a hand on his shoulder and said, "Mr. Grizzle showed me the film. You said something that scared the screaming meemies out of both him and Dallas Howard. What was it?"

Van shrugged and figured this would be as good a time as any to tell her his secret- the secret he'd told his parents the night they were killed. "I told him that if he kept it up he was going to find out exactly how far I can really be pushed."

"What are you talking about Van?" she asked. Van got the impression that she was just a little afraid of where the conversation might be going.

Van shrugged and decided to be completely honest with his aunt. "He wanted to know if I killed Mom and Dad and made up the story about werewolves to get out of it. I told him that I didn't make it up, but that I did put a silver knife into the base of the skull of one of them, so that should tell him exactly how far I'd go."

He watched his aunt's eyes grow large. "How did he find out about what happened?"

Shaking his head, Van said, "I don't know. But he had some pretty specific details about what the police think happened."

"What kinds of details?" Linda asked.

"He knew what the coroner's report said," Van told her. "When that didn't get the reaction out of me that he wanted he stooped to name-calling."

"Must have been some name," Linda said.

"Not really," Van told her. "It just surprised me, and I stupidly reacted to it."

"Exactly what did you say, Van?" Linda asked.

Van shrugged and said, "I told him that if he kept it up, he was going to have to explain to his daddy why he got his butt kicked by that queer." He looked up at her expecting to see condemnation, rejection, anything but what he saw.

"Do you think you're telling me something I didn't already know, Van?" she asked.

"Did Shelby tell you?" he asked, suddenly hurt by the

idea of his cousin telling his secret.

She shook her head and said, "No, Shelby didn't tell me. I have two eyes, I can see. And what I've been seeing lately is you and Brett dancing around each other to see who's going to say something first." Leaning back against the paddock fence she asked, "You mean to tell me that you broke Craig's arm because he called you a queer?"

"I never touched his arm!" Van protested.

"No, but the floor did when he hit it, twenty feet down the hall," she said. "There's more to it than just that, Van. I'm not sure what it is, but I'm going to find out. I told you that you are my family, and right now I see my family hurting. I don't like it."

"What else?" he asked.

"Well, there's the fact that I looked in on you about three this morning and you were not in your room. Your window was open, but I can't imagine you taking a twenty-five foot drop to the ground below. This morning there was blood all over your sheets." She stopped and looked at him. "Either you've started your period, or you hurt yourself somehow." With a wicked grin she said, "And last time I checked you aren't likely to be having a menarche."

Van felt himself blush. "I woke up this morning with blood all over my face and hands. I don't know how it got there," he told her.

She nodded and said, "You know you're grounded?"

"Yeah," he replied looking past her.

"Well, Gareth asked me to let you spend a few days with him. He has an idea about what's going on. I can't say that I believe him, but I'm willing to give him his way on this." She stopped and touched the side of his face, "You don't have to go, but I think it would be a good idea. Gareth says that you two talk a lot."

Van smiled weakly. "Yeah, we do."

"Good, pack enough things for a few days. He's picking you up at noon," she told him, turning away. Stopping with her back to him, she said, "And oh, Van?"

"Yes, ma'am?" he replied.

She reached into her pocket and pulled out something and tossed it to him. "He said you dropped this last night when you brought down that deer." Shaking her head, she said, "I don't understand what he's talking about, but he says that you've crossed some kind of line and need his help."

Van just nodded and replied, "Yes, ma'am." He looked down at the hammer in his hand. That would explain why he couldn't find it this morning.

~*~

Shelby looked over at Brett and the others sitting at the table for lunch. Things were very quiet at her usual lunch spot. She had no illusions as to why too. The big news around the school was that Craig's arm was broken- snapped both bones in his right forearm when he hit the floor. Somebody had managed to get a copy video of the fight from the office and uploaded it to the internet. Nobody was pointing fingers- yet, but the best money was running on it being Felicia Ballenger. That girl had computer skills like nobody else in the school.

Brett sat down, looked over at her and asked, "Did Uncle Alex talk to your mom?"

"About what?" she asked.

"He has to go out of town. He was wondering if we could move the movie night to your place?"

"Oh yeah," she replied, remembering her mentioning it. "She says that since Van is going to be staying with Gareth, it's okay." She stopped and smiled at him, "But you owe me big time. You are going to have to help me to clean up before and after."

Brett smiled and said, "You're on."

Several more people joined them at the table, some from the kindred, but not all- not the least of which was the head cheerleader, Carmen O'Brien. She wasn't quite as Brett would say, Shelby's arch-nemesis, but they'd had their conflicts in the past. To be fair though, Shelby recognized that she wasn't completely blameless in those conflicts. She looked over at Brett and said, "Caleb tells me that some of your friends are getting together at your house tonight after the game. I was wondering if Brandt Snow was going to be there?" The last she asked at nearly a whisper.

"Well, it's been moved to Shelby's," Brett said.

"Oh," the well-built brunette quietly commented. She seemed to consider her options carefully before asking, "Is Brandt going to be there?"

"Why are you worried about where Brandt is going to

be?" Shelby asked. She knew the girl had a quiet crush on her friend, but at the same time she suspected that she was afraid of the fallout of being a popular girl dating one of Reverend Johnson's favorite groups to hate. Of course her own interest in Caleb Johnson was going to cause enough strife on that front to maybe hide Carmen's stealth campaign to catch the attention of the kindred's quiet genius.

"Don't know. Just wondering," the girls said coyly as she munched on some carrot sticks from her lunch.

"Don't you have to cheer tonight?" Brett asked.

"Yeah, but I figured the party wouldn't really get started until after that. It won't even be good and dark until after the game, and everybody knows you can't start horror movies while it's still light out."

"She's got a point," Shelby said. Looking over to where Dallas was settling into a chair she asked, "With Craig out, what are our chances against County?"

Dallas just smiled and said, "I think probably better than most people realize. Craig's been off his game lately. Caleb is starting in his place."

"Good," Brett said. When everyone turned to look at him, he said, "Hey! I like to see my friends get ahead."

"Right," Shelby said unconvinced as she threw a piece of apple at him.

"So what movies are we watching?" Shelby asked.

"Thought we'd start off with classic Sam Raimi and the *Evil Dead*," Brett said.

"That's different. Aren't you starting Halloween a bit early? It's still almost a month away," Carmen said.

"Never too early for Halloween," Brett said. "Come on, it's the perfect holiday. We get to dress up in scary costumes, scare the snot out of each other, eat all the candy we want, and for one night of the year, extortion is legal." Brett smiled over at the head cheerleader and asked, "Does that mean you're coming?"

The brunette smiled coyly and said, "I think I might

do that. Beats having to sit and listen to certain people brag about how well they did on the field."

"Glad to have you," Shelby said, not exactly feeling it.

~*~

The sun was still about two hours away from setting behind the hills of Yeager Airport in Charleston, West Virginia, and Dace was already in a bad mood. He'd told Vic and Logan to find out where the nearest airport to Wellman was. The problem was that there were no flights from where they were into Huntington, so they'd had to settle for flying into Charleston nearly 80 miles away and then driving from there to the small town across the Kentucky State Line.

Even the interstate that wound its way out of West Virginia was bracketed on both sides with Autumnal mountains ablaze in reds and golds. The mountains felt old to him, older than even those of their ancestral home in Northern Europe, and definitely older than those where his family settled in Iceland. They were not as high nor as steep as the Alps of his youth, nor even the Rockies where he now lived, but they were far older, and for some reason that put Dace on edge nearly as much as the rising full moon he could feel just below the horizon

It took over an hour before they pulled off the interstate onto the secondary road heading toward Wellman. Passing through the narrow Silver Gap leading north between the mountains, Dace became even more agitated. He could feel something in the very land itself- something alive, and something very powerful. It was old- at least as old as the mountains themselves and it was asleep. He involuntarily shuddered at the idea of it awakening.

As they cleared the gap and the valley below opened up before them, Dace could see the lights of the town come on as the sun's last light faded from view. The valley widened out into a broad plain along the banks of the Ohio River, with another road and set of railroad tracks on the far side running parallel to the river. The mountains to the north and the south ran right up to the edge of the road effectively isolating the small community from the outside world. A second smaller valley opened up between the mountains on the North, and somehow Dace knew in his bones that it was there he would find his quarry.

"Where to first, Dace?" Vic asked from the passenger seat. He'd slept most of the drive from the airport and was just now realizing that they were at their destination.

Dace growled slightly and said, "First we find a place to hide the car. Then we go looking for the kid. We want to make sure that he knows exactly who is coming for him."

"Is that a good idea?" Logan asked. "Wouldn't it be better to take him out quickly, and be done with it?"

Dace shook his head and said, "No. We want to send a clear message to anybody who'd mess with us. You don't get to kill a Yarnvid and get away with it."

"If you say so, Dace," Logan replied from the back seat. "I'm not sure this is going to end well though. Vandyl doesn't know where we are and neither does Mathius."

"Are you scared of a single boy?" Dace asked as he drove into the small town.

"He killed Greg in a fair fight," Vic said.

"We don't do fair fights," Dace growled. "We're a pack. You're either one of us, or you're prey."

"So, how do we find our "prey" then?" Vic asked.

Dace pulled into the lot of a small strip mall and found a spot at the back corner. Putting the SUV into park, he pulled his phone from its case and started tapping its surface. "It's the twenty-first century. I got his aunt's name and address from the file where he was released into her custody. All I have to do is type it into the search maps app on my phone and we're on our way."

"But is he there?" Logan asked.

"What do you mean?" Dace turned to ask his brother.

Logan pointed to the cars moving along the road and in the parking lot. "It's a Friday night and he's a high school kid. Is he likely to be home now?"

Dace sat back and thought about what his brother said. He knew if he were the kid he wouldn't likely be home now.

Turning he asked, "What do you suggest then?"

"Find a place to hole up for a few hours, then later when he's more likely to be home, head over there and check things out." He looked back toward the East and grinned wickedly before adding, "It'll also give the moon a chance to get high in the sky."

Dace grunted and thought about what his brother suggested. It made sense. No use risking any more of his pack than necessary, and facing a sleeping house is always preferable to one that is wary. "How do you think we should kill some time?"

Vic pointed to a sign at the local eatery: **GO MOUNTAINEERS! BEAT GCHS MUSKETEERS!** "It's been a while since I saw a good high school football game." He grinned again and added, "Besides, you never know who we might run into."

~*~

Felicia Ballenger settled into the bleacher seat next to her mother as the two watched the game below. Okay, Felicia wasn't paying that much attention to the game- she had other things on her mind. Her mother on the other hand seemed genuinely interested in it. She was a tall beautiful woman with a grace and intelligence that Felicia always found a solid anchor in her life. In some ways she'd always reminded Felicia of an actress from the sixties famous for being involved in the first interracial kiss on broadcast television. Her mother's skin was a bit darker than Felicia's but was unblemished, giving her forty some odd years an ageless beauty that Felica hoped she'd inherited.

But these thoughts were only a distraction from the turmoil she felt swirling in her soul. She felt guilty about giving that file to Craig. It kept her from enjoying the football game on the field below. Which was a shame because Wellman was eating County alive. She felt guilty because Craig had gone and gotten himself seriously injured trying to use what was in it. Worst of all was that she was the only person in the school who knew where he got his information, and she was afraid that he'd try to hold that over her head. No, she knew he eventually would.

If her dad found out that she'd hacked his files, then she'd be in a world of hurt. Heck the whole file was completely out of his jurisdiction anyway. He'd been assigned to this area as a liaison with the local sheriff's departments to help them cope with the rise of meth labs and prescription drug abuse in the Appalachians, not keep an eye on a kid who may or may not have killed his parents. She knew he'd be really angry with her for that kind of breach of privacy, and was beginning to understand why. That little bit of information in the wrong hands had already caused a mess.

As if sensing Felicia's internal turmoil, her mother asked, "What's got you so distracted tonight?"

Felicia turned and smiled at her mom and said, "Nothing really. Just thinking about school, I guess."

"I heard about the fight yesterday. Were you involved in it in some way?" her mom asked cutting to the heart of the matter without realizing it.

Shaking her head, Felicia said, "No. I knew one of the boys- I'd helped him with an assignment for math, but beyond that, no."

"Then what?" her mom asked, giving her one of her *I know something is up* looks.

"I've been invited to a party after the game..," she said deftly deflecting the question.

"What kind of party?" her mom asked, crossing her arms.

"Just a bunch of kids getting together to watch scary movies and eat popcorn," she told her.

"Sounds a little tame to have you this kind of distracted," her mom said. "Are the parents going to be there?"

"Shelby's mom will be," Felcia said.

"What about her dad?" her mom asked.

Felicia shook her head and said, "I don't know. I think I heard that her dad was dead."

Nodding her head Felicia's mom asked, "So what is it you're not telling me?"

Felicia shrugged and said, "Shelby and her family are part of the Mountain Hearth Kindred."

"That group of Pagans to the East of town?" her mom asked.

It was Felicia's turn to nod. "Yeah."

"I see," her mom replied. "You know what the Bureau says about those people...," she let it hang there.

Felicia nodded and said, "I know what it says. I also know what I see everyday in school, and I don't see a bunch of racists looking to go out in a blaze of glory and take as many black folk as possible with them."

"I don't know," her mom said. "Maybe another time.

When I've had a chance to talk to some of the parents." Felicia knew that was as good as she was going to get today. She also knew that it had done its job. Her mom thought this was about something other than what was really bothering her.

~*~

Shelby watched as Brett went about the dusting around the house. Her mom had decided that if they were going to have this movie fest at her house, then it was going to be clean and that they wouldn't embarrass her with clutter. Hence the two of them had stayed home from the football game and had been cleaning for most of the afternoon. Van had already left to spend a few days with Gareth Bjargeir. She suspected it had something to do with his moodiness of late.

It was nearly seven when her mother stuck her head out of the kitchen and asked, "Shelby, why don't you ride to the store with me to pick up some extra pizzas?" Shelby knew that was mom-code for *I need to talk to you.*

"Sure, Mom," she replied. Turning to Brett she suggested, "I'm going to the store with Mom. Why don't you check the big screen and the Roku to make sure we're ready for tonight."

Brett nodded to her and said, "Good idea. It wouldn't be a good thing to get started and the system go on the glitch."

Shelby smiled and picked up her jacket as she headed toward the garage with her mom. "We'll be back shortly."

"Don't call me shortly!" Brett grinned as he squatted in front of the flat screen.

Shelby and her mom were silent until they'd pulled out of the driveway. Finally, her mom looked over and asked, "Have you told anyone about Van's situation?"

"Specifically?" she asked carefully.

"About the werewolf stuff," her mother said.

"No," Shelby replied, releasing a breath she didn't realize she was holding. "I mentioned to Brett, with an understanding that he wasn't to talk about it to anyone else, that Van had been in custody while the police investigated, but I'd never tell anybody about that."

"Well, someone did," her mom told her. "That was part of what set off that fight. Craig knew about Van killing the gang-banger, and he knew that Van said they were werewolves. I'm afraid that if Craig starts spreading those kinds of rumors, then it could make Van's life as miserable as Brett's."

It was something she hadn't considered. Van had managed to slip into the school's and the community's life so seamlessly that it seemed like he'd been there for years. He was already moderately popular, and several girls had approached Shelby to get more information about her cousin, obviously interested in scoring a new boyfriend. But, she realized that this was the kind of thing that could really make his life miserable, especially since she knew Craig to be a vindictive ass.

She considered her next words very carefully, The things she'd been sensing off Van lately had her more than a bit concerned. "Mom, what if there really is something to what Van said happened to Aunt Ellen and Uncle Dane?"

"You mean real werewolves?" her mom asked.

"I know it sounds far-fetched but what if it's not? Was Van hurt when they were attacked?"

Her mom shook her head and said, "Not according to the doctors. There wasn't a scratch on him."

"Is he really that good?" she asked.

"What do you mean?"

"It was at least four against one and none of them laid a hand on him, but he killed one of them. Is he really that good of a fighter?" Shelby asked.

"I don't know. Why don't you ask him?"

"Maybe I'm afraid of the answer," Shelby said honestly.

"Now what does that mean, Shelby?" her mom asked.

"Lately I've sensed something in Van that is more than just a little frightening. There's something just beneath the surface that's capable of terrible violence. I first sensed it when he stopped Craig and Dallas from putting Brett into a garbage can. I sensed it the other day when he and Craig fought. There's something feral and wild just beneath the surface. It almost got out the other day. Do you think that there really are werewolves and that he got bitten?"

Her mom pulled into a parking space at the local Kroger without a word. Killing the ignition, she turned to Shelby and said, "I don't know. If you'd asked me that yesterday, I'd have laughed at you...,"

"But not now?" Shelby asked.

Her mom shook her head and said, "Not now. Whatever it is, I hope Gareth can get to its source. He seems to think there is something else going on too."

"Is that why you sent him there for the weekend?" Shelby asked.

"That, and I didn't think it would be fair for there to be a party downstairs where he couldn't participate."

"What are we going to do?" Shelby asked.

"He's our kin and he needs us. We stand by him and help him any way we can." The tone of her mother's voice reflected her own thoughts on the issue. It was just good to hear it confirmed.

Shelby swallowed hard and nodded.

CHAPTER 6

Van put his bag down in Gareth's guest room and looked around. The house itself was an old rambling Victorian that had been restored to pristine condition. It was furnished with antiques from all around the world, and had a very homey feel to it. He couldn't help but notice the various pictures of the old man and his now deceased wife. As he descended the stairs back down to the foyer he noted the reverse order of the timeline of pictures. At the top were grandchildren, then the children grew younger as he came closer to the landing.

"Van, would you come into the kitchen please?" he heard the old man ask.

"Yes, sir," he called back and made his way toward the back of the home to find the old man setting various foodstuffs out. "Your aunt said that you haven't eaten yet. How does bacon and eggs, gravy and homemade biscuits with sliced tomatoes sound?"

Van smiled and said, "Like breakfast, but it does sound good."

Gareth chuckled and told him, "I like breakfast for dinner sometimes. Grew up in the deep south and it wasn't that unusual of an occurrence. I'll start the biscuits and you slice the bacon."

Van nodded and leaned against the counter, "Deal. Mom used to do that when we lived in Lexington. I always liked it."

"Good," Gareth replied. "We can talk while we cook. Get the buttermilk out of the fridge and I'll start the biscuits."

"Yes sir," Van told him, opening the large stainless steel

appliance. "What do you want to talk about?" he asked carefully.

"How much do you know about the legends of lycanthropes?" Gareth asked, going right to the point.

"What I've seen in the movies mainly," Van replied. "Although I did notice while reading Egil's Saga that there was a werewolf in that story."

"Not many people catch that one," Gareth said. "There are as many kinds of shapeshifters or skin walkers as there are legends. The movies play fast and loose with the details because they're more interested in telling a good story than trying to be accurate."

"So, you do believe me?" Van asked.

The old man chuckled and a gleam of mirth filled his one good eye. "Oh I believe you met something that can shapeshift into a wolf, but if it was an actual honest to goodness werewolf, I'm not sure. You said that some of them had tails and were like the ones from the movies, sort big beastly bipedal wolf-men?"

Van nodded and said, "Four were. The fifth, the one that seemed to be in charge didn't have a tail."

Gareth nodded as he pulled down a heavy stone bowl and began to fill it with flour and baking soda. "You see, what we traditionally think of werewolves don't have tails. Actually, very few of the ancient legends had wolves who could take a man-wolf form. Most simply became large tailless wolves. What you described sounds like an mananulf."

"A moon wolf?" Van asked thinking he'd translated the Old Norse word correctly.

"Very good," Gareth said, pouring buttermilk into the bowl. "The moon wolves are the descendents of Angrboda."

"The troll-wife who is Fenris' mother?"

"The same," Gareth told him. "Your parents did a good job of teaching you the lore. Your wit does them honor."

"Thank you sir," Van said blushing. "What other kinds of werewolves are there?"

Gareth shrugged, began to mix the ingredients into the bowl as he added, "There is the line that came out of King Lycaon and his sons whom Zeus cursed for serving him his own son for dinner. They simply take the form of a wolf on the full moon. Then there are those who are cursed by different gods for different reasons. Sometimes they can take a man-wolf form, but few of them have tails. And then there are the ulfhedinn."

"Wolf-skins?" Van asked.

Gareth nodded, "Again they are limited to the form of a wolf, but they do have tails. They choose to become a wolf for reasons of their own by means of a wolf-skin they put on."

"Does it really work?" Van asked.

Gareth reached up and touched the scar running down his left eye. "From what I've seen, yes."

"Is that why you were so quick to believe me when nobody else was?" Van asked as he took out the bacon and began to slice it into half strips.

"Gareth began to knead the dough and said, "Among other things." He paused for a moment and gave Van a deep stare with his one good eye. "There is more going on in Wellman than most people realize Van; and you've had the misfortune to step smack dab in the middle of it without even knowing it."

Van suppressed a shudder under the onslaught of that stare. "Like what?"

Looking back at the dough he said, "I'm not a liberty to go into too much detail. I can say that your little escapade last night put you dead in the middle of it."

"What escapade?" Van asked. "All I remember is a strange dream about chasing down a deer."

Gareth nodded and said, "I don't think it was a dream, Van. I don't know if you were far-faring from your sleep- which I tend not to believe- or if you have become some kind of shifter yourself, but you chased down that deer last night. More importantly, that stag was more than just a normal deer.

It was the incarnation of the spirit of the local land. By killing it, you tied yourself to the land, and managed to irritate some of the locals in the process."

Van listened to what the old man was telling him. "You mean, I've become a werewolf like those that attacked and killed my family?" That was something he hadn't considered and was a thought that was too dreadful to contemplate.

Gareth shook his head, wiped his hands on the towel next to the table and got down a rolling pin. "I don't know. I do know that the vaedvaettir was taken last night, and not by the pack of the wild hunt. Whoever killed it became the Wellman's guardian for the next year."

"Vaedvaettir?" Van asked. "I don't recognize that one."

"The hunt spirit. When the pack summoned the Wild Hunt last night it was looking to tie itself to the land, so as to better protect it. In doing so, the very spirit of the forests and the land around us took physical form. By killing it, by eating its heart, the pack would become one with the land."

"And you think that's what I did last night?" Van asked.

Gareth nodded. "I think you either sent out your fylgia form to kill it, or you went out yourself."

Van shook his head and said,"I've never done a sitting out. I have no idea what my fylgia form would be, or how to summon it."

"I thought as much," Gareth said. "Summoning the fylgia is something that it takes years of practice and study to be able to do, and it requires a pretty good understanding of magic. As far as I know, you've never shown any interest in magic."

Van shrugged and said, "My mom was the vitki in our family. I was content to become a thane like my dad."

Gareth grinned again, as he began to roll out the dough. "I thought as much. Your parents were good people, and they've raised a fine son. I hate it that you've gotten caught up in Wellman's more esoteric difficulties. You kids were supposed to make it out of high school before you got involved."

"I don't understand," Van said.

"When I chose this area to settle the kindred, I had to make some deals with the people already here. They were intrigued by the idea of a functioning kindred in the community but were wary of it as well. Let's face it, there tends to be a higher percentage of what we call the gifted among the followers of the reconstructed religions."

"So you're saying that there was already something different about Wellman before you and the rest of the original nine families came here?" Van asked.

"Yeah," Gareth said. "But you can't tell anybody about it."

"Like they'd believe me," Van replied.

"Things may change there, Van," Gareth said. "But for now, we have to keep it to ourselves."

"Why?" Van asked.

"Because, we don't want to attract outside attention. The advantage to Appalachia is that communities like ours tend to keep to themselves and not trust outsiders."

"I still don't understand," Van replied.

"You don't have to completely understand, you just have to keep it to yourself," Gareth told him.

"Okay," Van agreed. "Does my aunt know?"

"What?" Gareth asked.

"My Aunt Linda. Does she know there's something going on behind the scenes?" Van asked.

Gareth shook his head and said, "I don't think so. She's got a talent for seidr, but I don't think she's that sensitive."

"So what do we do?" Van asked.

"About what?" Gareth asked as he took down a juice tumbler and began to use it to cut the dough into round biscuit shapes.

"What you said about me and the land," Van said.

"First we determine if it was you, and exactly how it was you," the old man said. "Then we find out how tied to the land you really are."

"I don't feel tied to it," Van said.

"That's what we're going to work on this weekend. It's also why I wanted you here with me instead of with your aunt," Gareth said.

"I don't understand," Van replied.

With a sigh, Gareth looked at him with his good eye and said, "It's the height of the full moon tonight. If you've been infected and are out of control, I'd rather have you here with me, than at your aunt's with a bunch of teenagers watching scary movies."

Van nodded is head and said, "I hadn't thought of that."

~*~

The game had gone well for Caleb. Because Craig was out of the picture he'd gotten to play for the whole game and had helped lead the team to victory. Beating County was a major event in Wellman because they were so much bigger than their small independent school district. He'd been in a good mood as he drove his old pickup out the long winding road that led into the hollow where Mountain Hearth Kindred was located. Because of his mood, he barely noticed the full moon rising over the recently bare limbs of the hardwoods that lined the side of the road. Crossing Silver Bridge over John's Creek he pulled up the side road leading to the Stein's farm.

Several other cars were parked in the small side lot next to the barn. He recognized Dallas Howard's little Ford, as well as a black VW Cabriolet that belonged to Carmen O'Brien. There was an older Ram pickup he didn't recognize and a black Mustang that told him that the Snow twins, Brandt and Allison were there as well. Several yards beyond that was a cord of freshly split wood with an ax and a maul leaning against it. Caleb got the feeling that perhaps that wood was part of Van's punishment for fighting. Looking back at the cars on the parking pad he grinned slightly. He had no idea that so many of his classmates were interested in scary movies.

Grabbing his jacket he jiggled the handle on the door of his truck to make sure it would catch and climbed out. He knew he was eventually going to have to get that handle fixed, but for now it was only a minor inconvenience. As he stepped out onto the gravel parking area, he felt a shiver of cold run down his spine. In the distance, he heard a dog start to bay at the moon, as the hair on the back of his neck stood on end.

Quickening his step to the front walkway he made his way to the door and rang the bell. He was a bit surprised when Mrs. Stein opened it with a cup of hot cider in her hand. "Come on in, Caleb," the woman said looking outside. "Everyone is in the living room," she said handing him the cup of cider.

"There's popcorn, candy, chips and dip in there."

"Thank you, Mrs. Stein," he told her as he wiped his feet on the rug in front of the door. Looking around he noticed that the interior of the large log home was decorated with a rustic theme, complete with furniture made from rough-hewn wood. As he entered the living room, the first thing Caleb noticed was the huge stone fireplace that dominated the north wall. A large flat panel television and entertainment center was on the wall to the right, and there were several of his classmates drinking cider, pop, or hot chocolate and munching on snacks while lounging on the furniture.

He waved at Brett who was talking quietly to Allison Snow, and smiled over to where Shelby was refilling her plate with chips. Noticing his glance, the red-head blushed slightly and smiled back at him. There was a definite attraction between them, and that idea made his stomach do a quick flutter.

"So when does the movie start?" he asked Brett.

"Just waitin' on everybody to get settled with their snacks," the blond said nodding to Allison. Caleb briefly wondered if there was something going on between the two of them. For some reason he liked the idea of Brett finally getting his act together enough to get a girlfriend, and a pretty one at that.

Not realizing how hungry he really was, Caleb filled his plate with various snacks including some little hot dogs in sauce from a crock pot. Settling into a seat on the large overstuffed sofa next to Shelby he munched on the snacks as he smiled over at the red-head. "Is this seat taken?" he asked playfully.

Shelby smiled and replied, "It is now."

"Good," Caleb said as Mrs. Stein dimmed the lights and the movie began to play.

~*~

Logan Yarnvid had a bad feeling about this trip since they crossed the mountains into this small valley. There was something peculiar about the land that put his teeth on edge. Combined with the rising of the full-moon it took his being on edge to almost full paranoia. He kept getting the feeling that someone was watching over his shoulder.

Dace had picked up some information at the football game- which Logan had to admit that he enjoyed even though he had no stake in who won- about this Van Griffin they were after. Evidently he'd been in some kind of fight at school and had managed to toss the regular quarterback down the hall. That idea fit with his own impression of the boy from their previous fight. He was almost like another moon-wolf about to go through his first change. It made him wonder from whose bloodline he could originate.

They parked the SUV off the road near a bridge over a wide and deep creek. Hiding it behind a stand of trees, Dace said that anybody checking it out would think they'd simply gone fishing in the creek. The pull of the moon was strong and by the time they'd reached the top of the embankment, they'd shed their clothes and had let the spirit of Fenrir have his way.

Crossing a bridge with the unlikely name of "Silver" they padded their way into the woods on the other side and made their way past a sign that read: Mountain Hearth Kindred. This was both unexpected and yet explained a great deal. The boy had taken refuge with others who followed the hated Shining Ones.

A low mist rose from the moist leaves on the forest floor, and Logan could see the moonlight casting eerie shadows through the bare limbs of the trees. In the distance a dog of some kind whined and bayed at their scent. Logan had no illusions about the effect his kind had on the local psyche. Those that were sensitive to such things would know that death stalked this night.

Suddenly Dace signaled they should stop and sniffed

the ground. Logan and Vic took turns getting the scent too. There were wolves- real wolves in these woods and they'd marked their territory. Granted no wolf was a match for what Yarnvids were, but still there was a balance to the forest and their grandmother had always taught them to be respectful of it.

Dace nodded to the two of them and then indicated that they should continue on in the same direction. Within another two hundred yards they encountered another scent, this one completely unrecognizable. Whatever it was, it was touched by the moon, but beyond that none of them had a clue. They slowed their pace after that as they worked their way up the side of a mountain and then down toward the farm below them. At the top of their climb they found the remains of a huge stag that had been killed by something. Again they could not identify the spoor.

Descending to the farm below, the scent of fear began to waft upward from the log house. Logan stopped a moment and drank in the smell, reveling in the effect their very presence was having on the mundanes below. The animals around the farm were mewling softly, too terrified to call out to each other. Only a horse in the barn was making any real noise, whinnying and kicking his stall in fear.

With a howl Dace signaled they should surround the house- at least surround it as best a pack of three could. The only lights coming from inside originated from a large television in the front room, and a single light at the back of the house. The sounds of theatrical music along with a heavily distorted, "Join us," wafted from the house. Logan realized that some of the fear they were sensing inside was actually coming from silly high school kids scaring themselves with movies. He bared his teeth in the moonlight and grinned wickedly at that thought. This was going to be fun.

~*~

Gareth watched as the boy grew more and more agitated as the night progressed. He could almost see the outline of a beast in his shadow. As he paced up and down the living room floor Gareth asked, "What are you feeling?"

Van turned to look at him, the pupils of his blue eyes slowly contracting to vertical slits. "I don't know," he replied. "Something is here that's not supposed to be here."

Now, *that* caught Gareth off guard. "What do you mean?" Could the boy already be feeling the pull of the vordavaettir, the guard spirit? He knew it took awhile for the land guardian to become attuned to the role, and that it took a major threat to set off a warning this early in the stewardship.

"I mean that I can feel something wrong somewhere. There's an intruder somewhere in the den," the boy said. Gareth noticed as his ears seemed to grow to points and slide up the boys head.

"Den?" Gareth asked as the ears melted back down. He could tell this was going to be a long night.

"It's as good a word as any," Van said as he continued to pace. "Whatever it is, there's something here that's not supposed to be here."

"Where?" Gareth asked.

Van shook his head in frustration, his black hair lengthening and began to spread down his face and neck. "I don't know," he growled from between elongating teeth. Gareth noted with a smile that the boy's upper lip seemed to begin to split slightly.

"Van, sit down a moment," Gareth told him.

He turned his head to look at Gareth and whiskers began to grow from the side of his mouth. "Why?"

Gareth chuckled and said, "I think you probably need to take your shoes off."

"Why?" the boy asked again as he sat down in the rocker and began to untie his running shoes.

"I think you're likely to rip out of them soon," Gareth told him as the boy grew slightly. The light blue polo shirt he was wearing stretched tightly across his chest and shoulders, as his arms began to sprout thick black fur.

The boy looked at his hands as the fur grew down his arms. Gareth noticed that there was slightly darker black striped pattern under the fur, like a black tiger. He could hear the panic begin to rise in his face. "What's happening to me?" his voice dropped an octave.

"You are becoming something more than just Van Griffin. You're becoming something out of the sagas," Gareth told him. "Does it hurt?"

The boy looked at him and shook his head, "No. It itches though." As Van kicked his sneakers off, there was the audible sound of ripping cloth as his shirt and jeans tore from the mass he was gaining. There was a grace and elegance of motion to the boy's movements as he tore what was left of the shirt from his body.

The transformation was nothing like Gareth had ever seen, not in the movies and not with the ulf-hedinn. It wasn't the painful jerky transformations he'd seen in so many movies, and it wasn't the flash of one second being a man and the next being an animal that he'd once seen of the ulf-hedinn. It was a smooth, almost graceful flowing transition from man to something between human and great cat. From one moment to the next, Van had gone from teenage boy to nearly seven feet of black furred man-cat. There were stripes of slightly darker, almost blue fur that reminded Gareth more of a black Morris cat than a tiger. His face, although clearly still Van was now covered with the same rich black fur, with white whiskers. His bright blue eyes peeked out from under the now longer and thicker raven locks.

Claws were sheathing and unsheathing themselves from his fingers and toes. He was surprisingly calm under the circumstances, and Gareth couldn't help but notice the full moon shining through the large window of his living room, outlining the boy's head. A tail had pushed its way through the material of the running shorts, he'd evidently worn under his jeans. It was now curling and uncurling lazily behind him.

Suddenly Van turned to face him, fixing the old man with a stare that went straight to his gut. One word escaped from between the razor sharp fangs in his mouth, "Home." In a flash, the moon-cat was gone, leaving Gareth's door standing wide open.

~*~

As the night grew older and her friends became more and more absorbed in the movie, Shelby couldn't help but notice the miasma of fear that began to envelop not only the living room, but the entire farm. She found herself watching the room carefully. Carmen had managed to wiggle her way between Brandt and Allison and snuggled herself up against the large blond boy. Allison, on the other hand sitting with her legs pulled up under her and was holding her shoulders as she watched the movie. Dallas Howard was sitting across from her in a rocker, his knuckles nearly white as he gripped the arms of the chair. Even Caleb had taken his arm out from around her own shoulders and now had both hands tucked between his knees as he looked around warily. In the corner, she watched as Brett's eyes kept darting toward the gun case sitting in the corner, his hand occasionally reaching up to stroke the hammer pendant at his throat.

Suddenly the sounds of Faxi kicking his stall door broke through the eerie music of the movie. Shelby felt herself jump as her mother entered the living room looking half worried and half annoyed. "Something's spooked the animals, I'm going out to check on it," she said.

"Wait Mrs. Stein," Dallas said. "I'll go with you."

She smiled at him and said, "You stay and watch the movie. I won't be gone long."

"I'd still feel more comfortable if you had someone with you," the senior said. "I don't mind missing part of the movie."

"Or, Brett could pause it and we could all check it out," Allison offered as she looked to where Carmen had snuggled in close to her twin brother. Shelby couldn't help but wonder if there was a bit of territoriality going on there.

"It's probably just coyotes. We've been having some problems with them lately. It's the time of year when the young ones go out and start hunting by themselves and they're more than willing to take small livestock," her mom said.

"You got a rifle?" Dallas asked.

"Yeah, but I'm not about to hand it to you- not without your parent's permission," she said as she went toward the door.

Dallas nodded and said, "Still I'd feel better if someone went with you." He stood and asked, "Anybody else want to go?"

Everybody exchanged looks and then slowly nodded. Brett stood and said, "Good idea. Enough of us out there should scare them off." He paused the movie and added, "Come on."

Shelby extricated herself from the sofa and followed the others toward the back of the kitchen. As her mother opened the back door, a wave of fear washed through the house. She felt Caleb reach out and take her hand and found herself glad for it. To her side, she noticed a shudder run through Brett's shoulders as he pushed past the others to step out onto the back porch.

The first thing Shelby noticed was the full moon hanging high in the sky, it's light cutting eerily through the low hanging fog that was rising from the ground. Her mother hit a switch and the floodlights above the barn came on flooding the back yard with a harsh electric light. At the edge of the barn, she saw a large shadow melt back into the darkness. Another chill went down her spine.

"Hey! Get away from there!" Dallas said to her left. The senior then jumped down from the porch and ran toward where the cars were parked. To Shelby's horror, Caleb followed right behind him.

Both boys skidded to a stop on the other side Dallas' Fiesta, just at the edge of the pool of light that was being cast by the floodlights. A low growl emanated from the darkness beyond and then something huge lashed out into the light and grabbed Dallas yanking him into the darkness.

"Oh, hell no," Brett said beside her, jumped from the porch and ran toward the wood pile. Grabbing the maul leaning against the wood pile in both hands, he charged into the darkness beyond the surprised Caleb. Brandt was right behind him with the ax that had lain beside the maul.

"Brett! Brandt! No!" Shelby's mom yelled. Turning to Shelby, she said, "Get the rifle."

Without thinking Shelby nodded and ran toward the living room with Allison and Carmen hot on her heels. Grabbing the key from her pocket, she quickly unlocked the cabinet and pulled down her father's old hunting rifle. Rotating the lever forward she checked to make sure it was loaded and ran back toward the porch. In the distance she heard the sounds of a low growl and then a yelp of pain.

Skidding to a stop on the back porch she looked to where Caleb was pulling the bloodied form of Dallas from the shadows. Behind him, Brett was backing up holding the maul, blood dripping from its blade in front of him as if daring whatever was in the darkness to come out. Beside her, her mom took the rifle and aimed at the darkness.

The rifle barked and there was another yelp of pain as the boys made their way toward the dubious safety of the porch. Shelby couldn't help but notice the arc of blood that kept pumping out of Dallas' tattered throat. "Get him inside boys," her mom said.

Suddenly a crash from inside shook the very floor they were standing on. She heard both Allison and Carmen scream. Surprisingly strong arms pushed her aside and up against the outdoor freezer on the porch as Brett and Brandt charged past her and into the house. "Those boys are going to get themselves killed," her mother said. Pulling her up by the arm, she directed Shelby toward where Caleb was hauling Dallas up the stairs. "Give Caleb a hand with Dallas. See if you can stop the bleeding."

"Yes ma'am," Shelby said, turning toward the two boys. The sight of Dallas' ruined throat shocked her. His face was already ashen as he held a hand against the wound. Blood pumped from between his fingers in time with his heart beat.

"Oh my dear Gods," she said to herself as she ripped part of his shirt off to use to staunch the wound.

Low growls, crashing furniture, the occasional scream, and the sounds of the rifle barking inside the house shattered the night air. As she held onto Dallas' throat, she looked at Caleb and said, "Call 911. We need the Sheriff, an ambulance, and the fricken national guard if they can send it." Caleb nodded and reached the cell phone at his hip.

Suddenly the sounds of the fight were drowned out by a blood curdling scream that reminded Shelby of a woman in pain. From inside she heard Brandt yell, "Allison!"

"How many of these things are there?" her mother asked over the sounds of her reloading the rifle.

A second crash shook the whole house, as Shelby began to drag Dallas' limp form inside. Looking through the kitchen and dining room, she could see where the front door had been busted in. Brett was standing facing another huge hole in the wall where the picture window used to be. The maul in his hand was even bloodier and something was wriggling on the floor at his feet. It took her a moment to recognize it as some kind of clawed hand. "What the hell was that thing?" Brandt asked.

"Which one?" Brett said.

"The one that took the big one out the window," Brett said.

"I don't know, but I'm glad it was on our side," her mother said as she cocked the lever on the rifle forward chambering a new round.

"You sure about that?" Brandt asked.

"It pulled it off Allison," Carmen said.

"How is she?" Shelby's mom asked.

"Not good," Brandt said. Shelby took a moment to look around the corner to see where Brandt was holding his sister's leg while he tied a tourniquet just above the knee. "It went all the way to the bone."

"Caleb called 911," Shelby said. I can use some help with Dallas out here."

100

"Carmen," her mom said. "Help her."

As the girl got up to come to help Shelby, another horrific scream echoed off the mountains around them. It was followed by a definite canine yelp of pain, and then silence. In the distance, Shelby could hear the sounds of a car skidding to a stop outside.

"Hello the house!" the familiar voice of Gareth Bjargeir echoed.

"Gareth!" her mother yelled. "In here!"

The old man came traipsing into the house carrying a shotgun in one hand and something bloody in the other. It took Shelby a moment to realize it was a human arm severed just beneath the shoulder. He tossed it down in the living room floor and said, "I found this outside."

Caleb looked up and said, "That was Brett with that maul. He charged past me, hacked into that thing and grabbed Dallas. Never seen anything like it."

"What were those things?" Carmen asked as she held Dallas' hand.

"Werewolves?" Brett asked.

"Where's Van?" Shelby's mother asked.

"He's at my place," Gareth said. Shelby caught the look that passed between them. It said clearly that they would talk later.

~*~

Agent Gerald Ballenger looked around at the devastation at the Stein farm. Four people were dead, one girl was likely to lose her leg, and there was some kind of wild animal on the loose. The front door and a large picture window had been smashed in, and the whole downstairs looked like a war had been fought inside it. So far, the best he could piece together is that members of the same White Supremacist gang that had attacked the sister of Mrs. Stein killing her and her family had come looking for retribution for the death of one of their own. Evidently they got more than they bargained for in a bunch of teenagers with axes, a widow with a shotgun and some kind of wild animal in the area.

One kid had his throat ripped out, and another had most of the flesh below the knee completely removed by what Sheriff Treybond thought was a cougar. The attackers had lost a left arm and a right hand to panicked ax-wielding teenage boys. From the best he could tell, when the attackers tried to retreat, they were attacked by Treybond's cougar. There were definitely large animal tracks in the area.

The sheriff wasn't happy about his involvement, but since these men were wanted for murder and had crossed state lines to commit it yet again, the Bureau wanted him to look into it. Gerald himself wasn't comfortable with the whole situation. These people were part of a religious movement that the Bureau's Project Meggido had described as adherents to a racist belief system, and were listed as dangerous. As a white man married to a black woman with a mixed-race daughter, that made them automatically a suspect to him. What he couldn't understand was why one group of white supremacists was attacking another.

"What do you think, Agent Ballenger?" Sheriff Treybond asked. She was a fiftyish woman with short blonde hair that was starting to gray. She had a figure that suggested a regular workout schedule. This was her second term as Sheriff, and she was a competent law enforcement officer.

"I'm not sure, Sheriff. This gang attacked Mrs. Stein's sister and her family this past summer out in Colorado. One of them ended up with a knife at the base of his skull for his trouble. Maybe they came here looking for revenge."

"What do you mean, a knife at the base of his skull?" the Sheriff asked.

"The son claimed they were werewolves and in the fight he managed to beat one half to death with a sledge hammer and then stick a thirteen inch silver blade through his brain."

"Werewolves?" Treybond asked with a snort.

"Exactly. You know how these religious fanatics are," he told her.

"Never had any problems out of anybody out this way before, Agent Ballenger. They've been part of this community for nearly twenty-five years. What makes you think they're fanatics?"

Ballenger smiled at the woman and said, "Read the Megiddo Report from the FBI."

"I have, Agent Ballenger. It was written by an administration that was trying to justify killing a bunch of people out in Texas. I don't put a lot of stock in that kind of garbage. From what I've seen, these are good, hard working people."

"Then how do you explain two boys who know how to use an ax well enough to take off a couple of limbs, and a woman who can put a six inch grouping in a man with a hunting rifle?" Gerald asked.

"This is Eastern Kentucky, Agent Ballenger. People around here can hunt and shoot, quite well. It's the nature of living in a rural area."

Ballenger shook his head and said, "If you say so. Still, I'd like to talk to the nephew."

"From what Mrs. Stein told me, he was staying the night with Mr. Bjargeir. Everybody here says that he wasn't present. To be honest, I'm more worried about a large cat that attacks five people in one night than where these people go to church,"

Sheriff Treybond said as she got into her car.

~*~

Van felt the sun begin to warm his body. He stretched out and nearly lost his balance as he realized he'd fallen asleep in the upper limbs of a tall elm tree. Looking down, he could see his body was smeared with blood and there was a rich copper taste in his mouth. "You awake up there yet, boy?" a voice called from below.

Looking down, he saw several men standing around the base of the tree looking up at him. "Who are you?" Van asked. Then looking around he added, "And how did I get up here?"

The men chuckled at each other. "Our new landvordr is a bit confused," the oldest man said. "Come on down. Gareth asked us to find you."

With a surprising ease, Van scrambled down the tree and turned to face the men. "Who are you?"

The older man smiled and said, "I'm Lars Wolfson. We're the ulf-hedinn."

PART 2
RUNEMASTER!

Interlude

The morgue was quiet and the lights were dim. Being a small rural county, Greenup had little need for the place to be staffed overnight. A coroner only came in when there was an active investigation, and at midnight on a Sunday night, there was little stirring in the sleepy little mountain community.

A small light appeared in the back of the room and Auda Dagnidottir slowly took form. She was tall, leggy, blonde, and had the kinds of looks that explained why so many of the Aesir and Vanir would spend time among the jotuns. She was the kind of woman who turned heads, mortal and otherwise. But this evening, the young jotuness was on a mission from her grandmother, and it would not do to dally too long. Crystal blue eyes raking the shining doors that lined the back wall of the room, she let her mind reach out to find the one she sought. Opening the steel latched door she pulled out the tray to reveal the body atop it. Crinkling her nose, she said, "Oh dear cousin, Dace. You reek of Vanir and Aesir magic. Exactly what have you gotten yourself mixed up in?"

Reaching out, she touched the forehead of her mother's sister's son and quietly chanted the song her aunt had taught her. She felt the power pour through her body to the corpse under her hand. After a few moments, she felt him move under her fingers.

With a gasp of air, Dace Yarnvid's body began to tremble and then to shift part of the way to his war form. Sitting straight up, Yarnvid looked at Auda and growled. "What have you done?"

Auda stepped back slightly and said, "Grandmother is not yet finished with you, Cousin. She commanded that I come and awaken you from the barrow to wreak vengeance upon the servants of our enemies."

As her cousin slid from the table, Auda took a moment to study the moon-wolf. The spell had partially shifted him into his war form so that he more resembled a wolf-like troll than either man or wolf. His skin and fur had turned a dark blue and he stood six and a half feet tall and weighed in at a good three hundred pounds. Turning, Dace looked at the other lockers and then back at Auda. "What about Vic and Logan?" His voice was a low growl.

Shaking her head, Auda said, "Their bodies are not intact. It would cause them more pain than do them any good. It is a limitation of the spell our aunt taught me."

Dace seemed to consider her words carefully before asking, "And where do I go from here?"

Auda reached into a pocket at the front of her dress and said, "Put this on first." Handing him a gold coin with a particular runestave engraved with a blood red filling on it attached to a leather thong she added, "It will keep you from being scryed. Part of the steading to the east of here has a vordavaettir, this will hide you from being detected."

"What killed us?" Dace asked again as he took the medallion with a clawed hand and slipped it over his head.

"I don't know," Auda said. "Grandmother wants us to find out more about what is going on here. No thurs knew that there was an entire community dedicated to our ancient foes. We need more information and Vandyl refuses to commit the resources necessary."

"So once again, Granny does what none of the others are willing to do," Dace smiled, revealing a mouthful of bluish canine teeth.

"That's why she's clan-chief of Ironwood," Auda said.

"Where do we go now?" Dace asked.

"There's a cabin prepared for you near a cave in the mountains just east of the here. I think the two will make a good place from which to observe the mortals and plot our revenge," she told him as she gestured. "As for me. I have plans that require a bit more contact with the humans."

As the huge, clawed, paw-like hand took her smaller one, the light in the room faded as the two stepped between the limbs of the world-tree. In a matter of seconds they'd traveled to the aforementioned cabin, leaving the morgue once again dark and quiet. Nothing else would disturb the sleep of the dead tonight.

CHAPTER 7

Caleb Johnson looked over at Mrs. Stein as he held the door frame in place while Brett nailed it to the support wall. "There's one thing about this mess, I just don't understand, Mrs. S.," he said.

"Just one?" the blonde woman asked as she leaned a foot against the base of the frame to hold it. Caleb was unsure if the tone of her voice was one of sarcasm or irony.

He smiled and replied, "Well, for now one that is particularly puzzling. Why are the police so willing to overlook all the evidence of what we really saw in favor of a story that has so many holes in it that the odds of it happening that way would drive most gamblers to drink. I mean let's face it: a rogue cougar took out all three of those one-percenters plus mauling both Dallas and Allison, sounds more far fetched than were-wolves."

"And what really did take out the werewolves, Caleb?" Shelby asked from the other wall where she and a rather silent Van were installing a new picture window to replace the one that had been shattered Friday night.

Caleb looked over to where Van was doing his best to concentrate on the seam between the new window and the wall. Caleb just shrugged and said, "If there are such things as werewolves, then why not werecats? And that one had some of the bluest eyes I've ever seen." He knew everyone in the room knew who he was talking about.

Next to him, Brett shrugged and said, "Call it the Buffy effect."

"Buffy effect?" Caleb asked, looking around and finding looks of confusion on everyone's face.

"Yeah," Brett said. *"On Buffy: the Vampire Slayer*, people were constantly attacked by vampires, werewolves, and just about anything else the writers could come up with, but nobody ever really noticed anything unusual in Sunnydale. I'd say we've got something like that going on here. People are willing to believe an improbable series of events over the simple truth because the truth makes them nervous."

"Brett, the truth makes a lot of people nervous," Mrs. Stein said without batting an eye.

Caleb shook his head and moved out of Brett's way while the smaller boy adjusted the frame and then began to nail again. When he was finished, Caleb commented, "Still, it makes you think."

"About?" Shelby asked.

"If something like what we saw Friday night can exist, what about other things? Are vampires real? What about faeries? Is magic real?" He sighed and added, "And what does that mean about the nature of God?"

"I'm sorry what happened has put you into a crisis of faith," Mrs. Stein said. "But it may also open your eyes to a larger universe around you."

"Did you believe in werewolves before Friday?" he asked the woman.

He caught her looking over to Van and the slight nod he gave her. Finally, she sighed and said, "I had my doubts up until Friday night, but I was starting to come around to the idea."

Caleb let go of the door frame as Brett finished up with hammering it into place. He had to admit that the blond was showing a skill set he never expected him to have. As he picked up the hinges to be installed next, he looked over at Mrs. Stein and asked, "What would make you start to come around? You weren't expecting to be attacked Friday, were you?" That idea genuinely bothered Caleb. He couldn't imagine the woman purposefully putting her daughter and her friends in that kind of danger.

"I did," Van answered.

"You don't have to..." Shelby interrupted.

"It's going to be all over school anyway. Do you really think Craig Blankenship is going to let this go?" Van asked.'

Caleb looked at the raven-haired boy and once again noted just how blue his eyes were. "Let what go?"

Van sighed and asked, "You know my parents were killed by the same one-percenters who attacked you guys?"

"Yeah, but I'm not sure what a one-percenter is."

Shelby smiled and Caleb wondered how he could get her to do it again. "Ninety-nine percent of motorcycle clubs are harmless groups of professional men and women who just like to get on their bikes and ride. But one percent are hard-core criminals and are willing to do just about anything, including murder, to get their way."

Van nodded and said, "That group that attacked us were some one-percenters from out west. But when they attacked my family in Colorado, they were werewolves. The police thought that I was making up the story to cover up my killing my own folks." He looked down and Caleb could see an aura of darkness seem to engulf Van. "I killed one of them in that fight. They came looking for revenge."

"You killed a werewolf?" Caleb asked. "What with?"

Van walked over to the small altar set next to the fireplace on the north side of the room. He picked up a long dagger lying there. As Van drew the blade from its sheath, Caleb noticed the way the tip was tapered sharply back across the top. "Mom and Aunt Linda have matching seax; both are made of silver. I stuck Mom's seax in the back of the skull of the lead werewolf."

"You fought one of those with just a knife?" Caleb asked incredulously.

Van shrugged and said, "A seax, a hammer," he gestured toward the small two pound sledge on the altar, and everything my sensei in Lexington ever taught me. I wouldn't let them surround me, and I always kept at least one of them between me and the rest. Caleb watched the color drain from

Van's face, and how his voice went dead when he talked about his parent's death.

"I didn't mean to drag up unpleasant memories..." Caleb apologized.

"It's okay," Van told him. "Hopefully Friday night was the last we'll ever hear of them."

"Why did they attack your family in the first place?" Caleb asked.

Van shrugged and said, "I don't know. At the time they weren't that willing to discuss anything but us dying, and I was too busy trying to make sure that didn't happen to ask them."

"Still, it's a good question," Brett said. "Maybe it's something you and Gareth can dig into."

"Maybe," Van said, his voice shifting to something soft and gentler. Caleb couldn't help but notice the quick flicker of the two boys' eyes toward each other.

"So what are you going to say at school?" Caleb asked.

"I suggest we keep to the FBI's theory, as ridiculous as it sounds," Shelby said. "I'm sure Brandt and Allison will go along with that. The real question is you and Carmen."

Caleb smiled and said, "Trust me, Carmen has no desire to be ridiculed, but I'll talk with her at church this evening."

"Didn't know she went to your Dad's church," Shelby said. Caleb could hear the trace of warning in her voice.

Caleb just shrugged. He knew that Shelby and Carmen had had their differences in the past. Some things he knew to stay out of, womenfolk's grudges was at the top of that list.

~*~

Shelby settled into her usual table at lunch where half a dozen people she barely recognized were sitting around listening to Carmen. "Never knew the little guy had it in him. As soon as poor Dallas screamed, Brett jumped down, grabbed an ax and rushed in after him. Brandt was right on his tail." Carmen shook her head and said, "I don't know who he hit, but there was a howl of pain and then he and Brandt were dragging Dallas out of the darkness. They'd already cut his throat though and he was spurting blood everywhere." She looked over at Shelby and added, "Shelby and Caleb tried to do first aid but it was too bad. I mean it's not like you can put a tourniquet on someone's neck. To be honest it was a nightmare."

"Yeah, one I'd like to forget," Caleb said as Shelby settled into her usual seat. Looking up at her, he asked, "Have you heard anything about Allison?"

Shelby frowned and opened the lunch box she'd brought- her mom's famous cabbage stew and a peanut-butter and honey sandwich. She told him, "We went to visit her at the hospital yesterday but she was still out of it from the surgery. They had to take the leg."

"What about Dallas' folks?" Carmen asked.

"Dad went to visit them after church yesterday," Caleb said. "They're doing as well as anybody who'd just lost their youngest child could be doing, I guess."

"Okay, exactly what happened Friday night?" Felicia Ballenger asked.

Shelby, Caleb, and Carmen looked at each other. Finally it was Carmen who said, "I don't think any of us really want to talk about it anymore. There was too much blood and too much death." Her eyes darted to where Brett was standing in line looking not a little lost and forlorn.

Carmen turned to Shelby and smiled as if to say she suddenly understood something. Shelby hoped that if she'd figured out what was going on between him and Van that she'd keep it to herself. As if reading her mind, it was Felicia who asked, "In that case, tell me if the rumors about your cousin are true?"

"What rumors?" Shelby asked carefully.

"Well, I've heard that he told the police in Colorado that werewolves killed his parents..." she let the statement hang there.

Shelby snapped her head around and stared at the other girl. "Where did you hear that?" she demanded softly.

Felicia smiled impishly, took a bite of her applesauce and said, "I'm not sure. It's just a rumor going around."

Suddenly Shelby caught a whiff of an expensive perfume on the air. In her mind's eye, an image of Felicia hacking into an FBI database replaced the world around Shelby. She watched as the girl pulled the file up on her home computer, downloaded it to a flash drive and put it in her purse. As quickly as the image was there, it was gone again. Something deep inside Shelby told her this was not an isolated incident.

"Well, I wouldn't put too much stock in rumors if I were you, Felicia," Caleb said. "You wouldn't believe some of the stuff I've heard going around about you."

"*Liiiiiike?*" Felicia asked as her brown eyes grew in size.

"Well, I heard that you and Craig Blankenship were seen out together," Caleb said as he stared over the rim of his cup.

"That's ridiculous!" Felicia protested- a bit too vehemently for Shelby's taste.

Across from her, Carmen snorted, "About as ridiculous as werewolves." Then, shaking her head, she smiled at Felicia and said, "Besides, I'm sure Felicia has a lot better taste than Craig Blankenship." Shelby wasn't sure if she was using the opportunity to deny the werewolf story or to get a jab in at Craig. Probably both. Craig Blankenship was at least one subject on which Shelby and Carmen could agree. He was a low-life, sneaky little bully. Van had made the top of quite a few of the school's less athletically-gifted student's hero list when he broke Craig's arm.

"Maybe we can find another subject to discuss," Caleb

said as Brett approached the table. Shelby watched as her best friend settled in, taking up the last seat. Suddenly a wave of regret hit her and she looked left to see Felicia blushing deeply as Brett joined them. Caleb smiled and asked him, "You ready to start your first day with Mrs. Devlin's class?"
Brett pushed a blond lock out of his eyes and said, "I guess so. To be honest, I'd almost forgotten about it."

"Understandable," Caleb said. Turning to Van he asked, "Hey, I'm going up to the Huntington Mall this afternoon. I was wondering if you," he paused a moment and looked at Brett and added, "or maybe you and Van, would like to go along."
Brett shook his head in regret and said, "Van can't. He's got a meeting with the Belfonte Hunting Club."

Caleb couldn't help the double take. "That's one of the most exclusive hunting clubs in the area. How'd he get an invite?"

Brett shrugged and said, "Not so much an invite as an interview. I guess someone told them about the wild hog he killed." Caleb got the feeling there was more to it than that, but he wasn't going to push. Instead he asked, "How about you? Wanna go to the mall?"

Brett smiled hugely at the idea. "Sure. Where are you going?"

"I've got to pick up an order at the bookstore for Dad. After that, I thought I'd drop by Books A Zillion and then Sportsman's Pro Shop."

"Two book stores?" Brett asked.

Caleb blushed and said, "The first is a Family Christian Bookstore. Dad only buys his books from there- says he wants to support small businesses that believe like he does. *Books A Zillion* is for me."

Brett smiled and said, "Sure. Sounds like fun." He looked over at Shelby for a second and then said, "And I want to check on some things at *Sportsman's Pro Shop*."

"You want to go to a hunting and fishing shop?" Shelby asked with a smile.

Brett nodded and replied, "Let's just say I want to check on a few things."

Shelby found herself surprised at her best friend wanting to "hang with the guys"- especially since it was a guy she was sort of seeing. Shaking her head, she said, "I'm not sure, but I think we should all be very afraid."

Among the others' grins and chuckles, Brett just smiled enigmatically at her and said, "Yes, you should."

~*~

Brett settled into his new seat in Mrs. Devlin's class. Seven other students looked over at him and grinned as if they knew something he didn't. It was both exciting and a bit scary, and Brett felt as if he were a rabbit trapped by a pack of wolves. He nodded and realized that the students in this class had something in common other than just being smart. Each and every one of them could best be described as on the edge of the school's social environment. Well, all of them except of course Bastion Davenport who was the youngest scion of one of the oldest founding families in Wellman. He was the youngest person in the class- Brett wasn't sure he wasn't still in junior high school- and smiled from his seat across from Brett. "Glad to see another dude in the class. This class was starting to feel like something out of a bad chick flick," he said in a voice that was wavering under the throes of puberty.

Brett waggled his eyebrows and said, "You may or may not change your mind about that eventually."

"Yeah, but being outnumbered two to one is estrogen poisoning," Bastion said as he ran his fingers through his thick locks of auburn hair. Brett smiled and realized that the in a few years, the cute little rich kid was going to be a knockout teenager.

Still, he laughed at the comment and then looked around as he realized that they were the only two males in the classroom. Brandt, of course, was not there. Again that sort of drove home his earlier observation about the students in this class being on the outskirts of the school's social environment. He'd fought hard for his recent acceptance and wasn't sure he wasn't giving some of it up to join the "gifted program" no matter how cool the field trips.

At the end of the opposite table was Shelly Silver, a junior. She was a thin girl with bobbed strawberry blonde hair. He knew that her dad was a professor at the Ashland Community and Technical College, and that her mom wasn't in the picture. She didn't have many friends, and was known for always having her nose in a book- usually the stranger the subject the better.

Next to her was Liselle Garvin. Another strawberry blonde but considerably more heavyset, yet attractive none-the-less. She was going to be one of those girls who always carried a few extra pounds, but did it attractively and with style. She'd been heard on more than one occasion to remark that the word diet was a four letter word and to never trust a skinny cook. To be honest, although she was a sophomore like him, he really knew very little of her. He thought he remembered Shelby describing her as "kind, but tough".

Across from both of them were two other girls that he only vaguely recognized. The first was raven-haired and he wasn't sure if she was Hispanic or Cajun. Her name was Carmelita so he suspected it was more of the former than the latter but he wasn't sure. The other was a short-haired blonde girl who was wearing a gray tee-shirt with a pink flower blossom over the left breast. He had no idea what her name was.

Across from him and Bastion was Phoebe Smith, the school's new age fluffy bunny. He and Phoebe had locked horns several times comparing Wicca to the Northern Way. She just couldn't get it through her head that Brett had as little use for her "Rule of Three" as he did for "Turn the other cheek." But still, her mom owned the largest "alternative bookstore" this side of Huntington. Next to her was the closest thing the school had to a real live goth chick. The truth was that even though Bethanne McMillan dressed all in black and tended to wear spider and snake motif jewelry, she wasn't all that depressing. She just liked spiders and snakes, and just about any other exotic animal she could get her hands on.

It was she that smiled over at him and finally spoke. "Don't let Bastion put too much of a scare into you. We haven't sacrificed him or Brandt to ancient tree spirits yet."

"Hey!" Phoebe protested.

"And we're not going to," Mrs. Devlin said as she entered the classroom. Brett was unsure how the woman may have heard the conversation through the thick metal door. She was a short, stout woman somewhere between fifty and a hundred. There was an ageless quality about her that made pinning down her true age nearly impossible. She had her blonde hair pulled back into a bun and there were just now streaks of silver running amongst the gold. She had the figure of someone who worked out regularly but was gradually losing the battle with a slowing metabolism.

To Brett's surprise, she turned and locked the door from the inside. Turning back around, she looked at the class and asked, "Has anyone told our new student about this class or what we've been studying?"

Every student including Brett shook their head. Then surprisingly enough, she leaned against her desk and said, "Good. I'm glad that you are at least following some of our rules." She gave Phoebe a long look that spoke volumes of some past transgression.

"You mean this isn't a gifted and talented class?" Brett asked confused as he caught himself reaching up and gently touching the hammer at his throat.

Chuckles went through the other students. "Oh, it's a gifted and talented class all right," Bastion said.

"Just what the gifts and talents are," the blonde girl said with a slight giggle as she lay down a copy of a Battle Royale, "is the real question."

"Patricia..." Mrs. Devlin said, her voice had a sharp warning tone to it.

"Well, I'm right," the girl who was evidently named Patricia countered.

With a sigh, Mrs. Devlin nodded and replied, "That's not how we deal with new apprentice candidates."

"Apprentice candidates?" Brett asked, getting a strange feeling in his gut.

The older woman took a deep breath and said, "Your little group out in that valley are not the only people in this town who believe in things different from the mainstream."

Brett raised an eyebrow but said nothing as Mrs. Devlin continued. "Wellman was founded by three families that settled this area after the Civil War. These families were headed by a very special group of scholars and old world philosophers whose practices reached back centuries into rather esoteric studies."

"Let me guess," Brett interjected wryly, "They were part of the Hermetic Order of the Golden Dawn."

Mrs. Devlin gave him a surprised glance and shrugged before continuing, "Although Westcott would eventually leave to form the Golden Dawn in England, these three families were more closely connected to the Fraternal Order of the Golden Rosy Cross."

"So they were nineteenth century mystics," Brett challenged.

"They were nineteenth century mages, and sorcerers," Liselle said.

Brett looked over to where the girl was smiling and shrugged before asking, "And what does that have to do with this class?"

Mrs. Devlin smiled and said, "Each member of this class has been identified as possessing the mage talent."

Brett raised an eyebrow. This had to be some kind of joke. Somebody was trying to push his buttons, to embarrass him. He shook his head and said, "Yeah, right."

Devlin nodded and looked around the room. "I know it's hard to let down your defenses, Brett, but it's the truth."

Brett crossed his arms and cocked his head toward Phoebe, "I can see Phoebe willing to run this kind of joke. Although I don't know him from Thor's Goats, I can imagine Bastion doing it. But I'm surprised that a teacher, someone that considers my uncle a friend would be willing to go along with it. Quite frankly, Mrs. Devlin, I'm disappointed in you."

The teacher shook her head and said, "Even after this weekend, you're going to deny there's something supernatural going on in this community?"

Brett stopped cold in his tracks. "What happened this weekend?" he asked defiantly.

"Your friend Shelby's house was attacked by werewolves. You and Brandt went all medieval on them with a couple of axes."

Brett felt his blood turn to ice water in his veins. Reaching up, he again touched the hammer at his throat before asking quietly, "Where did you hear that?"

"Everybody in this room knows what really happened, Brett," Bethanne said getting up from her chair and putting a hand on his shoulder.

"I don't even know what really happened this weekend," he said. "How could you?"

"Because it's our job to know," she said. "Mrs. Devlin is teaching us what we need to know to eventually take our places with the adults studying whatever it is that makes Wellman different."

"That's the other thing, Brett," Bastion said. "There's a power source here in Wellman. We don't know what it is, but it makes magic much easier. That's the kind of information that we don't want outside forces to learn about." He gestured to the others, "We're sort of the outer circle. It's our job to study, and maybe to be eventually accepted as one of the six scholars' apprentices."

"Six scholars?" he demanded.

Devlin grinned and said, "There are six of us who are the primary researchers and defenders of the community, Brett. We want to protect whatever it is that makes magic easy here, and we want to study it as well."

Brett looked over at Brandt's empty chair and asked, "Does my uncle know what's really going on here?"

Devlin shook her head and said, "No. As far as he's concerned this is an elite gifted and talented program." She sighed and added, "But Gareth Bjargeir knows. It was part of our agreement with him that allowed your community to put down roots here."

"Why?" he demanded.

"Why what?" she asked.

"Why did you agree to that?" he asked. "It sounds like we're exactly the kind of people you'd want to keep out."

Devlin grinned and said, "To an extent you're right. Followers of reconstructed religions do tend to have a bit more sensitivity to these kinds of things. But at the same time, there was a connection to the Northern Way at the beginning; it was lost for a while, but Bjargeir and your community helped bring it back. Now with you, Brandt and a few others, we're cementing that connection again."

"So what do you want me to do?" he asked warily, still not fully trusting the situation. Something deep in his gut told him that they were telling him the truth, but at the same time, he'd grown wary over the years of trusting too many people. He knew how cruel some people could be. He wished at least Brandt were here, preferably Shelby or Van.

"For right now, just sit, listen and learn," Mrs. Devlin told him. "This class is a self-directed study. Watch what the others do, ask about what they're learning and find your own niche."

Brett nodded his head and settled into the class.

CHAPTER 8

"We can help you deal with being the vordavaettir, but we can't help you with the shapeshifting." Mr. Gearheart told Van as the two sat in in the older man's workshed out behind the house.

"Why?' Van asked confused.

"Because we don't do it the same way," the older man said. According to Gareth, Mr. Gearheart was the pack leader of the ulfhedinn, the group of werewolves that had been the land guardians until Van's ill-timed first change. By killing the guardian spirit and eating its heart, Van had taken their place for the next year. The problem was that Van had only vague memories of the incident. Friday's memories were far clearer, and more disturbing to him.

"Gareth says that you shift using some kind of wolf skin. Is this true?" Van asked.

The old man nodded and reached up and touched the three interlocking voknut at his throat before he said, "They are artifacts passed down through the generations of our families. We are the descendents of the Allfather's Ulfhethnar- his wolf-skinned warriors."

"How is it that you are not part of the kindred, then?" Van asked.

The man smiled and said, "We have been here for almost a century and a half. Your kindred is less than fifty years old. Our pelts were given to our ancestors over a thousand years ago, and for that long time we've been charged with protecting the land of the scholars. When this town was settled at the end of the civil war, it was settled by three ancient scholarly families- one of which was from the Nordic tradition. We were asked and agreed to be their guardians."

"And now I've managed to upset that," Van said worriedly.

"We don't blame you for what happened, Van- at least not all of us. Something new is going on, and we aren't sure who is behind it. You've acted honorably, and you've done the job you didn't know you'd stepped into. But at the same time, it was our job for a very long time," the older man said.

"So you don't know what I am, or how I got this way either?" Van asked.

The man shook his head and said, "No. The best we can tell, you are some kind of moon cat."

"Not a werecat?" Van asked.

Gearheart shrugged and said, "I don't know. I don't know any werecats. But you have a tail, and most were-shifters who have man/animal form don't have tails. Only those who are tied to the Troll-wife of Ironwood have a hybrid form as well as a tail." He gave Van an apologetic look, and added, "But the only shifters we know connected to her, are wolves." With a smile he added, "You, my young friend, are no wolf."

"How did I get this way?" Van asked.

"We don't know. Gareth says that you don't recall being bitten when you fought for your family- which, by the way, is one of the reasons the other wolf-skins are cutting you so much slack; that's an impressive feat by itself."

Van shook his head, "No. I was neither bitten nor scratched. To be honest though, that fight didn't seem normal either. I was faster, stronger, and more alert than I'd ever felt up to that point in my life."

Getting up from his chair, Mr. Gearheart went to a cabinet and took out a jar with a pale yellow flower in it. Handing the jar to Van, he asked, "Do you know what this is?"

Van looked at the flower and smiled. He remembered his mother collecting it very carefully on several occasions. She said it did have certain medicinal values but had to be handled very carefully because it was also a lethal poison. "Aconite, or more commonly called monkshood or wolfsbane."

"It's lethal to werewolves," Mr. Gearheart said.'

"It's lethal to just about anything that eats it, Mr. Gearheart, whether it's a werewolf, a human, or a horse," he replied.

"That's true," Gearheart said chuckling. "But most poisons are not dangerous to werewolves, this one is. Just touching it can leave second or third degree burns on a wolf-shifter."

"Even the wolf-skins?" Van asked.

"Even wolf-skins," he said. "When you came out of that tree Saturday morning, you landed in a bed of it, and was unfazed. I have no doubt that if you eat it, it would kill you. But how about touching it?"

Van gave him a long studying look before he unscrewed the lid and carefully reached inside saying, "Well, as they say, in for a penny, in for a pound."

The touch of the flower was soft, and a bittersweet odor wafted up from the jar as he rubbed the flower with his fingertips, but felt no pain. "Okay, so I'm not affected by wolfs bane the same way wolf-shifters are. What now?"

Gearheart took the jar from him and recapped it, putting it up high again. Turning back to Van, he said, "We wolves belong to Odin. Perhaps you should look to another of the Elderkin for your mistress."

Van smiled and said, "Freyja?"

"She is, after all, the Keeper of Cats, and the First Chooser of the Battleslain. She gets the first half of the valiant dead, before the Allfather gets a look. And to be honest, she's a strong-willed woman who may have decided to take a hand in matters. Didn't Gareth say that your mother was trui to Od's Wife?"

Van nodded. Mr. Gearheart was right. Van's mother was a very gifted seidr worker and at the same time had declared herself to belong to Freyja. "Yeah, she was. Dad wasn't quite trui, but he was pretty close to her as well; her and Skadi."

"A woman and her mother, or at least her stepmother. I

would say that you should look for your answers to what you are and how you became that way among the Vanir, not the Aesir. "

Turning toward the door Van asked, "Then what can you tell me about being the land guardian?"

"Normally, the responsibility is divided among the members of the pack who took part in the hunt. We are pretty scattered around the surrounding area and when there's an intrusion the ones closest to it, usually feel it first."

"I didn't feel the moon wolves coming into town, but did when they attacked the kindred," he told Mr. Gearheart.

"It takes a while to become accustomed to what's happening. It can be a subtle feeling, one so subtle that none of us felt you until your fight with Craig Blankenship," Gearheart told him.

Van smiled wanly and said, "I'm never going to live that down, am I?"

Gearheart shook his head and said, "Probably not. But he's going to have a lot harder time with it than you. He's the one who pissed his pants."

With a snort Van said, "There is that." Turning back to face the head of the wolf-skins, he asked, "So how do we start?"

"We start with you walking the perimeter of the land. That's why I suggested we use the cover of the hunt club. Your license is up to date, isn't it?"

Van nodded and said, "For everything except bear. Somehow I didn't see myself hunting bear and since the season is only two days long and only in a handful of counties south of here I didn't see any reason to waste thirty dollars, especially since there are a limited number of permits and it would be selfish of me to take something I have no use for and someone else wants."

Gearheart laughed and said, "I can't fault your thinking, and I think we can get away with not having a bear permit. So what do you say we start walking the woods later in the week?"

"Sounds good, Mr. Gearheart," Van said.

The older man nodded and said, "Glad to hear it."

~*~

Brett was still trying to process everything he'd been told today in Mrs. Devlin's class. The past week had really shaken him to the core. Yeah, he studied galdr, the rune magic of the ancient Norse, and even practiced it, but to this point any success he'd had could easily been dismissed as simple, "luck" which he knew deep down was its own source of magic. Friday night had been magic in its purest form, and had seen the death of one person he considered a friend and another had lost her leg, not to mention his best friend's house getting trashed. He was no longer sure what reality was, and considering his past infatuations with living in a fantasy world, that left him more than a bit concerned for his own sanity.

"You seem to be thinking deep thoughts," Caleb's voice brought him back to the present as he rode in the other boy's old pickup. He hadn't realized it but they'd already crossed the river once and were making their way down the Ohio side toward Huntington.

"Just trying to cope, I guess," he admitted to Caleb.

"I think I understand. It took a lot of nerve to do what you and Brandt did the other night," he said. "When did you grow brass nuts the size of bowling balls?"

"Interesting term coming from a preacher's kid," Brett said.

"I've always had a way with words," Caleb replied. "Still, it was surprising. You just about gave Mrs. Stein and Shelby a heart attack when you charged into that living room."

Brett blushed and said, "It was stupid. I wasn't thinking of anything except for a friend getting hurt."

"You two saved lives that night," Caleb said.

"Not enough," Brett replied.

"Don't be so hard on yourself," Caleb told him. "You're what, sixteen? You did more than most sixteen-year old guys I know could have."

Brett smiled wanly and asked, "Are you going to the funeral tomorrow?"

Caleb nodded his head and said, "Yeah, the coach wants the whole team there. Only person who's getting a pass is your favorite senior."

Brett nodded as he watched the bare limbs of poplar and oak flash by on the highway. "Uncle Alex and I will be there. I think most of the guys from the kindred will be. He was a friend, we need to stand with his folks- if they'll have us."

"I don't know why they wouldn't," Caleb said. "Even my dad says that you guys can't help it that some nut job comes looking to kill a kid they missed a few months ago," Caleb told him.

Brett just nodded, and said, "I guess that I'm so used to being on the outside, that it seems strange to me."

Caleb actually laughed and said, "You were on the outside because you wanted to be, Brett. I think your friendship with Van has done you a lot of good. Speaking of which, were you actually flirting with Allison Snow Friday Night?"

Brett laughed and said, "Actually, no. She was asking me about getting into the gifted classes. I think she's still irked that her brother is in the TAG classes and she's not. She likes to think that she's the smart one in the family."

"C'mon," Caleb replied. "Everybody knows that it's going to be a showdown between you and Brandt for valedictorian in three years. What makes her think she's that smart?" Brett chuckled and replied, "I think she thinks she's smarter because she's a girl."

"Could be," Caleb responded. "Still..., she is kinda cute."

"Thought you had eyes for Shelby," Brett accused him, somewhat shocked at the idea of him trying to get a date with his best friend while eyeing another girl.

"Oh I am," Caleb replied quickly. It was clear he realized he was in danger. "I was just thinking that you need a date, and Allison would be good for you."

Brett looked at the other boy stunned. Had he really submerged that much of his personality? No wonder someone wasn't getting the clue! Finally, he said, "No. I've got my eye on someone else." He let it stand at that.

"Look, about Shelby..." Caleb began.

"What about her?" Brett asked.

"I'm just not sure if she's into me. I keep getting mixed signals," Caleb replied not taking his eyes off the road.

"She likes you," Brett told her. "It's just she's concerned about the whole dating outside the kindred thing."

"You mean she doesn't want to date me because I'm a Christian?" Caleb asked incredulously.

"That's not quite it, but sort of," Brett tried to explain. "We have a different outlook on life and on matters of faith. And there's a lesson to be had in history about it, that has her concerned."

Caleb gave him a disbelieving glance, "Lesson in history?"

Brett nodded, "Yeah. Queen Sigritha of Denmark had been approached for her hand in marriage by Olaf Tryggvason, a powerful warlord who was working for the Church at the time. Things were going well with the negotiations up until just before the wedding when he insisted that she convert to Christianity. She quite firmly told him that he was welcome to follow whichever God he chose, or none at all, but she was not going to give up the faith of her forefathers. He promptly slapped her in the face, and called her a heathen bitch. Eventually, her father and her sons hunted him down and killed him for it, keeping the spread of Christianity out of the Nordic regions for another three hundred years."

"What's that got to do with Shelby?" Caleb asked.

Brett grinned and said, "She likes you and would hate to see me, or Brandt, or worse yet, Van have to hunt you down and gut you."

"Smart ass," Caleb replied.

Brett nodded saying, "I've been accused of that in the past."

After several moments Caleb asked, "Seriously, Shelby likes me?"

"Yeah, she does. But like I said, she's worried that your faith would come between you- at least your dad's faith, that is. He's not exactly a fan of the kindred."

"I know," Caleb said, the regret clear in his voice. "And he'd insist that any girl I dated be a member of a church somewhere, preferably, his. Something about being a good example for the members."

"Exactly," Brett replied. He paused for a second and then carefully added, "And she's worried about how much of your interest in her might be an attempt to break away from your dad. You know what kind of reputation preacher's kids have- and you haven't exactly gone out of your way to dispel the stereotypes."

To Brett's relief, Caleb laughed and said, "It's the hair. Everybody sees it and thinks I'm this bad-boy, or bad-boy wannabe."

"I guess that could be part of it," Brett said cautiously. He wasn't about to tell him that his hair was actually one of his more attractive features. Some guys didn't take too well to that. "It does sort of make you look like that guy who played Thor in the movies."

Caleb grinned widely and, in the tone of someone confessing a treasured wickedness said, "I know." Then his face changed and he asked sincerely, "So what do you think I should do about Shelby?"

Brett shrugged and said, "Ask her out. All she can do is say no, then you can move on."

Not seeming to be satisfied with the answer, he suggested, "Well, you could put in a good word for me. Let her know I'm okay."

Brett laughed and said, "I have put in a good word for you. I've told her I think you're a good guy. Still she's cautious, and I can understand why. I think you're going to have to earn her trust, and that's something she doesn't give easily, and something if she has from another she will not betray."

"You talk like you've told her a few secrets," Caleb said.

"We're best friends, what do you think?" Brett replied sarcastically.

"Best friends with the prettiest red-head in the school," Caleb jabbed. Then he seemed to consider something and said, "Oh...,"

"Oh, what?" Brett asked, suddenly worried.

"Nothing," Caleb said non-concomitantly. "Just something occurred to me."

"What?"

"Nothing really," Caleb said. "So you have put in a good word for me?" he suddenly changed the subject. "I appreciate that, man."

"No problem," Brett said neutrally, trying not to let his concern of what Caleb may have figured out eat at him.

"Got another question for you," Caleb said after a several moments of silence.

"What?" Brett asked, trying to keep the dread out of his voice.

"Who would I need to ask to get permission to hunt up on Silver John Ridge come deer season?"

"I'm not sure where that is," Brett said, glad for the change of subject. "Remember I wasn't raised here."

Caleb nodded and replied, "That mountain that runs behind the farms that make up your kindred."

"Oh, that," Brett said. "I'm not sure. According to Shelby each of the farms there own all the land up to the little creek that runs along the base of the mountain. After that, I think she said that Mr. Bjargeir owns up to the ridge-line. At least that's what I think. You can always ask him."

"Do you think he'd let an outsider hunt there?"

Brett shrugged and said, "I don't know. Probably."

"I think I'll talk to him tomorrow then. I've heard the game up there is good."

Brett smiled and said, "I wouldn't know. I don't hunt very much." He shook his head and said, "At least not like you and Van. I had no idea he was as good with a bow as he is."

~*~

Gerry Ballenger looked up from the reports the Sheriff had sent over about the Stein attack. It was clear that the woman was unwilling to pursue charges against the Steins or the boys with axes, and he wasn't so sure he didn't agree with her. From all accounts- even from the kids who aren't part of the kindred- was that they were attacked and were simply defending themselves. The problem was that he had three dead one-percenters, and a dead kid, along with another who'd lost her leg, and that was getting the attention of his bosses upstairs.

"You wanted to see me, Dad?" his daughter, Felicia asked from the door to his study.

Gerry smiled at the sight of her. She and her mother were his everything, and he'd do whatever it took to make sure she got the best start to her own life. "Come in, Baby," he told her, gesturing to a comfortable chair in the room. "Your mom tells me that you asked to go to the Stein house last Friday."

He could see the worry in her chocolate brown eyes when she replied, "Yes, sir. She told me no, so I let it drop."

Gerry knew that wasn't like his daughter. If she really wanted something, she'd start working it from a lot of different angles. "Why did you want to?"

Felicia shrugged and said, "I don't know. It sort of sounded like fun. Watching scary movies and eating snacks." She crossed her arms carefully and continued, "I guess it was a good thing that I didn't go now, though."

Gerry nodded and smiled wanly, "How many of the kids there did you know?"

"A few," she said with another shrug. "Shelby is in my English class, and Brett was too until today. I've got math with Caleb, and Allison, the girl who got her leg chewed up. Dallas, the boy who was killed, I'd seen around school."

"What about Van? Was he supposed to be there?" Gerry asked.

His daughter shook her head and said, "No. He was staying

with Mr. Bjargeir, at least that's what Shelby told us Friday at lunch."

"So you spend much time with these kids, the ones from the Mountain Hearth Kindred?" he asked carefully. He didn't want to use his daughter as a source of information, but what she might know from passing could be useful in his investigation.

Again with the teenage shrug, "Not really. I thought I might want to get to know them better, especially...uh Shelby." Gerry recognized a lie when he heard it.

"What about Shelby?"

"She just seemed nice. Her and Carmen O'Brien have some kind of rivalry going, but they seemed to put it behind them for the movie night- although I'm not so sure that's not because Carmen is crushing on Brandt Snow."

"One of the boys with the axes?" he asked carefully.

Felicia nodded, and asked, "What's this all about?"

"I'm just worried about the people my daughter is getting involved with. I'd feel better if you stayed away from that group," he told her.

Felicia nodded and swallowed, saying, "Yes, sir."

Her quick acquiescence caught him off-guard. After a moment he said, "Glad to hear you say that. Now give your old man a kiss and let him get back to work."

As she rose from her chair to comply, he couldn't help but notice the relief in her eyes. His daughter had won some point that he didn't even know about. Normally, that idea wouldn't bother him, but for some reason, this time it left him very uneasy.

Watching her leave the room, he picked up the report from the Greenup County Coroner. It just made the whole situation that much more confusing. Dace Yarnvid's body had disappeared out of a secure facility over the weekend. It was too much of a coincidence that worked to make the Stein story that much more believable. Gerry didn't like coincidences, because he knew that in crime they seldom were. The worst part was that it was taking his resources away from his initial investigations- trying to stop the spread of meth labs and the abuse of prescription drugs in the area. This was a local issue and really shouldn't be absorbing his time.

Then he remembered his daughter had almost gone to that party Friday. He remembered the teen who had his throat ripped out and the cheerleader who'd lost a leg. That was just a bit more important than some meth-heads. Granted, the killers had been caught, but he still felt something deep down wasn't right. Something told him the story wasn't yet over.

~*~

Most of the damage from the fight in the living room had been cleaned up, if not entirely repaired. The patches were still obvious and there was some painting and staining that needed to be done, but for the most part the holes had been patched, and things were sort of getting back to normal- at least as normal as they could for Linda Stein. She poured herself her third cup of coffee as she waited both patiently and in dread for the sound of the back door opening.

It was time there was some truth between her and her nephew. Actually, shaking her head she thought, I can't say that. Van has been very truthful, just confused. But it's time we discuss what really happened to Ellen and Dane.

It was with some surprise when she turned around as his raven-haired form traipsed into the mud room, hung up his jacket book bag. Looking over at her, he asked, "Mr. Gearheart wants us to start walking in the woods later this week. Is that going to be a problem?"

Linda took a moment to study him closely. He didn't look any different than he had a week ago. He was still tall, fair, lithely built with a head full of shoulder-length raven hair. His face was still handsome, slightly longish with an upturned nose that was just starting to show the signs of becoming more aquiline like his father. It was the eyes though that stood out to her. They were almost an electric blue and there were times when the black pupils would contract into almost a vertical slit.

"Is that okay with you?" he asked again, and Linda realized that she'd been caught up in trying to find the difference she knew had to be there.

Feeling her eyes go wide for a second, she nodded, "I guess."

"Thanks," he said as he slid past her and out toward the hall leading from the kitchen to the rest of the house.

"Van?" she asked.

He stopped at the door and answered, "Yes, ma'am." His voice suddenly changed, to a wariness she hated hearing there.

"Can we talk for a while?"

He turned and smiled at her, his eyes still wary. "Sure. What about?"

Feeling the need to make both of them more comfortable she pointed to a chair around the table she said, "Sit down."

He said, "Sure. If you don't mind though, let me get a cup of that then," he nodded toward her coffee. For some reason that simple request surprised her.

She just nodded and took a seat across from the one she'd indicated for him. With his back to her, she watched his arms and shoulders flex under the black polo shirt he was wearing. There was a grace and strength to his movements that reminded her of the barn cat, Shadow. Finally, he turned and took the seat. His eyes growing serious, he asked, "What's wrong?"

"Nothing is wrong, I'm just concerned," she said a little too quickly for her own taste.

"Okay," he asked. "What has you concerned?" Then quickly he realized how what he said must have sounded to her, added, "Never mind. Stupid me. Your house gets wrecked by a pack of werewolves looking for me." Very quietly he looked down and asked, "Do you want me to leave? There's still an uncle in Mississippi I could try to go to..." He left it hanging there.

"Great Gods, No!" Linda burst out quickly. "Look at me Van," she said reaching out to grasp his chin and turning it toward her. "What I said at sumbel, I meant it. You're family. You're blood of my kin. I could no more turn you out than I could Shelby. I love you. But I'm scared."

"I know," he said softly.

"How do you know?" she asked suspiciously.

"I can feel it. I can hear your heart pounding with a slow dread in your chest," he told her, almost sheepishly. "You're afraid that there are more of them," he said. "And maybe just a little afraid of me."

"I don't understand you, Van. I'm not afraid, just confused." She picked up her cup and sipped it, feeling the hot liquid make its way down her throat, and giving her an excuse to swallow. "That was you in the living room Friday night, wasn't it. It was you who came bursting through the door and pulled that werewolf off poor Allison."

He nodded and looked up at her, the pain obvious in his eyes. "I couldn't let them hurt you, any of you. You're the only family I have left."

Linda smiled softly and replied with a chuckle, "I'm not complaining, Van. The Winchester wasn't exactly doing a whole lot of good against them. The only thing that really seemed to hurt them was Brett and Brandt with the ax and maul- and you. I'm just confused."

"How did you know it was me?" Van asked, seeming to ignore the comment.

"The eyes," she said. Under all that fur, your eyes stood out. I couldn't help but notice them." She sighed and said, "And I'm not the only one. Brett noticed, and so did Shelby and Caleb."

Sighing, he sat back in his chair looking pained and frustrated, "I was afraid of that. Shelby I trust. Brett, well Brett I'm growing to trust. But I don't know about Caleb."

"I think you can trust Brett, and probably Caleb. Of course I don't trust Caleb, but that's for far different reasons," she told him with a chuckle.

Van nodded and smiled, "And probably rightly so."

"What are you, Van?" she asked him out of the blue.

He shook his head, "I don't know. Gareth can't tell me much. He sort of tossed out the word manakottr, but even he wasn't sure. Mr. Gearheart suggested that I look for what I am among the Vanir."

"Why would Mr. Gearheart tell you that? Why would you even be talking to him about this?" she asked worriedly.

Van smiled and said, "Because there's more going on in Wellman than any of us know, and he knows something about it. The whole Belfonte Hunt Club does. That's why they wanted to talk to me. I've sort of stuck my foot into the whole mess. I don't know much, but I do know that for the next year, I'm supposed to be some kind of protector for the area."

"Will the cat, or whatever that was go away in a year?" she asked, not sure if she would be glad to see it go or not.

"I don't think so," he told her. I was becoming it before the whole mess with the deer."

"Deer? What deer?" she asked, not understanding.

So she listened as he told her about the deer, and how Gareth came to have his hammer. He told her what Gearheart had told him, and she found herself listening in disbelief. But something deep in her heart of hearts told her that he wasn't lying. In the span of less than a year, Linda Stein's world had turned upside down, and a whole new reality was threatening to invade and replace her sleepy little existence.

Finally, she looked at him and asked, "Just tell me this, are you any danger to Shelby or myself?"

Van shook his head vehemently. I'm still me in there. I'm more driven, my primal urges closer to the surface, but I still know who people are. I knew friend from foe Friday night."

She leaned back into her chair and asked, "Can you change at will, or does it have to be the full moon?"

Van shook his head and said, "I don't know. Gareth said he's never heard of anything like me."

"I could have told him that," Shelby's voice said from the hall. Linda spun to see her daughter standing there, books in hand. "You're one of a kind, Van."

"I didn't hear you come in," Linda told her daughter.

"He did," she pointed at Van with her head. "Didn't you Van?"

Van nodded and sipped his coffee.

"So can I join you or is this private?"

Linda looked at Van and asked, "Van?"

"I don't mind," he said. "It's her house too."

"And yours," Linda was quick to reply. "I meant what I said, Van. You're family. This is your home."

"What she said," Shelby confirmed.

With a sigh, Van asked, "What do you want to know?"

"How about how long has this been happening?" Shelby asked.

Van shrugged and said, "The best I can tell, the first time it happened was on Thursday night- which, by the way, was the first night of the full moon. I don't remember it happening. The only time it's happened and I remembered it was Friday night. I sensed you guys were in trouble."

"So this isn't how you killed that werewolf out west?" Shelby asked.

Van shook his head, "There was something strange about that fight, but I didn't change. This all started after I came here."

"You haven't been bitten by any big cats here, have you?" Linda asked half-heartedly.

Van actually chuckled, the first sign of mirth she'd seen out of him in several days. "No, ma'am. Most of the animals on the farm won't have anything to do with me."

"That would explain why Faxi is so nervous around you. To him, you smell like a predator," Shelby said.

"Probably so," Van replied.

"Still," Linda said. "I'm concerned. You don't know anything about what's happening to you, and nobody we know does either." She thought for a moment and then asked, "Do you think Mr. Gearheart could have been right. Have you considered doing a sitting out? Maybe that would give you some kind of insight."

Shelby gave Linda a surprised look and asked, "Aren't you taking to the whole mystical side of this kinda easily, Mom?"

Linda just shrugged. "Having a werewolf brawl in my living room has sort of opened my eyes to other possibilities. I mean, I've always sort of played with the idea of the mystical side of our faith, but now it's sort of hit us at home- literally. I would be a fool not to consider it."

"I could talk to Gareth," Van offered. "I mean, Mom had been after me to do a sitting out, but I never really felt like putting that kind of energy into something I wasn't sure was going to be that useful to me. Now things are different."

Linda nodded her head. "Okay. Talk to Gareth. Find out what you need to do."

CHAPTER 9

Brett silently cursed the weather as the sun shone down on the cemetery where it looked like half the school had gathered for Dallas. It was a beautiful clear fall day, and to Brett is should have been cold, windy and raining to match the feeling of sadness and loss he was feeling. Dallas had been a friend, not a friend for very long, but his first friend that was outside of Mountain Hearth Kindred. That was something special as far as Brett was concerned.

He only half listened as Reverend Johnson, Caleb's dad droned on about the gathering in heaven for the souls of the faithful. It was the usual platitudes meant to comfort the grieving, and he could appreciate the Howard family needing them. Some cynical part of his mind noted when the reverend switched over from comforting the afflicted to afflicting the comfortable and began to "troll for souls" as Allison had once described it. At that point, he shut out most of what the older man was saying and studied the crowd.

He hadn't exaggerated when he noted that it looked like half the school had turned out. The football team all stood together toward the back of the crowd that gathered in the cemetery along Highway 23. Some twisted part of his mind wondered about the abandoned coal mines that were supposed to criss cross this section of the town. Last year, a methane buildup in one had exploded and blown hole in the parking lot of the First Church of God.

Coming back to the present, Brett noticed Craig Blankenship standing there with the rest of the football team. I thought Caleb said he had a pass not to come. With a mental shrug to himself, he added, I can't fault a guy for coming to pay his respects- no matter how much I dislike him.

Most of the kids from the kindred and his uncle were standing with him, as was Mrs. Stein. Even Van was there to show his respect for a fallen friend. The only two who were missing were the Snow twins. He found himself standing between Van and Shelby, and for some reason both of their presences were comforting to him.

It was with a bit of surprise when Caleb's dad ended the service and invited the crowd to pay their final respects. He felt a hand on his shoulder and looked back to see that his Uncle Alex was standing there. With just a wan smile of support, he turned and departed with Mrs. Stein, leaving him there with his friends to file past the grave, and drop a flower. Brett found himself glad that they'd decided not to open the casket at the grave site. He didn't think he could handle the thought of seeing Dallas' body just before they covered it up. For him it was the stuff of nightmares. He'd already decided that when he went, he wanted to be cremated.

As they were leaving the parking lot, a man in his mid-to-late twenties came up to him and asked, "Are you Brett Bond?"

Brett turned around and nodded, "Yes."

The man who appeared to be out of breath replied, "I'm glad I caught you before you left. I'm Steve Howard, Dallas' brother."

"I'm sorry for your loss," Brett said, and found that he meant it.

"I've been asking around about what happened that night. They tell me that you and another kid charged in to rescue my brother," he said.

Brett nodded and replied, "I'm sorry I couldn't do more. By the time we got him out, they'd already..." he paused a moment as the memories of what he'd seen in the dim light, what he'd heard came back to him. The sight of Dallas with his throat spurting blood would haunt him for a long time. Finally, he said, "He was already injured. I wish I could have done more."

The man shook his head and with tear-bright eyes said, "I do too. But at least you tried. My parents want to thank you for that...I want to thank you."

Brett didn't know what to say. "You're welcome" seemed out of place. Instead he swallowed hard and simply nodded saying, "I'm sorry."

Seeming to understand, the man simply nodded and turned away. Stopping for a moment, his back to Brett he asked, "He didn't suffer, did he?"

Brett shook his head and said, "I don't think so."

His shoulders shaking, the man simply said, "I'm glad. Again, thank you." Then he walked back toward the grave site leaving Brett more than a little shaken by the encounter.

Reaching his uncle's car, he slid in without saying a word. Alex simply looked at him and nodded, asking, "You okay?"

Buckling his seat belt and then leaning back he sighed heavily and said, "I don't think I'll ever be okay."

As he started the car, Alex said, "I took the rest of the day off. We don't have to go back to the school, or even home if you don't want to."

"I'm glad," he said.

"Where would you like to go?" Alex asked as he pulled into line to exit the cemetery's parking lot.

"I don't know. Just out of Wellman for a few hours. I need to clear my head," he told him. "Maybe down the Double A."

"You want to go to Cincinnati?" Alex asked.

Brett just shook his head and replied, "No. Just away from here. Maybe talk."

The stunned look on his uncle's face told him everything he needed to know. With a nod and a determined look, he pulled out onto US 23 and headed North.

They'd traveled several miles down the road and nearly halfway to Cincinnati when Brett broke the silence with a single word, "Why?" It was a question that had been eating at him for a couple of years now.

"Why what?" Alex asked.

"Why do you think my parents sold me to you?" he asked before he could lose his nerve.

"That's not exactly what happened," Alex protested.

"You gave them money, and I came to live with you," Brett said. "That's pretty much selling me, if you ask me."

Alex sighed next to him, and said, "Your mother asked me to."

"What?" that answer caught him off guard. "Mama?"

Alex nodded and said, "She was afraid of what might happen to you if you stayed with the family. I don't have to tell you that it wasn't a very good situation."

"But why me?" Brett asked.

"Because you were different from the other three," Alex said.

"You mean different besides the fact that I'm smaller and..." he searched for a word to describe the intrinsic alienness he felt with his own family and finally just gave up and left the sentence hanging.

"Exactly," Alex smiled at him. "Your dad's brothers were starting to notice the difference. She'd overheard some things that worried her. Your grandfather had always sort of protected you. He scared the piss out of a lot of people, and none of them would raise a hand against you while he was still alive. But after he died, your mother and I talked, probably like we hadn't talked in twenty years. We came up with a plan and I think we were both surprised when your dad agreed to it." Brett knew that other people had always given his grandfather a lot of deference. He thought it was simply out of age and respect. He wondered what it could have been if not that.

"What did she overhear?" Brett asked.

Alex shook his head and said, "No. Those were things that were told to me in confidence. If you want to know, you'll have to ask her."

"Which I probably will never do because I'll probably never

see her again," Brett said.

Alex just smiled and said, "Don't be so sure. If the Norns decide you need to be rewoven back into that particular tapestry, you may not have a choice. Your orlog has a lot of momentum in a particular direction, you've started to change it some with your own right good deeds, but it will always try to pull you back onto that path."

"Weird things always seem to happen to me," Brett complained.

"Are you unhappy with living with me?" Alex asked out of the blue.

Shaking his head vigorously he said, "No! Not at all. For the first time in my life, I'm actually happy. Uncle Alex, you're one of the best things that ever happened to me!"
Brett noticed the tightness around Alex's eyes relax, "I'm glad to hear that kiddo," he said with a smile. "You know, you can tell me anything. I won't think less of you, and I won't put you out, no matter what it is."

"I know," Brett said. He knew what his uncle was driving at. A line that he hadn't yet crossed. He realized that he hadn't crossed it for just the reason Alex had mentioned. He was afraid of the rejection.

"They really were werewolves, you know," he said changing the subject.

"That's what Linda tells me," Alex said non-concomitantly.

"You believe us?" Brett asked, surprised at the idea.

"Linda Stein doesn't lie. She doesn't exaggerate, and she doesn't panic very easily. If she says there were werewolves in her front room, then that's cause enough for me to go out and buy some silver bullets for the Colt," Alex told him.

"Don't do that," Brett said. "You'll ruin the barrel."

"Huh?" Alex asked.

"Silver's harder than lead. You fire enough silver rounds through that barrel, and you'll destroy the rifling. Besides, at close range a shotgun is probably better," Alex told him.

Alex snorted and laughed, "You are full of the strangest little details, you know that, Brett?"

Brett felt himself smiling and actually meaning it. Then before he could lose his nerve he blurted out, "I'm gay."

Alex simply smiled and said, "I know. I've known for quite a while, you know. Like I said. I'm not going to put you out because of something you can't help."

"That means a lot to me, Uncle Alex," Brett told him.

"You're my nephew, and I love you, Brett. Any time you have something worrying you, I'll be here to talk."

"Thanks," Brett told him. "Thanks for everything."

Alex just nodded and then pointed with his head toward a sign. "How about IHOP for supper?"

Brett nodded and said, "Sounds good to me."

~*~

The morning sun was coming through the leaf-bare trees making dappled shadows on ground as the mist was slowly burning off. It was a cooler autumn than any in Craig Blankenship's recent memory- not that at eighteen he had much more than recent memories- and he was grumbling about having to be out in the woods looking for good places to set up for muzzleloader season when it started in a couple of weeks. He wasn't going to be doing any muzzle-loader hunting- hell with his arm in a cast, he wasn't going to do much of any hunting this year. That was just one more thing that fag, Van Griffin was going to pay for.

He'd already started talking to people about what he heard about the little creep claiming to have killed a werewolf. The only problem with it was the attack on Shelby Stein's house caused a few people to actually start to believe that garbage. Sometimes he thought this world was completely messed up. That whole bunch of weirdos out there that called themselves the kindred, whatever that was, were being treated like just folks even though they were worshiping false gods and making sacrifices to graven images. He didn't understand why the city fathers didn't run them out of town.

He'd been walking along the ridge line just north of the hollow above that used to be called Silver John Hollow, as his dad and brother were scouting on the other side of the ridge to stay out of what now was private property. Craig had no intention of asking anyone from that group for permission to hunt on their land no matter how good the game. On the other side of the ridge was public land where anybody could hunt and the game was almost as good. He marked a few spots on the map his dad had given him, holding the pencil gingerly in his right fingers. The arm still ached, and the doc had warned him not to overdo it. When he had hit the floor, he'd snapped both the radius and ulna in his right arm and nearly dislocated his shoulder.

Craig continued along the ridge line trying to clear his head and decide what to do next. He was supposed to graduate at the end of this school year and was being considered for a football scholarship to UK. The problem now was that he wasn't going to get to play anymore for the rest of the season. That was going to hurt his chances, and the thought just twisted his guts up tighter.

Up ahead he saw the form of a shapely woman with long blonde hair in a ponytail wearing a khaki jacket and pants and a hunter-orange vest kneeling on the ground looking at something. Even from this distance, Craig could see she was quite attractive and smiled to himself. "Whatcha find?" he called out.

She held up a hand and said, "Stop. You'll trample the tracks." Her voice was strong and as she spoke the wisps of her breath became apparent in the cold autumn air.

"Huh?" Craig asked stopping where he was. "Whatcha find?"

"Come and see, but watch your step. There are big cat tracks all up and down this area."
Intrigued, Craig crept forward, carefully stepping around the tracks he could now see in the soft moist earth at the top of the ridge. They were huge and deep, suggesting an animal well out of proportion with what a wildcat or a cougar in the area would be. As he got closer to the woman, he made out the small Kentucky Department of Fish and Wildlife Resources patch on her shoulder. "I heard that there was a report of a cougar attack outside of town the other night," he said.

The woman nodded and said, "That's why I'm here. I'm investigating if they're true or not." Craig took a moment to admire the package. She was blonde, leggy and had a rack on her that rivaled anything he'd seen or felt in high school. He smiled at the fact that the top button of her shirt had come open while she was kneeling forward.

"One of my classmates is dead and there's a girl who lost her leg. Of course there's a large cat in the area," he said hotly.

She turned and smiled up at him saying, "And it would seem that you're right. Now the question is, what kind of cat?" Standing she dusted off her hands and said, "I'm Auda Dagni." Craig noticed her looking nervously at his hip where he had a Ruger strapped to it. Her own hand rested easily at her belt where she had an automatic holstered. "What are you doing out here?"

He shrugged and said, "I'm with my dad and my brother. We're scouting the area for good places to set up a tree stand."

"You always come out scouting armed?"

"When there's a cougar out in these woods that's killed three people and maimed a fourth? You bet your sweet ass I do." Looking down to where the pistol was worn so he could cross draw it with his good arm he said, "It's legal. Kentucky is an open carry state."

Ignoring the comment, she asked, "Got some ID on you?"

He nodded and reached into his back pocket for his wallet. Pulling it out, he fumbled with it with his injured hand, finally managing to get it opened, the whole time catching himself trying to steal glances down the front of her blouse. Finally, handing her his hunting and drivers licenses, he said, "Here you go."

She nodded looking at the ID and asked, "How'd you hurt your arm?"

"Fight at school," he said without missing a beat.

"You don't sound too ashamed about it," she replied.

"You should see the other guy," he lied.

At that, she glanced up at him and something in Craig's mind told him that she knew he was lying. With a nod she said, "Be careful out here. If this cat really is a killer, that Ruger probably won't do you much good. Cougars are ambush hunters, it'll try and take you from behind."

"I'll keep my ears and eyes peeled," he said.

"Now can you tell me how far I am from the farm where the cat killed those people?" she asked.

He turned and pointed down the ridge into the Hollow

below. "Down there in one of those. Don't know which one."

She smiled and nodded saying, "Thanks." Without another word, she headed back down the trail he'd come up, leaving Craig shaking his head.

He hunched his shoulders and continued following the path along the ridge wondering if those things were real, and watching for good places to set up a tree stand.

~*~

What Craig did not see was the bluish form that silently followed him just below the ridge. The creature that was once Dace Yarnvid had smelled Craig long before he'd seen him, and had felt the anger festering in his soul before that. He stalked the boy carefully, wondering what was bringing him out into the woods on a cold early October morning.

Black eyes watched as the boy stopped and marked a spot on the map, noting the heavy caliber pistol on his hip. He smelled no silver in that gun and had his doubts if even silver could stop him in his new form. The draugr were known to be nigh indestructible, more than a match for a human with a handgun. He moved closer and a shift in the wind brought another scent to him: wolf and man together.

Slinking back into the mists below the ridge, he waited until the boy was well out of hearing distance before he changed directions and followed the other scent. It wasn't wolf, it wasn't human, and it wasn't a werewolf like Matthias Gevaudan, his former pack leader. Instead it stank of Aesir magic and Dace would go miles out of his way to take down anything to do with the Aesir and the Vanir.

After nearly half an hour of searching for the spoor he found it deeper in the valley, making its way along the base of the ridge, deep in a pine thicket. A single wolf was loping along, sniffing at the ground as if following a trail. Dace noted when it gave a patch of monkshood a wide berth and then moved on, still tracking some spoor.

Crouching low, he stayed downwind of the mysterious wolf as it worked itself deeper into a ravine where a mountain stream cut its way down from higher elevations to wind along the outside perimeter of the woods that separated the developed lands from the undeveloped.

For just a second Dace caught a whiff of the spoor the wolf was following. It smelled of cat, and of man, and of Vanir magic. He suppressed the low growl that threatened to well up in his throat, and he knew would warn the other wolf of his presence. Instead he crouched even lower to gain a stronger hold on the scent. Once he was sure he could recognize it again, he stood back up and began to stalk the wolf.

He followed it back up the ravine to the top of the ridge. In the distance outlined against the sky, he could see the boy he'd been stalking earlier talking to a man and another boy. Dace realized it must be the father and brother he had told Auda about. He'd sense the excitement in the boy that Auda's presence had generated. She had that effect on men, and few could resist her charms. A boy that age never stood a chance. He was sure he was describing her in no uncertain terms to the others.

Dace turned his attention back to the wolf he was tracking. It was no more a normal wolf than he was and it stank of the magic of his hated foes. More importantly, it was tracking something that smelled of Vanir magic. He had no idea for what purpose it was tracking the other creature, but he could kill it and then find the other creature himself, and eliminate it as well.

Slowly he worked his way closer as the two disappeared deeper into the ravine and out of the sight or sounds of any nearby humans. He closed with it as it reached the base of a tree that stuck out over the ravine and began scrambling up the loose packed earth. Silently he leapt forward, his claws extended.

He felt them bite deep into the animal's throat as he ripped back pulling chunks of flesh and bone away from the body and effectively keeping it from howling for help from any pack that might be nearby. As the body twisted under his assault he pulled it to him, slung back its head and bit deeply into the wound. The blood had a strange taste to it; somewhere between human and animal. It was rich and sweet and full of power.

The animal fought to get away from his grip with a strength that surprised Dace, but he was stronger. He was faster, and he would not be denied. He lapped at the rich red liquid as it poured from the wound filling him with its power. When the wolf's limbs ceased to push away from him and went limp, he buried his face deeper into the neck nearly chewing the head clean from the body. When he was sure it was dead, he casually threw it up over the edge of the tree stump and heard a satisfying thud as the body hit the ground.

For long moments leaned against the moist earth of the ravine wall, reveling in the taste of blood in his mouth, the smell of the rich dark earth, and the thrill of the kill. Slowly, he came back to his senses and other smells started to intrude on his awareness. There was the odor of a rotting carcass- a deer he guessed, and the bittersweet smell of aconite. He pulled himself up the thick roots of the tree and looked around.

To one side there was the rotting carcass of a huge deer with a rack of antlers to send most hunters into despair that it had been taken by an animal. To the other side, the wolf he'd killed was gone. There, lying in a bed of deep purple flowers, was the form of a well-built man in his early twenties. He was wearing only a wide belt made of wolf fur and his throat was completely torn out and most of the musculature of his neck and shoulders were gone. Dace smiled at himself and considered the feast he offered.

Stepping up to pull him from the weeds, he felt the burn of the aconite and jumped back. Deep red burning welts worked their way down his lower legs as the wolf's bane made its way through his system. Looking down at the corpse he realized that it had already been poisoned by the flowers in which it lay. With a frustrated growl, and a growing numbness in his lower legs he lashed out the nearest large form.

His claws bit deep into the side of the tree and he felt it rock and then crack under the force of the blow. Slowly it toppled forward and down into the ravine as the moist ground gave way, sucking him down with it.

CHAPTER 10

Shelby and Van knocked on the hospital door and waited for a reply from inside. It came with a weak, "Come in."

She led Van into the room that was filled with flowers and balloons, and Allison was sitting up in bed, a sheet pulled up over her lower body. Standing in the room with her was a tall man in a three piece suit along with Allison's dad. The man looked vaguely familiar, and Shelby thought she remembered seeing him the night of the attack. He was tall with black hair and blue eyes and a classical nose with a strong jaw. He had a very official look to him, and something told Shelby that he was not here as a friendly visitor. Next to the bed, Allison's and Brandt's dad stood wearing a UK sweatshirt and jeans. The stranger was asking, "And Van Griffin wasn't there at all?"

"I wasn't where?" Van asked from behind her.

The man turned surprised at seeing him. "Are you Van Griffin?" he asked.

Van nodded and said, "Last time I checked." Shelby couldn't help but smile at the snark. "If I join my friend's Dungeons and Dragons game, I might be someone else though." Then he asked again, "I wasn't where?"

The man reached into his jacket and showed Van an ID that read: **FBI**. "I'm Agent Ballenger from the Federal Bureau of Investigations. I'm investigating what happened at your aunt's house."

Shelby raised an eyebrow and asked, "Funny, I don't recall you actually coming out to the house since the night of the attack."

"I'm just getting the investigation started," Ballenger said. She could sense in him that he was getting pressure from higher up to investigate. She could also feel his discomfort with the people in the room. It was as if he saw Shelby, Mr. Snow, even Allison and especially Van, as some kind of threat.

Shelby nodded as Van leaned against the door and said, "Hello Mr. Snow, hello Allison." His voice sounded very controlled. Shelby could sense the cat in his soul going into defensive mode.

Both of the Snows nodded and greeted Van before Ballenger asked, "Where were you on the night of the attack?"

"With the kindred's gothi," he replied. Then tilting his head, he asked, "I'm curious as to why you are so worried about this now. The FBI was disinterested in the whole thing when these same men murdered my parents. As a matter of fact, you tried to blame me for it. Now, you are still chasing after me when everyone at the scene tells you I wasn't there? What gives?"

"Just following up on all possibilities, Van," Ballenger said. Shelby could sense the challenge in his choice to use Van's first name. He was reminding Van that he was an adult.
Van nodded his head and asked, "Well, they aren't going to be attacking anybody else. They're dead."

Ballenger nodded and said, "And so is another boy, and Miss Snow here was attacked as well. We need to know what set all of this off." He looked at Van and asked, "Do you have any idea?"

Van shook his head and said, "I have no idea why they attacked us in Colorado. I assume they came looking for me because I had the bad graces to survive their attack and kill one of them. You guys wouldn't believe me when I told you what happened then, so I'm not sure why I expect you to believe me now."

"Van..." Mr. Snow warned.

Van caught the tone in the man's voice and looked over. With a very sincere and contrite voice he said, "I'm sorry, Mr. Snow. You're right. I'm breaking the peace, and making both Allison and you uncomfortable. I apologize for my bad manners." Then, turning to Allison, he patted her good leg and said, "I'm very sorry for what happened to you Allison. If there is anything I can do to help, please let me know." Then, looking up, he said, "Please excuse me." He turned without another word and left the room.

Shelby found herself furious at Ballenger. She could sense the distrust from the man. It was nearly knocking her down. He was going to think the worst of whatever was said no matter what. He looked over at Mr. Snow and asked, "What did he mean by breaking the peace?"

"He is a guest in this room, and it was bad manners of him to argue with you here, Mr. Ballenger," Shelby told him.

"I didn't quite mean for him to leave," Mr. Snow said. "I just wanted him to think about what he was saying."

"He knows that, Mr. Snow. He left because at the moment he wanted to make sure that he didn't act any more rudely than he already had."

"You people have some strange ideas," Ballenger said.

Shelby shrugged and said, "I don't expect you to understand them." Then turning to Allison she said, "Do you want us to come back later?"

Allison smiled weakly and said, "It might be a good idea." She reached out and touched Shelby's hand and asked, "Can you ask Mister Bjargeir to come by when he has a chance? I have something I want to ask him." Shelby could see in her mind what it was. She had no illusions whatsoever about what did this to her leg and she wanted to know if she was going to turn into it.

"Sure," Shelby told her. "I'll stop by his shop on the way home."

"Thanks," Allison said.

"What do you want to ask Mr. Bjargeir?" Agent Ballenger asked.

"It's a religious question," Allison said. "I don't think the FBI would be interested in it."

"I'll catch you later," Shelby said as she headed out to

find Van.

"Thanks, Shelby. And tell Brett that I'm never going to forgive him for getting into Mrs. Devlin's class before me," Allison said. It was a weak joke, but Shelby knew that Allison was trying to change the subject with Ballenger.

Unerringly, she headed down the hall to where she knew Van had taken himself. It was as if she had a homing beacon on her cousin and could follow him anywhere. Since the night of the attack, her mind was opening up to whole new vistas of possibilities. It was almost as frighting to her as what Van had become was to him. She found her tall dark and brooding cousin to be the only person sitting in an otherwise empty waiting room. There was a cloud of anger over him that she suspected would have made just about anybody else very uneasy. With a smile she stood in front of him and said, "Well, that went well."

"Mr. Snow was right. It was rude of me to take my frustrations out on Ballenger while in Allison's room. I know better than that, and I've been taught to act better than that. Dad would have blistered my butt for it."

"The cause was sufficient," she borrowed one of Brett's favorite expressions. She was unsure where he picked it up, but he loved to use it. "Wanna go get some frozen yogurt? There's a new place just up from The Eye in the Well. Allison wants me to ask Mr. Bjargeir to stop by."

Van nodded and followed her to the elevator. He waited until the door closed and then said, "She's worried about turning isn't she?"

"I think so," Shelby said. "She's not stupid. She's seen all the movies."

"Did it bite her?" he asked.

"I don't know. When yo...uh, the cat pulled it off of her, it was hunched over. There was blood on its mouth, but that could have been from what it did to poor Dallas," she replied. "Could you tell?"

Van shook his head and said, "No. I'm still too new to

my senses and the antiseptic smell was playing havoc with them."

Shelby nodded thoughtfully. "Van, I can sense the cat in you. I couldn't sense anything in her."

Van shrugged and replied, "And of course you told me that seidr workers always know these things."

"You betcha," she replied. "And don't you forget it."

"I've got a question for you," he said carefully.

"Go on."

"What do you think Brett would say if I asked him out?" he asked almost too low for her to hear. The complete change of subject had caught her so off guard that she had to actually think for a second about what he'd asked her.

Shelby smiled. She'd been wanting the two of them to get past their reticence and finally decide that they were as well-made for each other as she thought they were.

"I think he'd say yes," she told him.

"Has he talked to you about me?" he asked.

"Do you want me to tell him about us talking?" she countered.

"Not particularly."

"Then it's only fair that I keep what he tells me to myself as well," she told him. She'd spent almost two months balancing between both boys expressing what they were feeling toward the other to her, but not to each other. Sometimes boys could just be dense. "I think that you two should sit down and talk." She quickly added, "With each other and not me."

"Okay, okay," Van said, his mood improving. "Maybe I'll ask him out this Friday night."

"And how do you plan on going out with him?" she said, pulling the keys to her mom's truck from her purse.

Van blushed and said, "You've got a point. I just got my license and your mom hasn't put me on her insurance yet."

With a grin she said, "Maybe we can work something out. A double date?"

"With you and Caleb?" he asked.

"Sure as heck not going to be me and Craig Blankenship," she told him as she unlocked the cab and crawled up behind the wheel. "Come on, Cuz, let me buy you a frozen yogurt."

As they pulled down the long winding road that came off the mountain where the hospital was located, Van seemed to slip back into a depression. She could feel it threaten to wrap around her like a wet blanket. As she entered US 23 just above the bridge leading into downtown Wellman she asked, "What is it Van?"

"What's what?"

"You're mood is suddenly like a rainy Saturday afternoon," she told him.

He shrugged and said, "I was just thinking about mom and dad," he said.

She shook her head and told him, "The other thing you should remember about seidr workers, is that you shouldn't lie to us."

Again he shrugged and said, "I was just thinking that if I hadn't come here to live then Dallas would still be alive and Allison wouldn't have lost her leg."

"And if we had planned the movie on a different night then they'd have attacked when we were all at the house alone. We might not have heard them coming. We could all have ended up dead," she told him.

"You're not helping," he told her sarcastically.

"I'm not trying to," she replied. "What is is, and what is becoming is becoming. We can only control our own actions and let the Norns do the rest. It doesn't do any of us any good to second guess what has happened so far. All we can do is live our lives with the dignity we have."

She took a deep breath and sighed. "Look. Some people who know what's going on in the town might blame you for this. Others may just write it off. But anybody messes with you, you send them my way. We can't have you bouncing football players down the hall every day. Coach Grizzle might start getting upset."

"Yeah," he said with a smile. "That would hurt our chances at the state playoffs."

"So what are you going to tell Mr. Bjargeir?" she asked.

He grinned and said, "That old man knows more of what's going on around here than any of us. I'm sure he already suspects that she might be worried about that."

"I wonder if the leg would grow back?" Shelby asked. "That would take some explaining to do."

"I don't think so," Van said. "At least not in human form. I know that werwolves heal faster than humans, but without it attached I think even in wolf form she would still not have it. I think."

"That's the problem. All we have are I thinks. We don't have any facts, just guess work. And the real question is whether or not all of this over," she told him as they pulled into the parking lot of the antique shop that Mr. Bjargeir owned. "Something deep in my bones tells me no."

"I'm glad I'm not the only one who feels that way," Van told her as she turned off the engine. "I can feel something out there and its not friendly."

"Is this part of being the land guardian, you were telling Mom about?" she asked.

He shrugged yet again, and said, "I don't know. It could be. It might just be me being paranoid. You know the FBI is convinced that I'm delusional."

She grinned, "After last Friday, I have no doubts about what happened to you in Colorado and no doubts about what happened Friday. Those things are real and this is not yet over." She crawled out of the Ford and looked up at the sign over the front door. Next to the name there was a picture of a single eye staring out of a well standing under the limbs of a great tree. She smiled and thought that Mr. Bjargeir always did have a good sense of humor.

The first thing that she noticed as they entered the shop

was feeling like she had stepped back in time. As the door closed behind them, a buzzer beeped twice followed by the chiming of the bells attached to its frame. In the back, Mr. Bjargeir came out from behind a tall maple dining room cabinet that he was working on. He smiled at them and said, "Van, Shelby. What can I do for you?"

"Allison Snow asked us to stop by and see if you would stop by her hospital room soon."

He wiped his hands on a towel in his apron and said, "Well, I planned to stop by this evening after I close up shop. Did she say what it was about?"

She looked around the shop and asked, "Are we the only people here?" she asked.

"Just the three of us and the house-wights," he said.

She nodded and told him, "I think she's worried about what happened Friday night and whether or not she might be infected with lycanthropy."

Bjargeir nodded and said seriously, "I'll make it a point to stop by and see her."

"We appreciate that," Van said.

"How're you holding up, Van?" Bjargeir asked.

Van shrugged and said, "I'm coping. I'm still trying to sort out the feelings this stuff is generating inside me. I'm afraid before it's all over I'm going to be as irritable as a bear with a sore paw."

Bjargeir laughed and said, "More like a cat." He reached up and touched the scar running under the eye patch he wore over his missing eye. "Trust me, you don't want to mess with a bear. But I think you'll settle into it just fine." Then turning to Shelby he asked, "How about you?"

Shelby smiled and said, "There's some other stuff going on I want to talk to you about later." She grinned even wider and said, "The kind of thing a good Odin's man like yourself might be able to help me with. But for now it can wait. I'm not in danger of turning into a giant cat."

He grinned back at her and said, "Understood. I'll try

and stop by later this week."

"The FBI is investigating," Van said. "I'm afraid I was rather rude with Agent Ballenger and came close to breaking the peace in Allison's hospital room."

"I wish some of you young folk would get it through your heads that breaking the peace only applies to someone's steading, or to the Thing. You don't have to walk on eggshells all the time. Some of the best news I've gotten in recent years is that you kicked the crap out of Craig Blankenship. If Ballenger crossed a line and you called him on it, then good."

"He didn't cross a line, but he was definitely afraid of us," Shelby said.

Both Van and Bjargeir turned and looked at her. "How do you know?" Van asked.

She shook her head and said, "Like I said, a seidr worker knows."

Bjargeir raised an eyebrow and then said, "Your aunt was one of the most gifted seidr workers I've ever met. If you have her gift, then that could be a genuine blessing for the kindred. Do you have any idea what he was afraid of you about?"

She shook her head and said, "I don't know. For some reason he saw everyone in that room, including Allison, as a threat."

"I'll talk to the sheriff," Bjargeir said.

"Not sure what good that's going to do. He's a Fed," Van replied.

Bjargeir smiled and replied, "Son, don't you know that the county sheriff is the most powerful elected official of any office in the US?"

"As a matter of fact, no," Van said.

Bjargeir smiled and nodded his head. "Feds operate in a county at the sheriff's discretion. She can toss the lot of them in jail if she decides to, and there's not much that anybody can do about it."

"I didn't know that," Van said.

"Most people don't. But I don't think that's going to

happen. What is it about this particular agent that's setting off your intuition?" he asked.

"Mainly that he was scared of us, and I don't mean just Van or even me. He's scared of the whole kindred for some reason," Shelby told him.

Mr. Bjargeir nodded and stroked his white beard as if thinking. "It could be he's read Project Meggido. That's got a lot of garbage in it about us being a hate group and linked to the Nazi Party and other such nonsense."

"Really?" Van asked.

Bjargeir nodded and said, "Yeah. It was written in the nineties when certain people in the media were trying to create boogey men they could prosecute. They had a lot of help from the *Southern Poverty Law Center* who, at the time, had labeled anybody who followed the Norse faith as a racist. They've been sued into putting a caveat on that claim now, but in reality they're no better than the racists they claim to track.

"And you think that Ballenger is influenced by that?" Shelby asked.

Mr. Bjargeir shrugged and said, "Quite possibly. Some of what some groups among the folk believe could be be misconstrued as racist- especially if you were looking to be offended and if you wanted to take something out of context. That's why Mountain Hearth Kindred has never gotten involved in the whole "one drop" argument. We'd rather spend our time living our lives than worry about whether or not a single drop of Nordic blood was enough to make you one of us. We'd rather judge people by their deeds."

Shelby nodded and said, "Well, do you think that Allison has been infected?"

The old man looked to Van who shrugged as if to give some permission. "I've talked to Van and I've talked to some other shifters I know. They tend to think that the ones who attacked your steading were moon-wolves, not werewolves."

"What does that mean?" Shelby asked. "And what's

the difference?"

Bjargeir smirked and said, "Not much really. But moon-wolves are descended from giants and get their ability to shift from their bloodline, not from being bitten. If a werewolf bites you, it's possible that you could be infected- if you survived, which is not an easy thing to do. But if a moon-wolf bites you, he'll just kill you. Could you turn into a moon-wolf if he bit you and you managed to survive? Possibly, but I think the bite would have to be deep. According Kurt Snow, the doctors said the wound hadn't been gnawed on, but the muscle had been clawed away." He shrugged and said, "Moon-wolf or werewolf it's still horrible for a sixteen-year-old girl to lose her leg."

"What does that make you, Van?" Shelby asked her cousin.

He shrugged and said, "I don't know. Maybe a moon-cat? I've definitely got a tail, and it's got a mind of its own." He grinned and blushed at the last comment.

"We think there might be even more at play with Van than just lycanthropy or even ailuranthropy as Van's case may be. We're looking into it."

Shelby nodded and said, "Good. But I really think Allison and her dad could could use some reassurances."

Mr. Bjargeir fixed her with his good eye and asked, "You bucking for a promotion in the kindred, girl?"

Confused, she asked him, "What do you mean?"

"You are sounding like a gythia or even a steward. Are you looking to fill a spot in the future?"

She shook her head and said, "No sir. I was just thinking about someone who could use some help."

He laughed and said, "That's what the steward does, girl." Then he paused a moment and said, "I think your mom and I need to have a talk, too." She and Van looked at each other, worried. "From what I'm hearing, we've got ourselves a whole crop of kids growing up who are taking on quite a few responsibilities without being asked to. I don't like to let talent go to waste."

"Uh, I was just relaying a message?" Shelby said suddenly sheepishly.

Bjargeir nodded and said. "Well, I'll stop by and talk to the Snows just as soon as I close up shop. Now you two go on and get out of here. I'm sure you've got better things to do than sit here and talk to a crotchety old man."

Shelby and Van both nodded and decided to beat a hasty retreat before he got any more ideas.

~*~

Despite the run-in with Mr. Ballenger, Van still enjoyed his time with his cousin. And of course getting the little bit of an answer from her that he did concerning Brett had been good news. But to be honest, he liked spending time with Shelby. She really was a calming influence on him and had been the cousin to whom he'd told all his secrets when they were younger. And he had to admit that he'd found himself not dwelling on his parents as much lately. It seemed that the events of that horrible Friday evening had given him some kind of perverse closure. The men who'd killed his parents were dead and he felt his parents' spirits could now rest in peace in the halls of their ancestors.

It was later that evening when he was sitting at the small desk in his room putting the finishing touches on an essay for his English class that there was a knock at his door. He looked up to see Brett standing there looking a bit sheepish. "Your aunt said I could come on up."
Van smiled and pushed back from the desk. "I'm sorry, I didn't hear you come in."

"Van, this house has solid log floors. Hearing through them is nearly impossible."

Van shook his head and smiled saying, "Not for me." He looked back at the computer and said, "But I guess I was so caught up in that essay I was tuning everything out. What's up?"

"Uncle Alex and I went for a drive today after the funeral," he said. "We talked a lot."

"About?" Van asked.

He shrugged and said, "Family, why I'm here. The kindred, Shelby, you."

"Me?" Van asked, suddenly worried. "What about me?"

"He thinks I should talk to you," Brett said carefully.

"About?" Van asked.

Brett looked down at his shoes for a moment and then back up at Brett. "I was wondering if you wanted to go to the movies this Friday night. He says I can use his car."

"Okay," Van said. "But what about me?"

"Van," Shelby stuck her head in the door. "Brett just asked you out on a date."

Van looked at Shelby and then at Brett and asked, "You sure?"

Brett nodded, and Van could hear the other boy's heart beating in his chest. "I wouldn't have asked if I wasn't sure."

Van was stunned. Did Brett actually beat him to the punch on this one. "I just wanted to make sure. I mean this is a date, not two friends going to the movies?"

"If you don't want to..." Brett said, suddenly nervous.

"No!" Van said, "Uhhh... I mean yes. Yes, I'll go out on a date with you Friday night."

"Now see? We don't have to double date," Shelby said. "And you get stuck watching whatever bad sci-fi movie Brett wants to see without me."

"Shelby..." both boys said in unison.

"What?" I was just pointing out that you have lousy taste in movies, books, and music," Shelby said. Then with a twinkle in her eye she added, "But not in boyfriends."

"We haven't gotten that far yet," Brett said.

"You realize this is going to be all over school by Monday," Van said.

"How come?" Brett asked. "Shelby's not going to tell anybody."

Van thought about it for a moment and realized Brett was right. "Not that I care if people find out, but it would make life more difficult on you."

"People have pretty much stopped trying to put me in garbage cans now," Brett said.

"Really?" Van asked. "Must be word getting around about you and that maul."

"Maybe," Brett said. He came in and sat down on the bed. "Shelby says that you went to talk to Allison today and had a run in with Agent Bellenger. You do realize that is Carmen's dad don't you?"

Van shook his head and said, "No. I didn't. I hadn't put two and two together, I guess. She's black and he's white, so I guess it didn't register."

"She's actually bi-racial," Brett corrected.

"Yeah, but she doesn't make a big deal out of it so I tend to think of her as another girl in school I have to dodge."

"Poor Van," Brett teased. "Such a handsome guy that he has to dodge all the girls looking to trap him with their feminine charms. We all should have such problems."

"Hey, you're the one who just asked me out," Van countered. "I'm just saying that there have been several girls at school who've been on the hunt for a new boyfriend for quite a while." Leaning back in his chair he added, "And I can think of one who I have been told has got her eye out for you. Come to think of it, she gave me a message for you."

"Who?" Van asked.

"Allison Snow," Van said.

"What makes you think that?" Brett asked.

"She told me to give you a message," Van countered.

"No, Dipwad, what makes you think that she is interested in me?' Brett asked.

"Shelby said that she was very attentive at the movie that night. I was beginning to wonder if I had competition."

"What do you mean competition?" Brett asked, surprised.

"I've been thinking about asking you out for a while. It's just I suddenly started growing ears and a tail and that sort of distracted me," Van replied.

"So you think I really might be boyfriend material?" he asked.

"I wouldn't have said yes, if I didn't think so," Van replied. "You know I wouldn't lie to you. I owe you a deep debt."

"Me?" Brett asked. "What kind of debt?"

"I wasn't here to defend the steading. You did it for me," Van said.

"You showed up," Brett said.

"But you held down the fort until I got here."

"Your aunt wasn't exactly sitting idly by," Brett said.

"Nordic women have always defended their homes."

"You would have done the same for me," Brett said, thinking about it.

"I guess I would have," Van finally said. "So, what time will you pick me up on Friday?"

"Well, I got two tickets for the nine-fifteen showing of Imperial Entanglements."

"That's PG-13," Van said.

"We're over thirteen," Brett replied.

"Now that you mention it, we are," Van said with a smile as he stood.

"Uh uh," Shelby said from her room. "You know what mom said, Brett. Door has to stay open and no snogging."

"Are you listening?" Van asked.

"Of course," Shelby said.

"You know I'm going to get you back for this," Brett told her.

"I'm sure you will. But for now, I get to have a bit of my fun. After all, I have had to listen for you two pine over each other since September. I deserve a little fun for my long suffering," she told him.

"I'll remember this next time you're with Caleb," Van said.

"Haven't decided how far I'm going to let that go yet," Shelby replied.

"Seriously?" Van asked.

"Seriously," Shelby said. "I like the boy, but I'm not so hot on the crap his dad spews. And after what Mr. Bjargeir told us today, I'm rethinking a lot of who I associate with."

"IF YOU THREE ARE GOING TO YELL AT EACH OTHER ACROSS THE HALL, TAKE IT DOWN TO THE LIVING ROOM!" Linda shouted up from the stairs. **"I CAN HEAR EVERYTHING YOU GUYS ARE SAYING!"**

"Busted," Van said with a wry grin.

"You finished with that?" Brett asked, nodding his head toward the computer screen.

"As finished as I'm going to be," Van said. "It's really sort of a fluff assignment."

Brett nodded and said, "Then why don't the three of us go down to the living room so Mrs. Stein won't yell at us?" As Van pushed the chair back he asked, "What was Allison's message?"

"Oh, that she wasn't going to forgive you for getting into Mrs. Devlin's class before she did," he told him, putting the chair back under the small pine desk.

Brett became silent for a few moments as he seemed to consider something. "I think the three of us need to talk, maybe add Brandt too."

"All of us?" Shelby asked coming out of her room. "You turning kinky on us?"

He shook his head and said, "No. But I think it's something important to the kindred."

"Yeah, we need to talk about that too. Mr. Bjargeir said something today that has sort of got me thinking."

"You too huh?" Shelby asked.

"Yeah, me too. Especially after Friday night."

"I can always call and ask him over," Shelby said.

"Might be a good idea," Brett asked as they headed down the polished pine stairs.

His Aunt Linda was coming out of the kitchen with a pot holder in her hand. "I just put on a pot of milk to make cocoa."

"Thanks, Mom," Shelby said. "We were going to call Brandt over to talk. Is that okay?"

She gave the three of them a strange look. "I thought this was about something else." She looked back and forth between Van and Brett.

Van shrugged and said, "That's settled. We've got a date for Friday night. This is about kindred stuff and what happened Friday."

"Kindred stuff?" Linda asked. "You guys already taking up positions in the kindred now?"

Van felt himself blush again. "It's nothing like that."

"Really?" Linda asked, crossing her arms skeptically. Then, looking at Shelby, she said, "Go ahead and call him. Although I'd be surprised if his folks let him come over here now."

"Nobody blames you for what happened, Aunt Linda," Van reassured her.

"Not quite true," Linda replied. "I blame myself. If I'd been paying more attention then maybe I could have stopped Dallas from running out that night."

"And if you had two heads you'd be an Ettin," Brett replied. "What happened happened. If we try and second-guess ourselves we'll go crazy. Trust me on this, I kept blaming myself for stuff until my Uncle Alex kicked me in the butt about it. I think that Brandt will come." He looked over to where Shelby was dialing the number, "Tell him I'm here and want to talk to him, too. Tell him I'm going to spill the beans to you three."

"What's this about then?" Aunt Linda asked.

"There's a lot more going on Wellman than people know. We've gotten caught up in it, and it's only fair that the people involved know what's happening. None of us have taken any oaths to keep Mr. Bjargeir's secrets and so we aren't bound by his oaths."

"That sounds rather defiant," Aunt Linda said.

"Not really. I'm not so sure that Mr. Bjargeir hasn't arranged it this way. Come to think of it, it's the kind of thing someone who's fulltrui to the Allfather would do to both keep his oaths and to protect his people," Brett said.

"So you think that maybe Gareth left a hole in the line of oaths to give you room to act?" Linda asked skeptically. "It may be that he thinks you're too young to give an oath."

Van shook his head and said, "I don't think so. Gareth has told the Death of Balder enough to know the Warning of Mistletoe in that one." He looked at the others and said, "But nobody has asked any oaths of me about what I've been told. Maybe it's an oversight, but I don't think so. I think they're counting on my good sense and self-preservation."

"Okay, you guys are starting to scare me," Linda said. "Although the idea that my nephew can turn into a raging werebeast should scare me more, it doesn't."

That caught Van off guard and he could tell that Aunt Linda regretted saying it the moment it left her mouth. Even Shelby gave her a startled look. "I would never hurt you or Shelby, or anybody else I care about." Van said softly.

"I didn't mean it like that, Van," Linda said. "I mean that I'm not frightened that you are what you are, and some part of me thinks that maybe I should be."

Van shoved the hurt of her comment deep down and nodded. "If I thought you'd hurt me, do you think I'd ask you out?" Brett asked him.

Van shook his head and smiled, "No. I don't."

"Brandt is on his way," Shelby said. She kept giving her mom a disturbed look. "Van, I'm not afraid of you," she said clearly.

"And neither am I," her mother protested. "But if you think about it, we should be."

"I understand, Aunt Linda," Van said. "Let's forget about it."

"For now," Linda replied. "We need to talk about it, Van."

"I know," was all he said. Then turning to Brett he asked, "What is all this about?"

"I've got some information about what's really going on in Wellman." Looking around at the others and then up and down at Van he continued, "And I suspect your recent excursions with the Belfont Hunt Club may have given you some insights yourself. I think it's time we compare notes." He quickly turned to Shelby and said, "And that's not an opening for one of your snarky remarks."

"Would I do that?"

"Yes," Van, Brett, and Linda all answered simultaneously.

CHAPTER 11

Brandt Snow was exhausted both physically and mentally. He'd watched his friend get killed and this his twin sister get mauled by a werewolf. He'd stood by his family while his sister had her leg removed, and then the FBI had come by and stirred up all kind of crap trying to pin this on Van. He had just left a meeting with Mr. Bjargeir at the hospital with Allison where he tried to reassure the family that Allison wasn't going to turn into a ravenous werewolf come next full moon when Shelby had called wanting to talk to him. She said that Brett and Van were there and they all wanted to compare notes. At first he was afraid that his parents weren't going to let him go, but his dad had finally nodded and said, "Just be careful, and stop by the house and take the Colt with you."

It wasn't a big deal and his house was on the way there anyway so it wasn't really out of his way. He barely noticed the black sedan sitting off the road as he crossed Silver Bridge but didn't think much of it. He did start thinking about it though when he saw it following him down the lane and passing slowly as he pulled onto the parking pad at the Stein farm. He reached into the console and pulled out the heavy Colt and strapped it to his hip before getting out of the car and going to knock on the door.

When Shelby let him in, he looked back over his shoulder to see the black sedan turning around as he closed the door behind him. "What's wrong?" she asked.

He shrugged and said, "I think I was followed here." He looked at the other three and said, "From John's Creek."

"Black Dodge?" Brett asked.

"It was black. I didn't get the make or model," Brandt said. "But it could have been a Dodge."

The other three looked at each other and then shrugged. Mrs. Stein said, "There's nothing we can do about it now, but maybe Shelby and Van can follow you home in the truck to make sure you get there okay."

Brandt blushed and took off his jacket and unhooked the Colt from his belt and handed it to Mrs. Stein. "You had better take this until then."

"Are you afraid of me, Brandt?" Mrs. Stein asked.

He shook his head and said, "No, ma'am. But with that cat still out there, Dad doesn't want me out at night unarmed." He looked directly at Van and they all understood that if Brandt wasn't sure about Van's secret, he at least suspected it. His IQ did, after all, start with two.

"We need to talk about that," the tall raven-haired youth said. "I'm not going to hurt you or your family."

"I was there, Van," Brandt said. "I saw yo...uh...that cat came through the door, yanked that bastard off my sister and knocked it out the window. I'm not afraid of the cat, but my dad's not so sure." He looked at Mrs. Stein and said, "Uh...excuse the profanity."

"The cause was sufficient," Mrs. Stein quoted Brett.

He turned to Brett and said, "You've got half the kindred using that expression and none of them have any idea where it came from do they?"

Brett just smiled and said, "If they want to find out, then they can look it up."

"That's neither here nor there," Mrs. Stein said. "Brett said he's discovered something about what is supposedly 'really'" she made little quotation marks in the air with her fingers, "going on in Wellman. He said you know something about it."

It slowly began to sink in what they were talking about. "We're not supposed to talk about that, Brett. That's part of the understanding to be a part of it."

"Well, what's really going on got Dallas killed and your sister's leg mauled. I didn't take any oath about what I would say, especially not to keep it secret when it threatens either me, my family, my friends, or my kindred. Those come first. I'm not talking about going out and blabbing it to everybody, but we need to compare notes because I get the feeling this isn't over yet," Brett said.

"I don't know..." Brandt vacillated.

"Well, just come and listen. You don't have to say anything, but what you find out from us may make a difference with you and your sister," Van suggested. That caught his attention. He didn't want anything else to happen to his sister. Devlin's class had already started building a wall between him and his twin and he didn't like it and he knew she wasn't happy about it either.

"I'll listen," he said as he joined them at the large oak dining room table.

Van settled into at one the chairs with the grace of the cat that Brett suspected was part of his soul. "I'll start," he said. "You're right. I was the one that pulled that werewolf off your sister. I also would never hurt any of my family or friends. That was my second change and the only one I remember."

Brandt nodded and said, "Makes sense."

"To you, maybe," Brett countered.

Brandt shrugged and said, "Well, I've been at this a bit longer than you have."

"What does that mean?" Mrs. Stein asked.

"How about we let Van finish first," Brandt suggested and reminded himself to keep his mouth shut.

"There are a group of shifters living here in Wellman. They're called the ulfhedinn and they say it's their job to protect the area. According to them, they've been here longer than the kindred and are protecting something important." He sighed and said, "And they're fulltrui to Odin."

"They're not part of the kindred?" Brandt asked, surprised.

"No. According to their leader they've been here since the town was founded after the Civil War. They don't know what they're protecting, just that they've been doing it for the city founders since then."

Brandt nodded but said nothing.

Brett however said, "There's a handful of mages studying something powerful here in Wellman. Mrs. Devlin's class is sort of a training school to pick out the next generation of scholars. Evidently each of them pick a student to study under them and they are eventually replaced by their pick."

"How many are there?" Mrs. Stein asked.

"Six or seven. According to Mrs. Devlin, they originally had a follower of the old faith as part of their founding number but he left. That's why they agreed to let the kindred settle here, to replace something they felt was missing," Brett told her.

"That must be who the ulfhedinn work for," Van said. "But on my first shift, I screwed up and managed to make myself the land-guardian instead of the pack of wolves to whom the duty was supposed to go. But since I haven't taken an oath to whomever they serve, I'm sort of a wild card."

"Was it one of the uflhedinn that attacked us Friday night?" Brandt asked.

Van shook his head. "No. Those were moon-wolves, not ulfhedinn or werewolves."

"What's the difference?" Brandt asked. He looked at Brett and said, "We haven't covered the differences in shifters in class yet." Turning back to Van he asked, "And how can we tell them apart?"

"Tails," Van said. "According to what I've been told, there are ulfhedinn who are humans that shift into wolves by wearing a talisman, usually a belt made of wolf skin. Werewolves have been cursed with lycanthropy and when they shift they don't have tails. But moon-wolves are descendants of Angrboda the Troll-wife who gave birth to Fenrir, Hel, and Jormungandr. They are natural shapeshifters and have tails."

"And what are you then, Van?" Brandt asked.

Van shrugged his shoulders and said, "I have a tail. I'm a cat, and I'm pretty much in control when I shift. Mr. Bjargeir calls me a moon-cat, but he admits that he's just applying a term to me that makes sense and has no evidence that he's right. And he told us that it wasn't likely that Allison would become what attacked us."

"What can you tell us?" Mrs. Stein asked.

"I can tell you that Brett is right. Some of us are better at the magic side than others, and each of us have different approaches to it," he replied.

"What's your approach?" Brett asked.

Brandt shrugged and said, "Galdr." Then, nodding, he added, "Rune work."

"Yours?" Shelby asked with a smile.

Brett shrugged and said, "I don't know. I've been watching the others. I've thought about trying some different kinds of spells, but haven't decided on which ones I want to try first. I get the feeling that experimenting on my own could be dangerous."

"You have no idea," Brandt said. "I'm surprised nobody has warned you yet."

"Warned me about what?" Brett asked.

"There's something here in Wellman, it's what the founders are studying, but it makes magic work more easily. Be careful what you try to do, because it might just work better than you expected."

"That's good to know," Brett said.

"You're being awfully calm about this," Shelby said to Brett. "I would think that if you found out magic actually worked, you'd be out casting fireballs or something."

Brett gave her a hard look and said, "Not hardly. I've been researching werewolves so much lately that I've sort been letting my spell study go. To be honest, I'm a bit frightened by all of this." He looked over at Brandt and added, "And I'm not sure I trust everyone involved."

"What did I do?" Brandt demanded.

"Nothing," Brett said. It was clear that there was something he wasn't saying and Brandt knew it.

"What about you?" he asked Shelby.

"Me?" she shrugged. "I'm just a seidr worker."

"Have you done any sitting out?" Brandt asked knowing that seidr was a much more passive form of magic.

She shook her head and said. "No, although I suggested that Van do it to see if it could give him some insight into what he's become."

"What exactly can you do?" Brandt asked. "How much control over the cat do you have?"

Van said, "I haven't tried shifting deliberately." '

"Don't you think you should try?" Brandt asked.

Van said, "Haven't had an opportunity to try much. I don't want to do anything in the house, I've had my fill of replacing doors and windows, and I'm not sure I'm not being watched when I'm outside so I haven't tried."

"There's always the barn," Mrs. Stein said.

"Faxi is already scared to death of me," Van said. "I don't want to panic him."

Mrs. Stein nodded and said, "I hadn't considered that. It's probably why he's nervous around you. He thinks you smell like a predator."

"There's always our garage," Brandt told them.

Van shook his head and said, "No. I don't want to put your family at any more risk than they've already been."

"I thought you said you were in control," Brandt said.

"I am. But I don't think all this mess is over yet. I don't want any of my scent near your place right now," Van said. Brandt hadn't considered that. What if Van was right and there was still something out there gunning for him. It wouldn't do to bring that to his house.

"I understand," he said. "We could always go out into the woods," he offered. "It would also give us a chance to find out if it was linked to the kindred or if you can transform anywhere."

"I tend to think that he can transform anywhere," Mrs. Stein said. "He said that this mess with the land guardian came after he shifted, not before. Besides, he tossed a quarterback twenty feet down a hall on school grounds. That's not part of the kindred."

"Good point," Brandt said. "And there are supposed to be wards in the school that keep unwanted magic out."

"I didn't know that," Brett said.

"Most of the students don't. Not even the ones in Mrs. Devlin's class. It was something Bastion and I figured out ourselves. Doing magic outside of the classroom but still in the school is like trying to cast with a wet blanket over you. It's possible but it doesn't come off very well and the power is cut way down."

"When have you been using Galdr on school grounds?" Shelby asked.

"Let's just say that there were some things I wanted to make sure happened, and a little rune work helped," Brandt said.

"Like what?" Shelby demanded.

Brandt shook his head and said, "I'm not saying."

"You're one sneaky shit you, you know that, Brandt Snow?" Shelby said.

"That's what my sister keeps telling me," he replied.

"What does all this mean though?" Mrs. Stein asked. "What's really going on?"

Brandt shrugged and said, "I'd say that Van and Brett arriving has influenced some kind of balance of power. That has attracted outside forces."

"Us?" Brett asked.

Brandt nodded and said, "Neither of you were born into the kindred. Both of you are living with a parent's sibling, a mother's sibling at that. I'm told the scholars like to have everything balanced just so. About twelve years ago some kind of tragedy occurred that threw everything out of balance. Best Bastion and I can figure out, it has something to do with what happened to his mom and why his dad ran off with that girl. That sort of put things out of whack and maybe Van and Brett are supposed to bring them back into balance."

"What can you tell us about that?" Shelby asked.

"More than I'm going to. It's Bastion's story and I'm not going to drag his family's name through the mud. You can talk to him, or I can bring him into our conversation. But he's not part of the kindred so I'll leave that up to you guys."

"We'll think about it," Mrs. Stein said. Brandt knew that she knew more about the tragedy surrounding Bastion's mom's murder than just about anybody else, but she was as tight-lipped as just about any other adult who knew the whole story.

"What about testing Van's ability? We could always go out to Greenbo Lake tomorrow after school," Brandt suggested. "I think I can make sure nobody is around."

Everybody exchanged glances and then said, "Let's make it early Saturday morning. I've got plans Friday night," Van said.

"More important than finding out how much control you have over shifting?" Brandt asked.

"You know, I think so," Van replied. "I really do."

Brandt shook his head and said, "Must be a girl."

"Something like that," Van said with an enigmatic smile.

Brandt shrugged and said, "Let me know if you want me to invite Bastion."

Van and the others nodded. "We'll think about it," Mrs. Stein said. Then turning to Brandt he asked, "How much does your uncle know?"

"He doesn't know about Mrs. Devlin's class. They told me that much."

Brandt said, "I was told he doesn't need to know."

"We'll see," Mrs. Stein said. "I need to have a talk with Mrs. Devlin and Mrs. Davenport first."

"You know something about why the Devlins and the Davenports don't get along?" Brett asked.

"I know both of the ladies. I think I can get some information out of them."

"I hope so, Mrs. S.," Brett said. "I honestly hope so." Then turning to the others he asked, "Why don't we try to make it as early as possible on Saturday morning." He looked out the window of the house and said, "If there's anybody watching us, I don't think they'd expect a bunch of teenagers to be up that early on a Saturday." He looked at Van and Brett and gave them a knowing smile, "Especially if two of them have hot dates."

The other three looked at each other and said, "We'll be there."

~*~

It was late Wednesday afternoon before Caleb had been able to track down Mr. Bjargeir to get permission to hunt on the land he'd asked Brett about. When the man had described the tract to him, he had been impressed. It would appear that he was one of the biggest landowners in Greenup County. Everything from one ridge-line to the other in Mountain Hearth Hollow belonged to someone in the kindred. He owned the whole parcel on the north side from the creek to to the ridge top and it was prime hunting grounds.

He'd barely made it to church on time and his dad had taken him to task for not calling ahead. He'd told him that he was getting permission to do some deer hunting and that seemed to mollify him. He still wanted Caleb to call when he was going to be late. Caleb understood his dad's need to know that he was safe. Caleb's older sister had disappeared when Caleb was about three. Nobody knows what happened to her, as she just disappeared about thirteen years ago, supposedly to have run off with a married man. Add into it the recent events at the Stein's house, and his dad was doubly worried. Still, he was glad that his father hadn't pressed him about who he was asking permission of to hunt on their land. It would have just been more explaining to do.

Pushing those thoughts from his mind, he stopped to look around the base of the mountain just as the sun was climbing over the eastern ridge the next morning. He looked at his watch and saw that it was nearly six thirty. He figured he had about half an hour to head up this gully to look for a place to put his tree stand, a half hour to walk back, and then ten to fifteen minutes to get to school without being late. He was supposed to have a date Friday night after the ballgame, with Shelby and didn't want any phone calls to his dad that might give him reason to ground him.

He looked up at the gully and at the stream at the bottom of it as it cut its way down the mountain. The water was cloudy and since it hadn't rained recently, he figured there'd been a rock slide to disturb it. He made it a point to be extra careful as he climbed. The last thing he wanted to do was walk around in muddy jeans all day at school.

He hefted his backpack with his first aid kit in it onto his back and decided instead to work his way up alongside the gully. That meant the going was going to be steeper, but it also would let him avoid slipping and sliding along the red clay of the gully. By the time he was halfway up, he started getting an uneasy feeling. Something was watching him and it was none too friendly. He wished he'd brought his dad's Smith and Wesson with him but he was heading to school afterward and bringing a gun on campus, even if he left it in his truck, would be a major no-no.

As he reached the top of the gully, he could see where the sides of the gully had collapsed under a large mountain ash and had slid down into the stream. A foul odor suddenly caught his attention and he looked around before nearly puking where he stood. The form of a disfigured dead man lay on the ground in a what looked like a patch of purple flowers. His throat was completely gone and his head lay off to the side, a startled look on his dead face. There were traces of some kind of skin rash all over his nude body. Off to the other side of the patch was the carcass of the biggest deer Caleb had ever seen.

Suddenly something growled behind him. Instinctively he ducked and leapt forward. Landing on his feet in the middle of the flowers next to the body, he spun around to see what had growled.

His blood ran cold as the morning light revealed something out of his worst nightmares. The creature was as tall as the werewolves who'd attacked Shelby's house the other night, but he wasn't completely transformed. There was much more of the man to him than wolf, and he glowed an eerie blue in the morning light. Huge blue-black claws were extending from the massive paws' nail beds. Something ate at Caleb's mind telling him that this creature was not exactly alive. He tried to look away, tried to find somewhere to run, but found himself strangely transfixed by the hulking beast that was looking at him with blood lust in his eyes. He was nude and Caleb couldn't help but notice that the cold morning air wasn't doing anything for the creature's bits and pieces. He shook his head and wondered if he was going insane and if he really wanted that to be his last thought on earth.

As the behemoth recovered from its swipe at him, Caleb noticed that it stepped forward just a bit, but then quickly drew its feet back from the flowers like they had burned him. Caleb looked around at the flower bed, noticing that it spread out several yards in every direction. He stepped deeper into it, putting the corpse between him and the beast who began to stalk around the edge of the patch. It was then that Caleb noticed the large fur pelt lying next to his feet.

He didn't have much time to pay attention to it as the creature futilely swiped with its massive paws at the empty air over the patch, as if trying to strike him from a distance. After several of these useless attacks, it raised its head into the air and howled mournfully before loping off into the woods along the ridgeline. Realizing he was going to be late for school now, he reached into his pocket and pulled out his cell phone. He flipped it open and dialed 911.

Caleb wasn't sure why he did it, but something told him that it wouldn't be a good idea for the police to have the fur pelt. So, after telling them that he'd been attacked by an animal, but was okay and that he found a dead body, he hung up the phone and picked up the pelt. It felt soft in his hands and slightly oily. He ran his fingertips through the fur and felt a static charge build up.

He decided that it would be a bad idea to leave the patch of flowers until the sheriff got here so he rolled the pelt up and put it in his backpack under his first aid kit, and waited. It wasn't more than thirty minutes before in the distance he could see several sheriff's cars pull up into Shelby's yard. Oh yeah, that was going to earn him points with his girlfriend's mom. His phone rang and he answered it. "This is Sheriff Treybond. Exactly where are you?"

"On the ridgeline behind the farms. I can see your lights from here." He began waving one arm in the air as he spoke into the phone.

After a moment or so she asked, "Is that you waving?"

He nodded and realized that she probably couldn't see that, so he said, "Yeah."

"Whatcha' doin' up there, boy?" she asked.

"Lookin' for a place to put a deer stand," he told her.

"Figures," she said back into the phone. Hold on and we'll be up there as soon as we can find a trail."

"There's not one. I came up the side of the gully," he told her.

"Great," the woman said. "Just great."

"How do you think I feel?" he asked. "I'm already late for school and that means I'm probably going to get grounded and I have a date tomorrow night."

It took the woman almost another hour to get there, and by that time the stench from both the body and the deer carcass had overcome the adrenaline surge that had sent him into the patch. However, he had already decided that he was not going to come out of that patch until there were several armed people around him.

As the team came over the edge of the gully, he warned them about the tracks they were about to obscure and told them that was where the creature that had attacked him had been. He knew they wouldn't believe him when he described it. But there was something in the sheriff's eyes that made him rethink that conclusion. She took everything he said seriously and confirmed that the tracks looked huge. Another of the deputies found several more wolf tracks and some more huge cat-like tracks at the deer carcass. This was getting weirder and weirder. It took another hour and a half before they released him, and he felt a bit sheepish about asking a deputy to escort him off the mountain. But to be honest, that thing had scared him so badly, that he was willing to swallow a bit of his pride and ask for it anyway.

By the time he was leaving, a hot blonde from the Department of Wildlife was arriving to look at the tracks. Now talk about a rack. That woman had a wild and primal look about her that sent his teenage hormones into overdrive. Yeah, he might be dating Shelby, but that didn't mean he was dead, and this woman had looks that could wake the dead. When she smiled at him, he felt himself react to her on a very visceral level.

The deputy noticed him watching her, smiled and said, "Thought you said you had a girlfriend?" The bigger man took his arm and indicated the path all the recent traffic had started wearing into the gully. "Come on, Romeo, let's go."

Caleb grinned and replied, "I have a girlfriend, I'm not neutered." Then as he started to follow the deputy he added, "And Romeo and Juliette died. If I'm going to base a relationship on a fictional couple, I think I'll make it Morticia and Gomez." The man laughed and led him back to his truck.

~*~

Brett had a lot on his mind, so he failed to notice most of the buzz going around school about Caleb finding a body. As he slid into his usual place at the lunch table, he barely noticed that Felicia Ballenger had once again joined their table, he was too busy studying some notes he'd borrowed from Bastion. He fully intended to try out some of his own ideas this Saturday when he and Shelby took Van to the lake to figure out more about their raven-haired friend's feral side.

"Whatcha' reading?" Felicia asked.

Brett didn't bother looking up as he studied the spell, that Bastion had suggested. It was simple, associative magic, required few components and should work if he understood the principles correctly. Without looking up, he said, "Just some notes Bastion Davenport loaned me to get me up to speed in English."

Felicia nodded and turned back to the conversation with Shelby and Caleb, as the other boy continued, "I'm so hosed when I get home. I'll be lucky if my dad doesn't ground me for being late to school."

"It wasn't your fault," Shelby said. "What would he expect you to do, just ignore what you found?"
Caleb shook his head and said, "No. But, it doesn't help our situation any."

"We have a situation?" Shelby asked. Her tone brought Brett out of his concentration and he looked up.

Evidently, her tone wasn't lost on Caleb either. He shook his head, "I just meant with my dad's attitude toward the kindred."

Shelby raised an eyebrow and said, "We talked about this once already, Caleb. I won't try to come between you and your Dad, but I won't give up my faith for anybody."

Caleb shook his head and said, "Not asking you to, Shelby. I'm just saying that with a body found so near the kindred, near your house..."

"What do you think I or my mom or Van had something

to do with it?" she asked, her tone becoming flinty.

"No!" Caleb protested. "It just doesn't look good to my dad."

Shelby leaned back in her chair and crossed her arms. "I can appreciate what you're saying, Caleb." She looked over to where Felicia was listening. "But I won't let your dad, or you, or anybody else besmirch my name."

"Did you actually just use the word besmirch?" Felicia asked in awe.

Shelby shot her a warning look. She turned her gaze back to Caleb and said, "If being seen with me is more than you can handle, maybe you should find another date for Friday night." She then got up from the table and left.

Caleb started to rise, and Brett told him, "Don't. If you chase after her, you'll just make it worse. Let her calm down and then try to talk to her."

"I didn't mean that I didn't want to date her. I just have to worry about my dad too, and although I know you guys had nothing to do with it, the bodies do seem to be piling up out at the kindred. It doesn't look good."

"Has anyone seen Van?" Felicia asked.

Brett turned to look at her and raised an eyebrow. "Not since this morning," Brett said. "Why?"

Brandt actually reached over and put an arm on Brett's shoulder. It was a simple reminder to not lose his temper. "He wasn't in French class," Felicia said.

As if summoned by their conversation, Van walked into the cafeteria, his face a dark cloud of anger and frustration. Brett watched as several people simply got out of Van's way as he got in line to grab his lunch. "What's got his panties in a wad?" Carmen asked.

"Don't know," Brett said, watching the tall, thin boy work his way through the line. After a couple of minutes, he paid the cashier and then looked over at their table and sighed. Then to everyone's surprise, he went to an empty table in the corner and started shoveling food into his mouth.

"This is not good," Brandt said quietly. "Go check on him, Brett," the blonde told him.

Brett got out of his seat, took his lunch and joined Van.

"You okay?" he asked as he sat down.

Van said nothing, just kept shoveling food into his mouth, barely taking time to chew it. Then, taking a long swig from the carton of milk ,he wiped his mouth on the back of his hand and said, "I just got out of a three hour grilling with Felicia's father in the principal's office. They did everything except for charge me with murder."

"What?!" Brett asked. "What's this all about?"

"Caleb found a body up on the ridge above the farm this morning," Van said. "Since it was so close to our farm, guess who Agent Ballenger wanted to talk to first?"

"A body?" Brett asked in surprise. "What kind of body?"

Van gave him a smile and said, "What kind do you think? Their throat had been ripped out."

"And Ballenger thinks it's you?" Brett asked looking back over to where Felicia was talking to their friends. "Any idea who it was?"

Van shook his head and said, "No. I can't even get a time frame of when it was supposed to have happened. They wanted to know every place I was, and who I was with from the day after the attack on the house until this morning."

"What did you tell them?" Brett asked.

Van shrugged and replied, "I told them where I've been, the best I can remember, and who I was with."

"So they can compare your timetable to the time of death?" Brett asked.

"I assume so," Van said. "Ballenger doesn't like us. He doesn't like the kindred and he sure as hell doesn't like me."

"What are you going to do?" he asked.

"Aunt Linda is getting a lawyer," he told her.

"What are you going to do in the meantime?" Brett asked.

"I'm not sure what there is to do," Van told him. "I

haven't done anything wrong."

Brett looked back over his shoulder to their regular table and said quietly, "And yet, Felicia Ballenger keeps hanging around us."

Van looked up and nodded, "That's why I'm sitting here."

Brett started digging into what was left of his lunch and decided to let Van say what he would when he was ready. After several moments, he finally looked up at Brett and asked, "We still on for Friday Night?"

Brett smiled and said, "You bet."

"Want to ask Caleb and Shelby to double?" he asked.

"Don't think that will be a good idea right now," Brett said. "Caleb's not handling what happened too well, and that may start to cause problems between him and your cousin. She left here not long ago, more than just a little angry at him."

"What about?" Van asked.

"He's moping over how his dad is going to react to him finding a body out near the kindred. He thinks his dad is going to forbid him to see Shelby anymore."

"I'd hate to see that happen," Van said. "For Shelby's sake. But if his dad is as bad as Agent Ballenger, it might be a good idea to write him off. Not sure we would want to associate ourselves with someone like that. It could drag the rest of us down."

"Now who's quoting verse and scripture?" Brett teased.

Van looked around to make sure that nobody could hear him and said, "Brett, I turned into a giant anthropomorphic cat and killed four werewolves. Maybe we should pay a bit more attention to the condition of our souls. Maybe the gods are trying to tell us something."

Brett nodded and held up a hand. "I'm not arguing. I'm just pointing out that I'm usually the one making those kinds of comments. When the rest of you start, then it's time to really pay attention."

"What about Saturday? Are we still on for that too?"

Brett asked.

"I'm up for it if you are," he said. Then something hit him. Van wasn't asking about the trip to the lake. He was asking something far more important. He reached across the table and gripped Van's elbow. "I'm not afraid of you Van, and I know you aren't a murderer."

Brett watched the tightness around Van's nearly electric blue eyes relax. He smiled and said, "Thanks, Brett."

Brett leaned back in his chair and asked, "Now what are we going to do about Caleb and Shelby?"

"Nothing," Van said. "Let them work it out between them. If they can't work out something like this, then they don't need to be dating. No use in tearing each other up for something that can't be. If they want it to work, it'll work. They just have to decide how much they want it."

"I want to try some things out on Saturday, too," Brett said non-noncommittally.

Van looked up and from under his raven locks asked, "Oh?"

"Just a few things, Bastion Davenport and I have been talking about. He's sort of helping me get up to speed in Ms. Devlin's class."

"Gonna start throwing fireballs?" Van asked with a slight smile.

"If I thought I could," Brett replied. "In a heartbeat. But for now I'm going to try and keep it simple."

"That's usually for the best," Van replied. "Start simple and build up. After a while, you start to figure out how profound simple really is."

"That from the Havamal?" Brett asked.

Van chuckled and said, "No. From my sensei back in Lexington."

"Sounds like good advice."

"I think so," Van replied looking directly at Brett. "That, and if you don't ask, the answer is automatically no."

Brett might have been socially inept, but he recognized

exactly where that comment was aimed. He blushed, smiled, and said, "Let's just take it slow."

"I'm fine with that," Van told him.

Before Brett could reply, Brandt came over with what was left of his lunch, straddled a chair and said, "Ever get the feeling that you're being watched?"

Van glanced up at the security cameras in the cafeteria and said, "All the time."

Brandt chuckled and said, "I mean by someone else." He looked back over his shoulder to where Felicia was talking to Carmen and Caleb. "I'm not sure I trust certain people right now."

"Smart man," Van said. Then looking over at Felicia he asked, "You still coming out with us on Saturday?"

"Wouldn't miss it for the world," Brandt told him.

"Good," both Van and Brett said simultaneously. It was important to Brett that Brandt understood that Van wasn't responsible for what happened to his twin.

~*~

The house was quiet as Caleb entered it. It had been a long day, and he knew he was going to be in for it when he saw the light on in his dad's study down the hall. He really was too tired to deal with this, but he guessed he was going to have to face the music sometime.

Football practice had been subdued and Caleb had actually managed to play fairly well, as focusing on his game skills kept him from thinking about having to talk to his dad tonight. He looked down at the bag of the Colonel's extra crispy and all the fixings and smiled to himself. At least it was sort of a peace offering.

He headed down the hall and knocked on the study door. "Is that you, Caleb?" his dad called through the thick oak.

"Yes, sir. I brought dinner."

"Come on in," he heard his father say and then the squeaking of the office chair. As Caleb came into the room, he saw his dad turning around to check the clock muttering, "What time is it?"

"It's just after seven, sir," he told him.

Nodding at the clock his dad said, "So it is." Then spotting the large bag in his hand he smiled and asked, "Think I forgot about dinner again?"

"It's been known to happen," Caleb said with a grin.

His father smiled and said, "Well, you'd be right." Then blushing, he added, "Sorry about that."

Caleb looked past his father's shoulder to see the title of his sermon: The Occult and the Bible. He suppressed a sigh and knew that even if he skated by what happened this morning that his father was very likely to start a new crusade against the Mountain Hearth Kindred. "Want to take this into the kitchen, or you gonna be up all night working on your sermon?"

"We can eat in the kitchen," his dad said. "Sounds like you've got something on your mind."

Caleb just shrugged and replied turning down the hall and saying over his shoulder, "More like I expect you have something on yours."

"You think you know me that well, huh?" his dad asked following him down the hall.

"I know the school called you this morning about my being late."

"And why were you late?" his dad asked him. Caleb knew he was trying to give him either enough rope to untie the knot he'd gotten himself into or hang himself.

He began to put out the tub and other fixings on the table. "I went up to check on where I wanted to put the tree stand. Found a body up on Silver John Mountain, called 9-1-1 and had to wait until the police got there."

Sitting down, his father seemed to be unfazed by the admission. "I know. I got a visit from Agent Ballenger of the FBI. He was concerned that this was the second time you've been at the scene of a murder. He also said that your description of the animal you saw was," his dad stopped for a moment to think before he finally finished, "extraordinary."

"Yes sir," Caleb said, swallowing.

His father leaned back in his chair and seemed to study Caleb for a while. "Wanna tell me about it?"

Caleb shrugged and said, "It was big, it was hairy, and vaguely wolf-shaped. It walked on two legs and was a dead blue."

"Dead blue?" his father asked.

Caleb nodded, "Yeah, it was like no color I ever saw in anything alive."

His father just nodded his head and the two sat in silence for a long time, the only sound between them being the soft chewing of the food. Finally his father said, "You know that demons are real?"

Wow! That came out of nowhere and was not what Caleb was expecting. Finally, he shrugged again and said, "I really hadn't given it much thought."

His dad sighed and said with a catch in his throat, "Trust me on this, Caleb. They're real." Lowly he added, "But I think you're already starting to suspect it's true on your own. What happened to that poor Howard Boy and Snow girl, I think sort of drove home to you that evil does exist in this world that it can't always be explained away by man's science." This conversation had suddenly taken a left turn into the *Twilight Zone* as far as Caleb was concerned.

"I won't argue that what I saw that night and this morning fits any science I know, Dad." He took a sip of his soda and added, "Was it a demon? I don't know. The thing this morning didn't smell like brimstone and fire, it more smelled like something dead. But then again, I was standing next to a dead body and there was a dead deer not twenty yards away. Why did you bring it up?"

Again, he watched as his dad seemed torn in what to say. Finally, he took a deep breath and said, "Because I got a first hand experience with it fourteen years ago."

"When Sis left and Mom died?" Caleb asked. His father had never talked much about why his sister had left, only that as far as he was concerned, she was dead. He'd heard stories that she'd run off with Bastion Davenport's dad the night Bastion had been born and his mother died.

Caleb's dad nodded his head and said, "When I said your sister is dead, I meant it. Her body is walking around out there but what came back from that trip to Cincinnati was dead." The cold dead tone of his father's voice sent a chill down his spine.

"Dad, you're scaring me," Caleb told him.

"Good," his father said. "You should be scared. Strange things are going on in Wellman, and you should be scared; scared for your life, and scared for your soul."
Caleb shook his head and said, "Dad..."

"I'm serious here, Caleb. There are dark creatures only talked about in legend inhabiting this town. They're centered around the Devlins and the Davenports."

"Not the Mountain Hearth Kindred?" Caleb asked in surprise.

His father shook his head and chuckled, "My problems with the Mountain Hearth Kindred are doctrinal based, they don't have anything to do with what happened with your sister- except for Ellen Griffin, and that was only because she helped clean up the mess your sister left."

Who's Ellen Griffin?" Caleb asked.

His dad chuckled again, "You didn't know? She was Van's mother. Before she and her husband moved to Lexington, she was a local nurse and midwife. She literally cut Bastion Davenport from his dead mother's stomach."

"Maybe you should start from the beginning. How do you know all this? Exactly what are you talking about?"

"Just that there is more to this town than you know about. Your sister got caught up in it somehow," he told him with a sigh. "I'm not going to say Kelli was innocent. Far from it. She started messing around with a married man, and she knew that was wrong." Caleb noted that it was one of the few times he could remember his father using his sister's name. "But Paul Davenport was no angel either, and the fact he abandoned his wife and son doesn't say much about him." He sighed and said, "I guess we all failed our children on that count."

"What do you mean that Kelli's body is walking around out there dead?"

His father chuckled sadly, and Caleb could see the tears that were threatening his eyes. "Exactly what I said. Kelli died on that trip to Cincinnati. What came back was a walking corpse. It wasn't my daughter any more. It was some kind of thing with the strength of twenty men. It took a great deal of pleasure in torturing your mother before going off to join Paul Davenport in whatever unholy things they did to poor Elizabeth Davenport. The only thing that saved Bastion was that the Griffins lived next door, and Ellen went to investigate." He sighed again and added, "That was just another part of the tragedy. Van's mother was simply a midwife doing what she had to do, but because of the Davenports' influence they blamed her for not saving Elizabeth. But to be honest, from what I heard from Sheriff Treybond who was just a deputy at the time, was that the woman was dead when Ellen Griffin got there."

"Are you saying that my sister is some kind of monster?" Caleb asked.

His father shook his head and said, "No. Your sister is dead. Whatever is in her body now is the monster."

"And what has this got to do with the Mountain Hearth Kindred?" Caleb asked.

His dad gave him a strange look and said, "Nothing."

"I thought you were going to blame them for what's been happening. I thought you were going to ground me for being up on their property, to tell me to break my date with Shelby tomorrow."

His father chuckled low and said, "Son, you're of an age where you can start to make some decisions of your own. As long as you remember you're a child of the one true god, and don't make me a grandfather before you finish college, I can deal with a little rebellion." He shook his head and added, "To be honest, Caleb- and maybe I should have told you this before- but I'm very proud of the kind of young man you're turning into." He smiled, "Yeah, I wish you'd cut your hair, but so far that's the biggest thing we've locked horns over." Shrugging, he added, "And if you're dating one of the girls from the Kindred, it's just an opportunity to bring her to Christ."

Caleb shook his head and said, "Dad, I don't think that would be a good idea. They don't take well to attempts to convert them."

"Just keep living your life the way you are, Caleb. There's conversion and there's giving an example by living. I'd say you're doing a pretty goo job of that so far."

~*~

Later that night in the cabin she'd provided for him, Dace told his cousin, "The boy was there the night I died." She'd come up to berate him for being seen, for putting her mission into jeopardy.

"He didn't kill you," she said.

"How do you know?" Dace demanded as he stalked the room where he was staying. The place was bare of anything to suggest someone was living there. Dace slept in the closet of the cabin's single bedroom.

"He had the smell of innocence about him. He's never taken a human life." She stopped and grinned before adding, "He's an innocent in more ways than just that."

"Keep your mind on business," it was Dace's time to warn her.

"Oh, I am. It's just that there are so many attractive young men around here."

"Yeah, and remember, sixteen will get you twenty in this state," he told her.

She gave him a sour look and said, "No. Sixteen is fair game. Besides, you really think there's a prison that can hold me? I'm as free to do as I please as you are, Dace."

"Anyway," he dismissed those thoughts. They made him uncomfortable. "What are we going to do about the kid?"

"He didn't kill you," she replied.

"Maybe he knows who did," Dace countered.

"What did," she told him.

"Huh?"

"I talked to Agent Ballenger today. He's convinced that kid that killed Greg did it. He doesn't know how, but he's convinced Van Griffin has something to do with it." She put her hands on her hips and asked, "Exactly why did you and Logan, and Vic come up here?"

"To take out the kid for killing Greg," Dace told her.

She nodded and asked, "Exactly how did that happen?"

Dace shrugged his massive shoulders and said, "I'm not

sure. He was faster than a human should have been. He was stronger too, and he knew how to fight. He told Greg he was going to kill him, just before he sunk that dagger in his spine."

Auda nodded and added incredulously, "And you let him live?"

"Matthias called the retreat. Vandyl wouldn't let us go after him later," Dace told her.

She leaned back against the bare table in the kitchen just off the living area and said, "Grandmother will be having a talk with Vandyl about that. Sometimes he gets too full of himself because his name is remembered. Well, Granny's name is remembered far more than his, and she won't be happy about that." She smiled and said, "You did the right thing coming after him. Now we just have to figure out how to take him out." She shook her head and added, "And, how to deal with this kindred. We really don't want them to come to the attention of the Shining Ones. I think maybe that is why Vandyl ordered you to kill the parents. They were getting close to re-awakening the old powers."

"What do you want me to do?" Dace asked his cousin.

"I want you to find out what this boy, Caleb knows."

"How?" she asked.

"He's seen you. That's bound to give him nightmares. Use that."

Dace nodded and gave her a feral grin. He hadn't considered one of the powers given to his new form as all that useful, but maybe it was. He could far fared into the boy's dreams and maybe discover a few things. He could also leave a bit of a reminder that he was there while he was doing it. "I'll do it tonight, cousin," he told her.

"And I will work on what I can find out about this Van Griffin. There is something not right here. When you awoke, you stank of Vanir magic. I do not wish to become too entangled with that. They brought down the walls of the high yard with nothing but their voices."

"Do you think that Od's Wife has become involved?"

"Don't think so," Auda said.

"Why not?" Dace asked.

"Because too many of us are still alive. When she goes after what she wants, or what she sees as a threat, it is usually destroyed rather completely. Remember what she did to win back her property after your great grandfather stole it."

Dace shuddered at the thought of forty thousand of what he'd become, raised for no other purpose than war. "I'd rather not," he said.

"My point exactly," she told him. "We must tread carefully. The kindred's gothi is a follower of the Hanged God. That we may be able to use. He does have a reputation of not always protecting his pieces as he should."

"You will move against him?" Dace asked.

"Possibly. First I have an idea of who to point at this Van Griffin to at least put a leash on him. If he's more than he seems, then he'll survive and I can point Agent Ballenger at him. If he's not, then he'll be eliminated."

"What's that?" Dace asked.

"I believe I heard it referred to as a good ol' country boy ass-kicking."

Dace grinned hugely at that thought.

~*~

Van didn't like lawyers. He'd been assigned a public defender when he went into the system back in Colorado, and the woman had been next to useless. The only reason he hadn't been charged with murder back then was because the police simply didn't have the evidence. Now he found himself talking to another lawyer, this one at least seemed to be a bit better informed. "So exactly what did the police ask you?" Mr. Collins asked him.

"They wanted to know where I was from the night of the attack on this house all the way up to this morning."

"And where were you?" Collins asked.

Van shrugged and said, "The night of the attack I stayed with Mr. Bjargeir. The next morning I came home and helped put the place back together. After that, I spent Sunday in my room working on a term paper. Monday and Tuesday, I was still suspended so I stayed here and kept up on my school work. I went back to school on Wednesday, and after school I went with Shelby to the hospital to see Allison. There I met and got into an argument with Agent Ballenger," he stopped and looked at the man and said, "Whose daughter, by the way has, suddenly started hanging around with our group at school. Then we stopped by Yoasis for a frozen yogurt, and then to Mr. Bjargeir's shop, the Eye In the Well, to tell him that Allison asked him to come by."

"Why would she do that?" Mr. Collins asked.

"Because he's our gothi. I guess she needed some spiritual comfort. I know I would if some kind of big creature had just ripped off my leg."

"Okay," the man said. "What about last night?"

"Last night I worked on an essay for English. Then Brett and Brandt came over and we all talked for a while. They went home, and I went to bed. I went to school this morning, wait, we stopped at Mickey D's for a sausage biscuit and an OJ on the way." He reached into his shirt pocket and handed the man the receipt. "During the third period I got pulled out of Algebra

Two and sent to the office where Agent Ballenger did every-thing but accuse me of killing someone up on the mountain."

Mr. Collins leaned back and said, "The victim was Donny Kaizer, a local man who works at the railyard. Ever meet him?" He handed Van a picture of the guy. He was tall, ruggedly good looking in his early to mid twenties with a crop of straw blond hair and light eyes.

Van shook his head and said, "Can't say that I have. Most of the people in town I know are either other students at school or are from the kindred."

Collins nodded his balding head and said, "I under-stand." From what Sheriff Treybond is telling me, the victim died of some kind of animal attack."

"Then why accuse me?" Van asked.

Collins took a deep breath and said, "I'm not sure. Ballenger has cited the Megiddo Report as reason to put you under suspicion."

"That's the second time that has been mentioned to me, Mr. Collins. I'm not sure exactly what it is."

"It's a report the FBI did after they killed all those people in Waco in the nineties. It's very inaccurate and has been criticized several times as being a political hatchet job, but there are some people in the Bureau who won't let it go. Usually, they're looking for racists behind every crime."

"Agent Ballenger thinks I'm a racist?" Van asked.

"He thinks the whole kindred is," Collins told him.

"That pretty much confirms my estimation of his intel-ligence, then," Van said.

"Maybe, but he could still cause you problems if he chose to. The RICO laws are pretty broad and he could bring them to bear on the whole kindred," Collins said. "That's why Mr. Bjargeir has engaged my services for this investigation. If you're charged with a crime, then I'm your representation." Van nodded. "I need to ask something else, Mr. Griffin," the man said. "And it's going to be a difficult question, but I need you to answer me honestly."

Van nodded again and said, "I'll do my best."

Collins nodded his head and said, "What attacked you in Colorado?"

Van chuckled low. He wasn't sure if it was from hysteria, or actual humor. He looked the man straight in the eye and said, "Werewolves, Mr. Collins. I know nobody believes me, but they were werewolves."

"Ballenger can use that to force a psychological profile on you, Van. Are you willing to undergo a pre-emptive one with a psychologist I know?"

Van looked at his aunt and cousin, and then back at Collins. "What's it like?"

"Just asking you questions, son. Some of them might be difficult to answer though. Sometimes people don't like to talk about loss."

"Questions about Mom and Dad?" Van asked.

"Some. Some about your relationship with them. Some about your relationship with your aunt and your cousin, and even your friends at school." He looked over at Linda and said, "And some about your love life."

Van chuckled again. "That one's easy. Non existent- for now."

The man raised an eyebrow and said, "That's unusual for a boy your age, your build, and your looks."

Van chuckled and said, "There's someone with whom I've got my first date Friday night."

"Ever?" Collins asked.

"Ever." Van replied.

"Who's the lucky girl?" Collins asked.

Van looked at his aunt and his cousin before turning back to Collins and replying, "Brett Bond."

Collins smiled and replied, "I see." After a moment he asked, "Did your parents know you are gay?"

"I told them the evening they were murdered."

"By werewolves?" Collins asked.

"By werewolves," Van told him.

Collins nodded and then changed directions, "I'm curious, Van. How does a fifteen year old boy fight off four werewolves killing one of them?"

Van nodded and said, "That's a fair question." He stood up and walked over to the family altar and took down the hammer and the silver seax that was his aunt's match to his mom's. "With these," he said. Then stepping back, he hitched up the legs of his jeans and did a tornado kick. "And a third dan black belt in combat style shoto khan karate." He blushed and then added, "Of course that kick isn't from shoto khan, but it gets the point across." He didn't tell the man that he'd learned the kick on a dare from Shelby when they were kids watching reruns of the Power Rangers.

"Impressive," Collins replied.

Van blushed and sat back down. "I'm not defenseless, Mr. Collins. My parents, especially my dad, wanted to make sure I could defend myself." He shrugged and added, "We just never expected it to be against werewolves."

Collins nodded and said, "Still, I wouldn't mention it to anybody else."

Van said, "It's already all over school, sir. I'm not sure how, but the contents of the FBI's investigation is being spread around school."

Collins wrote something in his notebook and then nodded again. "I'll look into that. If there's a leak in the Bureau, it can taint just about anything they charge you with."

"Are they likely to actually charge Van with a crime?" Shelby asked.

Collins shook his head and said, "I don't think so. Not with the coroner's report stating it was animal attacks. The fact that your friend Caleb Johnson described a blue werewolf attacking him this morning, would support the idea of a tainted investigation."

"He didn't tell us that," Shelby said quietly.

"I'm sorry. I thought you had a copy of the report."

"I do," Linda said. "I haven't shared it with my daughter

or my nephew yet."

"Well, he did," Mr. Collins said. "And if the information came from Ballenger's office, he could be in a world of hurt."

"Let's hope so," Van replied.

"Strange sentiment," Collins said.

Van shrugged and said, "Not really. I don't like being spied on, and I don't like my personal business being spread across town for every Tom, Dick, and Harry to gossip about. If he leaked the report, I hope they hang him up by his bal..." he looked over at Shelby and his aunt and corrected himself, "His short hairs."

Collins laughed and replied, "Me too, Van. Me too. There's no place in law enforcement for personal prejudices, and Agent Ballenger seems to be full of them."

CHAPTER 12

Brett smiled to himself as he pulled the dark blue polo shirt over his head and smoothed out his blond hair- he'd gotten it cut yesterday afternoon while Van was meeting with his lawyers. He looked at his reflection in the mirror and checked his teeth. He looked at the can of body spray on his dresser and thought better of using it. Van had very acute senses, and he knew that a little would go a long way.

He checked his wallet to make sure he had enough money for dinner and the movies and then slipped it into the back pocket of his jeans, and pulled on his sneakers before heading out his bedroom door and down the stairs. When he reached the bottom, he found his Uncle Alex standing there at the door to his office. The tall blond man smiled at him and said, "Looking good."

"Thanks," Brett said with a smile.

"Come into my office. I want to talk to you," Alex said turning back toward the large room with his computer, books and a killer stereo.

Brett nodded and followed him. To his surprise, Alex took one of the comfortable wing back leather chairs and gestured toward the other for him to take. Taking a deep breath while Brett sat, Alex said, "I want to talk to you about tonight."

"Yes sir," Brett said with some trepidation.

"First off, I want you to know that I'm glad you felt comfortable enough to tell me that you're gay. Secondly, to let you know that I'm pleased that you've at least chosen someone we both can respect for your first date."

"Yes, sir," Alex said wondering where this was going.

"Thank you."

Alex sighed again and said, "I'm sure you know about the birds and the bees and such as far as boys dating girls and things."

"Yes sir," Brett said.

"But I want you to think about something when you're out tonight. I'm sure at some point, if you and Van keep seeing each other, that things are going to get intimate. Maybe not tonight, maybe not even the next date," he paused and shook his head and said, "and we won't talk about a third date. But there's something I want you to ask yourself if you find yourself with things going faster than you expect them to."

"What?"

"I want you to remember to respect yourself as much as you should respect your date. Ask yourself if this were a girl, would you let things go this far this fast? Would you have the same respect for a girl that let things go this far?"

"Sir?" Brett asked.

Alex smiled nervously and said, "Boys are geared differently than girls. It's easier to get their motors up to speed, and sometimes things can go faster than they expect."

Brett smiled and said, "In other words, don't let my little head take over and do the thinking for my big head?"

Alex smiled and nodded saying, "Exactly." Then blushing deeply, he got up from his chair and went to his top desk drawer and took something out. "And mind you, I'm not giving you permission to have sex. But if things do start to get out of hand, I want you to be protected- both of you." He handed Brett two silver foil packs.

"I put a box of these under the sink in your bathroom. I want you to put these in your wallet, and I want you to change them out at least once every two weeks. Just throw the ones in your wallet away after two weeks and get two new ones."

"Sir?" Brett asked.

"Most guys don't realize that the friction of keeping these in their wallets can damage them. Best to be safe than sorry."

Brett blushed and took the foil packs and put them in his bill-fold. "Thank you Uncle Alex," Brett said. Then looking into his uncle's eyes, he said, "For everything."

"You're quite welcome, Brett. Now go and have fun."

"Yes, sir," Brett replied, leaving the study.

"Ten minutes later he was pulling into the Steins' drive. He shuddered slightly at the fresh bleach stains on the parking pad and along the walk leading to the back porch. Memories of the night Dallas had been killed threatened to well up into his mind. Savagely he crushed them down, wondering how Van held up to seeing them every day.

He was met at the door by Mrs. Stein who had a mischievous grin on her face. "Good evening, Brett," she said.

"Hello, Mrs. Stein. Is Van ready?"

"He'll be down in just a minute. Come on in," she said. "I was just cleaning the rifle." She grinned broadly.

As he passed into the door, he saw the cleaning materials on the coffee table as well as the Wnchester she'd been firing the night Dallas had been killed. "Is that a hint?" he asked.

She smiled back at him as she slowly loaded the deer rounds into the side of the gun. "Does it need to be?" she asked, smiling.

"It's just dinner and a movie, Mrs. Stein."

She laughed and said, "I know. But let's just consider this a dry run for when Caleb picks up Shelby for their date tonight."

"They got that worked out?" he asked.

She shrugged and said, "I guess so. I'm not sure what the issue was, though."

"Ask Shelby," he told her.

"I will, she replied, putting the gun back into the locked cabinet. "Where are you guys going?"

"Thought we'd have dinner at Ruby Tuesdays and then go see that new sc-ifi flick."

"Well, I expect him to be home by midnight," she said.

"Or he'll turn into a pumpkin," Shelby said from the kitchen. She looked over to the gun cabinet. "Mom!"

Mrs. Stein just shrugged her shoulders and said, "Your turn is coming."

Before Shelby could reply, Van came down the heavy log stairs sliding his wallet into his back pocket. His face was a bit flushed and Brett briefly wondered at that. He was wearing a black polo shirt and blue jeans with white sneakers. His raven hair had been brushed to a high sheen, and Brett could see the hammer he wore around his neck nestled into the cleft of his collar-bone, and couldn't help but notice how his jeans clung to him in the most interesting places. Some small part of his brain realized that he was starting to see Van in a whole new light, and he liked it.

It wasn't that he hadn't always been attracted to Van. Hell, he'd been carrying a torch for him since before Van moved to the kindred, but he was just now seeing him not only as something attainable, but seeing him as something he was worthy of. It was a fundamental change in his whole world view, and Brett was finding that he liked it.

Van looked over at his aunt and shook his head, then turning back to Brett he said, "Sorry about that. But she's taking her role as my guardian pretty seriously."

"Damn right I am," Mrs. Stein said. "You're my sister's son, and now my responsibility." Then turning to Brett she said, "But I think this is going to be okay. Just as long as you two are home by midnight."

"Or else, Van will turn into a pumpkin?" Brett asked mischievously.

"More likely a cat," Van said snarkily, but Brett thought he caught a bit of bitterness too. "But that's another reason we need to be home early. We need to be out at the lake by six a.m. Don't know about you, but I need my beauty sleep."

"You get any prettier, and the girls at school won't be able to stand it," Shelby told him.

"Let's get out of here while we can," Van said to Brett.

"Sure," Brett told him and held the door open as Van pulled on his jacket.

"Van, remember what we talked about," Mrs. Stein said.

Van blushed and nodded, "I will."

Once they were out in the car, Brett turned to Van and asked, "You get the 'I'm not giving you permission to have sex, but if you do, make sure you're protected' lecture too?"

Van blushed and nodded, "Complete with a box of condoms."

Brett chuckled, started the car, and said, "Van, I'm not in any hurry. We said we would go slow. To be honest, I'm still adjusting to the idea that you're gay and that you actually like me. In some ways that's harder to get past than the idea that you turn into a giant werecat of some kind."

Van raised an eyebrow but said nothing as they pulled out of Wellman and headed the three miles into Ashland. The silence wasn't really oppressive and for some reason it seemed natural, amiable, even. Neither boy seemed to have the need to fill it up with idle chatter.

When they got to the restaurant and were seated, Van looked over at him and asked, "What makes you think that you're not likable, Brett?"

Startled by the question, he said, "What do you mean?"

"You said you were surprised that I liked you. Why wouldn't I? You're good looking, the smartest person I know, and you're far braver than I am. You charged into the dark to rescue Dallas with nothing but a maul. What's not to like?"

Brett shrugged and said, "I guess until you came along and knocked some sense into me about not picking fights, that maybe I thought I deserved to not be liked."

Van shook his head and said, "All I did was point out some things. You did the hard work yourself. I can't take credit for that." He reached across the table and took Brett's hand and said, "And I'm serious. You're handsome, nice, smart and brave. You should be proud of yourself. I'm the lucky one that you actually are interested in going out with me."

Brett snorted derisively, "You've got every girl in school short of Shelby throwing herself at you."

Van shrugged and replied, "And none of them hold a candle to you."

"Do you two think this is the right place to be having that conversation?" a man at the next table asked. "Some people are trying to eat."

Brett turned to see a man who looked to be in his late sixties. He was a tall, hatchet thin black man who had a head full of white hair. His wrinkled face frowned at them.

"Didn't mean to disturb your meal, sir," Van said neutrally, but Brett could catch a hint of a warning to it too.

"Well, you did," the man looked up at the waitress and asked, "Can you move the sissy-boys somewhere else? I'm trying to eat here and I don't want to have to hear them try to get into each other's pants."

The poor girl looked at Van and Brett helplessly. Before Brett could tell the man exactly what he thought, Van broke in and said, "It's okay. If you want to move us, that's fine."

The woman nodded and mouthed, "Thank you."

Two minutes later, they found themselves in the back corner of the restaurant between two large picture windows. "Sorry about that," Van told the woman as he settled into the seat.

"No, I'm sorry, and I appreciate your understanding. I didn't mean to eavesdrop, but I overheard part of what you were talking about. Nothing you said was inappropriate." She smiled down at Brett and started to say something but seemed to change her mind. Finally, she took their orders and left the table.

The rest of the evening went quite well as far as Brett was concerned. The movie was good. It had the right amount of action, comedy and cool sci-fi in it, and he enjoyed sitting in the back row of the theater holding Van's hand. The taller boy even held his hand all the way out of the theater and to the car. The look on his face was almost daring anybody to say anything.

As they climbed into the car, Van looked over at Brett and asked, "About Monday?"

"Yeah?" Brett asked back.

"How do you want to handle this?"

"What do you mean?" Brett asked.

"I guess I'm asking if you want to go out with me again, or do you want to see if you want to see other people?" Van asked.

"I definitely want to go out again, Van," Brett said. He shrugged and added, "As for seeing other people, do you want to?"

Van shook his head and said, "Not really. I like you, Brett. I've liked you for a long time. I just haven't had the nerve to say anything until now."

"Me too," Brett replied. He smiled and added, "You know, I think I owe your cousin though. She listened to me talk about you constantly but kept what I said to herself."

Van chuckled and replied, "Me too. Same reason."

"She's so going to kill us," Brett said.

Van nodded, "Maybe. Right now I think she's a bit infatuated with Caleb though, so maybe not."

"About Monday," Brett said.

"Yeah?"

"Are you ready to come out to the school?" Brett asked.

Van shrugged and said, "I don't think I'll have too many problems with it."

"Yeah, something about kicking the crap out of Craig Blankenship gives you a bit of a rep."

"I'm serious here, Brett," Van said. "I may have a rep, but you don't. If you want to keep this on the down low, I will understand."

Brett looked at him and asked, "Are you ashamed of me?"

"Hell no!" Van said rather vehemently.

"I'm not ashamed of you, or what I am. I am the way

the Gods made me. If you are willing to be seen with me, then trust me, I'm more than willing to be seen with you."

"It's just that you've worked hard for your recent acceptance," Van added with a serious tone, but Brett could see a pleased sparkle in his eyes. "This is going to change both our reputations whether we like it or not."

Brett reached across the console and took Van's hand. "Our deeds stand for themselves, Van. I can look Hel in the eye and tell her that my manhood is intact, and I can look your lady in the eye and tell her the same thing."

Van simply smiled and said, "Something told me this was right." Then as if what Brett said had suddenly sunk in, he asked, "What do you mean, my lady?"

"I mean the keeper of cats," Brett said. "Whether you realize it yet or not Van, you have been touched by the Vanir. They've laid claim to you."

Van seemed to think about it for a moment before he said, "I think I'd rather someone else laid claim to me." He grinned.

"Thought as the cat you'd be the one marking your territory."

Van looked around to make sure that nobody had heard the remark and said, "I think you've been reading too much shifter romance fiction. I'm not looking for someone to dominate. I want a partner, not somebody to answer to my every beck and call. I need someone who can meet me need for need, not submit meekly like a good little sub."

Brett chuckled and said, "I'm not sure I'm the one who's been reading too much fiction. I wasn't thinking that at all. I'm not interested in being your sub. I've been that for far too many people. I don't want to dominate you either. I want to be an equal partner."

Van grinned and Brett noticed the slightly elongating fangs and said, "Good it sounds like we're on the same page."

Brett started the car and put it in gear, saying, "Good."

"You still haven't answered me about Monday," Van

said. "Do you want people to know about us?"

Without taking his eyes off the road, Brett said, "Hel yeah. I want to shout it from the rooftops. But I get the feeling that part of that is simply my inexperience with this kind of thing. So let's just take it slow. You wanna come up and hold my hand, that's fine. But I don't want to do anything that might get either of us in trouble for PDA at school."

"So holding hands is okay, but no kissing," Van said with a grin.

"Van, we haven't kissed in private yet. How do you even know if either one of us are good at it?" he asked playfully.

"Do you intend to find out?" Van asked.

Brett teased him, "I don't know. Your aunt has that rifle. I'd hate to end up with a bullet in my gut for kissing you."

Van shook his head and said, "I can't believe she did that."

"I can. Your aunt has a definite possessive streak in her. She swore over the Well at the Allthing that you were part of her family. Actually, I'd have been disappointed in her if she hadn't."

"Brett," Van asked seriously. "Are you going to kiss me goodnight?"

Brett glanced over to Van and realized that maybe the rock steady young man he'd always imagined Van to be, might have a few insecurities of his own. He smiled and asked, "Do you want me to?"

"I've wanted to kiss you since we first met," Van said. "So yeah."

Brett nodded and was a bit surprised to realize that he might actually be the more centered of the two in this relationship. "Then kiss you I shall." With a grin, he added, "And I'll do my best to make sure it surpasses the kiss at the end of *The Princess Bride*."

Van laughed aloud. "I'll settle for something less dramatic, but more heartfelt."

"Then heartfelt you shall have, my kitten," Brett replied.

"Kitten?" Van asked.

"Would you prefer pussy?" Brett asked.

Van raised an eyebrow at the double-entendre and said, "No."

As they pulled into the Stein home several minutes later, Brett looked over and asked, "Do you want me to walk you to the door?"

Van smiled and said, "I think I can make it. But I do want that kiss."

Brett leaned over and obliged the request. It was everything he imagined a first kiss to be and more. It started as something gentle and slow, but before long deepened into something long and lingering that sent electrical pulses along his spine to areas of his body that, if he let it go on much longer, would be demanding attention. He was both relieved and frustrated when Caleb's pickup pulled in behind his car.

As the headlights flashed inside and the floodlights from the barn came on, Van pulled back and said, "Busted."

Brett nodded and grabbed another quick peck and said, "But it was at least heartfelt."

"Heartfelt wasn't the only place," Van said with a smile as he got out of the car. "I'll see you tomorrow at six at the dam."

Brett smiled and said, "Can't wait."

Then he heard the passenger door to Caleb's truck open and Shelby climbed out, teasing her cousin.

~*~

It had been a good evening all around as far as Caleb Johnson was concerned. He'd played well, and managed to score at least once during the game, and had a key interception that he ran for a thirty yard gain. And things were better on the Shelby front. He'd at least managed to convince her to go out with him after the game to Jerald-Dan's for a hot dog and a snow cone. It was a start, and he had to admit that there was a bit of an ego boost in having the hottest red-head in school on his arm at the little hot dog shop for everybody else to see. It was an ego boost, but he wasn't going to let it go to his head. He liked Shelby for herself, not because she looked good on his arm. It just didn't hurt that she did.

Catching Van and Brett making out in the front of Brett's uncle's car was a bit of a surprise, but it did sort of make quite a few things fall in place in his head. It explained why Van had turned down offers from so many girls at school, and why Brett had suddenly seemed to get his act together socially.

He wasn't planning on going and blabbing his mouth about it though. He knew that if he caused any problems for Shelby's cousin and her best friend, it would likely sour things between them permanently. And he was at least honest enough with himself to admit that although the sight of them in the car had startled him, and left him a little uncomfortable, he didn't have his dad's generation's reaction to boys dating boys. As long as neither of them tried to put the moves on him, he was okay with it. And who was going to mess with two guys who had a reputation for being able to dish out some serious damage- Van with his karate, and Brett with a maul?

He got home just barely before his own curfew and after saying good night to his dad, he crawled between the sheets of his own bed and found himself falling asleep before he knew it.

It was sometime well after three o'clock when he awoke and realized that he wasn't alone in his room. There was something standing at the end of his bed. Something big. Something hairy. Something not quite human. He slowly opened his eyes, but found himself unable to move his body. He tried to call out as he saw the creature from the other morning leering at him in the light coming from under the door. "You're awake," it said in a rough gravelly voice. "Good." It leaned over him, and he could smell its breath that stank of rotting meat and of dank earth. "Now we're going to have some fun."

Caleb struggled to move but found himself unable to lift even the quilt over his body. He struggled to cry out, but nothing came from his throat. "Tell me about the boy," the creature whispered next to his ear.

Suddenly, Caleb felt the bile threaten to rise up from his stomach at the stench of the breath, but the only muscle in his body that seemed to be working was the pounding of his heart. The creature pulled away, and Caleb could see him wait for him to answer, but no sound would come from his throat. He mentally wondered, What boy?

The creature seemed to chuckle at some unknown joke. "The boy who lived." Maybe the joke wasn't quite so unknown after all. "The boy who killed my brothers."

Suddenly images of Van floated through Caleb's mind. The images of him tossing Craig Blankenship down the hall, of him at the fall festival, and of him and Brett kissing in the front of Brett's uncle's car all paraded themselves across his vision.

"That's who I'm talking about, boy. What do you know about him?" he whispered again, and Caleb was afraid he was going to choke on his own bile.

Suddenly the image of the huge cat creature who'd come crashing into the Stein's living room and roaring like a predator flooded Caleb's mind and the thing in his room recoiled at its sight. "So that's what happened. Something new has come to the mid-realm."

The creature sat back on its haunches and seemed to think about it. Then it leaned into Caleb and said, "I'm not going to kill you yet, boy. You and I are going to become good friends. But for now I'm going to leave you with something."

The horrible face leaned in close and to his face, and then ducked its head. Still unable to move, Caleb felt the searing pain as fangs meant for ripping and tearing sank into his throat. Then there was a faint sucking sound just before he felt the creature pull back from the wound and then licked it. Then with a long claw he reached out and cut something into Caleb's chest. The pain was excruciating as he made first one line down the skin over his sternum. Then he made two slashes one either end of it one slashing downward from the top and one slashing upward from the bottom. Then he crossed the first line, and finally two more lines on either side of the whole mess. With each cut he chanted something in a single breath. When he finished, he said with a low growl "You're mine now, boy. I can find you anywhere you go. No matter how far or fast you run, I can find you and catch you."

Caleb struggled to move, to scream for help, but found himself unable to resist, unable to fight back. The creature withdrew across the room, its blue fur glowing in the soft light. Reaching into the shadows, it drew out a small object and tossed it onto the foot of Caleb's bed. "A little something to remember me by, pup. Payment to your father." He laughed and said, "It's about all you're worth." Then the darkness took the creature.

The compulsion to stay still suddenly gone, Caleb sat bolt upright in bed and fought back the scream of terror that threatened to awaken his father. He reached up to rub his neck and his chest as the horrible odor slowly faded from the room. Turning on the light, he pulled his hand from his neck and looked to see it covered with his blood.

Nearly running to the bathroom at the end of the hall, he flung the door open and turned on the light. As he winced in pain at the sudden light, he saw his eyes seemed to glow an eerie amber before settling back down to their normal brown. He looked at his throat and could find no sign of the bite. But there was a wicked looking scar on his chest where the creature had left its mark.

Suddenly he felt weak, and cold, and began to shiver. He flung the toilet lid up and started to puke into the bowl. It went on for long moments before he felt his father slowly pressing a cold cloth to his head. "Caleb?" he asked. "Are you all right?"

Caleb looked up at his father through fevered eyes and said, "It bit me." Then the darkness took him.

~*~

Van was surprised at how good he felt, even at five thirty in the morning. Yes, he'd been out late last night, and yes, Shelby had teased him about Brett, and yes, he'd been so wound up that he'd barely been able to get to sleep, but he found himself not feeling any ill-effects from it. Maybe there were some advantages to being what he had become.

Shelby, on the other hand, looked over from behind the steering wheel of the truck, her travel mug of coffee sitting between her legs and said, "I hate you."

"What did I do?" Van asked as he looked out the cold October morning at the trees as they whizzed by on Route 1.

"Nobody who was out as late as we were last night should be that chipper this early in the morning," she said.

Van shrugged and replied, "You could have stayed home."

"Should have," she said bitterly as she sipped her coffee. "Wasn't much of a date. He picked me up after the game and we went to Jerald Dan's for a hot dog."

"It was a group date out in public. It was safe for both of you," Van replied.

Shelby shrugged and said, "I was expecting a bit more for a first date."

"Then tell him that," Van replied. "We're not all like you. We can't read minds."

"I don't read minds," she protested. "I just get feelings and hunches."

"Well, don't play games with him. If you like him, tell him. If you want to do something other than go for a hot dog, tell him," Van replied.

"After our argument, I just got the feeling that he wasn't going to invest a lot in the date in case things don't pan out."

"Define 'pan out'," Van said suspiciously. "You think he was expecting to get laid?"

"Van!" Shelby protested.

"It's a fair question," Van defended himself as Shelby

drove through the winding mists that led down to the lake.

Again she shrugged and said, "I get the feeling he was hedging his bet against us not working out."

Van nodded his head and replied, "Ah, he's a bit gun shy, I'd say."

"Gun shy?" she asked.'

Van looked at her sharply and said, "You have a reputation for a temper. That scares some boys off. You're also independent, and will speak your mind and aren't going to hang off his arm as a trophy. I'm not sure he knows how to take that. Give him some time."

"And there's a problem with strong women?" she asked darkly.

Van held up his hands and shook his head and said, "Not as far as I'm concerned. Remember, my family was leaning toward the Vanir. But someone like Caleb who's been raised outside of our community may have difficulty adjusting to it."

She glanced at him and he could tell she was thinking about what he had to say. "I know. I really like him. It's just he gets a bit antsy about his dad. But last night, he told me his dad gave him his blessings to date me. I guess that's a good thing." Shelby shook her head and continued, "I'm still not sure I'm comfortable with the fact that his dad is so against us that he resigned from the inter-faith board in town."

Van nodded and said, "You'll have to decide on your own what to do about that. You either have to accept him or move on."

"That's not very helpful," Shelby protested as she slowed the truck.

"Maybe. Would you prefer I beat him up for you?" Van asked with a straight face.

"No, I wouldn't prefer you to beat him up," Shelby protested. "What a thing to suggest."

"Then you have to reach some kind of resolution."

Shelby just nodded as she pointed to Brandt's Mustang. "There's Brett and Brandt."

"Good," he said as she pulled into the small parking lot.

"I guess there's no need asking how things went last night?" Shelby asked.

It was Van's turn to shrug. "We went to dinner, then a movie, and then he kissed me good night."

"Some kiss," Shelby told him as she pulled into the spot and turned off the engine.

"I wanted heartfelt and he gave it to me."

She chuckled and said, "Never took you for a romantic, Cuz."

Van simply opened the door and climbed out of the truck. He noticed that both Brandt and Brett looked a bit worse for wear and once again Van realized that there might be some benefits to what he'd become. With a smile he put an arm around Brett's shoulders when the smaller blond came up to him. Looking at Brandt and then Shelby he asked, "Which do we want to try first, my shifting or Brett's fireball?"

"I'm not going to be trying to cast a fireball," Brett said. "I don't think such a spell exists. I'm going to try something else though."

"What?" Brandt asked.

"Some wardings on the four of us and our families," he replied. "Something to turn back any actions made against us with ill intent."

Brandt gave him a surprised look and asked, "Where did you find a spell like that?"

"Been playing with building runestaves for quite a while. Just never thought of actually trying it as a spell. I've got the disks already prepared. Just have to redden them and sing the runes." He shrugged and said, "That might take us a while, so why don't we try and get Van's control issues sorted out first."

"Anybody thought about what to do if I can't control it?" Van asked.

"Thought you said you had it under control," Brandt replied.

Van shrugged and said, "I think I do. But like I said, I haven't tried to actually change on purpose. I don't know if I can, or if trying to change against the moon is a bad idea."

"Now who's been watching too many bad shifter movies?" Brett teased him.

Van smiled back and said, "Touche." Finally he clapped his hands together and asked, "How do we want to do this?"

Looking around, Shelby said, "It looks like we're the only ones here right now. Why don't we go over to the shelter and work from there. Somehow I doubt we're likely to run into any early morning campers this time of year." Little wisps of steam rose in the cold morning air and Van realized he was not looking forward to stripping down to a pair of running shorts. The days may still be warm, but the mornings had frost on the grass.

Van nodded and grabbed his bag out of the truck and said, "Let's go and get this over with." The others fell in behind him as they made their way to the large structure that was used for meetings and gatherings. Although the doors to both the kitchen and the meeting area were locked, the open dog-trot between offered them a modicum of cover. Setting down his bag, he kicked off his shoes and began to pull the Henley he was wearing over his head. "What do you think you're doing?" Shelby asked.

"I don't want to tear up my clothes," Van told her. "I do gain mass and size when I do this. Almost ripped up my new pair of sneakers the last time I changed."

His cousin blushed and said, "I hadn't thought of that."

Van smiled and said, "Don't worry. I'm wearing a pair of running shorts under my jeans. I won't embarrass you too much."

He looked over to where Brett was standing watching him. The blond swallowed hard and nodded. Suddenly, it was Van's turn to blush as he realized just how much he was going to expose himself to his newfound boyfriend. "I'd say, Shelby wasn't the only person to not think this through," Brandt teased them as he stood in the doorway of the dog trot.

Van shrugged and shucked his jeans. "Nice," Shelby teased.

Laying the jeans across his bag, he asked, "Now what?"

"Now you change," Brandt said.

"How?" Van asked.

"How should I know? You're the moon-cat." Brandt said.

"What were you thinking about that Friday night?" Brett asked.

"I was upset, agitated. I could feel that something was wrong in the den."

"Den?" Shelby asked.

Van nodded. "My perspective seemed to shift. I was sensing something wrong in the area I was supposed to protect."

"Think about how you felt then," Brett suggested. "Think about what happened. Try to relive it."

Van nodded and reached into his memories. He tried to think about what had happened that night. How he felt the moon pull on him, how he felt the need to defend his home. But nothing seemed to happen. He simply stood there shivering in the cold October morning air.

"Well?" Brandt asked.

"Well, I can't seem to reach it," Van said frustrated.

"Maybe you can only do it on the full moon?" Brett asked.

Van shook his head and said, "I don't think so. I can feel it just beneath the surface, I just can't reach it."

"Relax," Shelby said. "Try again."

Van nodded and closed his eyes. Again, he reached for what he felt just under the surface. He reached for the animal that was hidden in his soul. "Freyja, if you did this to me, help me now please," he whispered under his breath.

Suddenly he felt something wrap around his legs.

Opening his eyes and looking down, he saw a long-haired white cat winding between his feet. The cat looked up at him and mewled softly. Forgetting why he was there, he reached down and petted the now purring animal.

As his fingers touched the soft fur, suddenly a door opened in his mind. Through it, he saw himself in layers. On the top was Van Griffin, underneath that was the half-man half-cat he'd knew that he could become. Yet underneath that, was another form, that of a large housecat the size of a cougar. And beneath all of that was the white light that was his soul. Peering through that column of light were a pair of intense electric blue eyes.

In his mind's eye, he could see a hand reach into different levels of who he was and pull out one after another form, finally settling on the man-cat form. Suddenly, he felt his skin begin to itch all over, his hearing became more sensitive, and his muscles seemed more powerful.

"You did it!" Shelby's voice cut through his sensory overload.

He opened his eyes and looked down on his friends as he felt his tail swishing back and forth behind him. Most of the color had gone out of the world, everything seemed bright and shiny to him. He looked down at his arms and could see a pelt of thick black fur, marked by darker blue-black stripes underneath. As the white cat leaped down and ran off into the woods, he flexed his hands and three-inch razor sharp claws erupted from slits in the tips of his fingers.

"Van?" he heard Brett ask. "Can you understand us?"

Something seemed to click in his brain, something primal, something instinctual. A need to protect infused his soul, a need to mark. He leaned forward to the smaller blond boy and ran the sides of his face against his head and shoulders. He could smell the subtle shift in his scent. Now he could smell himself on Brett and that was the way it should be.

"Van?" Shelby asked.

Turning on her, he again felt the pull to mark her so

that he'd know she was part of his glaring. He reached out and pulled her to him, and did the same thing to her as he'd done to Brett. He wasn't sure why he did it but she seemed incomplete without it.

"If I say something, is he going to rub himself all over me?" he heard Brandt ask.

Turning to the other blond, he asked, "Do you want me to?" The sound of his voice was strangely accented and a bit muffled by a genuine fear of cutting his tongue on his teeth. It was followed by a purring noise escaping from his throat.

"You can talk like that?" Brett asked.

Van felt his tail whip straight up behind his back and begin to curl and uncurl. "It's difficult," Van replied. "I have to concentrate and make each word carefully," he said between razor sharp teeth." A purr of amusement escaped his throat.

"So you aren't some slavering beast out to eat us," Brett told him in and I told you so tone.

Van shook his head. "Things are different. The way I see things, the way I hear things are different. It feels like part of me is quieter."

"Which part?" Shelby asked.

Van shrugged, "I don't know. Now it all seems to be about instinct. I have to concentrate to think, to act on thought instead of out of instinct."

"What are your instincts telling you to do, Van?" Shelby asked nervously.

He looked over at Brett and felt the pull he'd felt last night threaten to exert itself again. With a smile that felt strange on his lips he said, "You don't want to know." He felt his tongue lick the outside of his lips.

Brett gulped and blush, and Van could hear his heart begin to beat faster. He began to sweat slightly and Van could pick up the faint shift in pheromones that suggested something pleasant indeed. "Uh, we'll talk about that later," Brett replied.

"What else?" Shelby asked, slightly amused.

"All of my senses are hyped up. I can see clearly, I can hear clearly." He looked over at Brett and down below his waistline and added, "And I can smell everything."

"Is there anybody else nearby?" Brandt asked.

Van gave him a look of curiosity and then let his senses roam. He could detect some of the campers snoring nearby, and there was a couple down on the pier sharing a thermos of coffee. He could hear the steady pat of a runner on the trails, but nobody close enough to hear or see what they were doing. He shook his head and said, "No."

"Can you change back?" Shelby asked.

Van thought about it. Again he closed his eyes and pictured himself in the same layers as before. This time it came to his mind clearly. He reached down into the column of light and pulled out the human form.

"Wow!" Brett said.

Opening his eyes, his vision returned to normal and he could see Brett looking him up and down. "Don't accuse me of reading too much shifter fiction again, Van. You literally marked Shelby and me." Then, giving him a grin, he added, "I'm not sure if that's a good thing or bad considering she's your cousin."

It was Van's turn to blush. He added, "She's part of the glaring."

"Glaring?" Shelby asked. "What's a glaring?"

"A colony of cats," Brandt interrupted. "That's not a word I expected you to use.

Van shrugged and said, "It's not a word I expected to use either. It just came to mind." Then looking around he asked, "Where's that little house cat that was just here?"

They all looked around in confusion trying to find it. "I don't know," Shelby said. "Maybe you scared it off when you shifted."

In the distance, Van heard the sound of a woman's laughter that reminded him of tinkling glass.

Looking to the others, he asked, "Did you hear that?"

"Somebody laughing?" Brandt asked.

"Yeah," Shelby said. "Why wouldn't we?"

"Because I heard the same laughter the morning I killed that sow."

"Interesting," Brandt said, stroking the blond peach fuzz on his chin. Then turning to Brett he asked, "Can you top what we just saw?"

Brett just shook his head and said, "I don't think so. What I had in mind was a bit more subtle. It is supposed to turn ill intent back on whomever acts against us."

"Sort of a karma spell?" Shelby asked.

Brett snorted and said, "More of a warding designed to build orlog. If someone acts with good intentions toward us then it will rebound on them as well. But if they do something to hurt us, it will rebound completely on them."

"Best of both worlds," Brandt said with a smile. "I like it. Where did you come across that kind of spell?"

"I got the idea from the *Havamal*," he replied. "One of the words Odin knows."

"You think you can make it work?" Brandt asked. "Vitkors and vitkis have been trying to figure out those spells for centuries."

"I said I got the idea for it there, not the spell," Brett replied. He looked over at Van and said, "Put your clothes on and let's grab a picnic table." Looking over at Brandt he asked, "Can you start a fire in one of those metal barbecue grates? I brought the stuff in your trunk."

"Was wondering about why you did that," Brandt replied.

"And now you know," Brett said snarkily.

"Whoever says knowing is half the battle is going to get beaten," Shelby replied.

They all turned to look at her in surprise. Finally, Van shook his head and took her by the arm saying, "Come on. Let's let Gandalf and Merlin mix their magic."

It didn't take long for the other two to get things set up.

As he pulled a bottle of red looking water from the back of the trunk, Brandt said, "I brought the war water you asked me for."

"Good," Brett said. Then looking over at them he reached into his pack and pulled out four little Dixie cups. "For this spell to work right, I need you all the fill the little cups if you know what I mean."

"What?" Shelby demanded.

Brett blushed and said, "I need just a few drops."

"Brett...?" Shelby asked.

"I'm serious Shelby. It's meant to protect all four of us and our families." He grinned and said, "The bathroom is open over there." He pointed to the public restrooms.

Shelby gave him a grumpy look, snatched the cup from his hands and then went stalking off to the ladies room."

"You guys can either go behind a tree, or to the bathroom," Brett told them, handing them each a cup.

"You're serious?" Van asked.

Brandt nodded and said, "He's serious, Van. I sort of know what he's after. He's on the right track." Then looking over at Brett he said, "This is more spae work than galdr."

Brett shrugged and replied, "Maybe, but by combining the two, I should get a pretty good spell."

"Are we inside the area of whatever it is that you were telling me about that makes magic easier?" Van asked.

Brett shook his head and said, "No, and I want it that way. I don't want anybody to sense the casting until it's over. When we go back into town, hopefully whatever force is amplifying the magic will kick in then. Then it will be too late to pinpoint it."

Van just nodded as he stepped around the tree. "Just a few drops?"

"Yeah," Brett said.

"Okay."

Five minutes later, Brett was mixing together a red paste made from the red water Brandt had brought, some paint, the contents of the four cups and several other ingredients. Placing it in a tin cup on the grill, he took out four disks with a runestave carved into them. Although each base stave was identical, under each one was a different series of runes. The first read, VAN. Then was, SHELBY, followed by BRETT and finally, BRANDT.

"You really thought this out, didn't you?" Brett asked, picking up each of the disks of wood. He smelled one of them and then asked, "But why oak?"

Brett shrugged and replied, "It's Thor's tree. I get along with Thor."

Brandt just nodded and replied, "A bit surprising, but I can understand that. Why not in metal?"

"Because I'd want to do it in iron if I did, and I'd have trouble explaining to Mrs. Stein why I wanted four iron disks."

"Maybe you should apprentice to mom," Shelby suggested. "If this works."

Brett smiled and replied, "Maybe I will."

As the ink came to a low boil, Brett took it from the grill and mixed in a dollop of honey and said, "Okay, here goes." He took one of the disks, the one with Shelby's name and said, "Ladies first." Taking a tiny brush, he began to fill the runes with the ink, singing each one with a single breath. When he was finished, he handed it to her and said, "Don't lose this. Put it under your pillow tonight, then you can leave it on your dresser. Just don't let your mom throw it away."

Shelby took the disk and said, "I don't feel any different."

"Why should you?" Van asked. "Nobody wants to hurt you."

"Except Carmen O'Brien," Shelby said quietly.

"I don't think that's much more than just two girls who dislike each other. I don't think she'd really wish you harm," Brett said.

He then went back to work on the other three. By the time he finished, it was well after ten in the morning and people were slowly starting to come into the park.

Looking around Van said, "Maybe we should pack it in.

How does breakfast at IHOP sound?"

"Sounds good to me," Brett replied.

"Then let's get cracking. This little cat wants to be fed," Van told him with a grin.

CHAPTER 13

"I don't know where else to turn," Clark Johnson said from across the table where he was sitting with Gareth Bjargeir at the local IHOP.

Gareth nodded to the man and replied, "I'm not sure why you came to me, Clark. You've made no secret about how you feel about the kindred."

"My problems with your people are doctrinal, not personal, Gareth," he said. "But God help me, you're my only real hope. You understand these things better than anybody I know. I was helpless to save Kelli, or my wife, but I'm not going to lose my son too."

"We had nothing to do with what happened to Kelli," Gareth said.

"I know," Clark told him. It seemed that the man had gone through some kind of epiphany over the years. "At first I blamed everybody, even God, for what happened. But I got over that. I got to thinking about that, and realized this is somehow tied up in all the secrecy around the Devlins and the Davenports." He sighed and said, "Yeah, you guys worship different gods than I do, but I can't say that you've ever acted against the people of this community. Gracious, Ellen Griffin was driven out of town because of her helping it; and the fact that your entire kindred turned out to man the sandbags in '93 hasn't been forgotten either."

Gareth nodded. There was more to Clark Johnson than he'd realized. Either he'd really had a change of heart over the years, or he was a damned good liar. The thing was, Gareth had no idea as to which. He sipped his coffee and asked, "What do you want me to do?"

"That thing bit my son last night, Gareth. It bit him on the neck, but I can't find the wound. Caleb said it carved something in his chest, but I can't see it."

"Have you taken him to the hospital?" Gareth asked.

Clark shook his head and said, "No, he's at home in his bed. But I probably should. He's running a low grade fever, and puking up something unpleasant."

"How do you know it wasn't just a fever dream?" Gareth asked.

Clark took something off the table and slid it toward him. "I found this on the foot of his bed. Caleb said it left it for him, as a reminder that he was his." Gareth looked down at the small piece of gold. It looked like a piece of flattened gold coil that had been broken off. Looking closely at it, he could see the small indentation at the break point and understood. It was payment. He sighed and pushed it back over to Clark and said, "What did he say it was for?"

"Payment to me," Clark said.

Gareth nodded and frowned. This was not good news. The creature had claimed Caleb as his own. He would now answer anytime it called- no matter where he was. "We have to kill this thing, Clark. Your son is in more danger than you realize."

"He's going to be like Kelli?" Clark asked.

Gareth shook his head and said, "I don't know. Maybe, but maybe far worse. I need to talk to him, and I need someone else to talk to him."

"Who?" Clark asked.

Gareth frowned and said, "The last person either you or her mother wants in Caleb's bedroom."

"The Stein girl?" Clark asked. "Why her?"

"Because she has a gift for seidr, and right now we need it to find out the nature of whatever this thing is," Gareth said.

"She's a witch?" Clark asked.

"Not quite," Gareth said. "Seidr is more like being a medium, a clairvoyant, and a telepath all rolled into one. Ellen Griffin was a very gifted seidr worker, and it seems that Shelby has inherited the same gift."

"What do we need to do?" Clark asked.

"First we need to visit Caleb, then I need to talk to Shelby," Gareth told him.

Before Clark could reply, Gareth looked up to see Shelby enter the restaurant with her cousin, Van, Brett Bond, and Brandt Snow. With a smile he said, "Well, speak of mischief."

"What?" Clark asked and turned around to see the waitress going up to seat the foursome of young high schoolers. "How did you know she'd be here?"

Gareth shrugged. "I didn't. I just suggested IHOP when you called because it was local and I hadn't had breakfast yet."

As the waitress seated them, Shelby saw the two men and came over, "Hello Mr. Bjargeir." She turned to Clark and said, "Mr. Johnson."

Gareth chuckled and asked, "What's got the four of you out on a Saturday morning?"

Shelby actually blushed and said, "We went up to Greenbo Lake this morning to do some exploring."

"Did you find anything interesting?" Gareth asked.

"Quite a bit, actually. I'm looking forward to talking to you about it later," she said, looking over at Clark suspiciously.

Gareth smiled and said, "I've got an errand to run after breakfast, but that shouldn't take more than an hour. Why don't you and Van stop by my shop around noon. You can tell me about it then."

Shelby nodded and said. "Yes sir." She looked over at Clark and said, "Mr. Johnson, please tell Caleb that I'll call him later."

Clark smiled up at her and said, "I think he'd like that, Shelby."

The reply seemed to catch Shelby off guard but she

quickly recovered. "Have a good one, gentlemen." She then turned to rejoin her friends.

"What was that about?" Clark asked.

"Not here, Clark," Gareth said. "You have no idea how sharp young ears are these days." He looked over at the table and saw Van looking dead at him. He blushed slightly and then looked back at his menu.

~*~

"What can I do for you, Craig?" Auda asked the boy across the desk from her. Sheriff Treybond had been kind enough to loan her an office at the county jail. She was ,after all, helping with the investigation.

"I was sort of wondering..." Craig Blankenship began. "...I was wondering if it's safe to go in the woods now? Has that cat been caught?"

Auda smiled and leaned back in her chair letting her uniform shirt stretch tightly across her bosom. She was using a magic far older than that of the Vanir, or even of her own people. She was using magic understood by every male on the planet old enough to realize that there was a difference between men and women. She felt the top of her shirt separate slightly giving the boy a glimpse of her cleavage. "The cat hasn't been caught, Craig. Parts of the woods around here are still dangerous."

"   Well..." he asked, rubbing his hands on his palms. Auda smiled at herself, "Could you tell me which parts I should avoid. I mean, where is it most likely to be hunting?"

Ahh, there was more to this than just him wanting to go hunting. He might not realize it yet, but Auda knew what he was looking for- a place to dump a body. "Well, I'd stay out of the area below the ridge-line along Silver John Mountain. That's where a lot of the tracks seem to be," she told him. "But remember most big cats have large ranges. I think this one is male so his range could be as large as sixty square miles around that area."

"That would cover most of the town," Craig said.

Auda nodded and added, "And remember, they're crepuscular."

"What does that mean?" he asked.

"It means that they are most active at twilight, dusk and dawn. And it means they're likely to be in the woods the same time as the deer hunters," she told him.

He nodded and said, "Well, thank you ma'am. I appreciate the information."

"You drove all the way down here to find that out?" she asked. "That's something you could've just as easily called about."

The boy shrugged and said, "I was down here anyway, so I thought I'd pop in and ask."

She smiled at him, recognizing a lie when she heard it. Looking up at the clock and realizing it was nearly noon, she said, "It's lunch time. Why don't you join me over at Micky D's and you can tell me what's really on your mind, Craig."

He smiled and blushed at the suggestion. She was sure his mind was going exactly where she wanted it to go. He was, after all, an eighteen-year-old boy, a football star, and a legend in his own mind. Auda could use that, and she maybe could have a little fun on the side. After all, troll-wives did have a certain reputation up to which she entirely planned to live. "Sounds good to me."

"Let me get my jacket," she said, standing and grabbing the olive-green garment from the back of her chair.

Ten minutes later they were settling into one of the booths in the back of the restaurant and munching on the fare. "So, why did you really come to see me, Craig?" she asked over her shake.

He smiled and said, "Well, I do want to know about the cougar. My little brother will be out there and I want him to be safe."

"And?" she asked, stretching the word out sensually.

He shrugged and admitted, "And I wanted to see you again."

She nodded and said, "I thought so."

"Look, it's not what you think," he protested. "I'm not a stalker." He shrugged again, "I just like a woman who likes the woods as much as I do."

She nodded and said, "Seems to me you got quite a few of those who live in that community at the foot of the mountain, some of them your own age."

"What? Those freaks at the kindred?" he asked.

"I take it you don't like them?" she replied, locking eyes with him.

"They're a bunch of New Age nutjobs," he said. "I wouldn't go out with one of those girls to save my life."

"Oh, and you think you might go out with me?" Auda asked with a sly smile.

"You're, at least, real," Craig replied without a hint of embarrassment.

"Real?" she asked.

"You don't go in for all that new age crap about the elderkin whatever that is, or talk about worlog, or meegin, or weird crap like that," he told her.

She smiled and said, "No. I don't do that. But my question is why do you think you could go out with me?"

"I...uh...I..I just thought that..." he nodded toward her bosom, "Well...you keep showing..."

She laughed lowly and said, "Relax Craig. I'm not going to bite you. Not yet at least." She looked down at her shirt and said, "Because you keep seeing more of these, you think I like you?" He nodded and blushed deep red. "You're right about that." Leaning back in her chair she said, "The question is, what do you have to offer me? I mean, you're a high school senior- granted you are of age of consent- but I'm a grown woman. What would you bring to the table." She smiled and leaned in close and asked quietly, "Or the bed?"

~*~

"So, how did it go?" Bastion Davenport asked over the phone.

"Enlightening," Brandt told him. "Did you know that Brett and Van are dating?"

"No," Bastion said surprised. "I thought Van was straight."

"So did I," Brandt told him. "But keep it to yourself for now."

"What spell did he cast?" Bastion asked.

"I didn't recognize it. It mixed aspects of galdr with traditional magic. I'd swear some of it was even kitchen magic like Liselle uses.

"Do you think it worked?" Bastion asked.

"Don't know. It was subtle, not something I expected from Brett. It's a warding spell, designed to turn ill intent on anybody who acts against the four of us."

"So what do we have to do, wait and see if Craig Blankenship and some of his goon squad start falling down the stairs or something?"

"Something like that," Brandt told him.

"Is he ready to break the pact?" Bastion asked.

"I don't think he even considers himself part of the pact. His justification was that he took no oaths to protect the Six's Secrets."

"He knows about the Six?" Brett asked.

"Sorry. He only knows the general information Mrs. Devlin gave him. He doesn't know that they are even called The Six."

"What now?" Bastion asked.

"Now we wait," Brandt says. "If his spell works it could be spectacular to watch."

"It won't affect the Six," Bastion said. "They're too strong."

"Maybe," Brandt told him. "But it could upset a lot of apple carts. I think that it will work against the normals first."

"Who should we watch?" Bastion asked a bit worried.

"I'd be sure to keep an eye on Craig Blankenship. Maybe Reverend Johnson, and probably Felicia Ballenger too."

"You think it'll affect her? You think she means you guys ill?"

He heard Brandt pause for a moment before he said, "Her, no. But her dad, definitely. Watch her to find out if anything happens to her dad. I think the spell was made to return small ills for small ills and large ones for large. That man has a major hate on for Van and anything to do with the kindred."

"Okay," Bastion said. "By the way, I got some more information about my father today."

"What did you find out?" Brandt asked.

"He disappeared to New Orleans right after I was born. Evidently he lived down there for several years before moving to Atlanta, and then Louisville."

"He's that close?" Brandt asked.

"I think so."

"You gonna try and contact him?"

"He killed my mom, and ran off with Reverend Johnson's floozy of a daughter, what do you think?" Bastion asked.

"I think that curiosity will eventually get the best of you," Brandt told him.

"Maybe, but not anytime in the near future," Bastion told him. "Have you told Van about his mom and mine yet?" he asked.

"No. Haven't had the chance. It's not the kind of thing you can bring up casually. But I think I can eventually work it in. Suggest that what he's become might be inherited."

"Good idea," Bastion said. "Does his aunt know?"

"I don't think so. Some secrets are not likely to get shared, not even between sisters. The fact that she was a moon-cat is probably near the top of the list." There was a pause before he said, "How are you doing?"

Bastion swallowed and said, "Pretty good. No extra hair yet."

"That could mean a lot of things, Bastion," Brandt said with a hint of a tease in his voice.

"Not down there, you idiot. I'm talking about anywhere else." Bastion blushed. "That happened a few years ago."

"TMI Basty. TMI!"

"You're the one who brought it up," Bastion teased him. "You sure you don't want to give it a try?"

"First off Basty, you're thirteen. Second off, I have no problems with you liking guys and girls both, but I'm strictly interested in the fairer sex."

"Just teasing you, Brandt. I didn't mean anything by it," Bastion suddenly said, worrying that he may have crossed a line. Most people wouldn't realize just how fragile Bastion's self-esteem was or just how much he valued his friendship with Brandt Snow. He wished it could be more, but realized that Brandt wasn't going to swing that way.

"It's okay, Bastion," Brandt said. "Just what you're suggesting could get me in a lot of trouble."

"I know," Bastion said.

"Good," Brant told him. "Keep me informed on what else you might find out."

"Will do," Bastion said. "Talk to you later."

"You too."

Bastion hung up the phone and looked down at the file he'd managed to copy from his grandmother's computer. He looked at the picture of the handsome blond man with eyes the same shade of blue as Bastion's. "We will eventually meet Paul Davenport, and you will pay for what you did to my mother. And if I can find the little slut you ran off with, so will she." He noted the auburn fur that began to appear on his hands, and smiled coldly.

He hadn't been totally truthful with Brandt, and he genuinely felt bad about that. He'd been shifting now since the Friday night that Van Griffith had killed those werewolves. Now he needed to talk to the other boy, to find out more about what both of them had become.

~*~

Brett, Van, and Shelby entered the Eye in the Well and looked around. Shelby was feeling a little worried. She'd tried to call Caleb, but his cell went straight to voice mail. She'd left a message, something in the pit of her stomach told her that all wasn't well. She barely noticed that Mr. Bjargeir was not in the main showroom.

"Mr. Bjargeir?" Brett called.

"Down here, in the basement!" the man's voice called from a black door in the side wall dividing the two halves of the building. "Turn the sign and lock the door!"

Beside her, Brett nodded and turned back to the door and did as the old man bade before the three of them tramped down the old wooden stairs. "Be careful of that second to last step. It's higher than the others!" he called as they reached the first landing on the steps.

Sure enough, one of the wooden stairs was indeed higher than the others. It was the kind of thing that could throw off your balance. As they reached the bottom, they noticed a musty odor coming from beyond the dividing wall that separated the rest of the basement from the stairs. Mr. Bjargeir was sitting at a table with several books in front of him. A single hundred watt bulb burned above the table, but was unable to completely dispel the gloom of the huge basement. Across from him, looking sickly in its yellow light, sat Caleb.

"Caleb?" Shelby asked.

He stood from where he was sitting, and said, "Shelby!"

Without thinking, she rushed to the boy and hugged him. "Why aren't you answering your phone?" She felt something different about him. There was a pain in him that wasn't there before. Pulling back she looked into his sunken eyes and asked, "What's wrong?"

The other boy pulled his phone from his pocket and showed her the screen. "No cell service down here." He was sweating profusely, and was shivering.

"Shelby," Van said. "Come here."

"What?" she turned to her cousin and asked. Suddenly his eyes had gone to the same electric blue that she saw in the cat.

"Shelby, come here," Van said. "Something's wrong."

"Van?" she asked. "Then turning back to Caleb she saw something dark flash in his eyes. A low growl escaped his throat. "You're scaring me. Both of you!"

"Mr. Bjargeir?" Brett broke in, putting himself between Van and Caleb. "What's going on?"

"Caleb needs our help," the old man said. "We need to find out exactly what has happened." He looked back and forth between Van and Caleb and added, "You two can figure out who can piss higher on the tree later." He pulled a heavy sword from under the table, and added, "And the first one of you who throws a claw is going to deal with three feet of silver."

"What's going on here? Brett asked.

"I'm trying to figure out what bit Caleb here," Bjargeir said.

Shelby spun on the boy next to her. "Something bit you? When? Where?"

"Last night in his room," Reverend Johnson said, coming out of one of the little rooms just beyond the gloom.

"Can you describe it?" Brett asked, suddenly curious as he stepped toward Caleb.

"Brett," Van warned. There was an intense, almost animal reaction between him and Caleb now.

"Van, calm down." Brett said.

"How can I calm down when every fiber in my being is telling me you and Shelby are in danger?"

Shelby looked over and saw him flexing his hands as black fur seemed to grow and then disappear on his arms. Wicked looking black claws were extended from the tips.

"You want to explain that?" Reverend Johnson asked, suddenly noticing Van's reaction.

"Not particularly," Van said, pointing with his eyes toward where Caleb's hands were growing large and hairy.

"Maybe you should wait upstairs, Van," Mr. Bjargeir said.

"Like hell I am," Van said between sharp teeth. "He smells like death, and like a wolf."

Mr. Bjargeir sighed, and said, "I was afraid of that." Looking at Shelby and Brett, he said, "Okay, you two stand over next to Van."

"No," Caleb said. "Not Shelby."

Suddenly, Brett grabbed the sword off the table and pulled Shelby back toward the wall housing the stairs. "That's enough, both of you!" he yelled. "Caleb, Mr. Johnson, Mr. Bjargeir sit down." He turned to Van and said, "You too, Van. You two want to see who's alpha? Well right now, I am."

"Brett?" Van asked.

"We need to find out what's going on here and if you two start going at each other with more balls than brains then there's no telling who could get killed, infected, or what. I won't allow that," Brett said angrily.

Caleb sat down in his seat sullenly, his ears growing hairy.

Brett turned to Van and said, "You too, Van. If we're going to get to the bottom of this, we're going to have to use our brains."

Shelby had never seen her small friend like this before. She realized that he'd been developing a stronger sense of confidence, but never anything like this. She watched as Van approached the table cautiously, his eyes never leaving Caleb. Brett simply nodded and turned back to Caleb and then asked, "Okay, describe the thing that bit you."

"It was like the werewolves that attacked us. Except it was more human. Not quite like the ones in that television show you like, but more human than the ones who attacked us. It bit me, carved something in my chest and then left this. He said it was payment to my dad." He tossed a small piece of gold on the table.

"Anything else?" Brett asked.

"It was blue."

"Blue?" the blond repeated.

Caleb looked at him, obviously trying to describe something that didn't make any sense to him. "It was this dead blue color, like somebody who'd suffocated or something."

Brett nodded and looked to Van and then back to Caleb. "What's your beef with him?"

"He doesn't smell right. It makes my stomach churn," Caleb told him.

Turning to Van he asked, "And you?"

"He smells corrupted, like something dead. He smells like the things that attacked us," the raven-haired youth told them.

Brett just nodded again and then looked at Mr. Bjargeir for confirmation. The older man just grinned at him and said, "You're doing fine, Brett."

Brett sighed and said, "From what I've read of the lore, it sounds like a draugr ."

"Drawgur?" Reverend Johnson asked.

"A reanimated corpse that comes back from the dead to harass the living. They're sort of like a cross between a vampire, a zombie, and even an undead wizard."

"The paper said that the body of one of the attackers disappeared from the morgue in Greenup. Do you think that could be your draugr thing?" Reverend Johnson asked.

Brett stroked his chin and said, "It could be. It would be awfully powerful though. Having the power of a werewolf and a draugr at the same time would make him very strong." He turned to look at Caleb and added, "And explain what's happened to you."

"Okay," Shelby said as she let what Brett was saying sink in. "But why do Van and Caleb suddenly want to tear each other apart?"

"Because of the forces involved," Brett said. "As the

land-guardian, Van senses that Caleb has been tainted. Caleb senses the draugr's hatred for Van because Van killed the were-wolf."

"You killed a werewolf?" Reverend Johnson asked.

"Four actually," Van said.

The reverend turned to Mr. Bjargeir and said, "And you're okay with that?"

The old man turned his good eye toward the reverend and asked, "What would you do to the vampire who turned your daughter?"

"Kill it," Johnson said without thinking.

"Those werewolves killed Van's parents, and attacked his home," Brett told him. "Killing them makes sense to me." He then gave the reverend a strange look and asked, "Your daughter got turned into a vampire?"

The reverend nodded sadly and then added, "It was be-fore you came here." Then he sighed and said, "I just can't shake off the idea of killing people like you folks can." He turned to look at his son, and added, "Especially teenagers."

"Well, I got news for you," Brett said. "The only possi-bility of breaking the curse on Caleb is for him to kill the were-wolf who infected him. The problem with that is as the draugr, he has made him his thrall. He can't act against him."

"Made him his thrall?"

"That was what the payment was for. He was paying the man-price for making Caleb his," Brett said.

"You catch on fast," Mr. Bjargeir said.

"I read a lot," Brett replied. Then he looked to Caleb and asked, "You said it carved something in your chest?"

"Yeah, but Dad or Mr. Bjargeir can't see it," Caleb re-plied, unbuttoning his shirt. He looked over at Shelby and blushed and then opened it up to reveal what looked like a runestave carved into his chest. It was scarred over, but it looked raw and painful with highlights of dead white skin over angry red welts.

It was three parallel vertical lines with the center one

being slightly shorter than the outer ones. At the top of that one was a short line slashing down about forty-five degrees to almost touch the outside line on the right. At the bottom it was mirrored to the left. A third line slashed down through the middle of it at the same angle but nearly touching both the left and the right.

Brett whistled lowly and said, "That looks like it hurt."

Caleb nodded and asked, "You can see it?"

"Of course he can see it," Shelby said.

"What do you see?" Mr. Bjargeir asked.

Brett took a pencil and paper from the top of the desk and drew out the stave. "It was risted by claw and reddened with his own blood. Powerful."

"What does it mean?" Mr. Johnson asked.

"It depends on in which order they were carved and sung," Brett told him.

Caleb shook his head and replied, "I can't really tell you. Once the first line was carved I was hurting too much to really tell which lines were which."

"Makes sense," Van said.

Brett raised an eyebrow at his boyfriend. "It speaks."

Van blushed and said, "I am in control of the cat, Brett. It's not the other way around."

"Could have fooled me five minutes ago," Shelby said.

"I was caught by surprise," Van replied.

"Do you sense anything off of it as the land-guardian?" Mr. Bjargeir asked.

Van shook his head and said, "Only that he's a wolf and has been tainted by the draugr. The cat doesn't like either of those."

"I bet," Shelby replied with a smile. Turning to Brett she asked, "Why do I get the feeling that I've stepped into one of your favorite television shows?"

"Which one?' Brett asked with a smirk as he studied the runes. "The one with the female lead who falls in love with a vampire, or the one with the high school kid who gets turned into a werewolf?"

Shelby shook her head and gave him a warning, "Brett." Caleb growled at her side.

"Look, I'm trying to figure out how this stave was put together. We may be able to break the thralldom if we do."

"Not the curse?" Caleb asked.

"Which would you rather be, enslaved to a draugr for the rest of your life, or just turn hairy and chase Van once a month?"

"Brett!" Van protested.

Mr. Bjargeir chuckled. "It would seem that we've got a pretty good crop of kids coming up, wouldn't you agree, Clark?"

The other man just grunted.

"Well?" Brett pressed Caleb.

"I would rather not be anybody's slave." He sighed heavily, looked toward Van and added, "That includes the moon."

"You feel up to trying to take down the creature that did this to you by yourself?" Brett asked.

"If I have to," Caleb replied.

"And here I thought you were bright," Brett said under his breath.

"I heard that!" Caleb protested.

"I don't care," Brett replied and stuck his hands in his pockets before looking at Van. "Ready to go?"

"Huh?" Van asked.

"I can work with ignorance, but I have no desire to be around somebody who is looking to get himself killed and doesn't care if he takes other people with him," Brett said. Turning to Reverend Johnson he added, "After he's gone, give me a call and I'll see what I can do to make sure he doesn't come back as a draugr too."

Shelby could see a twinkle of amusement in Mr. Bjargeir's eye as he asked, "Do you think you could break the thralldom?"

"Given enough time to study the stave, very possibly.

It's powerful, but it's also kind of obvious. I just have to figure out the exact order they were carved to get this effect and then change it." He looked over at the Reverend and added, "Of course you have to give the gold back to the draugr."

The reverend nodded, and then asked, "How do you know about all this kind of thing?" He looked over at Mr. Bjargeir and asked, "Is this what you've been teaching them?"

Mr. Bjargeir chuckled and said, "This is magic, Clark. I don't have a magical bone in my body."

"I learn fast, Mr. Johnson. When I was accepted into the kindred, I started to read up on the more esoteric side of the faith. There are enough books out there about rune-work, and combine that with having read all the sagas- some of them several times- I can start to put things together. Then we were attacked by those werewolves and I sort of went into overdrive reading about them." He gestured toward the drawing on the table. "I've seen examples of runestaves far more complicated than that, and understood them. The problem is that this isn't just rune work, or I'd suggest someone else to help you. He's better at galdr than I am, but this is also blood magic." He said quietly, "And that's something I'm starting to understand better than I feel comfortable with."

"Blood magic?"

Brett nodded and said, "He used Caleb's own blood to redden the runes. That tells me that he wanted it tied to Caleb's soul. That's going to start affecting him on a primal level." He shook his head, "I wouldn't want to be living in your house come next full moon."

"You mean I could hurt Dad?" Caleb asked the fear in his voice evident.

"I mean that the draugr can make you do whatever he damn well pleases. I suspect that tonight you'll spill your guts about this conversation to him."

"How?" Caleb demanded.

Brett sighed and said, "Like this." He reached out for the blade he'd put on the table and sliced his hand on it. Both Van and Caleb growled at him. He ignored them, took the pencil, and wincing, dipped the tip into the wound. He then retraced the rune on the paper, singing each rune in a single breath. When he finished, he connected five more runes to it singing each one of them. Then he reached across the table and handed the paper to Caleb. When the tall boy took it, he said, "Start doing push-ups."

A look of surprise, then of fear suddenly flashed across Caleb's face as he dropped to the concrete floor obeying Brett's command. The small blond shrugged and said, "You'll keep doing that until I tell you to stop."

"What in God's name?" Reverend Johnson came around the table toward Brett. Again, Van growled and stepped closer. Brett shrugged and said, "When you took that gold piece you accepted the deal. When he took that paper, he accepted the command. Brett shook his head and said, "Magic is dangerous, and once it has touched you, you are susceptible to it."

"Make him stop!" the reverend demanded.

Brett shrugged and said, "Okay, Caleb. You can stop." He turned on his heel and said, "You coming, Van?"

"Brett!" Van demanded.

Brett stopped and did not turn around, but simply asked, "What?"

"Help him!" Van demanded.

Brett turned around and watched as Caleb scrambled to his feet looking confused. "I can't. He doesn't want to listen right now. Maybe after he's been under the control of the draugr he'll listen to what I have to say, but by then it'll probably be too late."

"I'm listening!" Van and Reverend Johnson said simultaneously. Realizing what they'd done, they both looked at each other sheepishly.

Brett sighed and said, "Break the thralldom and kill the draugr. The only way to break the curse is for him to kill the draugr himself. That'll get him killed if he tries it."

"What do you suggest then?" Mr. Bjargeir asked, suddenly making himself heard.

He looked at the reverend and asked, "Can you deal with your son as a werewolf?" He held up a hand and said, "I don't mean a werewolf who's out of control and killing people left and right. I mean as someone who has been touched by magic older than your church. He will be as much in control of himself as Van, but he won't be the pure little boy anymore. He'll be a creature of the moon."

Van shook his head and asked, "How is it you know so much about this all of a sudden?"

"Because when we figured out what you were, I started researching shifters. I figured out the difference between the wolf-skins, the moon-wolves, and werewolves after we talked the other night. When I saw that runestave it all started to make sense. Caleb's a werewolf now. According to legend the only way to break the curse is to kill the werewolf that started the line." He looked at Caleb and said, "I like Caleb, and as impressed as I am with his athletic ability, he's no match for a draugr. And to be honest, if he's a moon-wolf, that means the progenitor of his line is in the realm of the Gods. I don't think all of us combined could bring her down. If we're going to kill the draugr, then we're all going to have to work together, and that will make your kill null and void."

"And why would you want to help?" Mr. Johnson asked.

Brett shot him a look of contempt and replied, "Because he's a friend. Because this bastard killed a friend of mine, he killed another friend's parents, he left a third friend without her leg, and now he's infected a fourth friend. I think it's time to start hurting him back."

"How do we kill a draugr?" Caleb asked.

"You either force him back into his grave, or burn him to nothing. Since he was never buried, that means we only have the second option. You need a flame hot enough to reduce him to ashes," Mr. Bjargeir said.

"Only thing around here that I can think of for that is out at the steel mill," Van said.

"Oh, I can see how that will go now," Brett replied sarcastically. "Excuse me foreman, I need to dump this struggling blue skinned werewolf into one of your furnaces. Do you mind? This isn't the movies. Those furnaces are watched very closely all the time. That's millions of dollars worth of steel coming out of that plant."

"Do you have any ideas?" Van turned to Mr. Bjargeir and asked.

"I'm not sure. If we could get him in a flame, maybe we can ward it to keep him there until it burns out. If they've already done the autopsy, then they'd have drained the blood, so he would be getting pretty desiccated by now," the old man said.

"All of this is just speculation isn't it?" Caleb asked.

Much to Shelby's surprise, it was Mr. Johnson who said, "No, Caleb. The dead do walk. I've seen it with my own eyes." He turned and looked at Brett and then Mr. Bjargeir and asked, "How long do you need to study that thing?"

Brett shrugged and said, "I don't know. Not long, a day or so at the most. I need to figure out every possible combination and order, and which one would have the effect we're seeing. There are six or seven lines in that rune, depending on how you count them. I recognize at least three runes right off the bat. We're talking anywhere from fifty to a hundred different options to explore."

"Do it," Van and Caleb said simultaneously.

"Bossy, aren't they?" Mr. Bjargeir said.

"You don't know the half of it," Brett replied.

"I'm curious as to why you three can see that thing but Gareth and I can't," Reverend Johnson said.

"Because, like Mr. Bjargeir said, you don't have a magical bone in your body. I'm studying to be a vitkor- a wizard, Shelby is a seidr-worker, and Van is the land-guardian."

Reverend Johnson shook his head and said, "I'm not sure I can handle all this. I don't understand it." He stopped and looked at the four teenagers and said, "I won't say I don't believe it. I had to believe it after what happened to Kelli, but I don't understand it. First it took away my daughter and now my son. If you can help him do it, I don't care if he turns into a Labrador Retriever once a month, just don't let him die."

Shelby watched as the three boys exchanged glances. Something seemed to pass between them as they closed ranks even with them being on opposing sides of some kind of mystical gulf. She could feel something primal deep inside all three of them reach across that gulf. A promise was made and acknowledged between them. It was something she couldn't understand, something that was tied deeply to what it meant to be male, to be brothers on a level she could not fathom.

Finally, she sighed and asked, "What now?"

Brett looked at her and said, "Now, you and Mr. Johnson take Caleb home and feed him. He looks like Helheim warmed over. I'd say his body is still adjusting to whatever the curse is doing to it. I'll take Van home, and then I'm going to start running every combination of these runes as I can to see what I can come up with."

She nodded and looked over at Mr. Johnson and said, "Well, let's go get some chicken soup into him." She turned to Van and said, "Tell Mom where I am."

Van nodded and looked to Brett and asked, "What do you want me to do?"

Brett frowned and said, "For now, I want you to try and figure out some way we can burn a body hot enough and quick enough that that bastard can't get away." He stopped and said, "And remember about those disks. You know where they go and why."

"Unde..." Van began to say but Brett shook his head. "Don't say it. What Caleb doesn't know, he can't give away." He turned to the brown haired boy and said, "Sorry, Dude."

Caleb just nodded and said, "I understand." Then he smiled weakly and replied, "And thanks. For everything."

"It's what friends do," Brett replied. For some reason that comment seemed to please Mr. Bjargeir very much, and that surprised Shelby.

CHAPTER 14

Agent Gerald Ballenger hated lawyers. They always made his job that much more difficult, and he had very little use for the one standing in front of him, handing him a court order. "You'll find everything there in order, Agent Ballenger. The court has ordered you to turn over all records of your access to my client's case in Colorado."

Gerald nodded and said, "No problem. The Bureau should have this information in their log files."

"The order also includes logs of your home computer," Mr. Collins said.

Ballenger shrugged and said, "That's easy. I've never accessed his case from my home computer."

"That's not what the documents the Bureau has turned over to us say. According to them, you accessed and downloaded a copy of his file a week before the attack on his home."

"Why would I access the file of a kid I knew nothing about then?" Ballenger asked.

"That's what we're trying to find out, Agent Ballenger. But my client's confidential information that was contained in that file has become public knowledge at the school," Collins said. "That's why Sheriff Treybond sent me her deputy to clone your hard-drive." He pointed to a female deputy behind him with a laptop.

Ballenger felt something drop in the pit of his stomach. He could probably get the Bureau to fight the court order but by the time he did, it would be too late.

Ballenger nodded and said, "Come in. I'll take you to my office where the computer is."

"Thank you," the deputy said.

He showed the woman to his office where the computer was and gave her the password she needed to access it. As she set up, he turned to the lawyer and asked, "What's all this about, Mr. Collins? I'm simply doing my job trying to find out who killed that man up on the mountain near that hate-group."

"This is about your own prejudices, Mr. Ballenger," Collins said. "You have no evidence to tie Van Griffin to those murders, yet you insist on grilling him for three hours. Furthermore, sensitive information about my client's file from Colorado has been released to the general population of the school."

"What information?" Ballenger demanded.

"His description of the attackers who killed his parents," Collins said. "Don't you find it odd that not long after you were transferred to this area that the same one-percenters managed to find their way to him?"

"The Bureau didn't have anything to do with that. It was a coincidence," Ballenger told him.

"Perhaps. But it would seem that, in spite of a coroner's report that the man killed up on the mountain was killed by an animal, and a description by another young man not part of the kindred that corroborates my client's description, you still felt the need to question him for several hours. Now we find out that someone has released details from a sealed investigation. That is probably just a coincidence too."

Ballenger shook his head. This was not going to end well. He knew he could make a call to the DoJ, and possibly get a monkey wrench thrown into this situation, but that wouldn't help him deal with what he was originally sent here for- dealing with the meth and prescription drug problems in the area. He was damned if he did, and damned if he didn't. And it looked like this particular lawyer had some pretty powerful connections, so it could get nasty. "I'm simply doing my job," he said.

"Like those rogue IRS agents in Cincinnati who took it on themselves to audit groups who disagreed with certain political ideologies were doing their jobs?," Collins asked. "You are basing your investigation on Project Meggido which has best been described as laying the groundwork for another Waco. You are using it to paint all people of the Nordic faith with the same broad brush of racism and trying to convict them with innuendo and falsehoods. It's my job to protect their civil liberties, including their First Amendment rights. If you have any evidence linking my client to the murder of Mr. Kaizer, then that is what you need to pursue, but harassing my client for his religious beliefs is against the law."

"You don't find it odd that this kid claims that werewolves killed his parents. Then, after moving here, there is another murder and the people linked to the one member of that white-supremacist gang he managed to kill show up and get themselves ripped apart by some large animal?"

Collins smiled at him and said, "And yet several people who were at the scene describe exactly the same thing and you still want to pursue my client."

"I'm an FBI agent, I'm not a monster hunter. I don't track down what doesn't exist."

Collins shook his head and said, "I see. Well, if there's been a breach of security that has tainted this case against my client, I can promise you, Agent Ballenger, there will be legal repercussions for yourself and the bureau."

By this time Ballenger had had enough of this nonsense. "Fine. Do what you feel you need to do. Until then, I'm going to carry out this investigation in my own way."

"Fair enough, Agent Ballenger," Collins told him. "And I'm going to act to protect the interests of my client and his family."

Ballenger stopped a moment and looked at the man and then asked, "Tell me, Mr. Collins, how does a widow with no visible form of income afford an attorney of your caliber?"

Collins smiled at him and said, "My services are on retainer with Mr. Bjargeir, who is a sizable landowner in the area and a man of no small means himself. I work for the Mountain Hearth Kindred as a whole as part of that contract."

Ballenger nodded his head and said, "And does an attorney who has argued before the Supreme Court believe in werewolves?"

Collins chuckled at him and said, "I've seen a lot of things during my fifty some odd years on this Earth, Agent Ballenger. Do I believe in werewolves? I don't know. But I know what the report from the coroner says killed poor Mr. Kaizer. I know what the FBI's own report said about the campsite where the Griffins were killed, and I know what each and every person who was at the Stein home the night they were attacked said. I may not believe it, but I'm not willing to rule it out either."

"Then you have a far more open mind than I do, Mr. Collins. I see a group of people who have gathered together to recreate the culture of one of the most violent peoples in history- a people who cut a swath across Europe killing robbing and raping everything they came across. I don't consider the Vikings a good role model for children."

Collins smiled and said, "Then you don't understand them. I've talked on many occasions with Mr. Bjargeir about what they believe. They are building a community based on the ideals of honesty, hard work, hospitality, and self-reliance. Theirs is an ancient religion that was dominate in Northern and Western Europe when Christianity swept through with the sword, killing anybody who wouldn't convert. Perhaps you should actually get to know them before you condemn them."

Ballenger chuckled and said, "I'm not interested in getting to know people who reject my daughter just because she's part black."

Collins raised an eyebrow and said, "So far, you're on the only person I've heard say that. As I recall from my interviews with Allison Snow, your daughter had an invitation to the Stein home the night it was attacked. She said that your daughter said her mother said she couldn't come." He smiled wickedly and said, "It makes me wonder who is really honoring diversity, Mr. Ballenger."

~*~

It was well in the evening when Caleb got back to his home with his father and of all people, Shelby. He couldn't help but feel glad that she was there for him right now. The fact that she and his father seemed to be getting along surprised the hell out of the young football player and he was trying to keep conversation at least swung in directions that wouldn't cause any conflict.

And to be honest with himself, he felt like crap warmed over. His joints ached, he was tired, and for the life of him, he couldn't get warm. If it wasn't for what he'd seen and felt last night being confirmed by the others, he would have been tempted to think the whole thing was some kind of fever induced hallucination. But he knew it wasn't. He could feel the wolf settle into his soul. What surprised him was that it seemed to be more in conflict with the taint of the draugr than it did with his own soul. And for some reason it liked Shelby.

He watched as his dad and his girlfriend went to work in the kitchen and before long, strains of a popular country band came from the radio. He briefly wondered if he should be concerned when he realized that she was singing about digging two graves.

The fact that Shelby and his dad was hitting it off so well unnerved Caleb just a little bit. He'd always imagined his father being damned set against him dating someone from out at the kindred, and Shelby had already made it clear how she felt about people trying to convert her. As he lay back on the sofa, he wondered if he really was so sick that he was either hallucinating, or if they just felt it was bad enough to put their disagreements aside. Either way, it worried him.

The next thing he knew, his dad was shaking him gently awake to the smells of chicken, spices and fresh bread. "Wake up, Caleb. Dinner's ready."

"What?" he asked confused but feeling somewhat better.

"Your girlfriend can cook," his father told him. "Quite

well, I'd say."

Caleb sat up and rubbed his eyes as he tried to wrap his head around all the things that happened in the last few days. Looking up, he saw Shelby setting a plate of homemade biscuits on the table. "Eat up now, Caleb. I don't often cook, so you'd better enjoy this and don't expect it to be a regular thing."

His dad looked over at her and asked, "Really? Not even if I paid you?"

She laughed and said, "Not even if you paid me. I've got too much going on in my life right now. Mind you, I'm not against helping my mom out in the kitchen when I can, but it's not something I enjoy." She put her hands on her hips and looked at Van and said, "So, you'd better enjoy it."

He nodded and said, "I will." Getting up from the sofa, he joined his dad at the dining room table, something they rarely used.

After a quick and simple grace, which he was surprised that Shelby didn't object to, they dug into the soup and biscuits which were quite good. "This is good, Shelby," his dad said. "Thank you for the help."

She laughed and said, "I think Brett wanted me out of his hair so he could study that runestave."

"You two are close?" his dad asked.

"He's my best friend," she said.

Caleb's dad nodded and said, "Good to see boys and girls who can be friends. It's an important life lesson for both sexes."

She smiled and replied, "I know. Brett's kind of special too."

"He's originally from Alabama?"

"Georgia, actually," she told him. "He lives with his uncle now."

"His parents?" Caleb's dad asked.

"Not in the picture," she told him. Her voice wasn't exactly hard or even off-putting, but it was clear that it was something she wasn't going to talk about. Caleb understood that there was some kind of difficulty with Brett about his parents, and he didn't like the subject brought up. But as far as he was concerned, his Uncle Alex, the counselor at the high school, hung the sun, moon, and stars.

Caleb's dad seemed to get the hint and changed subjects. "So what are you plans after graduation?"

She grinned at him and said, "I'm not sure. I'm only a sophomore. I'm thinking of studying veterinary medicine at Morehead. I could commute back and forth and keep helping mom around the farm."

"We could always use another good vet. A couple of the ones we have I wouldn't trust to save a cockroach."

"Me neither," Shelby said. "Mom takes Faxi, our quarter horse all the way to Huntington to the vet to keep from having to use anybody local." She chuckled and added, "And that way, both Caleb and Van can use me as an MD."

"Hey!" Caleb protested.

"I'm teasing you, Caleb."

"It *is* funny when you think about it," Caleb said.

His dad seemed to catch on to the idea that neither he nor Shelby wanted his situation to get him down. With a grin he added, "I wonder if Sheriff Treybond will make me get you a dog collar?"

"Let's hope not," Shelby said. "Might be hard to explain to Coach Grizzle."

For some reason that comment seemed to amuse not only Caleb, but the wolf he felt in his soul. Then he remembered something. "That reminds me. I've got something you need to give to Brett or Mr. Bjargeir. I don't know what it is, but I got it from near Mr. Kaizer's body. I think it may have something to do with what's going on."

"What is it?" she asked as he got up and ran upstairs to his bedroom. Grabbing his backpack from the chair at his desk, he dug through it and pulled out the fur pelt he'd found. Suddenly he could smell the wolf that the pelt had once belong to. It rose up in his mind and challenged the wolf he felt in his soul. The room faded from around him and he found himself in a great forest. He could smell new fallen snow and wet earth. The scent of pine was nearly overwhelming. In his mind's eye, he saw it slowly shift into a one-eyed old man with a grizzled beard. Then it turned into Donny Kaizer.

"Son?" his father called from the door.

Coming out of the vision that seemed to overwhelm him, he asked, "Huh?"

"You seemed to be somewhere else there for a second," his father said. "And you started to get hairy."

Caleb shook his head and said, "Sorry, Dad. I need to give this to Shelby."

"What is it?" his father asked.

"I'm not sure, but I think it's important." Then remembering what Brett had said about the draugr coming to him tonight, he added, "And I think I need to do it tonight before I go to bed- before it's too late."

His dad seemed to understand and then said, "Okay." He walked across the room and took Caleb by the shoulders and added, "But whatever you're going through, I want you to know that you're not alone."

"I understand, Dad," Caleb told him. "But we have to work with what we've got, and right now, we've got so many problems we can't even keep up with them. Something tells me that it would be a bad idea to let the draugr get his hands on this." He smiled at his dad as he went out of the room and back downstairs.

Shelby was standing at the foot of the stairs and he handed her the pelt. "Give this to either Brett or Mr. Bjargeir. I found it near the body."

"Why didn't you give it to the police?" she asked.

He shrugged and said, "I don't know. It seemed like the right thing to not let them know about it." He turned to look at his dad at the top of the stairs and said, "Maybe what happened at your house has gotten to me on some instinctive level, maybe I'm just being a prick, but I think maybe one of those two would know what to do with it."

She nodded and put the pelt on the back of the sofa. "Okay, now, you go and eat. You need to keep up your strength." She looked over his shoulder and said, "And if he gives you any lip about eating or starts acting out of line, hit him on the nose with a rolled up newspaper." For some reason, Caleb found that to be a lot funnier than it really should have been.

His father's reply of "Yes, ma'am," didn't help matters either.

~*~

After dropping Van off at his place, Brett returned home, tossed his jacket on the bed and sat down at his desk with a pen and paper and started a chart to help him keep up with which combinations he'd tried with the runestave. It was two hours later and the sun had already sunk behind the western mountains when his uncle came to the door.

"Whatcha' working on?" he asked.

Brett looked up at the tall, good looking blond man and said, "Something Mr. Bjargeir asked me to figure out."

Looking down at his watch, Alex asked incredulously, "It's eight o'clock on a Saturday night and you're up here going through old runes?" He sat down on the bed and asked, "How was your date last night?"

Realizing that his uncle had something on his mind, he turned the chair around and rubbed the back of his neck. "It went pretty well. We're definitely going out again."

"What about school Monday?" he asked.

"What about it?" Brett replied.

"You coming out of the closet officially?"

Brett shrugged and said, "I'm not getting on the intercom and announcing it to the school, if that's what you mean. Van and I are dating. If people figure that out, cool. If they don't, that's cool, too."

"Just wondering, Brett. You don't always do things in half-measures. But I think you're handling this pretty well." He glanced over at the notebook and asked, "What's that all about?"

"It's a runestave Mr. Bjargeir came across. I was trying to figure out exactly what it means."

"It's a bind-rune," he told him. "More specifically, it's a variation on the one that was used in the ancient times to bind the ulfheddin and the bearshirts to the Allfather."

"Huh?" he asked. "How do you know that?"

Alex chuckled and said, "You're not the only one in this house with an interest in the runes. Been studying them for years."

"Why haven't you said anything before?" Brett asked.

"Because I wanted you to discover things that interested you for yourself. I didn't want to influence your interests," his uncle said with a smile.

"Can you show me how it was laid down?" he asked.

Alex shrugged and said, "Sure." He stood and went over to the desk. "First you lay down the center stave. It's from this one you want to to build the others around. It's Issa. It binds and holds the recipient." He drew the line straight down the middle. "Then you turn it to laguz for growth and the moon." He drew a short line at the top of the stave coming down at an angle to the right. "Then it needs to be linked the cycle of life and death or in this case to the Allfather, so the best form for it would be eihwaz, for the World-tree." He drew another short line from the bottom of the stave up in the opposite direction forming a stylized "s".

"Next it needs to be linked to some kind of requirement or need, so we rist and sing that rune." He drew a slanted line across the middle of the stave singing softly "Naudhiz." Finally, you need to freeze the recipient and bind him to the rune. He drew two quick lines on either side of the stave running parallel to it and sang "Issa, issa." Then the weregild gets paid and the recipient is bound."

Brett nodded suddenly understanding how simple and elegant the stave really was. "How would another vitkor go about breaking such a rune?"

"Don't know if it's ever been broken before. But I guess you'd have to give back the man-price and turn the rune into something positive." He seemed to think for a moment. Then he added several lines to the center runestave to turn it into two diamond shapes sitting atop each other and the stave running through it as he said, "Ing." Then he added simple triangles to the middle of each of the outer lines turning them from issa to thurisaz.

Raising an eyebrow he said, "Now that's a pretty powerful stave. It directs harm outwards to anyone who attacks the core family." He grinned at Brett and added, "And since it evokes thurisaz, that's invoking your favorite of the Elderkin, Thor."

Then he shrugged and sat back down on the bed. "So what's this all about, really? This isn't just some idle curiosity. What's really going on, Squirt?"

Brett shrugged and said, "Mr. Bjargeir really did ask me to figure this out."

"Why?"

Brett considered the question. Deciding that he loved this man like a father and he deserved to not be lied to, he chose to come clean. "Because Caleb got bitten by a draugr werewolf and this rune was carved in his chest. We're trying to break it so that Mr. Johnson can give the draugr back the weregild and Caleb and Van can take down the draugr and we can burn its body."

"You're kidding?" Alex said.

Brett shook his head and said, "No. I'm not. You can call Mr. Bjargeir or even Mr. Johnson if you want."

"And just how do you think that Van and Caleb can take down a draugr?"

"Because they're a moon-cat and a moon-wolf respectively," he told him.

Alex shook his head and asked, "Does Linda Stein know about this?"

"Some," he said.

"Let me call her," Alex said standing. Then as if remembering something, he said, "Oh. I almost forgot. Your mother called today. She wants to come and visit this Thanksgiving."

"That's all I need," Brett said. "Can we talk about it after we deal with this situation?"

"You're really serious about all this?" Alex asked.

"As a heart attack," Brett told him as he stopped at the door.

"When I brought you to live with me, I had no intention

of putting you in danger, Brett," he said.

"I know, Uncle Alex. But we don't always have a choice about these things."

Alex nodded his head and left the room, presumably to call Van's aunt. Brett studied the rune his uncle had helped him to construct and smiled. It would serve several purposes. Now he just had to convince Caleb to let him carve more lines in his chest.

~*~

As he sat in the back row of the Wellman First Congregationalist Church, Craig Blankenship was particularly pleased with himself. Yesterday had turned into one hell of an adventure. He was still sore from his time with Auda- strange name if you asked him. She'd done things with him that no girl he'd ever dated had been willing to do and then taught him new things on top of that. He definitely had plans to see her again. He only partially paid attention to Reverend Johnson's sermon on the dangers of the occult, as he considered some of the things he and Auda had discussed after their other activities.

She was right of course. He shouldn't let Van get away with humiliating him the way he had. He had to teach the sophomore a lesson about who was top dog around the school, and he had just the idea of how to do it.

There was no way that the other teen was likely to follow him out into the woods, but there were ways of getting him there, not the least of which was his little friend Brett. It was already all over school that the two had been seen by Carmen O'Brien leaving the Cinemark in Ashland holding hands Friday night. He was right in his initial assessment of both boys, they were a couple of cock-sucking faggots. He was going to be doing the school, hell the whole community ,a favor.

He smiled and tried to force himself to stay awake as the good reverend droned on about how little things could lead a person away from God and down the path of paganism and satanism. Even half paying attention, Craig got the feeling his heart wasn't in it though. It seemed like he was just going through the motions. For minute, Craig wondered about that, and then his mind drifted back to the wonders he'd discovered in the wildlife officer's blouse.

It was an hour later when he and several of his friends were sitting around Jeraldan's munching on chili fries and talking when one of them brought up the rumor about Van and Brett. "You know, we really shouldn't put up with that kind of crap around here. This ain't San Francisco you know,"

Chris Mason, a point guard on the basketball team, had said.

"Well, what can we do about it?" John, his brother- a junior replied.

"Well," Craig suggested carefully. "We could take them out to the old mines, and well, we could make it clear that this is a God-fearing community and we don't put up with that kind of crap around here."

"Dude," John said. "Van's already kicked your ass once. Do you really want to give him another shot?"

Craig shot him a hard look. He didn't like to be reminded about that- he was still getting used to having the cast on his arm. He definitely didn't want to think about what he'd seen in the dark-haired boy's eyes that day. He laughed and said, "It'd be three against one," he said. Then he pointed with his head toward his car and said, "And besides, karate or no, a tire iron to the back of the head will take care of business."

"We don't want to kill nobody," Chris protested.

"Who's talking about killing?" Craig said. "I'm talking about messin' up that pretty face of his." He smiled wickedly, "And doin' a number on Brett that'll have him packin' his bags back for Georgia."

The other two looked at each other. Craig knew they weren't convinced but at least they were listening. "All I'm saying is that we grab Brett and take his ass down to the old mines and do a number on him. Then we send the pics from his own phone to Van and wait for him to show up. Step out of the woods, hit him over the back of the head with a tire iron and then stomp his ass. Afterwards, we let them walk back to town." Of course, he had no intention of letting the two fags walk back to town. He could always circle back and finish things off. Like Auda had said, "There were some things a man just doesn't let pass." And Craig very much considered himself a man now.

"When do you want to do this, then?" Chris asked.

Craig didn't want to let too much time pass. He was afraid that Chris and John would back out. But he wanted to give the situation enough time to grow. Come Monday evening, or Tuesday morning, he figured there would have been enough time for everyone in the school to hear about their little date. That way there'd be no sympathy for them when they went missing. Who knows, if the mine was deep enough then maybe everyone would think they'd run off together. "How about Tuesday? We can grab Brett after school. I'll get the spot set up at Miller's Cave Mine."

The other two nodded their agreement. Craig knew he was going to have to stay on them to make sure it happened. "There's no practice on Tuesday because of some kind of meeting the coaches have to go to, so that would be good," Chris said.

Craig smiled and said, "Good. I'll let you know when things are ready."

~*~

"What did you find out?" Auda asked her cousin as she appeared in a flash of light in the cabin where Dace was pacing back and forth.

"Oh a lot, Cousin dear. A whole lot," the big draugr growled. "The Griffin boy is definitely who we want."

Auda smiled hugely. "Go on."

"He's one of the Vanir's, a moon-cat," Dace grumbled to her, his voice sounding dry and raspy like sandpaper on hard oak. Auda knew that he was replacing the lost blood that the coroner had drained by feeding off his thrall. She wondered how long he could keep it up. The boy only had so much blood in him.

She smiled at him and said, "Well, I've managed to set a few things in motion too. I doubt that they will actually take out the boy, but they'll at least guarantee he's in a place at a time we can name. All we have to do is step in and finish the job if my young lover doesn't have what it takes."

"There's more," Dace rasped.

"Oh?" she asked.

"The boy didn't like to talk about it, but I can be pretty persuasive. That rune you taught me keeps him well under my control." He leaned back against the wall and said, "He tastes good too."

Auda raised an eyebrow but said nothing about the last comment. "Spit it out, Dace," she ordered him.

He smiled and she could see that his formerly blue-white teeth had began to yellow as he began to dry out further. "The boy's little butt-monkey playmate fancies himself a vitkor, and his cousin thinks she's a seidr-worker."

She considered what he said, "Maybe we should make sure they're there too when we take out the moon-cat."

"There's more," he said.

"What?" she asked.

"Evidently the boy's sister is one of the undead. She killed her mother and left here about thirteen years ago with her human lover."

"That's a surprise," she told him. "What kind of undead?"

He snorted and asked, "What kind of stories has every teenage girl in the country wet between the legs?"

"Vampire? Really?" she asked. "How?"

"Have no idea. He doesn't either. The boy said something about a trip to Cincinnati that she came back from changed. He was very young at the time and doesn't remember much." Dace smiled and added, "Trust me, I took a great deal of pleasure in digging up everything I could from his memories. He didn't like it, but that's just too bad. I had a good time."

Again Auda raised an eyebrow and wondered if her cousin really understood what he was doing when he was delving that deeply into his thrall's mind. If the boy's will was strong enough, that kind of link could cut both ways. "Anything else?"

"Yeah, the boy gave the wolf pelt of the ulfhedinn I killed to the kindred's gothi," he said. "I made sure I punished him for that too."

"Don't drink too deep or you'll kill him," Auda warned.

"I know what I'm doing, Cousin," he said. "He's going to be just weak enough to not give me any trouble." He shrugged and said, "Besides, I'm thirsty, and there's not enough deer around here to keep me satisfied."

Auda simply nodded. She didn't like where things were headed with her cousin. He would probably have to be eliminated when his usefulness was over. She would, of course, apologize to Granny about it, but it really couldn't be helped. "We want him strong enough to travel come Tuesday. Leave him be until then."

"He's mine," Dace demanded.

"I'm not arguing that with you, Dace. But if you kill him too soon, it won't get our revenge on the boy who killed you. You can drain him dry after Tuesday for all I care. But until then, leave him be."

He grunted at her.

"Say it, Dace," she demanded.

He shrugged his shoulders and said, "Okay. Now tell me about what you've got planned with your little boy-toy."

She smiled, "It would seem that Craig Blankenship has a real hate on for your moon-cat. It didn't take much to plant certain ideas in his head. I even put a little touch of glib-tongue glamor on him so he can be more persuasive in getting his friends to help him. When it's over, it'll be just another teenage hate-crime that got out of control. Three of the followers of the Shining Ones will be dead, and we'll be long gone with no one the wiser that we were here."

"Did you really seduce an eighteen year old boy?" Dace asked incredulously.

Auda smiled and said, "Actually, I let him think he was seducing me. It was easier that way. Besides, there's something to be said for youthful enthusiasm."

"What if it comes out later?" he asked.

She shrugged and asked "Where are they going to find me? This identity is temporary. I can be anybody I want to be."

Dace growled is assent. It was clear he wasn't happy, but he didn't have to be happy. If it weren't for Auda, he'd still be dead and in a grave somewhere waiting to serve their kin in the final battle. This way he at least got to be up and around-for a while longer that is.

CHAPTER 15

As he entered the building at Wellman High School, Alex Falkstal was still in a bit of shock from what Linda Stein had told him on Saturday night. He'd agreed that all the parents and Mr. Bjargeir should have a meeting, something they planned to do tonight after school. Still, it was a lot to take in.

He'd played around with the esoteric side of the faith when he was younger and had even learned the Futhark runes, but for him it was always more of a mental exercise. Alex loved puzzles and ciphers, and had studied them most of his life. To him the meanings of the runes beyond just their phonetic value had presented him with an intriguing puzzle to play with, but he'd never put much stock into it beyond that.

When Linda Stein had told him that her home really had been attacked by a group of werewolves, he'd been shocked, but knew the woman well enough to at least accept on some level that she was telling the truth. But Saturday's conversations, first with his nephew and then with Linda, had left him more that a little disturbed. Add in the phone call he'd received from his sister earlier in the day and he found his stomach was in knots. He was genuinely afraid that the woman would try to take Brett away from him.

As he entered the main office of the school, Coach Grizzle looked up from where he was munching on a doughnut and smiled. "Hey, Alex, got a minute?"

Alex smiled and said, "Sure Doug. Come on in." He unlocked the door and stepped inside. He and Doug Grizzle had always gotten along pretty well. They both took a holistic approach to how they wanted kids educated, and it had made them natural allies in the rough give and take of faculty politics.

To his surprise, Doug closed the door behind him and smiled sheepishly. "Look, I need to ask a favor of you," the thin, short, gray-haired man said.

Alex hung his jacket up on the tree behind his desk and said, "Shoot."

"Look, you're in good with the Griffin kid's aunt, right?"

Alex raised an eyebrow and said, "I don't know how you define "in good". We're good friends. What about it?"

"Well, after this year, I'm going to be losing some of the best players I've had in years. I may lose some of them before the season is out if they don't get their acts together. I was wondering if you could put a good word in with the kid about maybe trying out for football next year."

"I'll mention it. She and I are meeting this evening to discuss some family issues," Alex told her.

"You didn't know that your nephew is dating her son?" Doug asked, surprised.

Alex raised an eyebrow and said, "I knew it. I'm surprised you did though."

Doug chuckled and said, "Heather said that a friend of hers saw them coming out of the theater this weekend holding hands."

"I would think you wouldn't want the extra headaches that a gay player might cause on your team," Alex said.

Doug chuckled and said, "I don't care if he nails the whole defensive line if he can play as well as I think he can." He shrugged and added, "Might as well. Craig Blankenship managed to nail most of the senior cheerleaders this year and that has caused me a whole lot more headaches than this would."

"That's an unexpected sentiment coming from a football coach, Doug," Alex said with a smile.

Doug simply shrugged and said, "I'm here to teach history, and coach football. I long ago gave up trying to micromanage my player's lives. They have a certain code of behavior

I expect of them, and they know it. Anything else is none of my business."

Alex understood. Doug's daughter Heather was one of those senior cheerleaders, he'd mentioned. "I'll bring it up. Maybe not tonight, but I will definitely mention it to both him and her."

"That's all I can ask," Doug told him, heading out the door. He checked his watch and said, "I got cafeteria duty in two. Gotta go."

Alex smiled and waved as he sat down at his desk thinking that his world was getting weirder and weirder as he dove into his schedule for reviewing IEPs and 504s for his report to the state. Sometimes he wondered why he ever decided to leave the classroom and take a counselor's job. He really did prefer teaching science. Then he remembered the increase in pay and wondered if it was really worth it.

Somehow he managed to make it all the way to lunch before he realized that his outer office had been unusually quiet. As he exited the office, and headed toward the faculty lounge (after the new nutrition rules had been handed down from Washington, he'd resolved himself to bringing his own lunch every day) to heat up his soup and sandwich, he noted that things just seemed quiet. He told the secretary, Mrs. Garrison, "Headed to lunch, Maureen." The woman never looked up from her computer screen but simply waved to him as he left.

Entering the lounge he found Grace Devlin, the only other teacher there. "Hello, Grace," he said as he got his soup from the fridge.

"Afternoon, Alex," she said as she nibbled on some kind of sandwich.

"How's Brett settling in to your class?" he asked, to make small talk.

"Quite well actually. Although I knew he and Brandt Snow were friends, I'm a bit surprised at how well he's getting along with Bastion Davenport."

Alex chuckled and said, "Grace, the boys in that class are outnumbered significantly. I'm not surprised at all that they're banding together."

She chuckled and said, "You've got that right. With Phoebe Smith in the class, it's probably best if they present a united front. That girl walks around with a chip on her shoulder about male privilege."

Alex smiled as he watched his soup bowl do little off-center circles in the microwave. "It's good training for when they get to college."

She chuckled again, this time with a snort of derision. "You're right there. Sometimes I wonder exactly what it is some people are progressing towards."

"Something I think that even they won't like if they ever get their way," he told her, running a dollar bill through the pop machine.

"You have a point there," Grace told him. "By the way, I heard Brett has a boyfriend now."

"I don't know if it's at the boyfriend level yet, but he and Van Griffin are dating," Alex said neutrally.

To his surprise, Grace said, "Good. Van's been a good influence on him since he transferred here. Too bad it took losing his parents. Ellen Griffin was good people."

"How are the other kids taking the fact that Van and Brett have stepped out of the closet?" he asked, still neutrally.

She smiled at him, letting him know that she understood he was fishing for information without wanting to appear to be fishing. "For most it's not a big deal. This generation coming up seems to be pretty accepting of that kind of thing. I think in a few more generations it's not going to even be something to comment on. Yeah, I've heard some grumblings from some of the kids, but for the most part it's been nothing out of the ordinary."

"Glad to hear it," Alex said as he took his pop and soup to the table.

The rest of the lunch was spent on neutral subjects and

Alex realized that maybe he'd been more nervous about today than he let on. Talking to Grace and Doug had gone a long way in alleviating his fears for his nephew. Now if he could just get the niggling worry out of his mind about his own sister's visit during Thanksgiving.

~*~

Linda Stein set the coffee service down in the living room and smiled at her guests. Gareth Bjargeir had been a guest in her home for as long as she could remember, and of course she and Alex had been friends since before Max died. She smiled at that thought. Alex had introduced her and Max when they were in college together.

Even the Snows had been to her home on more than one occasion as they lived just down the road from them. But she never expected Clark Johnson to be visiting, and especially not about the subject at hand. But to be honest, she'd never considered the subject at hand to be one that would ever need discussing. It was too much like something out of one of Brett's favorite fantasy novels.

But Alex had asked to meet with all the parents and she understood that. Brett was something special to him, and he wanted to make sure that the boy was safe. She just wished she could reassure him the way he needed. Her own home had been attacked by werewolves and now Alex had been clued into what was really happening in Wellman.

"I appreciate all of you agreeing to meet with me," Alex said. "It would seem that I'm the last one to find out about what's going on."

"We thought you knew," Kurt Snow said.

"I knew what Linda had told me. I didn't know that our kids were starting to battle the forces of darkness," Alex said. "To be honest, it sounds like something out of *Buffy The Vampire Slayer*."

Clark Johnson snorted, looked at Linda, and said, "I could have used Buffy thirteen years ago, and so could have your sister."

"What happened to your wife and the Davenports was a tragedy, but really doesn't have anything to do with what's going on now," Linda told the man.

"Except, now it's my son whose life is on the line," Clark said.

"Exactly what is Caleb's situation?" Alex asked.

"That damnable creature is torturing him every night in his dreams. There's nothing I can do to stop it. There's nothing to grab onto, nothing to do but pray." Linda could tell the man was nearly at his breaking point. She would hate to see that happened. She may disagree with Clark Johnson on a lot of things, but it was clear that he loved his son, and she had no desire to see Caleb hurt in all of this.

"What are you going to do?" Alex asked.

"Your nephew is working on changing that blasted thing carved into his chest," Clark said.

Linda watched as Alex let things sink in. "You mean he's going to let Brett carve on him?"

"If it breaks the enthrallment, yeah," Clark said.

"I'm not sure I'm comfortable with all of this," Alex said. "So far, I've heard people that all my life I've considered rational and well-grounded talk about werewolves, spells, and runes. And I really don't want my nephew carving his initials into anyone's chest."

"What would it take to convince you, Mr. Falkstal?" Reverend Johnson asked. "Do you want me to ask my son to come down and shift for you? How about Van?"

That brought Alex up short. He seemed to think about it for a moment and then said, "Maybe."

Linda went to the stairs and called up, "Van, would you come down here?" She looked back over at the reverend and said, "No offense, Mr. Johnson, but right now, I trust Van's control better than Caleb's."

The man sipped his coffee and said, "I quite understand, Mrs. Stein. I'm not comfortable seeing my son change that way as it is."

She smiled and nodded as Van came down the stairs with Brett. She noticed her nephew was barefoot and wearing a pair of running shorts and a tank top. He grinned at her and said, "I heard."

Looking over at Alex he smiled, "You need proof. I

understand that." Then moving faster than she thought possible, he leaped from the stairs across the room to land in front of Alex. In mid-flight, his body shifted and changed to become the cat-creature that had defended this house the night it came under attack.

His body curled in on itself as he landed and then he turned around to face Alex and raised his head to look at the high school counselor with a mouth full of sharp fangs. "How is this, Mr. Falkstal?"

"Show off," Brett said from the stairs.

As Van rose to his feet to tower over the adults, he stared down at Alex and said, "Everything you've heard is true."

Linda watched as her old friend swallowed hard and looked around quickly. "Is this entirely safe?"

Van laughed and it came out like a soft purr, his tail curling and uncurling behind him. With a smile she noted that the rising and falling limb was giving poor Clark Johnson a rather rude free shot of his backside. "I'm in control of the cat, Mr. Falkstal, not the other way around."

"Well, maybe not of the tail," she said as she walked over. She pointed with her eyes at his backside and then to the reverend. Suddenly his body shrank down to his normal human looking form, and he said, "Sorry, Mister Johnson."

The man laughed and said, "No harm done."

"So do you believe now?" Kurt Snow asked.

Alex only nodded his head and swallowed hard. He looked at the others and asked, "Isn't there someone we could call for help with this?"

It was Kurt's turn to chuckle and ask, "Who you gonna call?"

"Did you just ask that?" Linda chided him.

The man smiled and said, "Sorry. Couldn't help it. It was too good to pass."

Linda shook her head and said, "Men." Then turning back to Alex she said, "But he's got a point. I'd prefer my nephew not get locked up for study somewhere, and I'm pretty sure the same can be said for Clark."

"So what are you going to do?" Alex asked, obviously trying to process what has been happening.

"We're going to let Brett change or at least try to change the rune on Caleb's chest. Then we're going to try and deal with the draugr."

"How?" Alex asked.

"We're working on it," Gareth Bjargeir said. "The body needs to be completely destroyed. We're trying to figure out how to do that."

"And you're going to let the kids do it?" Alex asked.

"We'll be there to help. But I don't think any of us have what it takes to do it," Linda said. "Our children have been given gifts to use. We might as well let them use them. We'll just be here to support them."

"Why do I feel like I just stepped into one of the Icelandic Sagas?"

As he descended the stairs, Brett chuckled and asked, "You're seeing the similarities too?" He stopped for a moment and then added, "Now you understand why I want to wait to deal with what you told me last night? It doesn't do any good to worry about it until this has been dealt with."

Linda couldn't help but think that was a very mature attitude coming from a sixteen year old boy.

Alex nodded and asked, "What now?"

Brett said, "Now I get Caleb drunk and then start cutting."

"Drunk?" Alex asked.

"Would you want me to start carving into your chest without some liquid courage?" Brett asked. "Besides, if he starts to shift on me in the middle of it, I'd rather his reflexes be a little off."

"Heaven help me, but that makes sense," Reverend Johnson said. He looked at Brett and said, "You have to be the most practical boy I have ever met."

Linda couldn't help but laugh at that. Brett had a reputation for being anything but practical, of having his head in the clouds and not looking where he was going. She noticed that several other people, including the boy in question, joined her in the laughter.

He looked up at her and asked, "Where do you keep the whiskey?"

She looked over at Clark who thought about what he had asked. Finally, the man nodded and she turned and said, "My husband had a bottle of Maker's Mark he bought for the '96 Championship game. It's never been opened."

"I can't think of a better use for it," Van said.

"I'll get it," Linda told them.

"And I need your seax too," Brett said.'

"Why mine?" she asked.

"Because it's silver and has been blessed," he said. "Van's mother's would be better, but yours will have to do."

"Mom's is upstairs," Van said.

"They gave it back to you?" Brett asked, surprised.

"No reason to keep it," Van said. "And it does have certain religious connections. It took a while but the Colorado State Police finally sent it to me right before I moved here."

"That would be perfect," Brett said.

"Why?" Reverend Johnson asked.

"Because it's already tasted moon-wolf blood, blood that's part of the line that turned your son," Brett said. He shrugged when everyone looked at him and said, "I'm working here not only from galdr but from associative magic as well."

"I'll get the bourbon," Linda said leaving the room.

~*~

Brett watched as Caleb made a disgusted face and handed the empty glass to his father. "Ugh," that stuff is nasty.

"Hey," Mrs. Stein said. "That stuff's expensive."

"Still tastes nasty, Mrs. S.," the boy said.

"How do you feel?" Brett asked him.

"Nervous," he said. "I know what's coming and am not looking forward to it."

"Do you think you need another drink?" he asked.

"Not if you don't want me to throw up on you," Caleb said.

"I think that's enough for now," Brett's Uncle Alex said. "There's an art to getting someone drunk enough to not feel pain without having them pass out sick."

"I think I'd rather be passed out, considering what Brett's about to do," Shelby said.

"I need him at least partially conscious," Brett said. "I need to know if it's working. I just don't want him focused enough to break the restraints."

"You're really going to tie my boyfriend to Van's bed?" Shelby asked.

"Well, when you put it that way," Brett said.

"Boyfriend?" Caleb asked looking over at Shelby. Brett noticed that he was already slurring his words.

She smiled at him and crossed her arms across her chest, hugging herself. Mr. Johnson put an arm around her and said, "I'm not entirely comfortable with this myself." He sighed, "But I won't lose another child. Whatever it takes to keep him safe."

"This is just the first step," Brett told him as he tied Caleb's free hand to the bed post.

"You guys realize that this could be considered child endangerment," Alex said.

Brett looked at Caleb and asked, "Do you consent?"

"To what?" the boy asked with a smile.

"To my changing the rune on your chest?" Brett asked

seriously.

Caleb nodded.

He turned to Mr. Johnson and asked, "Do you consent to my doing this?"

The man nodded and said, "Yeah."

"Won't do any good with the wrong judge," Alex said.

"Do you want me to stop?" Brett asked. "If I do, and that thing keeps feeding off him, I suspect he'll be dead within a week. Look at him."

His uncle stared at the shirtless boy tied to Van's bed. He was pale and gaunt. Brett had seen pictures of meth addicts who looked better. Brett knew his uncle couldn't see the angry scars of the rune or even the raw wounds where Caleb said the draugr kept drinking his blood.

"I'm just pointing out that the law may not agree with you."

"We'll deal with that when we have to," Mr. Johnson said. "Right now, let's get my boy out from under that demon's control."

Brett started to correct the man, but decided against it. Right now it wasn't as important as getting Caleb better. He looked over at Van who was standing on the opposite side of the bed and said, "If it looks like he's going to break the restraint, grab that wrist." He climbed on the bed and straddled the boy's waist, then nodded to Mr. Johnson and his Uncle Alex. "You two handle that one." Then looking down at Caleb, he said with a smile, "Normally, I'd require you to buy me dinner and a movie."

"Brett!" Shelby said.

But Caleb chuckled and said, "You'd have to get me a whole lot drunker than this."

"Sense of humor intact," Brett said as he pinned the piece of paper with the new rune drawn on it to the wall above the headboard. Then taking the knife he said, "Once I start, I can't stop. Each line has to be done with a single stroke, and I'm going to have to reopen the old lines to purge them. Do you understand?"

Caleb nodded and squinted his eyes. "I understand. It's going to hurt like hell."

"Good," Brett said.

He then drew the seax from its sheath and went to work. As the knife cut into the other boy's chest and opened one of the old scars a black cloud began to waft up from the original wound. Caleb screamed, and then howled. Cutting into a friend like that was the hardest thing Brett had ever done. He felt the power literally pouring out of him into what he was doing. It was like running a marathon as he made each stroke, and each rune and watched the blood and smoke boil up.

Half way through the process, Caleb began to shift into his wolf form and started bucking and howling. In his mind's eye, Brett kept the image of Midgard's Warder, of Thor, forefront in his mind, saying a silent prayer for strength from him. With that, he felt strength pour into his limbs as he continued to fight to carve into his friend's chest. As he finished the runes on either side of the main stave and carved in thurisaz, he intoned Redbeard's name- calling upon his power to seal the rune.

As he exhaled the final rune song he heard another wolf in the distance howl in pain. He smiled to himself and thought, *Good. Now let you feel some of the pain, you bastard.* Then, in the sky above, he heard the rumble of thunder and the wolf became silent. He rolled off the half changed moon-wolf on the bed and leaned heavily against his uncle. "It's done."

"How do you feel, Caleb?" Mr. Johnson asked.

The boy tied to the bed turned to him, his eyes glowing the soft yellowish brown of a wolf, his teeth elongated and his body covered with hair except for the bloody rune carved in his chest shining silver in the light from overhead. Slowly his face turned back to normal. He nodded and said, "Tired, hurt, and like I'm gonna throw up." He suddenly turned his head and started puking up his guts.

Beside him, Shelby grabbed the garbage can and tried to catch the rain of half-digested bourbon, and black sickness that seemed to be coming up with the whiskey. A dark stench rose in the room, driving everyone out as the blackness pooled in the garbage can. "Don't let it get on you!" he told Shelby.

His friend nodded and stepped back as the blackness continued to rise into a cloud. Van turned and opened the window, turned the fan sitting in it around backwards and turned it on. The blackness seemed to fight the breeze for several heartbeats before the whoosh of air proved to be too much and it was sucked out into the cold October night.

"What the hell was that?" Kurt Snow asked from the door.

"The last remnants of the draugr's influence." He turned to Caleb and said, "Now to be completely free of him, you just have to give the coin back."

"What if he won't take it?" he asked.

"All he has to do is hold it in his hand," Brett said. "You're a smart boy. I'm sure you can get him to take it from you."

"What now?" Mr. Johnson asked.

"Now, we get Caleb cleaned up, and then we get him back to your house. Later, we go hunting," Van said.

"What's that on his neck?" Mr. Snow asked.

As Van untied the young moon-wolf, Caleb reached up and touched the juncture between his neck and shoulder. "It's where the thing has been drinking from me."

"Like a vampire?" Mr. Johnson asked.

"Something like that," Brett said. "I told you that draugrs were part vampire, part self-willed zombie, and part undead sorcerer."

"Is he likely to become a vampire now?" Mr. Johnson asked.

Brett shook his head and said, "He better not. That took a lot out of me. That rune should protect him from the draugr's influence from now on." He chuckled and said, "But I'm afraid that he may eventually find himself called by Redbeard instead."

"Redbeard?" Mr. Johnson asked.

"Thor," Alex said. "That's who Brett was calling on for strength." He gave Alex a strange look and asked, "An interesting choice. Thor isn't known for his interest in magic."

"Thor is a God. He can do whatever he damn well pleases," Brett told his uncle. I don't have a good relationship with Van's lady, or with Mr. Bjargeir's patron, but I have a pretty good one with Midgard's Warder. I called on who I thought would help me."

Suddenly lightning flashed across the evening sky and thunder rolled across the mountaintops. Alex held up his hands and said, "Okay. It seemed to work, so I'm not going to complain."

"What do you mean he might be called by Thor?" Mr. Johnson asked.

Brett shrugged and said, "He doesn't have to answer. But that's Thor's rune he's wearing on either side of that runestave. It's powerful and it's charged. The draugr took Caleb away from your God for himself. I took him from the draugr and gave him to Thor."

"Why did you have to give me to anybody?" Caleb asked sitting up, his head between his knees.

"Because I had to charge the rune. I could have chosen any of the Elderkin, but I chose Thor because I have a good relationship with him."

Much to everyone's surprise, Mr. Johnson said, "I won't complain. My boy is safe."

"No," Van said. "He won't be safe until we deal with the draugr. But he's his own man, now. That's more than he was this morning."

Alex sat down in the rocker across the room and said, "I can't say I believe it. I saw it with my own eyes and I'm still having trouble believing it." He looked up to Mr. Bjargeir and said, "Exactly what have we been teaching our children?"

"We've been teaching them the old ways, Alex. You know that."

He shook his head and said, "But I never expected it to come to this? I never expected my nephew to become vitkor."

"Are you upset with me, Uncle Alex?" Brett asked, suddenly hurt.

The tone of his voice must have gotten Alex's attention because his head snapped up and he rushed across the room to pull Brett into a hug. "No! Not at all. I'm very proud of the young man you're becoming. I'm just surprised by it all." He laughed and continued, "I guess I'm getting a lesson in faith."

He blushed and said, "I guess, I'd learned to mouth the words to our worship but I had let the faith go cold in my heart. You've reawakened that, Brett. I'm more upset with myself, maybe even a little ashamed."

" I think we can all say that to some extent," Kurt Snow said from the door. "We've seen miracles these past few weeks. It's time we started living the miracles we've seen."

"Just don't go spreading it around, please," Caleb said from the bed. "I'd rather not end up on the lacrosse team," he added with a weak smile.

"Then you'd have to start dating a werewolf hunter," Brett volunteered. "And she'd die tragically saving her friends' lives." He stopped and asked, "You actually watch that show?"

Caleb shrugged and said, "I've usually got nothing to do at ten o'clock on a Monday night."

Brett chuckled. After a while the chuckle became a laugh, and then the laugh became tears. It had been a hell of a few weeks, and he was on an emotional roller coaster. He didn't remember much more of that night.

CHAPTER 16

Bastion Davenport wasn't sure why, but some small part of his mind was telling him that he should keep an eye on Brett. He figured it was because some part of him figured that if he followed Brett, that would eventually lead him to observing more of Van, which was his goal this week. According to Brandt, Brett pulled off some pretty spectacular galdr and spae work yesterday. He did know that the boy looked like hell warmed over today. Whether or not it was a late night of passion with his handsome boyfriend (being a thirteen year old boy, that was something Bastion would like to know more about) or if it was from his mage-work, Brett Bond looked like he'd been put through the wringer. He'd barely stayed awake during class today, and even Mrs. Devlin had commented on it.

Being in the junior high side of the building usually left him without much chance to interact with his classmates in Mrs. Devlin's class, so when he spotted Brett coming out of the gym today after school, he took the opportunity to follow him back to the main building's parking lot.

Bastion had gotten good at moving unseen and unheard over the last few weeks since his first transformation. He was very much in touch with the cat in his soul and had learned to move like one. The increased grace, strength and senses had given him more than one opportunity to discover things about which he was not supposed to know.

It was the latter that had alerted him to something being off when Brett passed the gatehouse to the football field and a shadow stepped out behind the small blond. Moving more quickly that even he thought was humanly possible,

Craig Blankenship and Chris and John Mason slipped up behind Brett. Then out of nowhere, Craig cracked Brett on the back of the head and the boy went down like a load of bricks.

Bastion stepped back into the shadows of the gym and watched as the trio loaded Brett into the back of Craig's car and pulled out a roll of duct tape. It took very little time for them to do whatever it was to Brett they were doing and then all three piled into the car and headed out. He watched as the car pulled out onto the street running in front of the school and then over to US 23. It disappeared in the general direction of the old mines.

Just at that moment, he saw that wildlife management officer who'd been assigned to the area come out of the gym. "Ma'am!" Bastion called.

"Yes?" she asked with a smile.

"Ma'am, I just saw three guys hit Brett Bond over the back of the head and stuff him in their car!"

"What?!" the woman's eyes turned flinty.

"Did you see who it was?"

Bastion nodded, and said, "Craig Blankenship, and Chris and John Mason."

The woman began to curse furiously. "You got your cell phone on you?" Bastion nodded. "Did you see which way they went?" Again Bastion nodded. "Let me see your phone," she said.

Bastion shrugged and handed it to her. She smiled at him. He never saw the right cross that caught him across the jaw.

~*~

The first thing that Brett noticed was the smell. Something smelled like the old oil that his dad used to take out of their old beat up Chevy every once and a while. His dad always wanted to make sure that Brett knew at least some "manly" things. But Brett's heart had not been in it. Not so much because he didn't like to know how things worked- he did- but because his dad's attitude about it was that Brett was somehow a disappointment because he wasn't interested. He didn't realize that Brett was less interested in being slapped around than he was about how the engine worked.

The next thing he noticed was that he was cold and damp. He shivered from it and when he realized what he was doing, he tried to stop. That set off a throbbing in his temples that made Brett feel like his head was about to explode. He rolled over and groaned into whatever it was stuck across his mouth. He tried to reach up and pull it from his face, but found his arms were secured tightly behind his back. He looked down and saw that his feet were taped together too.

"Now the fun begins," he heard a voice from off to the side. He thought he recognized it, but before he could focus his eyes he felt a sharp kick to his side. Ribs cracked under the force of the steel toed work-boots. When the second blow hit, he felt the rib let go and it felt like somebody had stabbed him in the side. He tried to scream for help but only a muffled whimper came from under the tape against his mouth.

Rough hands grabbed him and pulled him to his feet. He tried to focus his eyes through pain but the darkness that pressed against his vision was as much from the pain as it was from wherever he was. He struggled against the arms holding him but couldn't move and when he tried he felt the stabbing in his side again.

"Uh uh, faggot," a voice said. Some part of his mind recognized it as Craig Blankenship. "You don't get away that easy."

He felt his face jerked around. He tried to focus his eyes

but only got a brown and tan blur against the darkness of wherever they were. In the distance, he thought he saw a faint light, but was unsure if it was real or a side effect of the pain.

About the time that Craig's grinning face finally came into focus, his head lit up with stars again as something slammed into the side of his face. He fell to the side only to be held up by someone else as another blow caught him on the other side. He felt something run down his face and realized it was probably blood. Then the blows rained down on him until the darkness took him again.

~*~

Shelby entered the front room of her house holding Caleb's hand. "Mom!" she called. "Do we have room for one more for dinner?"

"Shelby, I really should be repaying you for dinner. You've already cooked me one meal," Caleb said at her side.

"Oh pooh. You can take me to the Road House some time," she said.

"Mom?" she called again. Looking around she spotted a note on the table. She picked it up and read:

Shelby and Van, I've stepped over to the Snows' to help them get Allison situated. Be back soon. Love, Mom.

"Well," Shelby said with a wicked grin. "We've got the place to ourselves for a while."

"Looks like someone else is here," Caleb said pointing to a pile of clothes in the floor.

Shelby walked over and looked at them. The first thing she noticed was that they seemed to be in tatters. She recognized Van's new sneakers, and they looked like they'd been busted out from the inside. "What the heck?" she said.

"Shel?" Caleb said.

"Why would Van rip up his clothes?"

"Shelby?" Caleb said again.

"Huh?" she asked, turning to him.

He handed her a cell phone. "I think this is Van's."

Shelby took the small black device. "Look at the last message that's up."

Shelby turned it over in her hand and her blood went cold. There was a picture of Brett tied up and bloody. His face looked a mess and one eye was swollen shut. A set of hands pinned his face back and there was a long knife held to his throat. The message under it read:

Miller's Cave Mine. Come alone, or no matter what happens, your butt-buddy won't come out alive.

According to the readout, the message had been sent from Brett's phone.

Shelby dropped the phone and headed over to her mom's desk. She yanked out the center drawer, and turned it upside down. Taped to the bottom of it was a key. She grabbed it and went to the gun case. Half a minute later, she was chambering a round in the rifle. "Go upstairs and grab Van some clothes out of his closet."

Her boyfriend nodded and pounded upstairs.

"Which closet is Vans?" he called back.

"The one without the dresses in it!" she yelled at him as she scribbled a note to her mom telling her to check Van's phone.

By the time she was finished, Caleb was at the foot of the stairs. "Come on," she said looking up to see Caleb's ears begin to elongate. She shook her head and said, "Not yet. We still have to cross 23 to get to the old mine. It's on the river side of the highway."

She watched as her boyfriend took several deep breaths and the wolf features slowly faded. Finally he said, "Good thinking. We'll take my truck." Shelby nodded and placed the phone on the table next to the note to her mom.

As they climbed into the truck, Shelby looked over at Caleb and said, "This isn't your fight."

"The hell it's not. I owe Brett big time. Nobody's gonna hurt him and get away with it," he growled as he pulled the truck back onto the road. "Any idea what this is all about?"

"No," she said. "But Van's down there too. Think it might be a trap?"

"Of course it's a trap. Otherwise they wouldn't have sent the picture, they'd just hurt him and gone on," he said.

She nodded and told him, "I thought as much."

"What do you plan on doing with that thing when you get there?" he asked.

"I'm going to get my cousin and my best friend out of there. If I have to shoot some people, then I'll shoot them."

"Good," Caleb said. "I like a woman who's willing to defend herself and her friends."

"You don't know that half of it," she replied grimly.

As they pulled out onto the highway he asked "Do you know if Van even knows where the mines are?"

"I think so," she told him. He's been walking the town with the ulfhedinn. He told me that he can sense when something is wrong in the den."

Caleb nodded beside her as they tore down US 23 at the very top of the speed-limit. Shelby understood that if they got pulled over for speeding they'd be that much later, and having to explain the hunting rifle in the cab of the truck might prove to be difficult.

A couple of minutes later, Caleb pulled the truck off the old road that led to the mines and then over to the side of the road. "This is as far as we take the truck. We don't need them to hear it coming."

"Good idea," she told him, climbing down out of the cab and pointing the rifle toward the ground.

Caleb came around to the passenger's side of the truck and began to strip. Shelby had the good graces to blush as she watched him shuck his clothes down to his boxers. She didn't turn away, but she at least blushed as his body began to crack and pop and he grew in size. His face elongated and a wolf's snout pushed out from his handsome features. His ears became pointed and moved to the top of his head. The muscles under his skin writhed like snakes as his bones popped and rearranged themselves.

In a matter of seconds one of the creatures who attacked her house was standing in front of her. For a heartbeat, she feared for her life as he reached out and sniffed her. Then he licked her up the side of her face, turned and disappeared down the road.

Shelby smiled to herself, picked up the clothes and put them in her backpack with Van's and followed him as quickly as she could. She didn't have a cat's or a wolf's speed, but she could make good time. She hoped that anybody passing would think she was just out hunting.

~*~

Van followed the sense of the intruder he'd felt earlier. Something that had been masking its presence had dropped. It was big, it wasn't human, and he could sense a miasma of evil emanating from it. Deep down in his soul, he knew, the cat knew, and the land-guardian knew, that it was evil.

He hadn't taken his man-cat form, but had instead elected for the four legged version he'd seen in his mind the other day. He was a good four or five hundred pounds of black house cat when he crossed the four lanes of US 23 about two miles back. He knew that at least one car had skidded to a stop as he plowed across the road and up the side of the shale mountain that had been cut away to make room for the road. By the time they got out of their cars, he was already disappearing into the grove of trees at the top of the small cliff. He flicked his tail at them in defiance and made a bee-line for the evil that was holding Brett.

As he made his way deeper into the woods above the mines, he could sense the sun beginning to sink behind the mountains in the distance. The cat part of him thought this was good. He knew his vision would be better than theirs at night. He knew he had an advantage.
Somewhere on the wind he caught the scent of a wolf. He lifted his head and opened his mouth and stopped breathing for just a moment. Pulling back his lips, he felt the scent go straight to his brain. His cat instincts began to catalog the scents. Two wolves, another cat, two women, one he recognized as his cousin, three men, and something else he couldn't identify. Whatever the last thing was, it was powerful, but it was neither a threat nor an ally. It simply was. And then there was Brett and blood.

He worked his way down the low hill that led off in the direction of the intruder. Unerringly, he picked his way silently through the forest until he came to a clearing. A squared off hole in the side of the mountain that had a large iron gate standing open dominated his view. He saw two cars parked out front, but recognized neither of them.

He pricked his ears forward and the sounds of five heart-beats came from inside the mine. A sixth one seemed to be coming from one of the cars. Cautiously, he worked his way around the clearing until he came to the road that led down from the highway. He could hear the sound of someone running down that road. The sense that told him of intruders in the den registered "as supposed to be here".

He turned back and worked his way along the cliff face until he was at the entrance. Sitting down on his haunches he listened carefully.

"What if he doesn't come?" he heard a voice he didn't recognize come out of the darkness.

"Oh, he'll come," a voice he recognized as Craig Blankenship said. "We've got his butt-buddy with us."

"He doesn't look so good," a third voice said. "Maybe we should let him go."

"Not until we get Van here," Craig said. "Don't back out on me now."

"Okay," the third voice said in a tone that told Van he was having second thoughts.

A shift in the wind was the only warning he got. He rolled to the side just as a great clawed paw caught him in the side and slammed him against the shale surface of the cliff.

He twisted and reached into the light that was his soul and pulled out the man-cat form in mid-air as he bounced back toward the thing that had hit him. With a scream of rage, he raked it across the face with one paw and then rolled out of the way.

As the giant blue wolf-creature howled into the night, Van took a moment to study it. It was bigger than he was, and there was an aura of power and death around it. He could smell the anger and the fear coming off it. He could feel the hatred that it harbored in its undead heart for him as it charged him, arms out wide and claws extended. Van leaped to the side and struck out with a clawed hand, raking its dead flesh from its bones.

"What the hell was that?" one of the voices inside asked loudly.

"Beats me. Go check it out!"

"The hell I will," the third voice said. "You go check it out."

"Chicken-shit," Craig said. Whatever else he may have said was lost in the roar of the draugr as it charged Van.

With the grace of the cat that he was, Van side-stepped the huge creature again and lashed out with a claw, this time tearing away the back of its thigh. But the loss of the muscle didn't seem to slow it down. Even with the yellow of the bone showing through, it still moved the leg as if it were uninjured.

Suddenly a howl split the air and something came hurtling out of the darkness to smash into the creature. Both of them went tumbling into the mine entrance and out of sight. Van caught a brief whiff of Caleb's scent. He chuckled to himself and it came out as a low purr as he crouched and followed them into the darkness. It was where he wanted to go anyway. Brett was down there. He could smell him.

~*~

As Craig disappeared back into the darkness, Brett felt Chris come around behind him. He whispered into Brett's ear, "I didn't sign up to kill anybody or get myself killed.

Brett felt the cold metal of the boy's knife as it cut away the tape on his wrists. He looked over to his brother and noticed that John was nodding his approval. Barely able to move, Brett tried to stand and swayed uneasily on his feet. His chest was on fire, and he could barely breathe. He reached up and pulled the tape from his mouth wincing with the pain it shot through his chest.

Looking up to the roof of the cavern, he said quietly, "Hear me Midgard's Warder. I stand for our people. Lend me your Ase Strength" He reached up to the blood still trickling from the side of his mouth and dipped his finger in it. Drawing the Uruz Rune on his face singing the name of the rune. Then he repeated the gesture with the thurisaz rune.

He felt some strength return to his body as something out there answered his prayer. He still hurt like hell, but he could move, and managed to do so just in time as two dark forms came hurtling out of the darkness.

He saw claws and fur flying as two werewolves rolled across the cavern, one glowing eerily blue, the other a muddy brown with jagged streaks of silver running through its fur like lightning bolts. As they came to a stop in the middle of the room, Chris and John both scattered to either side. Brett was nearly pinned against the back wall as he dodged to the left and right to avoid stray blows.

The blue creature was covered in bloodless wounds and gashes all over its body. The other wolf was bleeding from several places but was still holding his own, the hatred and anger for his opponent shining in his golden eyes. Suddenly the draugr raised a great paw and back-handed the other werewolf into Brett's direction.

The brown werewolf hit the back wall with so much force that the rapport echoed off the walls as the shale wall behind him cracked and split. As the brown wolf struggled to his feet, the draugr charged him, claws out ready to do serious damage. Suddenly, the black clawed form of Van's mooncat came barreling out of the darkness and hit the draugr low in the back. Brett heard the sound of bones crunching as Van landed blow after blow on the creature. Slowly another sound came to his ears: the faint hiss of air or gas escaping from the crack in the wall and the floor.

He looked over at where Chris and John were standing slack jawed at the sight of the three creatures battling it out in the cramped quarters of the mine or cave or whatever it was. "Run," he hissed at the other boys. "That's gas."

John turned to look at him confused. "Gas?"

"Methane, you idiot! Get out of here before you suffocate!" he said, not wanting to warn the draugr. The kernel of an idea was starting to take root in his mind.

He dashed over to where the brown wolf was trying to stand, and grabbed him under the arm and shoved him back toward the darkness from which he came. He felt another sharp pain in his side as he half dragged, half carried the giant creature toward what he hoped was safety.

The wolf stared down into his face, and for a second, Brett thought he was going to lash out at him. But then it simply nodded its head and then sat down as it bones began to pop back into place. After getting his friend settled, Brett looked over to the growling and snarling forms where Van and the draugr were doing their best to rip each other to shreds. To Brett's horror, he realized that the draugr was dishing out a hell of a lot more damage to Van than his boyfriend was doing to it.

Without thought of his own safety, he dashed in and kicked the draugr once between its hind legs as it tried to bring its teeth to bear on the black cat's throat. He was surprised when the creature actually reacted and rolled off Van into the back wall, holding its hands between its legs. He guessed that, on some level, it was still a male. He grabbed Van and pulled him backwards. "Get out of here!" he growled at the moon-cat.

"What?" Van demanded.

As the draugr struggled to his feet, he grabbed one of Van's claws and carved two quick runes in his palm, singing them both quickly, one after another. When he finished, he turned to face the draugr whose blue tinted fur was rustling heavily as its back was against the crack in the wall. He grinned, and snapped his fingers.

Brett had told the others that there was really no such thing as a fireball spell. But this was going to be damn close. "Kennaz a Thurisaz!" he screamed at the wall behind the creature.

A small spark, no bigger than a candle flame suddenly appeared behind it. A burst of fire suddenly engulfed the draugr and lashed out toward where he and Van were scrambling to get out of the blast area. Looking back behind him, he saw the great wolf-like creature caught in a jet of hot blue flame that shot out from the wall. "Run!" he turned and screamed at the others as a wall of fire began to build behind them.

Like something from an adventure movie, six forms raced the oncoming fiery death and stumbled out of the cave's mouth just before a tongue of flame lapped greedily at the edges of the opening. "We made it!" Chris said.

"Uh, not quite," Craig said from the ground where he was staring at the moon-wolf and moon-cat, both of which had their eyes locked on him.

Brett chuckled and said, "No, we made it. You're in a world of hurt, Craig."

"I wouldn't count my victories just yet," a strange voice said from the clearing. He looked over to see a tall buxom woman with long blonde hair holding a pistol to Shelby's side while holding what looked like the Steins' rifle in her other hand. "There's still one more act to play out in this little drama you've cooked up."

She looked at Van and Caleb and said, "Change back or I shoot her right here."

The cat and wolf both looked at each other and then back to the blonde. Caleb was the first to change shifting down into human form where he was only wearing a pair of boxers. "Now you," the woman jabbed Shelby in the side again.

Brett watched as Van slowly took human form again. He tried not to notice too much that Van was wearing even less than Caleb.

"You three," she pointed to Craig and his crew, "over here."

Without a word Craig grinned broadly and joined the woman. The other two moved somewhat less quickly but still they joined Craig as the woman tossed Shelby's rifle to the senior. "Now, all you have to do is finish what you started," the woman said. "Then we can drop their bodies in there and go get something to eat." The way she said it was so casual, so nonchalant that it could have sounded as if she was discussing a homework assignment.

"Those bullets won't stop me," Van said through clenched teeth. "They'll just make me mad." He indicated Caleb with his head, "Same with him."

"No, the woman shook her head and said, "But they'll slow you down long enough for us to finish you off with this." She reached behind her back and pulled out a long wicked-looking seax. "It's just what the doctor ordered, silver."

"I didn't sign up to kill anybody," Chris protested.

"Well, you are now," the woman said. "Or you can join these losers and nobody will ever find your body either."

Brett looked at the woman, and for some reason found the entire situation to be ludicrous, as he watched the back door of the car behind her open and a form slipped out into the night. He briefly wondered what Bastion was planning. He shook his head and said, "Exactly how do you think this is going to play out? You kill us and dump our bodies in the cave? You think nobody will come looking for us?" He looked at

Craig and Chris and John, "Or do you think that you'll pin it on your teenage accomplices?" He chuckled again and said, "And of course we don't exactly want to see all of this get out either, not with two shifters being exposed. It's likely to blow up in all of our faces."

"I can walk away anytime I want to," the woman said, with a sneer. "I'm a Jotun born and bred. I can simply become someone else."

Brett shrugged and said, "Maybe, maybe not. But if the shifters are exposed, then that's going to start raising questions about other things and I'm willing to bet that you wouldn't want to see an even further increased interest in all things Nordic- not with that movie out, and the television series. People are starting to return to the Old Gods, this kind of thing getting out would probably give them even more attention."

Obviously intrigued, she raised an eyebrow and asked, "Then what would you suggest we do?"

Brett shrugged and said, "We could all go our separate ways. We killed your draugr. You may get one or two of us, but we will eventually bring you down, guns or no guns."

"And what about these three?" she asked looking at Craig and his friends who were standing there, stunned at the conversation.

"We could kill them," Brett said with a cold tone to his voice. Every eye in the clearing turned to look at him in surprise.

That was when Bastion struck. Screaming like a banshee, a smaller orange furred version of Van's man-cat came screaming out of the shadows and bore the woman to the ground. The rifle in Craig's hands barked once and Brett felt a searing pain run through his lower left calf and the bone shattered under the force of the round hitting it.

Brett's leg collapsed under him and Van and Caleb surged forward, neither one taking the time to shift but instead hitting the senior from either side like a couple of defensive ends taking down a quarterback. From somewhere near Shelby four shots rang out, and then the rifle barked again and the only sounds that broke the silence of the clearing was the heavy breathing of the teenagers.

Finally, the nude form of Bastion Davenport sat up, having shifted back to a human. Pulling back his fist, he punched the woman under him. "Sucker punch me will you, bitch?" She didn't make a sound. Instead, a growing pool of blood was spreading out from her head.

"What happened?" Caleb asked.

"You don't want to know, Brett said holding his leg as another wave of pain hit him. Through a haze of agony he said would someone call 9-1-1? Craig shot me in the leg."

"Oh my gods!" Shelby cried and ran over to him.

Looking down in the dim starlight she asked, "How bad is it?"

"I think it hit bone," he told her as she started applying direct pressure to his leg. "You're bleeding bad,she replied. Reaching into the backpack at her feet, she pulled out a green flannel shirt and wrapped it tightly around the wound. She tossed the bag to the two other boys and said, "Put these on."

"What about them?" he asked, nodding in the direction of Craig's group."

"The woman's shots went wild. She hit Craig twice and the other two once each. Looks like Craig got her," Shelby said.

"What are the odds?" he asked incredulously.

"Not in their favor," Bastion said, standing behind the sedan he'd crawled out of as he fished for his clothing.

"What do you mean?" Van asked the boy as he pulled on a pair of jeans.

"Brandt told me about the spell you cast. Sounds like it acted perfectly. Bad luck was paid for evil actions. Their fates were sealed as soon as they kidnapped Brett."

"You believe this stuff?" Caleb asked as he pulled on a t-shirt. Brett realized that the flannel shirt around his leg probably belonged to Shelby's boyfriend.

"Of course I believe it. I knew it was going to work as soon as I heard about it."

"And how come you can turn into a werecat too?" Van asked.

"Because, just like you, it runs in our family line. Both our mothers were moon-cats."

"And you kept this to yourself why?" Van asked.

"Nobody asked," he said with a smile.

"Is someone going to call 9-1-1 before I bleed to death?" Brett asked. "Damn, this hurts!!!"

Caleb fished into his pocket and said, "You got it, Bro."

~*~

Alex Falkstal listened incredulously to his nephew's version of the story. It was the real story of what happened, not the story Doris Treybond filed officially which was a twisted tale of teenage romance with an older woman, revenge, and homophobia. For some reason the sheriff was willing to let a lot of things pass, and that surprised him.

On the other hand, news was that Agent Ballenger was being relieved of duty and reassigned to Quantico in Virginia. According to the court documents, he'd accessed and disseminated poor Van's FBI file to the general populace of the high school through his daughter Felicia, who'd claimed to have hacked his files without his permission. Nobody believed that, though. The news that Bastion Davenport was a mooncat was a bit of a surprise to everyone involved- except for, evidently, the boy himself and Brandt Snow.

Alex had been dismayed by the doctor's report on what Craig Blankenship and the two other boys had done to Brett. Two broken ribs, a punctured lung, the orbital bone around his eye had been broken and the doctor said it was a miracle the eye had not detached. He had a broken arm, and a broken leg, the latter from the gunshot wound.

Alex's sister had not reacted well to the news that Brett had been kidnapped and beaten for being gay, and he suspected his brother-in-law had reacted even worse. He was worried that she was going to try and use that to regain custody of him. He'd already spoken with Van's lawyer, Mr. Collins, about that and they were working out a strategy.

Now, he was just helping his nephew get settled back into his room. Brett had insisted on not moving into the guest bedroom on the ground floor in spite of the cast that encased his leg. He was determined to not let this whole thing slow him down, and Alex had to admire his gumption.

As Brett settled into his chair and sighed, Alex asked, "Can you explain to me why you don't seem as surprised as the rest of us that out of six shots fired by Agent Dagni and crew, five of them hit other members of their gang and only one hit you?"

Brett smiled and asked, "Had you rather they hit us instead?"

Alex shook his head and said, "Of course not. But that doesn't explain why you don't find it wildly coincidental."

"Because of the spell we cast," Brett said. "It was designed to send ill actions back to the person aiming them at us. Craig and crew knocked me over the head, took me to an abandoned mine, beat me to a pulp and then, using my own phone, sent a picture to Van of them holding a knife to my throat. It's a good thing by the way that Craig's cast was in that picture. But, that's about as good a description of ill actions as I can think of. Then, when we were facing down with Agent Dagni, he shot me in the leg. When the spell kicked in, it kicked in with a vengeance," Brett told him.

Alex nodded, not wanting to think about how close he came to losing his nephew. He'd come to love Brett like a son, and if he'd lost him, he wasn't sure if he could have handled that. He was just worried now that he was still going to lose him. He smiled as best he could at the boy and said, "Your mom is definitely coming to visit for Thanksgiving."

"And here I was feeling better," Brett said sarcastically.

"I know how you feel, Brett. But you really have to see her, especially now."

"Now that she and Dad know I'm gay?" he asked.

"We'd have never been able to keep that out of the news," he told him. "It made the national networks."

"Great," Brett said. "Now I'm out to the whole world. I thought they were supposed to keep the names of minors out of these sorts of things."

"Only if there was sexual assault involved," Alex told him. "I asked Mr. Collins about that."

"We've been keeping that guy busy a lot, haven't we."

"Yeah, but he's just about sold Sheriff Treybond on the idea that Dagni faked the cat attacks. She's not wanting to dig too deeply, mainly I think because the Davenports asked her not to."

"How are they handling the idea that Bastion's a mooncat?" Brett asked.

"Not nearly as badly as I thought they might. He's been spending a great deal of time with Van though, learning how to control his change," Alex told him.

"Great, that's all I need, competition from the richest kid in school."

"I don't think Van is likely to see Bastion that way," Alex said. "He is after all, only thirteen."

"Doesn't matter how Van sees it. Bastion sees it as a cute guy who swings his way."

"Bastion's gay?" Alex asked.

"Bastion says he goes both ways. Brandt says that Bastion's been throwing himself at him for over a year now."

Alex smiled and said, "I think Van can manage to fight off the advances of a randy teenager. I think you're selling your boyfriend short. He did, after all, charge into danger to rescue you. Didn't he?"

Brett smiled and said, "Yeah, and that's something I'm not going to let Bastion forget until he's got his own girlfriend or boyfriend."

Alex sighed and said, "And now for the bad news."

"Yes?" Brett asked.

Alex reached into his pocket and handed Brett a flash drive. "Here are the assignments you missed while in the hospital. You've got a week to catch up on them."

Brett groaned.

EPILOG

The late October moon was rising in the East as Paul Davenport pulled off I-64 onto the connector leading into Greenup and then Wellman. He could feel the hum of something powerful pull him home, a home he'd not seen in nearly fourteen years, a home he'd left after Kelli had drained his wife and killed her and their unborn son.

When Paul had left Wellman, Kelli had been his master, and he her student. Now things were different. He'd become the master, and she the servant. But then again, she'd never been very focused, not as a witch, and not as a vampire. It had taken Paul only a few years to break her hold on him and to exert his on her. He was surprised at how easily she accepted the shift in roles. He always thought that she was a submissive at heart.

Later, as he pulled off the connector onto US 23 and headed north, he felt the pull that called him back here grow stronger. He knew it would be a bad idea to try and see his parents and definitely not Elizabeth's family. He suspected that the Sheriff would never make it to the scene before they started shooting.

It would be best to lie low. There was a hunting cabin not far from Silver John Mountain. It should be just fine this time of year as he expected none of his sisters or their money-grubbing husbands were likely to be using it. It was too much like roughing it for them.

He smiled wickedly as he thought about using the cabin where he had first nailed Elizabeth Devlin the week before their junior prom. Kelli would like the idea of her taking

314

over a place so intimately connected to his ex-wife. His mistress was so easy to please, and he felt good as he returned home. It was time he took over the reins of the family, even if he had to kill half of them first.

Made in the USA
Middletown, DE
15 August 2023

36620898R00187